DEVIL'S

~

GRACE

DEVIL'S GRACE

Elizabeth B. Splaine

GREEN PLACE BOOKS | *Brattleboro, Vermont*

Printed in the United States

10 9 8 7 6 5 4 3 2 1

GREEN WRITERS PRESS is a Vermont-based publisher whose mission is to spread a message of hope and renewal through the words and images we publish. Throughout we will adhere to our commitment to preserving and protecting the natural resources of the earth. To that end, a percentage of our proceeds will be donated to environmental activist groups and the author's focus on The Parkinson's Foundation. Green Writers Press gratefully acknowledges support from individual donors, friends, and readers to help support the environment and our publishing initiative. GREEN PLACE BOOKS curates books that tell literary and compelling stories with a focus on writing about place.

Giving Voice to Writers & Artists Who Will Make the World a Better Place

Green Writers Press | Brattleboro, Vermont
www.greenwriterspress.com

ISBN: 978-1-950584-73-4

COVER DESIGN: Asha Hossain Design LLC

THE PAPER USED IN THIS PUBLICATION IS PRODUCED BY MILLS COMMITTED TO RESPONSIBLE AND SUSTAINABLE FORESTRY PRACTICES.

Inspired by real events.

~

BE KIND (It's easy.)

—Anonymous child, handwritten placard posted in front of the Barrington, Rhode Island Town Hall

DEVIL'S

~

GRACE

PROLOGUE

~

August 2018

The summer had been unusually dry, but last evening's skies had opened and unleashed the wrath of God on the small Rhode Island peninsula known as Barrington. The sun was playing hard to get among the pines, casting shadows that danced and shimmered on the wet asphalt. It was four o'clock in the afternoon on a Monday, and Angela Brennan was five miles into her six-mile run. The first three miles were for her health, the fourth was for stamina, and the last two were punishment, plain and simple.

Cresting the hill on Chachapacasset Road (her kids never did learn how to spell the name of the road correctly), the expanse of Narragansett Bay sparkled before her, and Angela allowed herself a moment of quiet contemplation as she inhaled the exquisite scents of late summer. Freshly cut grass and the sun-baked seaweed of low tide—the smells of home. She unfastened her hair tie, letting her wavy blond hair cascade lazily down her back as she walked down the hill. Her long, tanned legs were tired from the run, yet maintained a bounce borne of endurance and purpose.

Approaching Barrington Beach, Angela expected to see teenagers eking out the last remnants of a summer filled with tanning, swimming, and furtive drinking. But to her surprise, the beach was barren, save for an old man about two hundred yards away, swinging a metal detector. She slowed her pace and surveyed the houses facing the water, then waved to a friend who sat reading on a balcony. Turning left, she jogged a half mile along the water's edge until she came to a dilapidated dock that extended from an abandoned home on Rumstick Road. After the elderly owner had passed away several years ago, the once-breathtaking home had become a pawn in an inheritance battle among the woman's grown children. The result was that no one maintained the grounds and the entire estate had fallen into disrepair. The old wooden dock, once a diving platform for local children, listed to the right and caution tape had been wound around it.

Ducking under the tape, Angela walked behind a secluded piling, squatted, and pushed a heavy rock until it rolled about a foot away from its original resting place. She then used her hands to claw through the sand until her fingers caught the edge of something hard. Glancing about to ensure she was still alone, Angela tugged at the object until the sand relinquished its hold with a violent sucking sound.

The gun was encased in heavy plastic, and she was meticulous as she unwrapped it. The plastic cocoon had done its job; the pistol was as pristine as the day she'd purchased it.

First, do no harm—a line from the Hippocratic oath she'd taken when she'd earned her medical degree from Dartmouth. And she wouldn't do any harm. Not any more harm than she'd already done. Not yet, anyway. Not just yet.

CHAPTER 1

~

May 2018

Angela walked down the hallway, her eyes glued to an iPad that contained recent lab results of the patient she'd just seen. Without looking up, she sensed someone walking behind her and assumed it was the nurse assigned to her clinic that day. "Who's next, Karen?"

"Your last patient today is Yolanda Hassan in room six, Doctor."

The perky voice drew a smile to her face, and Angela turned to find Liz Rumsey, her military-cut, platinum-blond hair standing at attention. Her sparkly green eyes crinkled at the corners, as if to compete with the toothy grin that took up most of her face. The individually dramatic features created an overall effect of masculine beauty that made people stop and stare.

"Liz, what are you doing outside of the surgical suite? I thought nurses were allowed to leave only on weekends," Angela joked.

"And even then it's a crapshoot with the recent on-call schedule."

Angela chuckled. "Seriously, what's up? I haven't seen you in clinic on your day off since you kidnapped me for our girls' weekend last year."

Liz offered a wide smile and nodded. "Oh yeah. I had forgotten about that. Tony did a great job keeping your birthday surprise a secret. Boy, that was a fun weekend, wasn't it?"

"Sure was. We need to do that again. It seems like we don't go out as much as we used to."

Liz crossed her arms and tilted an eyebrow. "That's because we don't."

"You're right. I'm sorry. With the kids' schedules and—"

"Yeah, yeah, I know. I miss my best friend, that's all."

Karen approached quickly and cleared her throat. "Dr. Brennan, Mrs. Hassan is waiting for you."

Angela nodded. "Sorry, Karen. Liz, you didn't come here to reminisce. What's up?"

Liz's smile dropped and she became clinical. "I wanted to let you know that Dr. Smythe is worried about Mrs. Sinclair."

Angela pulled a face in confusion. "Ava Sinclair? Why?"

Liz bobbed her head back and forth. "He's worried that her numbers are off."

"Her open-heart surgery was only three days ago."

"Well, she's vacillating between tachycardia and bradycardia, so her blood pressure's all over the place. Dr. Smythe is with her now and he requested I find you. He's kind of freaking out."

"Did you tell him her symptoms aren't unusual after surgery?"

"Of course I did, but remember, this was his first assist in an off-pump cardiac surgery so I think he's more nervous than usual."

Angela nodded, annoyed that the inexperienced surgeon was robbing her of valuable clinic time. Bernard Smythe had assisted in enough open-heart surgeries to know that Mrs. Sinclair's jumbled blood pressure was most likely her body's response to extreme trauma. Plus, Ava Sinclair had come through her surgery beautifully, and her grateful husband had poured praise over Angela in response. But reassuring young surgeons was part of the job as chairperson of Cardiac Surgery, so she knew she had to go, even if soothing Bernard Smythe's frazzled nerves meant that she'd have to stay late again to complete her clinical notes. It was her day to pick up the kids from the sitter, and she winced internally as she imagined asking Tony to do it. She removed her iPhone from her pocket and stabbed out a quick text instead.

"I'll finish up here and come over. Thanks, Liz."

"Of course. I'll wait with Dr. Smythe until you arrive. He's not going to leave until he's sure she's okay." Angela squeezed her arm and watched her best friend walk away before lightly rapping on the exam room door.

"Sorry to keep you waiting, Mrs. Hassan. It's good to see you."

"I wish I could say the same, Dr. Brennan. Don't get me wrong. You're a really nice person, but who wants to visit her cardiac surgeon on a beautiful day like today?"

"I cannot agree with you more. How have you been feeling since the surgery?"

"I feel great. It's nice to be able to breathe again, to spend time with my family without getting so tired."

Angela crossed to the sink and washed her hands. "That's good to hear. You had three blocked arteries, so I can imagine how tired you felt. Your heart was working harder to pump blood throughout your body—of course you were feeling exhausted. Deep breaths, please."

Angela placed her stethoscope against the patient's back, slowly moving it across as she listened to her lungs. She then transferred the instrument to the woman's chest and listened for a full minute to her heart. "Sounds fantastic." She glanced at her iPad. "Your blood pressure and blood oxygen numbers are strong, too. Seems like you're doing great. Based on what I've seen here today, Mrs. Hassan, I don't think I need to see you again for six months. How does that sound?"

A gap-toothed grin illuminated the woman's round face. "That sounds wonderful, Dr. Brennan."

"Okay," Angela laughed. "Get dressed and you're free to go. See you in six months."

Angela washed her hands once more—wash in, wash out, as she had been instructed—and made her way to Ava Sinclair's room. She knocked on the door and then pushed it open to find

Liz seated in the bedside chair and Dr. Smythe standing at the foot of the sleeping patient, his arms crossed and brow furrowed in thought. He was so focused that Angela was standing next to him before he became aware of her presence. They stood silently for a moment before Angela spoke. "Status?"

"Heart rate varies between 40 and 120 beats per minute with blood pressure and oxygen levels following suit. Shortness of breath and fluttery eyes when she's awake. I'm not sure if she's sleeping or passing out intermittently."

"Potential causes?"

Dr. Smythe took a deep breath, attempting to calm his busy mind. "Post-surgical heart arrhythmias are not uncommon, so that's a possibility. No fever, so I don't anticipate any infection. Genetic testing and EKGs ruled out any factors that might indicate long QT or Wolff Parkinson syndrome."

"Have you spoken to her when she's awake?"

"Yes, and she's coherent and doesn't complain of pain."

"Okay. Have you done everything you can do for her at this point?" Angela stole a glance at Liz, who smiled and nodded.

Dr. Smythe chewed the inside of his cheek as he considered her question. "Yes, but—"

"No buts. If you've done everything you can, then you need to let Mrs. Sinclair's body do its job and heal. Look at me, Dr. Smythe." The younger doctor tore his eyes from the bed. "One of the most difficult things I had to learn as a less experienced surgeon was when to do nothing. We're taught as physicians to do something, to fix the problem. No one teaches us when to back off and simply let the body do what it does best, which is heal itself. This is one of those times. You've done everything you can, as have I. Mrs. Sinclair needs to do her part now. It's her turn."

"But something doesn't feel right. I can't explain it—"

Without warning, a loud, monotone beep sounded and Mrs. Sinclair's body writhed in convulsions. The duty nurse rushed in with an emergency cart as Angela instructed Liz and Dr. Smythe to restrain the patient while she applied her stethoscope. "No heartbeat. Mrs. Sinclair, can you hear me? Mrs. Sinclair?" Angela examined the woman's eyes using her pen light. "Pupils dilated and fixed." The woman's body momentarily relaxed and then arched off the bed in renewed paroxysms.

"Dr. Smythe, initiate CPR."

"But—"

"Do it!" Angela ordered. "Liz, prepare the paddles."

Dr. Smythe placed his left hand on top of his right and intertwined his fingers. He repeatedly pressed down firmly on Mrs. Sinclair's chest as he counted aloud, her body bouncing with his movements. He breathed heavily as he worked, his eyes fixed to the heart monitor, willing it to start beeping. After thirty depressions, he stepped back to allow Angela to listen for a heartbeat. After a moment, she shook her head and looked at Liz. "Paddles charged up?"

"Yes, doctor."

Angela extended her hands and accepted the automatic defibrillator paddles, then applied them to Mrs. Sinclair's chest.

"Clear!"

The patient's body jerked once and then lay still. Dr. Smythe listened for a heartbeat and shook his head.

"Again." The defibrillation process was repeated two more times with no success. "One more time," Angela ordered loudly.

"Dr. Brennan," Liz said quietly, "I think she's gone."

"No," Angela said. "One more time."

"Dr. Brennan," Liz repeated. "You've done everything you can. She's gone."

A commotion erupted outside the door and Mr. Sinclair burst through, a frantic nurse trailing him. "I'm sorry, Dr. Brennan. I tried to keep him out, but he pushed me aside and said that—"

Angela held up her hand toward the nurse, indicating that the intrusion was okay. Stepping toward Mr. Sinclair, she shoved her hands in the pockets of her lab coat. "Mr. Sinclair. I'm so sorry. We did everything we could but—"

"But what? She's dead? How can she be dead? Two days ago she was absolutely fine. You said so yourself. And now she's dead?!" His voice was rising, and Angela knew from experience that she had to get him into a social worker's office as soon as possible.

Lowering the timbre of her voice in an effort to calm him, she said, "I'm not exactly sure what happened, but I think your wife had a stroke that led to another heart attack. We won't know until we do an autopsy."

Mr. Sinclair's eyes had been locked on his wife's face until he heard "autopsy." Stepping forward, he loomed over Angela and jabbed his finger into her face as he spat, "You will not carve up Ava's body any more! You've done quite enough!"

Angela glanced at Liz, whose tense face summed up the volatile situation. She then looked at Dr. Smythe, who stood in the corner of the room, face downcast. "Mr. Sinclair, again, I'm so—"

"If you say sorry one more time, I'll . . . I don't know what I'll do. Get out." He twisted a baseball cap in his large hands and stared at his wife's body as tears gathered in the deep lines around his eyes. Angela's heart seized. He seemed like a broken man who had nothing left to lose.

Angela set her mouth, nodded, and motioned with her head for everyone to follow her out of the room. Once outside, she asked Liz to contact a social worker to help Mr. Sinclair with next steps, or what her mentor had always referred to as "the business of death." Turning to Dr. Smythe, she noted that he refused to meet her eyes. Instead, he stared at the floor and leaned against the wall, his arms crossed over his chest. Angela cleared her throat and said, "I think Mrs. Sinclair suffered a subarachnoid hemorrhagic stroke caused by years of high blood pressure. And that stroke led to a fatal myocardial infarction. If I'm correct, her death was almost inevitable. There's no way we could have known about the aneurysm. This is not your fault, Dr. Smythe."

He shook his head, then raised his stony gaze to meet hers. "I told you something wasn't right. I knew, I *knew* something was really wrong. You say it's not my fault? I know it's not my fault, Dr. Brennan. It's *yours*."

CHAPTER 2

~

Tony Brennan's grip tightened on the phone as he responded to his general contractor's excuses. "I can't have this conversation with you one more time," Tony fumed. "Either get your guys on board or I find someone else. It's that simple, Rob. We're three weeks behind schedule and I'm getting calls asking for an update. They should be calling *you*. I'm just the poor schmuck who designed the damned house."

Sean, Tony's wiry, bespectacled business partner, snickered. Tony rolled his eyes and listened some more. "Just get them moving, okay, Rob? Thanks. Talk to you tomorrow." Tony shook his head as he disconnected. "Unbelievable!"

"Hey, man. That's why you make the big bucks," Sean commented.

Tony grinned, his even, white teeth glowing against olive skin. "We *are* bringing in ten percent on this two-million-dollar project."

"And this is just one project. I've got two more about half that size currently in negotiations." Sean extended his hand for a high five. "Not bad for two artists-turned-architects who don't know what they're doing business-wise, am I right?"

Tony was quiet.

"You're gonna leave me hanging, Tony?" Sean asked, palm still extended. Tony glanced at Sean's hand and slapped it. "Sorry, man. It's just . . . I was thinking back to when things were simple. I kind of miss that. Do you?"

Sean scrunched his face. "If by 'simple' you mean poor, then . . . no, I don't miss those days. The struggling artist thing worked for you but didn't really do anything for me. Besides, you can always go back to your painting if you like. Jesus, Tony. Angela makes like a gazillion dollars at the hospital. I wish I had a partner that made that much. Don't get me wrong, Melanie is a great wife and mother, but her salary as a school teacher leaves a lot to be desired."

"It's not about the money, Sean."

"It's always about the money, Tony."

Tony shook his head. "No, it's not—"

"Says the man with lots of money," Sean interjected.

Tony shot him a look and raked his fingers through his dark, wavy hair. "When I met Angela, she was in med school and I was finishing my masters in architecture. We made plans to take on the world together, just her and me. I supported us through her residency. We were poor, but it was good, you know? And then, surprise! Emily arrived, and things got more complicated. And then Liam came shortly after that. And then, all of a sudden, she's doing a post-doc fellowship in cardiac surgery and has opportunities presented to her that she's never considered before."

"What's wrong with that?"

"Nothing. But . . . it's just that life is crazy now. There's no rest. I feel obligated to build this business because she's so successful in her career. I kind of just want to take a break." Tony glanced at Sean, wondering if his friend could appreciate what he was trying to say. Despite his earlier comments about Melanie's salary, Tony knew that Sean and his wife shared a wonderful life with their children. On several occasions, Sean had shared with Tony that he wouldn't change a thing about his life.

As if reading Tony's mind, Sean asked, "Do you regret any of it?"

"Absolutely not! I would do all of it again in a heartbeat. But I might slow everything down just a bit, that's all."

Sean repositioned his glasses. "I don't know a lot of things, Tony, but I know for sure that life doesn't work that way. Besides, you two aren't getting any younger. How old was Angela when she had Emily?"

"Thirty-six."

"And that was twelve years ago. You're both pushing fifty, brother. Now is not the time to slow down. You can sleep when you're dead. Until then, keep on fighting the good fight, designing those houses for the incredibly well-to-do, and suck up all the shit that comes with it. You hear me? I've become accustomed to a certain lifestyle, and I don't care to give it up," Sean said as he pushed Tony toward his drawing board strewn with plans.

"Alright, I hear you. Seriously, thanks for listening. I'm not sure where all of that came from. I guess I've been thinking about it but didn't know how to say it."

Sean slapped Tony's back. "That's what friends are for. Just keep me in the loop, okay? If you're ever serious about hanging up your architecture license, I need to have time to find the next big thing and latch onto his or her coattails."

"Will do." Tony's phone chirped and he glanced at it. "Goddamn it."

"What is it?"

Tony blew out a mouthful of air. "It was Angela's night to pick up the kids and she has to stay late."

"Again?"

Tony looked hard at Sean. "Yes. Again."

"Sorry, bud."

Tony shook his head and glanced at the time. "Shit! I'm going to be late. I gotta go."

"Go," Sean said. "I'll lock up here."

Tony stuffed some plans into his backpack, grabbed his keys, and loped to his car. His office was in Providence, and it would take him at least thirty-five minutes to get to the sitter's house in Warren. Tony ran a red light and then gunned the engine as he sped onto I-195. Weaving around slower cars, he commanded Siri to dial the sitter, who answered on the first ring.

"Hello, Mr. Brennan. Let me guess. You're running a few minutes behind schedule?"

Tony grimaced. "Hi, Mrs. Stanton. Yes, and I'm so sorry. I'll be there soon." Tony glanced at the clock.

"I'll draw up a proposal for future tardiness, Mr. Brennan. I hate to do it, but in my experience, charging people for being late tends to help them focus. All of a sudden, picking up your children on time will become a priority."

"Understood. And I'll be happy to pay you whatever you think is fair for tonight."

"Money doesn't solve all problems, Mr. Brennan."

"I know. I didn't mean to imply that it did. I mean —"

"Okay, okay. Just get here when you can."

"Thanks." Tony hung up just as a Range Rover cut him off, forcing him to swerve wildly into the right lane. As he leaned on his horn, voicing his displeasure at the other driver, traffic slowed and then stopped. Up ahead one car lay on its side while another was in several large pieces strewn across two lanes of traffic.

Tony's shoulders slumped. "You gotta be fucking kidding me. Today of all days."

Three lanes shrank to one as he neared the accident site, and flow was slow but steady as cars alternated entering the single lane. He drove past the crash and saw a man lying supine on the ground, paramedics pressing his chest in a rhythmic pattern. A woman lay sprawled on a stretcher, one arm flung across her face. As Tony stared at her, she suddenly sat up and locked eyes with him. Her right eye was swollen shut and she gaped at Tony as if she were asking him how she got there. Startled, Tony averted his eyes and remembered his wife's admonition some years ago.

Angela had been working in the Emergency Department and was seven months pregnant with Emily when they had driven past a terrible accident. Tony had slowed to absorb the scene, and Angela had turned to him, her eyes earnest and questioning. "Why do people have such a fascination with gore and terror? It's like they can't get enough of it."

He had shrugged. "I guess people are curious. I know I am." She had stared hard at him as they had accelerated past the accident. "Tony, you realize someone might have died in that crash, right? If you were dying, would you want someone gawking at you, horrified?"

"Probably not."

"Do you know what my theory is? My theory is that humans are irresistibly drawn to the macabre because they don't see it in their daily lives. It scares them, but they have to look to reinforce the fact that they're safe, despite the fact that someone else isn't. They know that the person lying on the ground could very easily be them, so they're fascinated, yet relieved by someone else's horror."

Tony had never considered that perspective before and found that her words rang true. "You're not fascinated by the macabre?"

Angela had laughed derisively. "I don't need to be fascinated by it. I see it literally every day. Last night, a six-year-old came in with a gunshot wound and died. It's awful. Death, especially in children, is awful."

She'd turned her head toward the window and picked at a thumbnail, reliving the previous night. It was then he'd truly appreciated the emotional toll her work must take on her, how she must internalize each patient loss. And yet, until that moment, she had managed to compartmentalize so well. Tony had rarely seen Angela wear her worry, managing a smile regardless of what she might have seen or experienced at work. Tony had taken her hand and they had continued the drive in silence.

Despite that, here he was, so many years later, still rubbernecking at an accident scene.

Tony shook his head to clear it as the road opened up to three lanes. Glancing at his watch, he swore under his breath and depressed the accelerator as he realized exactly how late he was going to be.

CHAPTER 3

~

Angela peeked through the lead-glass windows that surrounded the front door and saw Tony's car pull in the driveway. She smiled, remembering how tiny Emily was when they had designed their dream home. They had poured all of their savings into the land and foundation, and had borrowed money from her parents to complete the structure. Like many homes in the area, it was clad in weathered cedar shingles and boasted two fieldstone chimneys and four dormers. A Belgian-block cobblestone path led to the enormous cherry front door, through which the children tumbled, scattering their belongings.

Angela stood in the expansive foyer, arms wide open. "Hi guys. How was your—"

"Can't talk now, Mom," Emily said as she held her palm out toward Angela, effectively warding off any possibility of a hug. A small sting of disappointment fluttered through Angela.

"I was just asking how your day was."

"Fine," Emily answered as she scrambled up the steps, two at a time.

Angela rebounded and turned to Liam, who was engrossed in his phone. "And you? How was your day, little man?"

Liam pushed some curly blond hair from his face with a hand that clearly had not seen soap and water all day. "Great,

Mom! It was great! Tyler poked his eye at recess and had to go to home. It was really gross but awesome!" He ran toward her, hugged her hard, and then dashed up the stairs as she tried to return the embrace, leaving her outstretched arms clasping air.

"Hey, hey! Don't make a mess, you guys!" Tony called after them.

"And dinner will be ready soon so please wash your hands!" Angela added as she transferred her hug to Tony. They stood quietly for a moment, enjoying the closeness and relative solitude. Angela inhaled his scent as Tony gently rocked her back and forth, a habit he'd had for as long as she could remember. Being hugged by Tony was like coming home to a warm house with a roaring fire and the aroma of a home-cooked meal. She sighed deeply and snuggled into his chest, remembering their life before children, when they would make love and then linger over a gourmet meal prepared while drinking too much wine.

"Rough day?" Tony asked.

Angela's mind relived Ava Sinclair's death and its aftermath. She closed her eyes and saw Mr. Sinclair's devastated face, his body sagging as he digested the horrendous news. Although the scientist in her was frustrated that Mr. Sinclair wouldn't allow an autopsy, the mother in her understood his rationale. His wife was gone, and understanding why she died would do nothing to ease his pain. "Yeah. You could say that."

"Want to talk about it?"

Angela smiled into Tony's shirt. "Not right now. Tell me about your day."

Angela noticed that Tony's body stiffened a little. "It was really busy. And not helped by your last-minute text to pick up the kids."

"I know, and I'm sorry for that." A buzzer sounded and she reluctantly pulled away. "That's the microwave." She took his hand and led him into the large, sunshine-yellow kitchen around which they had designed the rest of the house. Angela had left the overall design to Tony, but had insisted on light-cherry cabinetry, top-of-the-line appliances, and an island large enough to host a soccer team. Growing up with a mother who loved to cook and host dinners, Angela understood the importance of food and a quality kitchen in which to prepare it.

Angela removed the potatoes from the microwave. "Hey, can you grab the chicken and heat it up, please?" Tony crossed to the SubZero fridge and removed the premade dish.

"What's that?" Angela asked as she glanced at a manila envelope that lay on the black granite counter.

Tony put the chicken in the microwave and followed her gaze. "Oh, that? It's a contract from Mrs. Stanton."

"For what?"

"It outlines the financial implications of our being late to pick up the kids from her house."

Angela shook her head. "I don't understand."

Tony filled four glasses with filtered water. "It's simple, Angela. We've been late so many times that Mrs. Stanton felt the need to draw up a contract that states we'll be charged a dollar for each minute we're late to retrieve our children."

"Well . . . that doesn't seem fair. How many times have we been late?"

Tony paused, mid-pour, and pursed his lips. "This week? Let's see. It's Friday, right? That makes . . ." He counted on his fingers. "Five times, according to Mrs. Stanton."

"No. That can't be right."

"Believe me. It's correct."

"Well then, I guess we'll just have to pay her the overtime she's requesting. We don't want to lose her. Or, rather, we don't want her to fire us. The kids love her and she's so good for them."

"I agree, but I think we need to come up with a better plan for pick-up."

Angela tensed, sensing what was to come as she transferred the plates to the table. "What do you mean?"

"We've had this conversation ad nauseum. I know you're busy at work, but so am I. In fact, Sean and I are starting to turn away projects because we can barely keep up."

Angela pressed the intercom button twice, a prearranged signal that the children's presence was requested downstairs. A modern-day version of the dinner bell. Within seconds, she heard the distinct slam of Liam jumping off the top bunk of his bed, and then rhythmic thumps as he sprinted down the hallway and barreled down the mahogany spiral staircase. Smiling, Angela returned her attention to Tony. "If business is so good, then why don't you and Sean hire a third architect?"

"You know that's not—" Liam came sliding around the doorjamb in his socks, grabbing at the countertop in an effort to stop himself before crashing to the floor. He jumped up and put his fists on his narrow hips.

"What are you wearing?" Angela asked, looking him up and down.

"Do you like it? It's just like what the guy wore in that movie you and Dad like. What's it called? *Dirty Business*?"

Angela evaluated her towhead, sinewy son dressed in one of Tony's white dress shirts that fell past his knees. A black tie was draped around his neck and his eyes were hidden by the dark lenses of some Wayfarer sunglasses.

Angela stifled a laugh while Tony shook his head. "It's called *Risky Business* and you're a goofball. Come sit down. Where's your sister?"

Liam shrugged as he deposited himself at the table and started shoveling potatoes into his mouth. "I dunno. She was in her room last time I saw her."

Angela pressed the intercom button that corresponded with Emily's room. "Em, dinner."

"I'm not hungry."

"Come on, Em. We don't get many opportunities to eat as a family. Please come down."

"I said I'm not hungry."

Angela sighed. "Get down here please, young lady. Right now."

There was a long pause, followed by the angry exhalation of air her daughter had recently mastered. "Fine!"

Angela returned to the table and spread a cloth napkin across her lap. She and Tony watched in fascination as Liam ripped meat from the drumsticks that criss-crossed his plate. "Goodness, Liam, slow down. No one's going to steal your food. You don't have to eat so fast."

"Dad, you don't get it. Hunter and I were playing *Minecraft* and if I'm gone too long, he might kill my cow."

"I *do* get it, buddy, but if you choke and die because you're plowing food into your mouth, then you won't be around and Hunter will get your cow anyway. See where I'm going with this? You may as well slow down."

Liam grinned, his two front teeth too large in his nine-year-old mouth.

Angela looked at Tony. "What in the world is he talking about? Something about killing a cow?"

Tony and Liam responded in unison, "*Minecraft*."

Angela had no idea to what they were referring. "Yeah, I heard that. But what is it?"

Emily breezed in and sat heavily in the chair opposite Angela, then crossed her coltish legs. Angela noted that in the brief time Emily had been upstairs she had managed to braid her long brunette hair and style the braids into a crown that circled her head. "God, Mom, you're so out of it. *Minecraft* is an online game that little kids play with other little kids all around the globe."

"It's not for little kids!" Liam shot back.

Emily sneered at her brother before rolling her eyes. "Whatever."

"Is it safe?" Angela asked.

Tony made a face. "As safe as any online game can be."

"What does that mean?"

"What Dad's saying is that if you were around more, you'd know," Emily mumbled.

Angela rested her fork on the plate and sat up straighter in her chair. She placed her elbows on the table, then entwined her fingers and rested her chin on them as she gazed at her daughter. "What did you just say to me?"

Emily attempted to hold her mother's gaze but failed. "Nothing."

"Oh, no. It was definitely something, Emily."

Emily glanced quickly at her father. "Can I be excused?" Without waiting for an answer, she stood and ran from the room.

"Can I go too?" Liam asked eagerly, completely oblivious to the tension. "I finished my food." Angela waved her hand in his direction, dismissing him. She felt disappointment settle into the lines around her mouth. "Go." Liam wiped his mouth on his shirtsleeve, placed his plate in the sink, and bounded upstairs.

"That was my shirt he just wiped his mouth on," Tony said as he picked up a drumstick. "Oh well."

"You feel the same way, don't you?"

"About the shirt?"

Angela pushed mashed potatoes around her plate. "No. About my not being here. You think I'm not around enough."

"No, no. I'm not taking that bait, Angela. Don't put words in my mouth."

"You're right. That wasn't fair. But do you think that?"

"I think the real question is, what do you think?"

"I think that if I want to be a CEO one day, I need to commit to at least as many hours as I'm currently working, if not more."

"CEO? What are you talking about?"

"I was going to talk to you about this later, but . . . Maggie will be retiring soon, and she's asked me to consider putting my hat in the ring as her successor." Angela smiled tentatively, hoping that Tony would wholeheartedly support her.

"To be hospital CEO? Aren't you happy being a surgeon?"

"Sure, but she asked, so . . ."

"So you're seriously considering it?"

Angela tilted her head back and forth while biting her lip. "Yeah, I guess I am." She grinned again as she said the words aloud.

"Don't you need a business degree to run a hospital?"

Angela shrugged. "I asked the same question, and Maggie

said the hospital would fund my MBA. She said I could get my degree in less than a year."

"But having a business degree doesn't mean that you would know how to run the hospital. This is silly."

A rush of adrenaline surged and her excitement shattered into a hundred little shards of anger. "Silly?"

"Honestly? Yes. I was telling you that I can barely keep my head above water at work and you're telling me that you're going back to school to become a CEO, which means that we'll see you even less than we do now. And that's not saying much."

Angela nodded slowly as anger, sadness, and resentment jousted inside her troubled mind. "And there it is. The truth. You don't think I'm here enough."

Tony closed his eyes and breathed deeply. "Okay, yes. I don't think you're here enough. We used to share kid duty, Angela, but since you've become chair, you're gone by the crack of dawn and we're lucky if we see you by seven o'clock each night. Tonight was a perfect example. It was your night to pick up Em and Liam, and, last minute," he snapped his fingers, "you can't make it. With my current workload, I can't do any more than I'm already doing." Angela felt the blood rush to her cheeks. Tony wasn't wrong, but she felt his comments painted an unfair picture of her as a mother and wife. She stared at her hands as they wrung the napkin that lay in her lap.

"And that doesn't even include the conferences, talks, and symposiums that you attend throughout the year. I mean, Liam is relatively well-adjusted, but it's just a matter of time before he'll start testing us like Emily does. And what about Emily? She needs her mother now more than ever. Did you know she has a boyfriend?"

Angela's head shot up as a bolt of electricity ran through her. "What?"

"Yes. A boyfriend. Apparently his name is Max and they've been dating for a month. I only found out about it because Liam was reading her texts aloud in the car and she freaked out at him."

"I wonder why she didn't tell me?"

Tony looked steadily at her. "You and she haven't had a lot of girl time recently, Angela. Hell, you and I haven't had a lot of 'us' time either."

Angela dropped her head, eyes stinging with unshed tears as guilt cloaked her. "You're right, Tony. I should have been here for her first boyfriend."

Tony placed his hand over hers. Although her impulse was to pull away, she knew from experience that doing so would inflame the already precarious situation. "It's not just Emily's boyfriend. You're missing so many of the little things that make a family special, Angela. We only have the kids for a little while before they grow up and are gone."

Tears breached her lids and spilled onto her plate as she considered Tony's comments. Although she wanted to be angry at him, she knew that he was right. Being a cardiac surgeon took a lot of physical time, but it also took an emotional toll as well. Even when she was home, which was certainly less frequently since she had become chair of the department, her mind was often elsewhere: reliving a surgery, planning a presentation, or, God forbid, revisiting a patient's death. She hadn't realized until now the cost that she and her family had been paying for her absence. She wiped her eyes. "I know, and I want to be a part of it. But you know I've wanted to be a surgeon since I was a little girl. And I don't feel like I should have to sacrifice my dreams because of our family."

Tony quickly withdrew his hand, and Angela realized that she had misspoken. "Is that what you're doing, Angela? Sacrificing your dreams because of us?"

"You know what I mean, Tony. I want to be a great surgeon *and* have a great family."

"So what's this business about becoming a CEO?"

Angela blew her nose on her napkin and shrugged. "Maggie thinks I have more in me. That I'd be a great leader."

She looked at Tony and noted that his mouth was twitching, a sure sign that he was considering what she'd said. After several moments, his mouth stilled. "I can't disagree with Maggie. You *would* be a great leader. But tell me, do you really want to do this?"

Angela looked into his eyes and noted the small lines that had formed at the edges. He looked tired. "I do. But not at the further expense of our family. I won't do it if you think I shouldn't. And I promise that I won't hold it against you for telling me how you really feel."

Tony took some time before responding. "I love you, Angela. More than anything in the world except for Emily and Liam. If this is what you want, then we'll make it work. But you're going to be busier than ever, so I think we should take a mini-vacation to spend some time with the kids. We can explain everything to them then."

Angela tried but failed to stifle the smile that raised the edges of her mouth. "What about your firm?"

Tony raised his eyebrows. "I'll talk to Sean about hiring another architect and I'll cut back on my hours to be here more with the kids. I was just saying that I wanted to slow down a little anyway."

Angela wanted to jump up and hug Tony. But she still felt some tension in the air between them. "You wouldn't be slowing down by staying with these two."

Tony smiled openly, shattering the remaining uneasiness, and Angela felt her shoulders relax.

"I know, but it'd be different. And I could still work when they're in school."

"You'd do that for me? Become a stay-at-home dad?"

Tony winced. "That's a little dramatic, but yes, I would."

After such an emotionally intense day, her strain released in a torrent of love that caught her by surprise and brought tears to her eyes. "Do you know what you are?"

"A sucker?"

She kissed him and placed her forehead against his. "No. You're reliable and kind and the best father I know."

CHAPTER 4

“Clamp.”

Liz handed the instrument to Angela, who delicately occluded the internal mammary artery.

“I need more light here. Scalpel, please.”

Another nurse shifted the LED lamp to focus on the exposed heart whose pumping was inhibited by a stabilization system. “That’s better. Thanks.”

The scalpel slipped out of Angela’s gloved hands and clattered to the tiled floor. A fresh instrument was in her hand before she could request it, prompting her to smile underneath her surgical mask. “On the ball as usual, Liz.”

Liz’s green eyes smiled in return. “You know it.”

Angela carefully detached one end of the artery she would use to bypass the patient’s blocked one as Liz used a surgical sponge to soak up excess blood. Angela then made a small incision in the damaged artery above the blockage and attached the harvested organ.

“Body temp?”

“88.6.”

“Can we get that down, please?”

“Working on it, Doctor.”

Angela glanced at Liz over her mask. "Hey, I meant to ask you the other day in clinic but I forgot. Whatever happened to Mr. Right?"

"Who?"

"That guy you were dating who you said was—"

Liz glanced quickly at the other six people in the operating suite. "Really, Dr. Brennan, you're asking me this now?"

"Blood pressure 115 over 82, and stable. Pulse is 84 beats per minute. Pulse ox is 85 percent," the anesthesiologist noted as he stared at Liz.

Angela smiled and extended her hand for another clamp, which Liz loudly slapped into her palm as she targeted Angela with a death stare.

"Why not? We have no secrets, do we guys?"

Everyone chuckled except Liz.

"Teamwork makes the dream work," Angela noted as she clamped the other end of the artery to stop blood flow, and then detached it and guided the open end of the harvested organ to the small incision she'd made in the coronary artery. She then sewed the two together below the site of the blockage, thereby completing a new path for blood flow to and from the heart.

"So . . . what happened?" Angela prompted.

Liz cleared her throat while rolling her eyes. "It, um, didn't work out as I had hoped."

Angela smiled. "No more details?"

Liz raised her eyebrows and spoke with attitude. "Not in *here*. And if you continue with your current line of questioning, I might be forced to retaliate and regale the Dream Team here with a story or two about you."

Angela smiled broadly underneath her mask. "I'm sure they don't want to hear about that. I guess we'll need to go out for a drink soon."

Liz tilted her head and widened her eyes. "Now, why didn't I think of that?"

Angela laughed. "Liz, you're a good sport. Dr. Smythe, please suture the remaining incision sites."

The team was quiet as they observed the young surgeon carefully sew the areas opened by the scalpel. Once completed, Angela removed the tissue stabilizer, allowing full blood flow to resume throughout the heart.

"Body temp is 88.2. BP is stable at 112/80, pulse is 88 beats per minute, and pulse ox is 92 percent."

Angela nodded while removing the positioner that had secured the heart during surgery. "Right on schedule. Slowly increase body temp to normal and continue to monitor all vitals. Report to me if any problems arise. I'll be updating the family and then in my office dictating notes. Dr. Smythe, you got this?" Angela swept her hand over the patient's body, indicating that Dr. Smythe should complete the remaining details of the operation.

"Yes, Doctor. And thanks for letting me assist."

Angela held his eyes, feeling the rift that had not yet healed from the Ava Sinclair incident. She removed her latex gloves and used a pinky to pull down one side of her surgical mask. "My pleasure. You're a good surgeon. Just don't let it go to your head. After all, we're all replaceable. Remember to do a bang-up job on her bandage."

Dr. Smythe shook his head. "I've never understood why you say that."

"It's simple. What's the first thing that a patient does upon regaining consciousness?"

"Ask where they are?"

Angela smiled. "True. But after that, what's the next thing that a patient does? They look at their bandage. If we do a lousy job bandaging, then the patient assumes we did a lousy job on the surgery as well. Hence, a clean, white bandage that is applied neatly." She nodded at Liz, who winked in return, an unspoken gesture that meant "Job well done."

After placing her bloody apron and scrubs in a hamper marked "Hazardous," Angela scrubbed her hands, arms, and face in the large stainless-steel sink and donned her street clothes and a pressed white lab coat that sported her name in blue needlepoint. The jacket had been a gift from her parents upon med school graduation, every stitch sewn by her proud mother.

She spoke with the relieved family and then started the trek to her office. Her mind wandered to her family's upcoming vacation, and she allowed herself a moment of pure joy as she imagined sleeping in and sunning herself while spending time with her favorite people on the planet.

"What are you smiling about?" Liz asked as she fell in step beside Angela.

"Wow, you scrubbed up quickly."

"I have a date, actually."

Angela grinned. "I promise that I won't ask about it during our next surgery."

She felt Liz's eyes on her. "Yes, you will."

Angela laughed. "Yes. I will."

"So what's with the happiness that's exuding from your pores right now?"

"I'm just so excited about this vacation, Liz. I can hardly wait. An entire long weekend at the beach!" Angela stopped suddenly and faced Liz. "Listen, you're not mad that I raised the subject of Mr. Right in the O.R., are you?"

Liz waved her hand. "Are you kidding me? My love life is hardly the most interesting item that's discussed in there."

Angela laughed. "True, but the real reason I raised the issue is because I think that Savin has a crush on you."

Liz's entire face crinkled. "The English anesthesiologist? Are you kidding me? He's, like, sixty!"

Angela shook her head. "He's a wonderful man, Liz. You could do worse."

Liz shook her head. "No daddy issues here, sister. If anything, I like to date younger men. So if you're going to try to set me up, please focus on thirty to forty-ish. Deal?"

Angela smiled. "Deal. I'll get on it. If this date today doesn't work out, that is."

Liz rolled her eyes. "You're such a yenta."

"Someone's got to do it. You're too wonderful to be spending your life alone."

Liz stopped and regarded her friend. "You're good to me. Have a great vacation if I don't see you." They embraced and Angela smiled as she watched Liz walk away. Without turning around, Liz called out, "And don't forget about that drink. You're all talk!"

Angela smiled and removed her phone to check email. Turning the corner, she bumped into someone and mumbled, "Excuse me" without looking up.

"Is that how you greet a friend of so many years?"

Angela stopped and turned. "Frank! Oh my goodness, I'm so sorry! I didn't know it was you." She rushed forward and hugged the octogenarian physician under whom she had studied and perfected her craft. As she withdrew, Frank smiled, crinkles appearing around his rheumy blue eyes. His thick, snow-white hair stood at various angles and she was suddenly reminded of Santa Claus.

"I guess not," he retorted, squeezing her hand. "How's business?"

"Never-ending. You know what they say. The only two things that don't go south in a recession are healthcare and booze."

Frank chuckled. "I believe you learned that from me, my dear."

"On day one of my first rotation as an intern. How could I forget? Dr. Frank Toner charmed us and terrified us at the same time." It was true. Angela had returned home and told Tony about the scary, adorable man under whom she'd be studying cardiac surgery. Tony had questioned how one person could hold both titles, scary and adorable, until he'd met Frank and immediately understood. At six foot three, Frank was physically imposing, but it was his stoic manner and intellect that commanded attention and respect. Yet all of that could be cast aside when he laughed. His smiles and warm chuckles were inclusive and had a calming effect on both patients and interns alike. In Angela's opinion, there was no one in the world like Frank Toner.

"Just doing my job, Dr. Brennan."

Angela took his arm as they walked. "And you did it very well. To what do I owe the honor of your visit?"

"I wanted to let you know that I'm retiring, Angela."

Angela stopped to face him as a wave of caution swept over her. "Frank, that doesn't sound like you at all. What's going on?"

"Well, I am eighty-three."

"And?"

"The fact is that I'm sick."

"How sick?"

"Sick sick."

Angela opened her mouth to ask another question but Frank held up his hand. "That's all you need to know, Dr. Brennan. I know you're a busy person so I'm not going to keep you any longer. Remember, respect your patients. If you don't, you won't have a job. Go. We'll talk more later."

Angela paused, wanting to know more, yet afraid to hear it.

"Go," he repeated. Angela nodded, then watched as he slowly turned and shuffled away.

"Dr. Toner?"

The stooped man turned, his bushy eyebrows raised.

"You taught me everything I know."

A half-smile dawned on his weathered face. "That would explain why you're such a damned good surgeon then, wouldn't it?"

Although Angela didn't show it, pride welled up as she watched Frank walk away. Praise from Frank Toner was rare and, therefore, valuable currency in her psyche. Smiling, she stood a little taller as she completed the walk to her office.

CHAPTER 5

~

The sun shone brilliantly as Emily and Liam bodysurfed the waves at Truro Beach on Cape Cod. The air temperature was unusually warm for late May and the water had followed suit, allowing hearty, wetsuit-clad visitors early beach access after a hard winter. She and Tony had taken Emily and Liam out of school two days early and enjoyed a glorious, extended Memorial Day weekend filled with days basking on the sand as pods of seals frolicked offshore, and nights spent enjoying lobster around a bonfire as they huddled in blankets. While Tony and Liam had flown kites and ridden bikes, Angela and Emily had shared an afternoon at a spa, reconnecting through laughter and discussions about school, boys, and clothes.

After spending an evening playing family games, Angela and Tony had said goodnight to the kids and mapped out what their immediate future would look like, with Angela working and going to school while Tony made himself more available for the kids. The stresses of home and work life had been pushed aside, or at least put into perspective, as they rediscovered why they'd fallen in love years ago.

They awakened on their last day and rushed to the beach, eager to absorb as much sunshine and relaxation as they could.

"I don't want to leave," Angela moaned as she dug her toes in the sand, head tilted back against the chair.

Tony glanced at her and smiled. "Me neither. Let's stay."

Shielding her eyes with her hand, she looked at her husband. "If only it were that simple."

Tony shook his head. "You'd be bored in another week."

Angela grinned. "So would you."

"Mom!" Liam called. "Look what I found!" Angela shifted her attention to the shoreline where her son stood, outstretched arms holding something.

"What is it?"

"A jellyfish!"

"Liam, it might sting you! Be careful!"

Liam shook his head as he ran toward her. "It's okay, Mom. It doesn't have any stingers. It's just jelly. See?" The boy thrust it toward her face and she involuntarily reared back and almost fell over.

"Wow, honey. That's great. Why don't you put it back now?"

Angela watched Liam gallop toward the water, all gangly arms and legs.

Tony laughed. "He's like a Great Dane puppy, isn't he? Barely able to control his limbs."

Angela nodded, love surging as Liam gently returned the invertebrate to its natural habitat. "Hopefully he'll grow into those huge feet. He's definitely going to be as tall as your father."

"When are we leaving?" Emily asked as she sauntered toward her parents. Tony consulted his phone. "In about five minutes." Emily's hands found her hips. She jutted one to the side and pouted her lips. "But Liam and I are actually getting along. Can't we stay a little longer?"

"I need to get back, Em."

"You always need to get back, Mom."

"We all have responsibilities, right?"

Emily rolled her eyes at Angela before turning abruptly and returning to the water.

"Wow. She was so great the other day when it was just her and me. And now . . . ," Angela muttered.

"Yeah," Tony said. "Aren't daughters and mothers supposed to start having relationship issues around puberty? Isn't she testing her independence or something like that?"

Angela regarded her husband, eyebrows raised. "Well, I see someone's been reading some parenting books."

"She'll push harder, so be ready for it."

"Duly noted. And when is it your turn with Liam? When will he start testing you?"

They both watched as Liam removed a crab from the water, thrust it toward his sister, and then chased her. "I don't know. That kid is different. I'm not even sure he's going to go through that phase. But I guess we'll see."

Emily screeched and threw sand at Liam, finally sprinting back to the blanket and collapsing. "Mom, make him stop!"

"Liam, buddy, put the crab back. Let's start to clean up. We have a long drive home."

The nine-year-old deflated as he stomped back to the ocean to return his treasure, and Emily went into sulk mode as she dried herself and organized her beach tote. After returning to the rental home, they stripped the beds, cleaned the dishes, and within an hour were on the road back to Barrington.

The sun was waning in the sky as they headed west on Route 6. Fifty minutes into their two-hour trek, Tony realized that he'd left his sunglasses at the rental house and asked Angela if he could borrow hers. She removed a pair of Michael Kors glasses from her purse and handed them to Tony, who slipped them on and mugged in the rearview mirror.

"What do you think, guys?"

Emily removed one ear bud. "What?"

"What do you think of my new sunglasses?" Liam gave Tony a thumbs-up while Emily squinted at her father and shook her head before replacing her earphone and mumbling, "You're so weird, Dad."

"What do you think?" Tony nudged Angela, who'd been gazing out the window.

"What? Oh, you look stunning."

"What's wrong?"

Angela grimaced. "Reality is hitting me hard."

"What do you mean?"

"Remember I told you about my patient who died after the off-pump heart surgery?"

"Uh-huh."

"What I haven't told you is that Bernard Smythe thinks it was my fault."

"What? That's ridiculous. Didn't you tell me that there's no way you could have known about the aneurysm that killed her?"

"Yeah. The other cardiac surgeons agree and that's what I told Bernard, but . . . I don't know." She waved her hand in the air, swatting at the problem as if it were a fly.

"Angela, listen. You've told me in the past when things like this have happened to other doctors that it's impossible to identify all risk factors prior to surgery. You did the best you could, and she died. Maybe it was just her time."

Angela laughed scornfully. "That's crap, Tony. There is no 'it's just someone's time.' There's only success and failure in the operating room, especially when it comes to heart surgery. And I failed . . . badly."

Tony paused. "Okay, let's say that it is your fault. I'm really sorry that she died, as are you. Are you going to let the situation define you? Or is it going to be something that happened that you learn from and move on? Life is full of choices, Angela. This seems like a choice to me."

"Mr. Sinclair didn't have a choice," Angela mumbled.

"Who?"

"The patient's husband."

"Well, *you* have a choice, so what's it going to be?" Tony looked at Angela, and she was struck with how ridiculous he looked in the feminine, large-frame sunglasses. His unruly, beautiful hair flopped over the front of the lenses, and he suddenly grinned the smile that had drawn her to him so many years ago. The incongruity of their serious conversation with the spectacle of him wearing her glasses made her burst out laughing and she leaned toward him.

"What?" he asked, confused.

"Nothing. I love you, that's all. Come here."

He leaned in and grabbed a kiss before returning his eyes to the road. "It's about five o'clock and we're almost in Barnstable. We should stop for an early din—"

An explosion of light blinded Angela at the exact moment her brain registered the truck plowing into the driver's side of their Volvo. Her body slammed against the door while her head whipped to the left, the front airbag deploying, instantly breaking her nose. The force of the impact then whipsawed her head to the right, crashing against the side airbag. Turning to Tony, she witnessed her sunglasses bursting into little pieces as his face slammed against the airbag and then back against the headrest, his mouth bloody and agape.

The Volvo careened off the road, its steel frame creaking but holding fast as the car rolled twice. Screams erupted from the back seat and Angela watched in horror as Liam's body lifted and crashed into Emily before slamming against the roof and coming to rest on the floor.

Angela clawed at the airbag that was limiting her mobility, desperately attempting to find a handhold. Twisting in her seat as the car came to a sudden, violent halt in a field of newly planted corn, she met Tony's wild eyes. As her vision went supernova and then black hole, one thought permeated her waning consciousness. Liam wasn't wearing his seatbelt.

CHAPTER 6

~

"Tony, please keep your voice down. The kids."

A blinding flash of light stole her vision.

"I don't care if the kids hear us having an argument, Angela."

Pain sliced through her chest. Her lungs deflated like wounded balloons.

"It's just that we've been over this a hundred times, and—"

"It's simple, Angela. The job or us. Choose."

Magnificent hands gripped her chest and abdomen in an effort to restrain her.

"Tony, you know it's not that simple. And your ultimatum certainly isn't fair."

"Fair?"

She floated in a sea of glass and sky.

"I'm on a great path. I've been told that I have CEO potential."

Tony glowered, his chocolate-brown eyes smothered by bushy eyebrows.

"Don't look at me that way, Tony. You don't think that I could be a CEO?"

Her landing was hard, brutal, disjointed.

"That's not the point, Angela. It's never been the point. Liam, do you have your seatbelt on?"

~

Incessant honking roused Angela to consciousness. The sound drilled into her ears and reverberated through her head. A flash of pain spiked in her nose as she fluttered her eyelids, and when she attempted to raise her right hand, she noted that both arms were pinned. The copper taste in her mouth made her wonder if she'd forgotten to brush her teeth, and she couldn't remember what she'd just been thinking, but had the feeling that Tony was angry at her.

A loud groan overcame the blare of the car horn. *Where are the kids?* She couldn't remember. As she swam through the mental bog and opened her eyes, her eyeballs rolled around in their sockets. Making an effort to focus, she blinked repeatedly but could not still her eyes. With dull disinterest she realized that the moaning she'd heard was coming from her own mouth.

The sound of a siren pierced the haze and caught her attention, finally allowing her eyes to focus straight ahead. After a moment, she realized that she was staring at cracked glass. With studied effort, she turned her head to the left and saw her husband. His face was turned toward her and his eyes were open. As consciousness continued to gather in her rattled brain, she realized that Tony's breathing was shallow and quick. Recent events spiraled back and within a minute she was fully alert and focused.

"Tony—" She gagged and then vomited on the airbag that pinned her arms in her lap. "Tony, can you hear me? Oh my God, the kids! Liam? Emily!" she screamed.

Someone groaned in the back seat.

"Liam, Emily, is that you? Are you okay? Emily?"

Emily coughed and started to cry.

"Em, honey, it's gonna be okay. We're going to be alright. How is Liam? Liam, can you hear me? Liam?" Using all of her strength, Angela tried to free her arms. After three attempts, she realized that her arms were cemented tightly between the airbag and her lap.

Tony's breath was labored. He gasped repeatedly, his eyes flaring.

"Tony, do you hear those sirens? People are coming to help us, okay?"

In response, his eyes darted toward the back seat. "Emily is alive," she said. His eyes flared again, and she knew he was worried about Liam.

"Liam?" Angela tried again. "Emily, is Liam okay?"

"I don't think so," Emily managed between staggered breaths and sobs. An icy fear seized Angela, and she strained toward the back seat. The left side of her neck screamed as she forced it into an awkward angle, her brain attempting to organize the broken mass her eyes saw on the floor of the backseat. Liam lay face down, his arm twisted behind him at an impossible angle. His right leg was facing the wrong way, and a massive gash across the back of his head bled profusely.

"Liam! Liam!" she screamed. Angela thrashed her head back and forth as she tried again to free her arms so she could tend to him. Unable to move or speak, Tony hissed as his frantic eyes repeatedly flitted to the back seat. After several attempts, Angela stilled her futile efforts and leaned her head against the headrest as tears rolled down her cheeks. The sirens were crescendoing, the sound melding with the car horn to create a cacophony that assaulted her ears. Emily had retreated into herself and was crying quietly. Angela focused on the crack in the windshield, her eyes tracing the spidery web that had been created there. "I know you're asking me if Liam is okay. He wasn't wearing his seatbelt," she whispered as bile rose in her throat.

In response, Tony's body spasmed uncontrollably and his eyes rolled back. Panic overtook her and she thrashed again in her seat, desperate to help her family.

"No, no, no! Don't you leave me!" she cried. "Stay here, Tony. Stay with me!" She was commanding him, willing some of her strength into his fragile body. "Help is almost here, Tony! Don't—"

Angela stopped abruptly when she noticed the piece of plastic protruding from Tony's thigh. A section of broken dashboard had perforated his leg, likely his femoral artery, and he was losing blood quickly. A bizarre calm came over her.

"Tony, listen. I can't move my arms, but you need to put your hand on your right thigh. You're losing too much blood. Tony!"

His eyes fluttered open and then closed.

"No, Tony. Fight it! Don't go to sleep! Stay here with me. Tony, put pressure on your right thigh!"

Tony's eyes flew open, and for a moment, she thought he'd heard her and would obey. A jolt of adrenaline flew through her, and for a split-second, she imagined a scenario where Tony walked away unharmed. But instead, he smiled through broken teeth. His labored breath came in small bursts. As she watched, she realized with horror that she'd seen this behavior before in her patients, the look often coming immediately before—

"No, Tony! No!" she screamed, desperate to keep him with her. If he succumbed to unconsciousness now, she knew his chances of survival dropped substantially.

He closed his eyes as the sirens drew closer.

"Only another minute and help will be here! Please, Tony, please don't go." Her demands became pleas as the blood continued to seep from the gash in his thigh. She breathed unevenly through ragged sobs.

Opening his eyes once more, Tony appeared suddenly coherent. She watched with manic hope as he stared in confusion at the shattered windshield. He then settled his gaze on Angela, who smiled encouragingly. "That's it, Tony. I'm here. Focus on me. Help is coming. Can you hear it?"

Tony's eyes widened. He whimpered and then took a long, shuddering breath before speaking clearly. "I love you."

Angela felt a part of herself break away as she watched her soulmate fade, his breath coming in shorter gasps, further apart each time until they ceased altogether. She knew he was gone when his eyes lost their focus, the lids lowering slightly while his mouth fell slack.

A numbness took hold of her chest and crawled to her

extremities, settling in until she could no longer feel anything. A quiet rustling from the back seat attracted her attention, and she realized with a start that she could not entertain the luxury of acquiescing to grief. Her children needed her. Breathing deeply to steel herself against the rising tide of terror, she spoke evenly.

"Emily, how are you doing?"

Her daughter moaned and then screamed. Relief washed over Angela. If Emily was screaming, then she was alive.

"Emily, stop! Don't move. The ambulance will be here in seconds. It's important you don't move. Okay?"

"Okay."

A police cruiser skidded to a stop on the shoulder of the road next to the cornfield, followed by an ambulance and a fire truck. A pair of paramedics carrying a stretcher ran toward the car, and Angela directed them to focus on Liam first. The larger of the two men yanked Liam's car door open while the other one knelt beside Angela. Angela looked at him and noted that his eyebrows were too bushy and that he needed a shave. His nylon jacket had a spot above the left pocket and she wondered if it was dried blood. Or coffee.

"What's your name, ma'am?"

"Angela. Dr. Angela Brennan." A wave of nausea swelled and Angela swallowed in an effort not to vomit. The car horn stopped suddenly. The abrupt silence was disconcerting and made the paramedic's voice seem too loud in the quiet cornfield.

"Okay, Angela. I'm going to puncture the airbags so I can take a look at you. Okay?"

"My husband—" Angela trailed off.

"We'll get to your husband."

Angela craned her neck to see Liam, but the paramedic stopped her by placing a hand on her shoulder. She swung her head back toward him. His hand felt tender but strong, the touch of a competent clinician.

"Angela, I need you to focus on me, okay?"

"But my son—"

"My partner, John, will look after your son."

Angela looked into his brown eyes and nodded. They were the same deep hue as Tony's. "You need to check on my daughter."

"I will, as soon as I make sure you're alright."

The man stabbed the airbags and a whooshing sound filled the car. "Can you move your arms?"

Angela's hand found her broken nose and pain shot through her head. She nodded.

"How about your legs?"

Slowly moving her legs, she nodded again. "I'm okay. Please help my daughter."

Angela started to turn again to check on Liam.

"Dr. Brennan?" Hearing her professional title, Angela immediately returned her attention to the paramedic, who had stood. "As I said, my partner will take care of your son. I need you to help me with your daughter. Help keep her calm. Can you do that, Doctor?" He extended his hand toward her, and she noticed that his fingernails were clean and trimmed.

Angela's head leaned toward Liam, but her stare remained riveted on the paramedic. The man glanced at Liam and then returned his focus to Angela, his mouth set in a grim line. Her heart skipped a beat as she read his eyes and intuited the implication of his silence. After a moment, he said, "Can you help me keep your daughter calm, Doctor?"

Making an effort to close her mouth, Angela nodded and placed her palm against his. He lifted her gently out of the car and walked her several yards away before returning to open Emily's door.

"What's your name, young lady?" He touched Emily's arm and she screamed, shattering Angela's mental fog.

"Emily. Her name's Emily," Angela said quietly. Noting Emily's bloody face and terrified eyes, Angela desperately wanted to shove the paramedic aside to attend to Emily herself, but knew that he was in a better position to help than she was.

"Your arm is broken, and it looks like your leg is too. Listen, Emily, I'm going to tell you the truth. Getting you out of the car and onto the stretcher is going to hurt. But I want you to know that once you're settled in the ambulance, we're going to do everything we can to make you comfortable. Are you with me, Emily?"

Emily nodded, her trusting, expressive eyes touching Angela's soul. Angela noted that the paramedic looked at his partner across the back seat. The other man was kneeling next to Liam's broken body but he was making no effort to extract the boy. As a look of silent understanding passed between the two medical professionals, Angela felt bile rise in her throat. She turned away and stifled a sob, partially because she didn't want to upset Emily any more, and partially because she wasn't sure that she could handle seeing her daughter in so much pain.

"John, can you please help me lift Emily?"

"Sure, Dave."

While John and Dave prepared the stretcher, Angela turned back around and took in the severity of Emily's injuries. The vision of Emily's contorted face and broken bones overwhelmed her, and she sank to the ground as the men lifted the terrified girl onto the gurney. Emily screamed, and a sudden, raging desperation stripped Angela of all rational thought as she dry heaved and crawled toward Liam's side of the car.

Dave's calm voice carried to her, gently calling her back. "Dr. Brennan, Emily needs you. Why don't you ride in the ambulance with her?"

Angela stopped crawling. She glanced at Dave, and then at the tiny flattened corn stalks that surrounded the car. It occurred to her that the accident had ruined a farmer's hard work and she felt bad about it.

"I need to tend to my son and my husband . . ."

Dave crossed to her and knelt. "Angela, I'll make sure your son and your husband are treated well. I promise."

"Their names are Tony and Liam, in case you need to talk to them. Tony's my husband and Liam is my son." Her voice faltered. "He's nine years old."

Dave nodded and extended his hand. "Thank you for helping me, Dr. Brennan. Emily needs you now."

Angela glanced at the smashed Volvo and then at Dave. "Are they both really gone?" Her voice broke as she scanned his benevolent face, desperately searching for a glimmer of hope. She found none.

She felt the pressure of Dave's hand on her shoulder. "I'm afraid so. Yes."

Angela looked at the sky. It seemed extraordinarily blue with only one puffy cloud that hugged the sun. She allowed herself to be hoisted up, and suddenly became cognizant of stopped cars whose passengers had exited their vehicles to gape at the accident scene and its victims. She recalled a conversation she'd had with Tony years ago when she was pregnant with Emily and they had encountered an accident.

Anger, frustration, and helplessness rushed up her throat and she vomited on the broken corn. When she was done, she wiped her mouth on her arm and turned on the small crowd. "Are you happy now?" she screamed as they gawked. "Have you seen enough? Stop looking! *Stop staring*!"

Her fury dissolved into despair, and her knees buckled. As Angela lay on the earth, sobbing and gasping for air, Dave appeared in an instant, picked her up, and carried her to the ambulance.

CHAPTER 7

~

Angela perched on the edge of a chair at her daughter's bedside in the Emergency Department. Emily had been sedated upon verification that her vital signs were strong, and she now dozed fitfully, her broken limbs periodically twitching. The sporadic movement would almost draw her from sleep, but then her medication would respond and relax her once more. Angela couldn't take her eyes from Emily's angelic face. She wondered how she would tell her beautiful daughter that her life had been decimated in an instant. Angela sighed and realized that she had no idea what time it was or how long they'd been at the hospital. She had recently regained feeling in her extremities and knew that her body was coming down from an adrenaline high that had powered her through the initial trauma. Although she was exhausted, the buzz that lingered in her bloodstream had not yet allowed rest.

Angela glanced around the cubicle, reflecting on the time they'd been in the Emergency Department. Word of the accident had spread throughout the hospital, and several colleagues had stopped by to express their condolences and concern. Angela had received their kind words robotically, periodically murmuring appropriate responses, until the nurse manager had pulled the curtain around the cubicle to allow Angela and Emily some privacy.

She traced a finger along Emily's unbroken arm, envying a child's ability to trust others, to take them at their word. Along their journey in the ambulance, the paramedics had told Emily that she was going to heal beautifully. The assurances Emily longed to hear set her mind at ease, and Angela watched in dull fascination as Dave and John had coaxed a smile and a laugh from her. Emily had not asked about her brother or her father, and the medical professionals had offered no information. Movement and conversation had been swift, culminating in her being medicated as soon as possible upon arrival at the hospital. No time to think, ask questions, or envision a scenario in which everything might not be okay.

Upon arrival, Angela had undergone her own complete check-up and had been diagnosed with a broken nose, multiple contusions, and a minor concussion. Her nose had been set, and she had walked out of her emergency room cubicle with care instructions and a bottle of painkillers that could take down a horse. She had accepted the medicine but had yet to swallow a pill, wanting to ensure that she was completely coherent upon Emily's awakening. Her head throbbed but she remained determined to ensure her daughter's health before attending to her own.

Emily stirred and her eyelids flickered open.

"Hi, Ma," she slurred. Her tongue circled her lips as if searching for something.

Angela managed a wan smile as butterfly wings of relief fluttered through her. "Hi, baby. How are you feeling?"

"Thirsty."

"Oh, of course." Angela grabbed a small plastic cup filled with melting ice chips. She lifted her daughter's head, careful not to jostle her broken arm, and tipped some liquid into Emily's mouth. The girl sighed and lay back down.

"Thanks. My arm . . . hurts."

"I know, sweetie. They've taken X-rays and are going to set your arm in a cast soon. Your leg is going to require surgery, but it's going to be just fine."

Emily's face contorted. "Why surgery?"

Angela brushed Emily's long bangs away from her face and caressed her bruised cheek. She paused, trying to remember the last time Emily had let her touch her like this. It had been months.

"Mom?"

"Sorry, honey. Your knee is a little busted up, but I don't want you to worry. You're going to be fine. Go back to sleep."

Emily squinted and her eyes searched Angela's face. "Are you okay?"

Angela stared at the only remaining member of her family, unsure how to answer the question. Her eyes wandered about the small space, settling on the multilingual sign that promised patient confidentiality. *Am I okay? Not even close.*

"Physically I'm good."

Emily shook her head. "Your face . . ."

Angela rose and crossed to the mirror above the small sink. A ghost with bruised eyes, blood-matted hair, and a ridiculous bandage on her misshapen nose stared back at her. She imagined Tony grimacing and saying, "Hon, you need some work." Turning back toward her daughter, she found that Emily had already fallen asleep again, the short conversation having exhausted her.

"Dr. Brennan?"

Angela turned to find Bernard Smythe staring at her, his probing eyes full of concern. She lifted her hand in greeting and then pointed toward the curtain, indicating they should speak outside the cubicle. Once they were out of Emily's earshot, Bernard ran his hand through his hair. Angela examined the circles under his eyes and his wrinkled lab coat. He looked nothing like the dapper surgeon she was accustomed to seeing.

"Jesus, I don't know what to say. How are you doing?"

Angela shook her head. "Don't ask me that."

"I'm sorry, it's just that—"

Angela cut him off by waving her hand. She could deal with acquaintances trying to be kind, but not Bernard. Not now.

He fidgeted. "I just wanted to say I'm sorry about what happened."

Angela looked at him as if she hadn't understood his words.

He mistook her look of disdain for confusion. "About the accident. I'm sorry about the accident, and about your—well, about your husband and son."

Angela took in the familiar surroundings. Nurses and doctors jutting this way and that, seemingly aimless to the casual observer, but in actuality an efficient, competent symphony of movement that saved lives. She had always felt comfortable here, in her hospital, a second home of sorts. Until now.

In this moment the place felt foreign, and the words Dr. Smythe uttered, words she had spoken so many times, were weightless and meaningless. Letters making words that formed sentences that dissipated in the air, like so much helium. Regret flooded her, not for the accident, but for her part in promoting empty empathy as a physician. She felt guilty and searched for somewhere to rest her burden. Placing her hand on her protégé's arm, she said, "We can do better, Bernard."

"I beg your pardon?"

For a brief moment, Angela stepped outside of herself and reflected on conversations she'd had with patients, similar to the one Bernard was having with her. He meant well, but despite his heartfelt attempt, she understood his inability to find appropriate words to convey genuine sympathy. It wasn't his fault. Clinicians had to construct an emotional barrier in order to maintain their own mental health. It was too easy to get dragged under the rising tide of death and sadness their jobs often encountered. But now, being on the receiving end of platitudes, she had a unique understanding of the inadequacy of his words. She realized that no matter what she'd said to her patients and their families, no matter what profound or sincere words Bernard uttered in this awful moment, there simply was no phrase that could encapsulate the enormity of the horrific situation. Silence was underrated but was precisely what situations like this required. A person's presence was enough when words were superfluous.

"We need to do better, as physicians. We owe it to our patients. I believe you're sorry about my situation, but you need to find the words that help me truly believe that you mean it. Or don't speak at all."

Dr. Smythe took a step back, unsure how to respond. He'd been in similar situations, but not with another clinician, and certainly not with his mentor.

Angela firmly gripped his arm, her eyes boring into his. She realized that she sounded possessed, a mother raving with grief, but she didn't care. At that moment, her singular goal was to ensure that he had heard her. "Do you understand?"

"Angela, I got here as fast as I could," Liz said breathlessly as she rushed forward and embraced her friend. Angela released Bernard's arm, and he nodded once and rushed away, clearly relieved to be excused from the awkward encounter. "I would have been here sooner, but I was in surgery with Robert. What the hell happened? I heard that there was an accident."

Angela looked at Liz's pained expression and saw a reflection of own her grief. Not knowing where to start, she repeated Liz's statement. "There was an accident."

"I know. But how did it happen?"

Angela shook her head, blinking several times as she locked onto Liz's eyes. "I'm not sure. I think there was a truck. And it hit us on Tony's side. He was driving. Wearing my sunglasses. He looked so funny, Liz."

"Okay."

"Yeah. And then this truck . . . it came out of nowhere. And I couldn't move my arms. It was the airbag, you see. And Liam—" Vivid detail came hurling back and she watched her ragdoll son thrown about as the car tumbled through the cornfield. Her eyes followed in slow motion. "He wasn't wearing his seatbelt."

Liz's hands flew to her mouth and retreated just as quickly as Angela's eyes found the curtain surrounding Emily's cubicle.

"Emily needs surgery on her left leg. Liam crashed into her so hard that it shattered her femur and knee. The impact tore away all of her knee tendons."

"I'm so sorry, Angela."

Angela nodded dumbly and then looked past Liz at two nurses who were laughing. "I watched him die, Liz."

Liz tightened her jaw and crossed her arms. "Who, honey? Liam?"

Confusion overtook Angela for a moment. "Yes, actually. I watched Liam die, too, but I didn't know it at the time. I meant Tony. I think his neck was broken. He couldn't move. I watched him take his very . . . his last . . ." Angela shuddered as her breath came in short bursts.

"Oh, Angela." Liz collected her friend in her arms and held her, rubbing her back. Angela winced. Liz's touch felt too hard, like sandpaper scratching her skin. She pulled away.

"You know what his last words were?"

"Tell me."

Angela looked through Liz as she watched Tony die. "'I love you.' He said, 'I love you' to me right before he died." Her eyes focused on Liz's face again. "And it's strange, but I can't cry. Why is that?"

"You're still in shock, Angela. It's important that you stay here for a while, regardless of what's recommended to you. You're very well known in this place and people may be afraid to boss you around. But I'm not."

Dr. Stan Jacobs approached, a crisp white lab coat over his pristine blue scrubs. The chief of Pediatric Orthopedics looked imposing, almost god-like, as he strode toward them with his head high. The confidence he exuded strengthened her while simultaneously causing apprehension. He was followed closely by the director of the Emergency Department, a woman whose name Angela couldn't recall. Her employee badge said "Melba," and Angela suddenly remembered when they'd first met, she'd told Angela that an easy way to remember her name was to think of Melba toast. Melba seemed genuinely sad as Stan shook Angela's hand in greeting.

"Angela, I'm so sorry about what happened, but I want you to know that I'll be performing your daughter's surgery. I can't change what's happened, but I can fix your daughter's leg. It's going to require a titanium rod and a new knee though, so it's going to be a rough rehab road for her." Stan's voice sounded too loud to Angela's ears but she nodded, grateful that he'd taken Emily's case.

"Understood. Thanks, Stan."

He patted her back and smiled thinly as he entered Emily's cubicle.

Melba cleared her throat. "I'm sorry to bother you, Dr. Brennan, but I wondered if you'd mind following me while your daughter is being prepped for surgery. I need you to identify—"

Angela's stomach clenched, and before she could register what was happening, she had vomited on Melba's brown, leather pumps. Angela mumbled apologies as Liz dashed away, then reappeared with some towels and began clean-up. Melba smiled. "No worries, Dr. Brennan. No worries."

Although Angela knew it was a state requirement that she'd have to identify Tony and Liam's bodies before they were released for burial, she hadn't thought the moment would arrive so quickly. Her body took on a life of its own and began shaking. The more she tried to stop it, the harder it trembled. Her knees buckled and she sank into the chair that Liz had placed behind her.

A sliver of ice ran down Angela's spine and she looked desperately at Liz, who handed the sodden towels to a nurse and then silently slipped her hand into Angela's and squeezed. "You don't have to do this right now, you know."

Angela glanced at Melba, who nodded her agreement. Angela closed her eyes, reliving the accident. Although she had witnessed Tony's last breath, she hadn't seen Liam since before the crash and suddenly she felt an indescribable pull to see her baby one more time. "No. I want to go."

Liz frowned but nodded. "Okay. I'll go with you."

The path to the Morgue that she'd walked so many times as a physician seemed endless, yet was over before she was ready. The floor in the basement, scrubbed sparkling white by the hospital's talented janitorial team, mocked her with its jovial flecks that reflected the overhead lights. The cheery, bright-white walls took on an antiseptic quality that sickened her as her leaden legs threatened to cease movement. It was sheer will that propelled her forward.

"Thank God Emily's going to be okay," Liz offered as they crossed through the glass doors marked "MORGUE" and approached two steel tables.

"I'm not sure God has anything to do with this, Liz," Angela replied as she examined her own feet housed in paper booties she'd been given. She absentmindedly wondered where her flip-flops had gone and realized that they were probably still in the cornfield. Or the car.

"Are you ready, Dr. Brennan?" asked the assistant who stood stoically by the first table. Angela swallowed and nodded, then glanced at the woman's army-green scrubs, wondering if she chose such a drab color because of the work she did.

Angela inhaled the antiseptic scent peculiar to the Morgue as her eyes flitted between the two steel tables. Based on the length of the sheet that covered the body closest to her, Angela knew that she'd be seeing Tony first. The spotless white sheet reminded Angela of a Halloween ghost costume—only the eye cutouts were missing. She glanced at Liz, who slipped her arm around her friend's waist for support.

Angela nodded again, and the assistant slowly pulled the sheet down, careful not to disturb the body. Angela felt her breath expel quickly and without warning, leaving her gasping for air as if her solar plexus had been struck.

Tony's eyes and mouth remained open, as if he were singing. His warm, brown eyes had become milky and dull, and his skin appeared sallow. Angela slowly disengaged from Liz and approached the table. Her shaky hand found his thick, wavy hair and smoothed it as she regained her breath. When she found her voice, it sounded thick and far away.

"I love you, Tony, so much. I'm sorry."

She knew better than to kiss him. She didn't want her last memory of his touch to be cold and unreciprocated. Instead, she kissed her fingers and placed them gently on his colorless lips. Her eyes wandered across his face for the last time, and she realized that she felt disengaged from the entire situation, as if this nightmare were happening to someone else. Another version of her, perhaps, in another reality, and she momentarily wondered if sometime in the future she'd regret not being able to feel more. Or whether she would look back and be grateful for the emotional paralysis.

Glancing quickly at the assistant, she nodded. "That's my husband."

The young woman returned the nod and replaced the sheet before moving on to the next table. Liz was silent as she placed her arm around Angela's waist. Angela looked at Liz for reassurance and ground her teeth, anticipating the same physical reaction to seeing her son. The assistant gingerly removed the sheet from the top half of Liam's body, and Angela's insides shattered. The freeze started in her gut and worked outwards, followed immediately by the sensation of the ice cracking and falling away into nothingness, the black hole that was her new reality. She lost sensation in her limbs as her hands flew to her mouth, and Liz reacted quickly but quietly, brandishing an emesis basin. Angela shook her head and swallowed, determined to keep herself together for Liam.

"You okay?" Liz asked.

Angela heard someone whimpering and, with an exultant adrenaline rush, thought it was Liam. Only when Liz squeezed her hand did she realize that the sounds were coming from her own mouth. She forced herself forward until she stood by Liam, his once-perfect little form twisted and broken in unimaginable ways. His face, however, remained angelic, and if it weren't for the fractured body attached to the pristine head, Angela could have mistaken his death for a deep sleep. His curly, blond hair remained vibrant, one stubborn lock draping playfully on his forehead. A slight smile graced his pale, heart-shaped face, making her wonder if he now knew something she didn't. She smiled sadly in return and ran her finger along his ski jump of a nose.

"I love you, Liam. I'll miss you so much. Take care of—" A barking sob escaped her and she fought to regain her composure. Time stopped as she fantasized remaining with him, and she wondered how long the assistant would let her stay. After a period of time, maybe minutes or hours, she heard Liz clear her throat. Jolting back to the moment, Angela kissed her fingers and placed them on his cold lips. "Take care of Daddy," she whispered.

She looked to the assistant, who gently replaced the sheet. When Liam was completely covered, Angela slowly turned to a red-eyed Liz and nodded. "We can go." Steeling herself, she forced her feet, one step at a time, to walk toward the exit.

As they reached the door, Angela turned back and was surprised to see that the assistant was crying, her hand resting lightly on Liam's shattered body. Angela was struck that someone who dealt with death and grieving on a daily basis would allow herself to feel so deeply. The human reaction grounded her and helped her to focus.

"What's your name?"

Caught off-guard, the assistant used her sleeve to wipe her eyes. "Melinda Nuñez."

Angela nodded. "Thank you, Ms. Nuñez, for doing an incredibly difficult job very well. I appreciate your professionalism and kindness. The way you handled my two boys was gracious and thoughtful. I won't forget it."

Melinda Nuñez offered a surprised, tight-lipped smile. It was as if no one had ever thanked her before.

CHAPTER 8

~

Barring a short conversation with a patient's family, Angela had never spent any time in the hospital's surgical waiting room. As a clinician, if she knew the discussion would take longer than five minutes, she'd arrange a meeting in the conference room designed specifically for that purpose. Another surgeon was in that room right now, updating a family on their loved one's progress. Angela peeked through the window and noted that the family members were smiling. The surgery must be progressing well.

Angela glanced at the clock for the fourth time in as many minutes. Emily had been in surgery for two hours, and probably still had another hour to go. Hospital employees—some of whom she'd known prior to the accident, but most of whom she hadn't—had come and gone, each offering what they hoped were words of encouragement and comfort, none of which had found their mark. Their convenient phrases had bounced off of her as she smiled, sympathetic to their discomfort. Liz had remained with her for a while, sporadically silent and then chatty, until Angela had ordered her to go home and get some sleep.

"I can't leave you here by yourself."

"I'm not by myself. I have Emily."

Liz had smiled and taken her hand. "Yes. You do have Emily. I'll be back after I take a quick nap and tend to the cats, okay?"

Angela had paused, wanting to say how grateful she was to Liz for her years of friendship, personally as well as professionally, but she was afraid her raw emotion would initiate a cascade of tears that might not stop. Instead, she had hugged her hard and said, "You are a very, very good friend, Liz."

Liz had walked away, and Angela had sunk into a chair and fallen into a shallow, restless sleep. The next thing she remembered was hearing her name and realizing that she'd dozed off for a moment.

Jolting upright, she saw the hospital's CEO, Maggie Donnelly, standing in front of her, accompanied by another woman and a man. Maggie was dressed in her self-imposed uniform, a navy blue suit with a light blue button-down shirt accompanied by a single strand of pearls and simple gold earrings. She stood erect, a black portfolio in the crux of her elbow, as if she were rushing to yet another meeting. Angela had always admired Maggie's efficiency, in dress, leadership style, and time management. She exuded competence, and Angela found her strength comforting. As Angela attempted to stand through her post-sleep haze, Maggie seated herself in the adjoining chair.

"Don't get up, Angela. I was just coming to see how you are. I'm so sorry about what happened. Tony was a wonderful man and your son—Liam was it? I met him only once, but I remember his firecracker personality from the barbecue you hosted at your beautiful home last summer."

"Yes. Thank you," Angela mumbled as she struggled to remember the barbecue to which Maggie was referring. Her brain wouldn't clear and she wondered if her concussion was to blame.

"I understand that your daughter is in surgery with Stan Jacobs?"

Angela's mind returned to the conversation and she nodded.

"He's the best. She's in good hands."

"I know. Thanks."

"I need to run, but I just wanted to stop by and express my heartfelt condolences for your loss."

Angela glanced at the two people accompanying Maggie and noted their suits and trendy glasses. The woman's icy blue eyes seemed to look through Angela and the man appeared bored. Angela wondered who they were but couldn't summon the energy to ask. "Thanks for coming, Maggie."

Maggie patted Angela's hand and stood. "Once you're settled, let's get together and figure out next steps. No hurry. Take all the time you need. We'll transfer all of your patients to the other surgeons." She offered an efficient smile and turned, the two strangers following closely behind.

"Are you someone important?" a gruff voice asked.

Angela turned to find a man of about seventy years slumped in a chair four seats to her left, his layered, disheveled clothes at least ten years out of date. The graying cargo pants hung loosely on his bony legs and his torso was covered in layers: a faded black T-shirt covered by a red-and-black plaid flannel shirt and a dark zip-up hoodie. The gray stubble on his chin accompanied the shock of white hair that remained on his head, and his piercing blue eyes stared through her. His body was lean and the weathered skin on his stern face hung like a hound dog. Glancing at his arthritic, calloused hands, Angela surmised he was a retired blue-collar worker.

"No."

"I'm askin' because those people that you was talking to seem important."

"The woman I was speaking with runs this hospital."

"Who was the other people?"

"I don't know." Angela turned her body away from the man, attempting to disengage from the conversation.

The man harrumphed, displeased with her answer. "So you're not important but you know that lady?"

Irritated, Angela nodded and glanced at the clock. *How long was I asleep?*

"How do you know her, then?"

Angela sighed. "I work with her."

The man was defiant as he stuck out his dried, cracked lips. "I was right."

Angela looked at the ceiling, desperately trying to maintain her composure.

"Listen, lady, I'm just trying to be nice. Makes the time go quicker. It seems like you and me are in the same boat, waitin' on somebody. I just thought I'd make conversation. But never mind."

Angela was so tired. She closed her eyes and pictured Tony and Liam laying on the steel slabs several floors below, then visualized her daughter on the operating table. Her scalp prickled as she imagined something going wrong, a miscalculation of the anesthesiologist, a slip of the scalpel, an underlying risk factor the surgical team hadn't considered. Opening her eyes, she gasped and pulled away from the old man who was now seated beside her.

"Hey, hey. I'm sorry, hon. I didn't mean it. I didn't mean to make you so upset."

Angela was surprised to find that her body was trembling, and she was unable to speak. The man leaned toward her. He smelled of unwashed clothes and wood smoke.

"Honey, it's gonna be okay. We're all scared, but it's gonna be okay. You know why?"

Angela shook her head.

"Because He's with us." The man pointed to the ceiling, and for a moment Angela thought he meant someone on the floor above them. "God looks out for us, so we're going to be alright no matter what happens."

Angela drew a deep breath and found her voice. She felt like a child as she asked in a small voice, "Do you really believe that?"

The man grinned, a missing tooth glaring black among the remaining yellow ones. He placed his hand over his heart. "With all of my heart, mind, and soul. Your little girl's gonna make it through just fine. Wait and see."

"How did you know it's my daughter who's in surgery?"

"Because I heard you telling Miss Muckity Muck."

Despite the situation, Angela smiled at the description of Maggie.

"Somethin' tells me you're some kind of muckity muck too, but you're either too shy, humble, or stupid to admit it."

Angela regarded her unlikely ally, thinking that perhaps she had misjudged his intelligence.

"Well, which is it? You don't strike me as the shy type, and you don't seem particularly humble, if I may say so . . ."

"Definitely stupid," Angela answered.

"Oh, I don't think that's true either," he said. "What's the real story?"

Angela paused, unsure she wanted to further the conversation.

"It's okay," he urged. "I won't tell nobody."

Angela shook her head. He was persistent, she had to give him that. "I'm a doctor here. A heart surgeon. We were in a car accident earlier today. That's why—"

"You have the pretty nose bandage. I figured."

"Yeah. And why my daughter's in surgery for her leg."

"What's her name?"

"Emily."

The man grunted. "Nice name."

"It fits her."

"It must be weird for you sittin' on this side of the fence."

"What do you mean?"

"Well, you're usually the one doing the surgery, right? You're the one who walks out with the white coat, has all the answers, imparting knowledge on us lower beings." His tone had become high-brow and she felt a little miffed.

Angela raised her eyebrows. "Is that the way you see it?"

"Isn't that the way you see it?"

"No, not at all."

"Well, that's the way it comes across sometimes."

Angela thought back to what she'd said to Bernard earlier about how physicians must work harder to effectively communicate their thoughts. Then she considered the man sitting next to her and how she must appear to him. "Good to know. To answer your question, it is strange sitting on this side. I'm seeing things differently."

"That's good. Maybe you can make some changes around here. Like these chairs. They're very uncomfortable."

"I can't disagree with you."

"Angela."

She turned to see Stan Jacobs approaching her, his heels clicking loudly on the linoleum floor. In an instant she understood what the old man had been trying to tell her. Stan was intimidating in his designer shoes and bleached, white lab coat. He carried himself with haughty confidence and she wondered if he'd always been that way or whether he'd cultivated the demeanor through years of practice. With a start, Angela realized that Stan's presence meant that Emily's surgery was complete. Terror and relief battled for brain dominance as Stan rapidly closed the distance between them, but his wide smile put her at ease and she stood on shaky legs.

"Flying colors, Angela. She's doing great. Like I said, she'll have a long rehabilitation, but six to nine months from now she'll be running again."

The weight of uncertainty vanished as Angela breathed an audible sigh of relief and shook Stan's hand.

"I can't thank you enough, Stan. When can I see her?"

"She's in recovery room twelve if you want to go in now. She's still sedated though."

"Okay. Thanks."

Stan nodded, turned on his heel, and walked away. Angela's exuberance evaporated as the reality of her situation hit home. She would sit by Emily's bedside until her daughter awoke, at which point she'd have to inform her that her nuclear family had decreased by two.

Walking quickly toward the recovery room, Angela realized that she hadn't said goodbye to the man in the waiting room. In fact, she'd never asked his name or why he was there. The entire conversation had been about her. She retraced her steps and saw only a single woman seated in the far corner of the waiting room.

"Excuse me. Where did the man who was sitting here go?"

"What man?"

Angela's eyes scoured the small space. "There was an older man sitting here, rumpled sweatshirt, white hair. Did he go to the bathroom?"

The woman shook her head. "It's been just you and me for the last hour."

Angela blinked twice. "No. There was a man right there." She pointed to the chair where he'd been sitting. "And I spoke to him. Where did he go?"

The woman shrugged. "I don't know what to tell you."

Angela felt an irrational wave of anger rise but tamped it down when she thought about Emily waking up alone. "I have to see to my daughter, but if he returns, will you please tell him that Angela said thanks?"

The woman smiled. "Sure. If he returns."

CHAPTER 9

Although Angela steeled herself before entering the pediatric post-surgical recovery room, she still stopped short when she saw how frail and small Emily appeared in the large bed. An intravenous needle protruded from her daughter's left arm, and Angela visually followed the tube until it ended at a plastic bag hanging on a portable metal stand. A machine beeped regularly, indicating Emily's steady heart rate, and Angela noted that Emily's pulse was consistent and strong. The left side of Emily's face was black and blue, and a bandage over her left ear glared white against her brunette hair. Her entire left leg was wrapped in thick gauze covered with multiple ace bandages and was being held in place by metal pins attached to what looked like scaffolding, while her right arm was in a large, neon-green cast.

Angela permitted her mind to exit doctor mode and go into mommy mode, immediately regretting the decision; her chest hurt when she considered the daunting tasks her daughter would endure in the coming months. Not only would Emily have to grapple with the emotional toll of losing her family, but she would also be subjected to the significant physical exertion that rehabilitation would require. Angela determined that she must be brave in order to show Emily that their family, what was left of it, would persevere and remain strong. It was what Tony would have done if the situation had been reversed.

"Dr. Brennan, it's good to see you."

Angela turned to find a short, young woman standing behind her, a warm smile fixed on her wide, freckled face. Her mousy brown hair was tied in a no-nonsense ponytail that swung as she spoke, and her scrubs were decorated with Minnie Mouse dressed in various outfits.

Seeing the confusion on Angela's face, she added, "I'm Lauren Kirk. I worked one of your surgeries several years ago because your cardiac nurses were all sick. The flu, if I remember correctly. I wouldn't expect you to remember me, but I enjoyed working with you. Anyway, I'm sorry for everything that's happened. Your daughter is doing great, though."

Angela didn't remember Ms. Kirk, but she was impressed by how the young nurse was able to meld the positive and negative thoughts into words in such a kind way, her open smile confident and unfaltering. *Bernard and I could learn something from her*, Angela thought. "Thank you, Ms. Kirk."

"Lauren."

"Thank you, Lauren."

"My pleasure. Let me know if you need anything."

Angela lowered herself into a chair next to the bed and took Emily's hand. Stroking her sun-kissed fingers, Angela marveled at how much Emily's hands resembled her own, despite the chipped, blue polish on her daughter's nails.

"Hi, Em. I'm here if you can hear me. I'm not going anywhere."

She leaned her forehead against Emily's hand and started humming "You Are My Sunshine," the only song that had lulled her daughter to sleep when she was a colicky baby. The song carried her frazzled mind to a happier place and time and allowed her a moment of peace amidst the storm. Angela crossed her forearms on the mattress and placed her chin atop them, realizing that the hours of adrenaline release had left her utterly exhausted and literally unable to keep her eyes open.

She awoke several hours later with a blanket over her shoulders and a cramp in her neck.

"Welcome back. Can I get you anything?" Lauren asked as she swapped out Emily's empty saline intravenous bag for a new one.

Angela shook her head and gently rubbed her eyes, careful to avoid jostling her throbbing nose as she focused on Emily. Relieved to see her safe and sound, Angela yawned and looked at Lauren. "Well, maybe some ibuprofen, if you don't mind."

"You got it. I'll be right back."

As Lauren exited the room, Angela noted that the nurse walked with a slight limp. She reappeared almost immediately, carrying water and two dark orange pills in a cup.

"Here you go."

Angela glanced at Lauren's leg as she swallowed the painkillers. "Why are you limping?"

Lauren leaned down and lifted the pant leg of her scrubs to reveal a prosthetic limb. Angela's eyebrows shot up. "How did you lose your leg, if you don't mind my asking?"

Lauren waved her hand. "Oh, I don't mind at all. Osteosarcoma when I was thirteen. Fortunately, I was lucky, and it was caught before it metastasized to my lungs or something. All they had to do was amputate from my knee down."

She balled her hand into a fist and knocked twice on her prosthetic. "It's amazing what science has created. I hardly notice it."

Angela felt an unexpected camaraderie of loss with this woman half her age. "It must have been difficult, being a teenager when it happened."

Lauren frowned and tilted her head. "Yes, it was, but I got through it. Actually, it's why I became a nurse. The nurses that helped me were such amazing people, I knew I wanted to be just like them when I grew up. I wanted to make a difference in someone's life like they did in mine. You know?"

Angela didn't know. She had grown up in a family of physicians, and the expectation was that she would carry on the tradition. She had dreamed of becoming a surgeon since she was a girl. Not because she wanted to help people, but because it was the pinnacle of medicine. Holding someone's life in her hands was the ultimate test of skill, intelligence, dexterity, and power.

Although her father had wanted her to become a neurosurgeon, Angela had disliked the fact that, despite centuries of research, the brain was still such an enigma. She preferred the heart, which had been studied, mapped, and dissected since the fourth century BC, when Aristotle first identified it as being the most important organ in the body. Successfully repairing or replacing someone's heart brought her the greatest high she could imagine, but it wasn't until she worked closely with Frank Toner that she understood the importance of the vessel that housed the heart: the patient. He used to say, "Remember, you may hold her heart in your hands, but her hands are responsible for many hearts." Once Angela had broadened her scope to understand the larger picture, her commitment to healing had deepened, and she had found even greater reward in her calling.

"Are you okay, Dr. Brennan?"

Angela started, not realizing she'd been staring. "Oh, yes, I'm sorry."

"No need to be sorry. You've been through a lot. Oh, Emily's waking up."

Joy surged through Angela and she grinned like a child on Christmas morning as Emily's eyes flickered and then flew open. She attempted to sit up but Lauren moved like a cobra, and with a smile and a hand on her patient's shoulder, she gently returned Emily's head to the pillow.

"Whoa there, camper. No need to rush off. We're just getting to know one another."

"Where am I? What happened?"

"You're in the hospital and your mom's right here. Why don't I give you two a moment? I'll be back soon."

Lauren left the room and Emily turned toward Angela. "Oh, God, Mom. You look awful!"

Despite the situation, or perhaps because of it, Angela burst out laughing, and then caught herself. "Thanks. I think we both need a little touch-up."

Emily examined her science experiment of a leg. Her eyes widened and then wandered around the room. Angela knew that she was recalling sounds and visions from the accident. After several moments, Emily settled her worried gaze on Angela.

"They're dead, aren't they?" she asked, so softly Angela barely heard her.

Angela opened her mouth, but no sound emerged. She felt frozen, but realized that Emily needed an answer, so she forced a nod.

With the trust and hope only a child could muster, Emily rallied. "Are you sure? I mean, maybe they're okay. Maybe they're still in the car waiting for us to—"

"Emily—"

"—come back. Did the ambulance guys talk to them? Because sometimes Liam likes to play—"

"Em." Angela placed her hands over Emily's, which gesticulated wildly, as if she could conjure her father and brother back. "They died in the accident."

Emily's hazel eyes narrowed and burned brightly as she glared at her mother. "I don't believe you."

Angela flashed back to all of their recent arguments and felt her own temper flare. The rational part of her brain knew that she must work through the moment without using angry words. "Honey, I don't want to believe it either, but I saw them. They're gone."

The girl's face contorted, reflecting her roiling emotions. "Where are they now?"

"Downstairs."

"Where downstairs?"

"They're in the . . ." Angela hesitated, not wanting to say the word.

"Morgue?"

Angela was shocked. "How did you know that?"

"Jeez, mom. I'm not ten. I hear you talking to Dad all the time. Plus, that's where all the dead people go on TV shows."

Angela paused, not wanting to speak the truth. "Yes, that's where they are."

"Can I see them?"

"Absolutely not!" Angela recalled her own reactions in the morgue and couldn't imagine subjecting Emily to that horror.

Emily shrank into her bed, despair carving lines in her beautiful skin. For one ridiculous moment, Angela wished she could go back in time and undo the accident. Anything to take away Emily's pain.

"How did they look?"

"What do you mean?"

"Were they all bloody and mangled or . . . in pieces?"

"Emily Grace! What kind of a question is that?" Again, Angela had to swallow her anger and reminded herself that her daughter didn't meant to sound flippant. She was simply a child attempting to process information that most adults couldn't fathom.

Emily shook her head quickly. "I don't know. I'm sorry. I just want to know what they looked like."

Angela pictured Liam, his battered and broken limbs splayed under the sheet. Her mind's eye wandered to his unmarked face and she smiled sadly. "Liam looked peaceful, actually. And Daddy looked okay, too. I fixed his hair because it was kind of messy."

"That was nice."

"Yeah. He didn't like to have his hair messed up, did he?"

"No, he didn't."

Angela breathed deeply and gazed at her daughter. She took her hand. "Emily, we have each other and I'm incredibly grateful for that."

"I guess," Emily said as she removed her hand and stared at the wall. Angela's heart sank as fear of the unknown gripped her. *What if we can't forge a bond? What if Emily blames me for the accident?*

Lauren breezed into the room with some water and a small pill cup.

"Good news, my dear. We can remove that horrible catheter

in your bladder. The doctor wants to switch you to a less powerful painkiller, and he discharged you to a regular hospital room. We can get you out of here as soon as your room is ready."

"Hey, do you have a fake leg?" Emily blurted.

"Emily, please!" Angela admonished as she closed her eyes, embarrassed.

Lauren smiled as she removed Emily's Fentanyl IV. "It's okay, Dr. Brennan. You're right, Emily. I had cancer when I was a little older than you."

Emily's eyebrows came together. "Am I going to lose my leg too?"

"Oh, my goodness, no," Lauren said. "You're going to be just fine. In fact, you'll be good as new after your physical therapy."

Angela watched Emily consider Lauren's words. The nurse handed her the pill and water.

"Okay, take that pill. The medicine isn't as strong as the one you had before, so you might experience a little more pain the next few hours, but it's better for you in the long term."

Emily glanced at her mother, who nodded her assent.

"Knock, knock," Liz said as she entered the room. "How are you feeling, Em?"

Emily shrugged as she swallowed her pill. "Okay, I guess. Dad and Liam died."

The abruptness of Emily's blunt statement struck Angela like a gut punch. She drew a raspy breath, as if invisible hands were wrapped around her throat, crushing her larynx. Liz crossed to the bed and gently took Emily's bruised face in her hands.

"I know, sweetie, and I'm so sorry."

CHAPTER 10

Angela and Liz sat at a corner table in the hospital's food court, an island amidst a sea of activity. Patients' families and staff filled the space, the former taking a well-needed respite from their loved ones' bedsides while the latter enjoyed a break from work.

Angela watched Liz as she sipped her coffee. It occurred to her that Liz had more personal experience with death than she did. Liz's parents had died when she was a young adult, and she had put herself through college and nursing school by joining the army. Then, after graduation, she had fought in Afghanistan, so she had wrangled with death and its brutal aftermath various times. Yet somehow she had found peace, and Angela envied her.

"You're quiet," Angela said.

Liz smiled. "Well, I've learned that there's a time for speech and action, and a time for silence and stillness. But I haven't encountered this particular situation before, so I'm choosing the path that my mother so often recommended: if you're unsure what to say, say nothing. Just listen and observe."

"Makes sense," Angela said as she turned her attention from Liz and observed the orchestrated chaos of the cafeteria. She felt as if she were floating above the dining space. Her heart thundered in her chest, and for a moment she wondered if Liz could hear it. Her coffee cup burned the palm of her hand, bringing her focus back. She looked at her red palm, then replaced it against the steaming cup, welcoming the pain because it meant she was still capable of feeling.

"I don't know what to do, Liz."

"You don't have to do anything right now."

"Are you recommending that from experience?"

Liz looked at her. "Yes."

"Okay."

A baby wailed as its mother removed a bottle from its mouth.

"Do you want me to get you some food?" Liz asked.

"No, thank you."

Angela watched the mother remove the crying baby girl from her stroller and rock her back and forth. She remembered the feeling of Liam as a baby, soft and warm against her breast as he nursed. She started rocking, matching the rhythm of the mother as she spoke in a monotone. "I guess I need to figure out a funeral, right? How does it work? Are they buried together in one service with two coffins? Or should I have two services because different people may want to come? And what about Liam's school? I should call his principal. And my parents. I need to call my parents. I just don't know where to start."

The touch of Liz's hand made Angela jump and she stopped rocking, embarrassed. "We'll figure it out together. How about I call your parents?"

Angela looked directly at Liz, hearing her question but unable to process an answer. Her brain felt foggy, like she could think the answer to Liz's question, but couldn't quite bring the words to her lips. "I can't cry, Liz. Why can't I cry?"

"Angela, you need to give yourself some time. It hasn't even been twenty-four hours."

Angela shook her head. "Did you see them downstairs? Didn't Liam look peaceful?"

"He did."

Angela stared at the mother cradling her child and then raked her fingers through her hair. "Yesterday the kids were playing on the beach. Liam was chasing Emily with a crab. Everything seemed so normal. I didn't realize how wonderful 'normal' was. Before we left for vacation our biggest problem was how to pick up the kids on time. Work seemed so important." Her face contorted in confusion. "Can you believe that? We had trouble picking up the kids on time. And I was completely focused on becoming a CEO."

"What are you talking about?"

"Maggie asked me if I was interested in becoming hospital CEO. Tony was right. It was silly. So silly . . ." Her voice trailed off as she remembered the anger she'd felt when Tony had said that. He had been right. Her priorities were skewed.

"I didn't know you wanted to do that."

Angela spoke without looking at Liz, half of her mind still at the kitchen table with Tony. "That's the thing. I don't think I really did. Looking back now, I was going to do it just because it was the next big thing to achieve. It's so fucking ridiculous." Angela shook her head as if to rid herself of the memory.

"It's not, Angela. You'd be a great leader. You already are, but if you became CEO, you'd be a leader on a bigger stage."

Angela laughed derisively. "To what end, Liz? Nothing matters, really."

"Emily matters."

The words cut straight to Angela's heart and the mental fog lifted suddenly, as if a veil had been withdrawn. "Yes, that's true. And that's why I'm going to focus all of my energy on her. I'll get back to being a surgeon when I'm ready. But for now, I'm going to do the right thing and focus on my daughter."

"Sounds like a plan."

"Dr. Brennan?"

Angela looked up and saw a tall, attractive woman with salt-and-pepper, shoulder-length hair smiling down at her. "Yes?"

"I'm Katie Crowe. You operated on my husband, Bill, last year."

Angela forced herself to focus. Rallying her mental resources, she struggled but finally recalled the case. Seventy-something grandfather who required a triple bypass so he could ride bikes with his grandkids without running out of breath. "Oh, yes. Hello, Mrs. Crowe. How are you?"

"I'm fine, and thanks to you, so is Bill. We're here because our daughter gave birth to a beautiful baby boy yesterday afternoon."

Angela managed a smile. "How wonderful for your family. What's his name?"

"Liam. My daughter named him after my husband. Liam is Gaelic for William."

Angela blinked rapidly as the floor seemed to give way beneath her. Liz grabbed Angela's hand and interjected. "What a beautiful name, Mrs. Crowe. It was lovely to see you, but Dr. Brennan needs to—"

"Oh, of course. You're probably very busy. I just wanted to say hello."

"When did you say your grandson was born?" Angela asked breathlessly, feeling a mixture of confusion, worry, and curiosity.

"Late yesterday afternoon."

"At what time exactly?" Her voice was urgent as she wrung her hands.

"Let's see. Let me think. Um, yes, it was 4:58 P.M., to be precise. Why? Dr. Brennan?"

Angela could no longer hear her, or any other sound in the food court, as a whooshing sound washed back and forth through her head. The whooshing was replaced by a high-pitched tone that accompanied her vision narrowing to a pinpoint surrounded by bright white lights. The next thing she knew, Liz was catching her as she began to fall sideways from her chair. Liz righted her and said, "Breathe, Angela. You need to breathe."

"Is she alright?" Angela heard Mrs. Crowe ask.

"She's fine," Liz answered. "Just tired. Thanks for coming by." Angela watched Mrs. Crowe walk away, a concerned look on her face.

When Angela had regained her faculties, Liz leaned forward and said, "I'm so sorry, Angela. That was just awful."

"Do you think that's a coincidence, Liz? That a child came into the world at the moment my son was leaving it? And that he was named Liam?"

Liz inhaled deeply and shook her head. "It is strange."

"And that we happened to be sitting here when Mrs. Crowe came in? And the fact that it was me who operated on her husband last year? It's all so bizarre. I mean, have you experienced anything like this before?"

"Not exactly like this, but weird things happened before my mother died."

"What do you mean?"

"Well, you know she was sick for about a year before she died. And toward the end she would awaken and speak to the air, as if someone were in the room with her. When it was happening, I would try to talk to her, and she would look at me but not see me, you know? Eventually she'd come out of the trance and speak to me. When I asked her who she'd been talking to, she would name relatives who were long dead. It didn't strike her as strange at all, that she was having entire conversations with ghosts. It was as if she were straddling two worlds, like her soul had crossed over but her body hadn't. It happened more and more often, until she fell completely silent the hours before her death." Liz wiped her eyes. "At least she's in heaven, just like Liam and Tony."

Angela shook her head. "I'm not so sure."

"About them being in heaven?"

"About heaven, Liz. You sound like the guy I met in the waiting room when Emily was in surgery."

"What guy?"

An irrational anger rose quickly. "Some batty old man who was trying to make me feel better by telling me that I should have faith, that everything will work out okay. All I know is that half of my family is gone. Their bodies are lying on cold, steel tables downstairs, and I can't hold them anymore. I'll never see Liam grow up, graduate, go to college, get married, none of it. Tony and I were robbed of a chance to grow old together, retire, and just enjoy life."

Grateful to find an outlet for her frustration, Angela waved her hands wildly as she continued. "All this talk about God and heaven is bullshit. A fairytale to make the people left behind feel better." Her words hung in the air as she rolled her eyes. "Although, he did predict that Emily would come out of surgery just fine, and she did."

"So maybe he's right about the other stuff, too."

Angela focused on Katie Crowe as she laughed at something her husband said. Her anger dissipated, and a wave of sadness replaced it. "I could save Mr. Crowe but I couldn't save my own family."

Liz followed Angela's gaze. "It's an entirely different situation."

Angela sighed deeply. "Is it?" She looked at Liz and twisted her mouth.

"What's wrong?"

"There's something I haven't told you about the guy from the waiting room."

Liz leaned forward, concern etched on her face.

"What?"

Angela looked around before whispering, "He wasn't there when I went back to thank him."

"So?"

"He had vanished."

"What do you mean 'vanished'?"

Angela shook her head and shrugged. "I mean he vanished. One moment he was there and the next moment he was gone."

Liz stared open-mouthed at Angela, her eyebrows raised above large eyes. "Angela, you've been through a lot. Maybe—"

Angela rubbed her hands over her face and nodded. "I know. I could be losing it, but I'm telling you that when I went back to thank the guy, there was just a lady sitting there, and when I asked her where the man had gone, she said that it had been only her and me in the waiting room for the last hour. It was weird."

Liz closed her mouth, leaned back in her chair and crossed her arms. "There could be an explanation, but you're not going to like it."

Angela waited.

"Maybe that man was your guardian angel."

A disgusted look crossed Angela's face as she waved her hand toward Liz. Then she stopped and smirked. "Actually, now that I think about it, it makes perfect sense that my guardian angel would be a smelly, homeless man with a missing tooth and bad grammar. I bet his name was Archie Angelo."

Liz shook her head. "You never know. Someone was looking out for you and Emily yesterday. Don't dismiss that out of hand."

Angela tilted her head and squinted. "Here's a question, Liz. What kind of god lets a little, innocent boy die a horrific death? Answer: Not one I care to know." She stood up and started to walk away.

"Where are you going?"

"To my daughter."

"I'm coming with you." Liz had to speedwalk to match Angela's pace.

As they reentered the ICU and stood by her bed, Emily roused. "Hi, Mom."

A cloak of warmth surrounded Angela. She reveled in seeing Emily safe and awake. A brief vision of their new life together sparked hope, and she felt a rush of joy that threatened to overwhelm her as she stroked Emily's forehead.

"Hi, honey. How are you feeling with the new medication?"

"Weird."

"What do you mean?" Angela stopped stroking and placed her palm against Emily's forehead.

"I feel woozy and really, really tired. I can't catch my breath and—" She vomited.

Angela grabbed a towel that lay on the bedside table and wiped Emily's mouth. "Liz, she's really hot. Get Lauren."

"I had a strange dream."

Angela leaned forward and looked into Emily's eyes. They were glassy and her pupils were dilated. Panic surged and then relented as Angela forced herself into doctor mode. Her brain started running through potential causes of Emily's fever. "Okay, honey. You can tell me about it in a minute."

Angela reset the machine that was attached to Emily via electrical leads and grabbed a stethoscope to listen to her heart. Angela's breath quickened as she watched the numbers on the screen increase in response to her daughter's rapidly changing vital signs. The machine started beeping as Lauren stepped through the door.

"What's going on?"

"She has a fever. There could be an infection."

Liz shook her head. "It's too soon for an infection, and she's clearly having trouble breathing. I think—"

"I had a dream about Liam, Mom. He was standing in front of me and there was this light. This really bright light coming out of his chest and his fingertips, and he was so happy, you know? He was so incredibly happy." Angela tried but failed to focus on Emily as she mentally ran through the list of potential post-operative complications.

"Liz, she's hallucinating. It must be an infection." Turning back to Emily, she smiled tightly. "You're going to be okay, Em."

"I'm telling you, Angela. It's something else," Liz said as she stared at the numbers on the monitor.

"And I was happy looking at him. He wanted me to come to him—" Emily wheezed.

"Emily, I love you, but you need to stop talking, okay? It's important that you save your breath." Angela fought to quell her rising panic and forced herself to think logically. "Lauren, get Dr. Jacobs."

"I didn't want to go, but he was so happy," Emily whispered.

Angela stared at Emily but spoke to Lauren. "What was the medication and dosage of the IV painkiller you gave her?"

Lauren referenced her iPad. "Fentanyl, 20 milliliters per hour."

"And he was reaching for me, and Daddy was there." Emily vomited again. Angela grabbed an emesis basin and thrust it under Emily's mouth as she simultaneously picked up the already sodden towel. Her voice rose as she watched the color drain from Emily's face. "And the pill once you removed the IV Fentanyl?"

Lauren glanced at the iPad's screen and froze.

"Lauren!" Angela ordered. "What was the in the pill?"

Lauren blanched and shook her head. "Oxycontin, 30 milligrams."

A million pins pricked Angela's skin and she turned to Liz. "Oh. No, no, no."

Liz took two large steps toward Lauren and yanked the iPad out of her hand. Seconds ticked by as Liz scrolled through various screens. After an eternity, Liz's eyes met Angela's and she knew the truth. "It's too much," Liz said as she shook her head.

"By two, Liz. It's two times the dose she should have received." Angela held her breath as she quickly processed next steps. "Okay. We're going to—"

"So I went, and it was beautiful, Mom. It was amazing. But I was told to come back to say goodbye to you."

Angela's head swiveled to focus on her daughter, whose glazed eyes held a terrifying serenity. The room swirled and everyone disappeared as Angela's vision tunneled on Emily. "What did you just say?"

"It's okay, Mom. Everything's going to be okay." A small whistle escaped her lips as she struggled to breathe.

Angela's head started moving before she spoke. "No, no, no, baby girl. Lauren, where's Dr. Jacobs? Get a Narcan injection ready. She can't breathe."

"Mom, it's okay. They're here." Emily coughed and frothy sputum dribbled from her mouth.

Angela's mind broke as she watched Emily's body start to convulse, her gaze locked on something only she could see. Angela flapped her hands and raked her fingers through her hair in an effort to find relief from the explosion inside her head. She started hyperventilating and screamed, "She's dying! Liz, do something!" Liz ran from the room, issuing orders for the medication that would reverse Emily's overdose.

Angela grasped Emily's shoulders and screamed, "Emily, look at me. Look at me!" Emily's eyes rolled back and then returned to focus on Angela even as her lips were turning a light shade of blue. "I love you, Emily. You're strong. Fight it!" She turned toward the door and screamed, "Liz! Where's the damned Narcan!"

"I'm so happy here," Emily wheezed. "It's so beautiful. Liam and Daddy are safe." Angela started sobbing as Emily gazed past her and looked suddenly sad. "You can't come with me, Mom."

Emily's words injected Angela with renewed focus and suddenly every detail of Emily's face became crisp and clear. "No! Emily, I love you so much. Don't go. Please," Angela pleaded. "Baby girl! Please!"

Liz rushed in with a syringe and threw back the covers, revealing Emily's right thigh. She jammed the needle into her leg and depressed the plunger. Angela's eyes remained fixed on her daughter's face. Emily's back arched once and then she lay still, unbreathing.

Angela's face was a blank mask as she stared, unable to move or speak.

Liz's voice sounded very far away. "Initiating resuscitation procedure. Lauren, call the emergency team!" Time slowed as Liz came to the side of the bed and started performing CPR on Emily. Angela noticed the way Liz placed one hand on top of the other and intertwined her fingers, then placed them quickly but carefully on Emily's sternum. As someone pulled on her shirt to get her out of the way, Angela mentally counted along with Liz as she pressed on Emily's chest. With each depression, more sputum erupted from Emily's mouth and ran down her chin. Angela twisted the wet towel in her hands, desperately wanting to wipe her daughter's chin but knowing that she would just be in the way. When Angela's vision narrowed and she saw flashes of white light, she realized that she was holding her breath. She forced herself to inhale, then staggered to a chair and fell into it as a swearing Stan Jacobs entered the room with a team wielding an emergency cart.

"What the hell happened in here? Let us take over." Stan's words roused Angela and she watched Liz move aside to allow one of the emergency team to resume CPR.

Fury shot from her stomach to her mouth and she was unable to stop herself from leaping from the chair and stalking over to Stan. "You tell me, Stan! You tell me what happened! My baby is dying!" she screamed, jabbing her finger in his face.

"Angela, you should—"

She hit his chest with her fist. "I don't know what to do, Stan!" she sobbed. Pointing to Emily she screamed, "Do something!" and then dropped to the floor as her knees gave way beneath her. Angela felt herself being lifted and carried out to the hallway as she listened to the clinicians carrying out their emergency procedures. Liz's face appeared directly in front of her. Angela saw her lips moving but couldn't hear the words. Wails burst violently from her mouth as she grabbed fistfuls of her own hair and yanked repeatedly. Angela felt Liz gently take her hands and pull them away from her head. The wailing subsided and was replaced by Emily's last words playing on a loop in her mind. "You can't come with me, Mom."

Like hell I can't, she thought as she lost consciousness and sank to the tiled floor.

CHAPTER 11

Blinding light streamed through the window and pierced Angela's eyes. Instinctively she pulled the covers over her head and squeezed her eyes shut. *God, my head hurts.*

"Good morning. Or should I say good afternoon?"

Angela recognized the voice but couldn't place it, as the stuffing in her head muffled the speaker's words. Thoughts swirled around her mind, and she couldn't pin them down as her eyes opened and closed repeatedly.

"Daddy and I came as soon as Liz called us, Angela."

Right. It's my mom. Why is she here?

"I want you to know that we'll stay as long as you need. Daddy's been making some calls, getting things rolling."

What is she talking about? Angela reached to her left, feeling to see if Tony was awake yet. He wasn't in the bed.

"Can you please look at me?"

Angela sighed deeply, feeling like a chastised teenager. Removing the covers, she stared dully at her mother.

"That's better. How are you feeling?"

"Like I've been hit by a truck—"

The truth of her statement rolled her stomach and she managed to turn her head just enough so that she didn't vomit on the bed, but rather on the oak floorboards. "Oh my God. They're all gone," she breathed.

Her mother approached, sat next to her, and wiped her mouth with a towel. "Shhh, sweetie. Shhh."

"Where's Emily?"

Sally Barckett stared at her with wide brown eyes. Angela noticed that her mother's colored hair was coiffed perfectly, as usual, and her thin lips formed a straight line as she considered a response.

Another wave of nausea threatened, but Angela kept it at bay. "I mean, where's Emily's body?"

Her mother offered a disapproving moue while neatly folding the towel. "Her body, along with Liam's and Tony's, were released to the funeral home an hour ago, so they're in transport as we speak. We wanted the hospital to do an autopsy on Emily, but we were told that you'd been through enough. And you, well, you were in no position to argue."

Angela touched her nose and grimaced as pain flashed into her jaw. The bandage felt crisp and Angela wondered who had changed it. "Is Liz here?"

"Yes. She's downstairs on the phone with someone from the hospital. They want to talk to you when you're ready."

"About what?"

Her mother shrugged. "I'm not sure, but don't worry about that right now, okay?"

A scream clawed inside Angela's head, desperately searching for release. "What should I worry about then, Mom? I can no longer worry about my family because, oh yeah, I don't have one!"

Her mother quickly looked away and cleared her throat. "I can hear your father coming up the stairs. Let's see what he has to say."

The door creaked and her father entered. "There's my angel. How are you doing, sweetheart?"

Angela shook her head as a surge of anger swelled and then dissipated. "What day is it?"

"Friday."

"So, it's been . . ."

"Four days since the accident," he finished.

Angela blinked, amazed that she couldn't remember anything from the last four days. "What am I on, Dad?"

"Xanax. A fairly high dose. Both Liz and I thought it was a good idea after you collapsed at the hospital."

Angela scratched her head. "It's too much, Dad. I can't even think straight."

"You don't need to think straight right now, but I'll alter the dosage."

Angela stared out the window at the large oak tree whose leaves were coming into full bloom. *Tony loved that tree*, she thought absentmindedly.

Still staring at the leaves, she asked, "You know what Liam wanted to be when he grew up?"

She could feel the tension as her parents struggled for a response. "What?" her father finally asked.

"Happy." She grimaced. "That's what he always said when we asked him." She saw him in her mind, his goofy grin on Christmas day after unwrapping the bike they'd gotten him. She and Tony had used four rolls of wrapping paper trying to wrap it. Four rolls of gift wrap and two bottles of wine.

She turned to her parents. "Do you know the story about John Lennon?"

Her father shook his head.

"When he was about five years old his mother told him that happiness was the key to life. So when he went to school and was asked what he wanted to be when he grew up, he answered 'happy.' He was told by his teacher that he misunderstood the assignment. His response was that she misunderstood life."

Her father smiled as her mother stood and left the room, mumbling, "Excuse me" and dabbing at her eyes with a handkerchief. Angela returned her gaze to the leaves. Her father asked, "What about Emily? What did she want to be?"

Turning back to him, she sighed and tears gathered in the corners of her eyes. "Emily was more of an enigma. She had so many talents, it's hard to know where they would have taken her. She would have been a great doctor, but I don't think she would have chosen that path. She was always doing something with her beautiful hair. Maybe she would have been a hair stylist. Or a teacher, maybe? She was patient with everyone but her family." Angela envisioned her daughter smiling as they chatted while getting a manicure. Then she saw Emily rolling her eyes and stomping away from the dinner table following a disagreement. Angela wondered what role she herself might have played in Emily's impatience.

A knock sounded, and Liz entered. "Hey, you."

"Hi." Liz's empathetic look was like a knife to her heart. Angela almost broke down again.

"I just got off the phone with the hospital. Maggie to be exact. She wants to meet with you when you feel up to it."

"What for?"

"She didn't say. I assume to discuss some time off, who might oversee the Cardiac Surgery department while you're out, that kind of thing."

Anger burst through Angela's thin veneer of control. "I'm not taking any time off. I'll go to the funerals but then I'm going back to work."

"Angela, I don't think that's a good idea," her father offered.

She rounded on her father. "Why do people think it's a good idea to tell someone who has just lost everything that they *should* do this or *shouldn't* do that? Who are you to tell me what to do?"

"Angela, I've handled many surgical cases in which—"

Angela held up her hand. "Dad, with all due respect, I've handled many surgical cases, too. And let me tell you that you have absolutely no idea how I feel right now. How do I know that? Because *I* have absolutely no idea how I feel right now. So, please, back off, and leave me alone!"

Angela glanced at a silent Liz, whose eyes volleyed between

the two physicians as she struggled to find something helpful to say. "How's your pain, Angela?"

Angela touched her new bandage. "Dulled by the incredibly high dose of Xanax I'm on. Thanks, though, for changing the dressing."

"Of course. How about I make some tea?"

Angela nodded, knowing her friend was attempting to ease the tension. "That would be nice. Thanks."

As Liz left, Angela took a deep breath, regretting her harsh words "Sorry, Dad. I know you're just trying to help. I guess Emily got her impatience with family from me."

"It's okay, angel. You're right. I don't know what you're feeling, and I shouldn't tell you what to do."

Angela met her father's red eyes and realized that he'd been crying before coming in to see her. Upon closer examination, she noted that his shoulders were slumped and his clothes, normally so dapper, were wrinkled as they hung on his tall, slender frame. The dark circles under his blue eyes matched his gray, unwashed hair, and she suddenly appreciated how much the catastrophic loss must be affecting him. Not only had he lost both grandchildren and Tony, but he was going to have to witness his only child staggering through a horrendous valley in her life. Jim Barckett was a proud man, though, and Angela knew that he wouldn't want her to draw attention to his sadness or his current bedraggled state.

"Mom said something about you making calls?"

He cleared his throat. "Yes. I spoke with Nicholson's Funeral Home and scheduled a meeting with them for later today if you're up to it. If not, I'll go and report back."

"No. I'll go. Let's go together."

He nodded and rubbed his eyes. "God, Angela. I'm so sorry this happened."

"Me too." She held his eyes and noted that his expression altered from kindness to worry. His eyebrows gathered as he sat next to her and stroked her hand.

"What is it, Dad?"

He sighed heavily. "I'm not sure I should tell you this right now, but—" He paused so long that she slapped the covers with her hand.

"Damn it, Dad, tell me!"

"The Barnstable police called while you were sleeping and told me that the man who hit you was a landscaper coming home from work. Apparently, he was reading a text from his wife when he ran the stop sign. He was treated and released from a local hospital and was arrested immediately on charges of vehicular manslaughter. He's in jail pending a bail hearing."

Angela held her father's gaze, afraid if she looked away she would start screaming and never stop. "I see."

"They said that you're welcome to attend his bail hearing to make a statement about the accident."

"What sort of statement?"

"You're allowed to say what happened and the judge will take your words into account when determining if the driver is allowed bail and, if so, how much bail will be."

Anger surged like a rogue wave. "When's the hearing?"

"Two days from now."

Angela could feel the blood pumping through her veins and an empowering calm settled within her. "I'm going to go and make sure that he's put away for a long time."

"Don't get your hopes up, honey. We might have the best justice system in the world, but it's far from perfect. Depending on the circumstances, he might get released with no bail."

"You mean he just gets off scot free while my entire family is gone?"

"No. He'd still have to return for his trial, but he could walk free until then."

"Over my dead body."

"Why don't you get some rest while I chat with your mom and Liz. We'll plan out the next few days and update you when you're ready. Does that sound okay?"

Angela nodded. "Thanks for being here, Dad. I can't imagine what I'd do without you."

He smiled sadly and massaged her hand. "Angela, you're my daughter and I love you more than anything in the world. I'll be here as long as you need me. And then for a little while after that, too." It was their secret joke. When she was a little girl, he had said the same thing and remained true to his word. Even after she was married with a family of her own, he had ensured that she understood he was still available if she needed him, to the point that it had irritated her. Now, however, she found comfort in his perseverance.

Jim left the room and Angela closed her eyes, immediately reliving the accident. As she envisioned Liam's broken body in the back seat, her only comfort was that he most likely died instantly. Tony, however, had not been so fortunate. He had died slowly, and most likely in a certain amount of pain. But she was grateful that she'd had the opportunity to speak to him before he died. And his last words, "I love you," replayed in her mind as she stared at the oak leaves blowing in the late spring breeze.

Suddenly Emily's voice called to her, and for a moment, she believed that it had all been a colossal mistake, that Emily was in her bedroom calling her name. Emily's laughter echoed throughout the room, and Angela smiled.

"I'm glad to see you're smiling," Liz said as she placed a tray of tea and sandwiches on the bedside table.

"I can hear Emily, Liz. It's like she's in the room."

Liz glanced around the bedroom. "She's here, Angela. I'm sure of it."

Angela's eyes followed Liz's, wanting desperately to believe, but unable to allow her mind the respite. "How is that possible? Is it just my imagination? Or the meds?"

Liz shrugged. "It depends on who you ask. But since you're asking me, my answer is no, it's not just your imagination. She's here."

"But I can't hear Liam or Tony."

"They might come at a different time, or they might not come at all. One thing's for sure, though. If you're open to their visiting, then they'll come."

Angela nodded, then asked, "Do you own a gun?"

Liz paused before answering and stared at her. "You know I do. Ever since I left the military. Why?"

"I'd like to learn how to use one."

"Why?"

Angela considered the question. She had several answers but was not yet ready to share any of them. "I'm alone now and I think I should have one."

Liz evaluated her. "I'm not sure now is the time to be making decision like this, Angela."

Angela offered a sudden, disarming smile. "Just think about it."

"Okay. I'll think about it."

CHAPTER 12

~

Angela sat in the back of Tony's Tesla and watched the world whiz by. Her father had insisted that he drive to the hearing, and although she had originally declined the offer, she acquiesced when she'd woken up that morning hyperventilating from a dream she'd had in which she was repeatedly stabbing a stranger on the street. Her father turned up the jazz that was playing on the radio. The music drilled into her head until she thought she'd explode.

"Dad, please. That music is awful."

Jim glanced in the rearview mirror and turned off the radio. "Of course. Sorry, angel."

They stopped at a red light and Angela watched a woman in the car next them reach into the back seat to retrieve a pacifier for her baby. The woman turned and smiled at Angela, then looked away when the greeting was not returned. Angela's chest hurt when she looked at the baby, and she tore her gaze away to focus on a hangnail she'd been worrying for the last two hours.

They arrived at the courthouse and her father found a parking space directly in front. He paid the meter and helped Angela out of the car, ensuring that she was safely ensconced between Sally and himself as they climbed the steps leading to the entrance.

Angela felt her body involuntarily pulling back, as if it wanted to keep her out of the building.

"Are you okay?" her mom asked.

Angela paused, shook her head, and then sat heavily on the wide stone steps. She felt her father's hand on her back as she noted a woman with two young children and an infant walk by.

Her father leaned in. "We don't have to be here. We can go home."

Angela lifted her face toward the imposing building. Above the entrance was etched "Above all, truth and justice." Angela considered the phrase and reminded herself why she was there. Putting her pain aside, she slowly stood up.

"No, Dad. I want to be here. I want to look into the eyes of the man who took everything away from me. Everything." Her voice broke as she spoke and her parents grabbed her elbows as they moved forward.

A small press corps awaited her as they arrived at their assigned courtroom. When the reporters recognized her, they pressed forward, thrusting microphones in her face. Shocked that anyone would take an interest in her personal demise, she simply stared at them as they hurled questions toward her.

"Dr. Brennan, how do you feel about seeing the man that killed your family?"

"What do you think should happen to the man who killed your husband and son?"

"How are you coping, Dr. Brennan?"

Angela looked at her parents as she considered their questions. Her mother's face was twisted in distaste and sadness, but her father's was stoic, betraying nothing for the cameras. She blinked several times, trying to decide whether or not she wanted to speak. Finally, she said, "I don't know how I'll feel when I see him, but I think he should be treated as my family was treated."

"Are you saying that he should get the death penalty, Dr. Brennan?"

Angela stared in confusion at the young woman who had asked the question. "Is that a possibility?" Angela asked.

Seeing an opening, the reporter stepped in closer. "Probably not, but if it were, would you ask for him to be put to death?"

First, do no harm, Angela thought. Before she could answer, a young man called out, "How are you coping, Doctor?"

Angela's eyes swung to the reporter who appeared young enough to have stepped off a college campus. He had curly blond hair that he repeatedly swept from his forehead as he shifted from side to side. She imagined Liam at his age. *They could be brothers*, she mused. The young man took her attention as encouragement and decided to press his luck. "Do you miss your family?"

Without warning, a black rage erupted. Angela leapt forward and yanked the microphone from the reporter's hand, then hurled it across the hallway where it crashed into a column and split apart. Silence descended as her parents grabbed her arms to restrain her from attacking any further. Breathing heavily, she wrestled her arms away from her parents and stepped toward the reporter, who held his ground. Sneering, she leaned toward him and whispered, "Does that answer your dumb question?"

Without another word she threw open the courtroom doors and marched to the front row, seating herself heavily as she clutched her purse against her heaving chest. The crowd already gathered in the chamber jumped at the entrance, then settled back into their seats. Her parents were at her side in an instant, not touching her but casting worried glances at each other. After several moments, Angela said, "I'm fine."

"Okay," mumbled Jim, who gently reached over and took Angela's white-knuckled hand. "It'll be over soon."

A bailiff appeared and announced, "All rise. The honorable Christian Vasquez will hear arguments to determine bail for Jonathan Dale, who has been accused of causing the deaths of Anthony and Liam Brennan."

The judge's large face was lined from too many years in the sun, and his low-lidded eyes traveled tiredly around the courtroom as overgrown eyebrows threatened his vision. His jowls swung as he angrily evaluated the gallery of onlookers. He was clearly not pleased that the case was garnering so much attention. Angela tried to breathe but found that her lungs would not obey. Instead, small sounds escaped each time she attempted a breath. Jim turned and, seeing her distress, pushed her forward and slapped her back hard enough that all eyes found her. The surprise of her father's hard hand broke through the momentary paralysis and she drew a desperate, shuddering breath that shook her entire body.

"Ma'am, do you need medical assistance?" Judge Vasquez bellowed. Angela blanched as she realized that he was speaking to her, and she quickly shook her head, but not before the defendant, who had been entering the courtroom, locked eyes with her as he was led to his seat. His pale, bearded face was ringed with shoulder-length, stringy blond hair and he looked as if he hadn't slept in days. His eyes struck Angela as being too close together, and his lime-green sweatpants were too large, giving him the appearance of a blond rat drowning in a bowl of sherbet.

"Are you sure?" Judge Vasquez's bass voice boomed over the speaker system.

Angela tore her eyes from the defendant. Looking at the judge, she nodded again while her father gathered her in his arms. Her mother had removed a hankie and was dabbing her eyes while weeping silently.

The judge considered Angela a moment longer and then asked, "Are both parties' legal representation present?"

The courtroom door flew open and the assistant district attorney for the state of Massachusetts rushed in to take her seat at the prosecution table. "Sorry I'm late, Your Honor. Traffic." The judge regarded her drily and then glanced at his wristwatch to make the point. "Well, we're glad you could join us, Ms. Dunn."

He shifted his glance to the defendant's court-appointed attorney, who said, "I'm ready, Your Honor."

"Go ahead then, Mr. Kepner." The defendant's lawyer stood and said, "Your Honor, my client has never had so much as a parking ticket. He's a hard-working father of three who made a tragic mistake. And he's very, very sorry. We're requesting he be released on his own recognizance until his sentencing hearing."

The judge glared at Mr. Kepner and then reviewed some information on his computer screen. After a moment, he looked at the defendant and then at Mr. Kepner. "I understand that your client was texting when he crashed into the Brennan's car. Is that right?"

"Yes, Your Honor." The defendant had stood and spoken, despite Mr. Kepner's attempts to quiet him.

Upon hearing the voice of the man who had stolen her family, Angela's stomach clenched. His tone was quiet and thick with emotion. Angela closed her eyes and imagined hitting him with her car, then reversing and ramming him again.

"And I'm so sorry." Her eyes flew open and she watched his shoulders shake. Angela's hands balled into fists and she dug her nails into her palms to keep herself from launching across the space between them and strangling him.

"I'm sorry. You see, my wife was—"

The entire gallery jumped as Judge Vasquez's gavel came down with a reverberating thud. "What is your name, sir?"

Angela was certain that the judge knew the defendant's name and was confused as to why he would ask.

The defendant pointed to himself.

"Yes, you. What is your name?"

"Jonathan Dale, sir."

The judge leaned toward the microphone. "I do not care *why* you were texting, Mr. Dale. I simply do not care. You see, I'm not here to determine your guilt or innocence. I am here to set your bail. And that is what I'm going to do." He leaned back from the microphone and examined the gallery. "I know that all of you, every single one of you, have texted and driven, and I do not know what it's going to take to get you to stop. But I'm tired of hearings such as these because this was avoidable." He leaned forward again, his lips brushing against the mic. "*Avoidable.*" He sighed heavily and leaned back, and Angela found that she couldn't tear her eyes from his bulldog face.

"Ms. Dunn, do you have anything to say before I set bail?"

The ADA stood and shook her head. "No, Your Honor, except I couldn't agree more with what you just said."

The judge set his mouth. "Based on predetermined fees, I hereby set Jonathan Dale's bail at ten thousand dollars, plus another ten thousand at my discretion." He glared at the defendant. "That should give you twenty thousand reasons *not* to text and drive, Mr. Dale." The judge banged his gavel and stood. The bailiff's instruction to stand for the judge's exit was lost among the chitter-chatter of the gallery as they discussed the bail determination.

The entire hearing had taken less than two minutes. It had all happened so quickly that Angela had not had time to react to the fact that she had not been asked to speak. She rushed to the prosecution table and grabbed Fay Dunn's arm. "Hey, why didn't I get a chance to say something?"

"Oh my God, Angela. What are you doing here?"

Angela looked at her like she'd lost her mind. "What do you mean, what am I doing here?"

Fay shook her head quickly. "I mean, well, your father said that you were most likely not coming so I didn't plan on having you make a statement."

Jim intervened. "I left a message with your assistant this morning saying that we were coming."

Fay's frantic eyes looked from Angela to Jim. "I've been out all morning. I never got the message. My daughter was sick and I had to take her to the pediatrician. But you should know that the bail the judge set was fair."

Angela gaped at her in disbelief. "Fair? He'll be out before this afternoon." She looked over to see the defendant's attorney huddled with his client. A crying woman with two small children and an infant looked on. Mesmerized, Angela walked toward them while her father continued to speak with Fay.

As she approached, she heard her mother rush up behind her. "Angela, don't do something that you'll regret."

Without turning around, Angela whispered, "I have nothing left to regret, Mom."

Angela approached the crying woman, whose tear-stained face was red and blotchy. She stood no more than five feet tall, and her hair was pulled into a messy ponytail. She wore no make-up and struck Angela as an old woman trapped in a young woman's body. Angela looked at the children, who clutched their mother's skirt like baby monkeys. They were scrawny and wide-eyed, as if they weren't used to interacting with anyone beyond their family. Angela's eyes were riveted to the infant that lay sleeping in a car seat. The baby was covered with a light-green blanket. Angela couldn't tell if it was a boy or a girl.

"Are you Mrs. Dale?" The woman nodded. "How old is your baby?" Angela whispered. The woman wiped her face and said, "Six days." Without warning, Angela detached from her body and witnessed the scene unfold from above.

She turned to the defendant. "Hey!"

He faced her.

"I didn't get to speak at the hearing but I want you to know who I am. I want you to see what you've done. To see the destruction you've caused." Jonathan Dale's eyes became wild as he realized to whom he was speaking. He stuttered, but Angela held up her hand. "Shut up. Don't say a word. I hope you fry for what you did. If I could, I'd kill you right here, right now, in front of your children." She stepped away and looked him up and down. As if examining roadkill, she shook her head in disgust. "You're pathetic," she hissed before turning and stomping out of the courtroom.

CHAPTER 13

Angela exhaled while gracefully pulling the trigger. In teaching Angela to shoot, Liz had been very specific in her choice of words because she wanted Angela to compare the act of shooting to a ballet. Preparation for the act was deliberate and thorough, setting up one's target required precision, and the actual release of the bullet necessitated accuracy and calm. Liz had rolled the description into one adjective—*graceful*—when Angela had pressed her on the need for such care.

Angela's bullet found its mark. She smiled and lowered her weapon. The world made sense when she was at the range. One bullet, one target. Everything else faded to the background. The recoil of the gun surprised her each time, reminding her that every action had an equal and opposite reaction. The logic of that scientific principle grounded her. She found a sense of peace when she wrapped herself in it.

"Nice shot!" Liz said.

Angela looked at her friend and smiled. "Thanks."

Angela took aim once more but stopped when she felt Liz's eyes on her. She turned and removed her shooting earmuffs.

"What?"

"I was just thinking about Sean's eulogy for Tony."

Angela placed her gun on the small shelf next to her purse. "Yeah. It was nice. He was a good friend to Tony." She stared into the distance. "It's hard to believe that it's been six weeks."

"How are you doing, Angela? I feel like coming here helps you, but I'm not exactly sure why."

Angela's mind drifted to the hundreds of people who had come to the service to pay their respects. Mourners had filled the pews in St. John's and spilled out the door and down the lawn in front of the church. Many of her children's classmates had stepped to the podium to reminisce about fun times or poignant moments they had shared with Emily and Liam. Like a moth to light, Angela had been drawn in by their words, trying to make sense of how she had arrived at this point in her life.

"I think I feel somewhat in control here, you know? It's like you said, shooting requires careful planning and precision, much like surgery—"

"Or ballet." Liz smiled.

"Yes. Like ballet. Anyway, being here allows me a release, I think. Does that make sense?"

"It does."

Angela smiled and donned her earmuffs. Grabbing her pistol, she took aim and was surprised to find that her hands were shaking. She stepped away and lowered her gun, realizing that she was still thinking about her family's burial.

After the memorial service, the mourners had walked to the cemetery and stood at a respectful distance from Angela and her parents as the minister spoke. Except for the occasional cough or sniffle, the only extraneous sounds had been the birds that made the cemetery their home. Finally, after a group recitation of the Lord's Prayer, the caskets had been lowered into the ground.

Since the accident, Angela had experienced emotional extremes she had not known existed. One day she'd awaken full of hope, only to be thrown into despair when she remembered the crash. Other days she'd wake up angry, ready to destroy anyone who was willing to engage her in battle. Most of all, though, she felt that she was missing a part of herself she knew could not be recovered. A hole that would never be filled. Although her emotions were volatile, the general malaise that swallowed her caused the most distress. It was as if she could feel *only* the extremes. There no longer seemed to be a middle emotional ground, and that terrified her. She stared at the gun in her hands and realized that one of the things she liked about shooting is that when the bullet was released, the outcome was determined. A bullet could not be retracted, and she enjoyed the sense of finality.

"You okay?"

She turned to find Liz's concerned stare alternating between her face and her weapon, which had slipped in her grasp and was now aimed at her knees.

"Angela, maybe you should take a break. Put the gun on the shelf."

"No. I'm fine."

Liz tilted her head, a worried look on her face. "Are you sure?"

"Yeah."

"Don't make me regret that I taught you how to shoot."

Angela attempted a smile. "I was just thinking about how the town rallied to support me recently. I mean, the candlelight vigil at the pond in town center was remarkable. Remember how the gazebo was decorated with colorful flowers? And everybody gathered to share a moment of silence as the sun went down?"

"It was beautiful."

Angela's mind and gaze were far away as she continued. "And the glow of the candles? It was . . . so peaceful. And so kind." She turned suddenly to face Liz. "The kindness, Liz. That's what so amazing to me. I mean, my refrigerator is overflowing with casseroles and breads."

"And don't forget your parents, Angela."

Angela nodded. They had arrived and quickly taken charge, moving into the guest room, answering the door, dealing with well-wishers, writing thank-you notes, and ensuring she ate at least one good meal a day. They had entered her room at night when she called out for Tony and had sat vigil as she calmed and resumed a fitful slumber.

Angela focused on Liz. "And you, my friend, full of stories from the operating room and gossip from the medical staff. Always there to make me smile. And you brought me here. Thank you."

"Well, I have to admit that I thought you had ulterior motives in wanting to learn to shoot, but since working with you and helping you get your license and that new pistol, I feel better. You're a crack shot. Almost better than me." Liz grinned.

Angela returned the smile. "Almost." She glanced at her watch and started. "Oh, I have to go. I'm supposed to meet Maggie in twenty minutes."

"Yeah. I have to go, too. I have some notes to finish."

"Okay. Talk later." Angela unloaded her gun and packed it away, then hugged Liz and ran to her car, arriving at the hospital exactly on time.

Angela sat down in the waiting area of the hospital's executive suite and examined the magazines arranged in a perfect fan. Inside her office, Maggie spoke in muffled tones, allowing the astute eavesdropper only a word here and there. Suddenly, the door opened, and Maggie shook the hand of her visitor before turning to Angela with her arms open wide. She wore a black crepe suit over a white blouse, her only jewelry a pair of pearl earrings and a matching choker. Her auburn hair was styled in a short bob that accentuated her narrow face and high cheekbones. Tortoiseshell glasses framed large brown eyes, and her smile was easy and open as she approached Angela.

"Angela, so good to see you. Please come in." Angela entered the office and was struck with its opulence. Whereas her office was cramped, cluttered, and offered minimal outside view, Maggie's boasted cherry woodwork and overlooked a courtyard filled with dogwood trees. Maggie noticed Angela's reaction.

"You like it? It's a far cry from my old office, isn't it?"

"Yes. I didn't realize that you had redecorated."

Maggie looked around. “It was about time, Angela. This office hadn't been redone since 1979.”

“Well, it's beautiful.”

Maggie smiled and gestured toward a chair. “Please, take a seat. Can I offer you water or a soda? Coffee?”

“No, no. I'm fine. Thank you.”

“Well, let me say first how sorry I am about everything that's happened. The service was beautiful, a true testament to your wonderful family.”

“You were there?”

“Of course I was there. We were all there. The administrative team, I mean. You're part of our work family, Angela. We support our own. Did you get the flowers we sent? Your thank-you note was lovely. Unnecessary, but lovely.”

Angela had no recollection of flowers, but nodded. Her parents would have sent the thank-you note. “Yes. I received the flowers. They were beautiful.”

Maggie waved the compliment away and then placed her elbows on the desk and clasped her hands, leaning forward. “How are you coping?”

Angela never knew how to respond to that question. Did people want to hear the truth? *I'm so sad all of the time that I want to rip out my hair. I feel like my soul has been torn from my chest and stomped on. My head throbs as if a vise is squeezing it and I can't sleep without drugs.* What did they really want to hear?

“I'm well, thank you. Fine.”

“Really?”

“Well, there are good days and bad days. My parents have been a big help.”

Maggie nodded, her face a mask of concern. “And the man that hit your car? I heard through the hospital grapevine that you attended his bail hearing.”

Angela cleared her throat. “Yes, I did. The judge set bail at twenty thousand dollars and the guy was out the next day.”

“Will there be a trial?”

"No. My attorney told me that he pled guilty to reckless endangerment and two counts of vehicular manslaughter. He'll be sentenced in the coming months. She said that the court will let me know when the sentencing hearing is so that I can attend."

"I see. Do you need anything at this point? What can I do to help?"

"I'm not sure how to answer that, Maggie. There's nothing you can do. Except maybe get me back to work."

Maggie raised her eyebrows. "Do you think you're ready to return?"

"Yes. I'm not doing anything at home. I'd like to focus on someone other than myself."

Maggie placed her palms on the desk. "Okay then. Let's get you back to work."

A knock sounded. "Come in," Maggie called.

A man ushered a woman through the doorway and then entered the office, closing the door behind him. The newcomers stood, hands clasped in front of them, waiting for Maggie to make introductions.

"Angela, this is Darlene Rancon and Bud Blake. They stopped by to offer their condolences and see if you need anything else from the hospital."

Angela stood and shook their hands. "Nice to meet you."

Turning back to Maggie, she said, "That's the second time you've asked me if you can help." Maggie smiled. "I just want to make sure you have what you need before returning to work."

Angela turned and regarded Darlene and Bud. "Wait a minute. I remember you. You were with Maggie when she stopped by the waiting room when my daughter was in surgery. Who are you guys?" She turned to Maggie. "Who are they?"

Maggie smiled. "Darlene is part of our in-house Counsel team and Bud is with Risk Management."

"And why would I need anything from the hospital's attorneys or Risk Management?"

"You wouldn't, necessarily. But I just wanted to let you know that our resources are available to you if you should need them. Like I said, we're a family."

Maggie removed her glasses and held Angela's eyes for a beat longer than necessary as she removed a cleaning cloth from a desk drawer. "Now, let's talk about your returning to work. When would you like to start?"

"Monday if possible. I thought I could resume office hours for a week or so and then return to surgery."

Maggie nodded and rubbed her glasses with the cloth. "That sounds great, Angela. I'm glad you're feeling good enough to come back so soon. We've missed your smiling face and talented hands in the operating room. And I know for a fact that your Cardiac Surgery team misses your leadership. Speaking of which, have you considered my proposal about getting your MBA so that you can pursue a larger role here? After all, I'm sixty-three. I have to leave here sometime." Maggie replaced her eyeglasses.

"I have, and I've decided that I need to focus on what I do best, and that's fixing hearts. At least for now. I genuinely appreciate your guidance and faith in me, Maggie, but the accident has shown me that my priorities need to be better balanced."

Maggie clasped her hands and brought them to her heart as she nodded. "Of course. I understand. Please know that my door is always open and that the offer stands. The hospital would foot the bill for your schooling, and you'd have a new challenge."

"Thank you, really. You're very kind."

Maggie smiled broadly as she stood. "Well, I guess we both need to move forward with our days. I must meet with Darlene and Bud, and you, I'm sure, have a busy day ahead of you as well."

Angela paused, realizing that she had absolutely nothing to do for the rest of the day. "Yes, of course. Life marches on, doesn't it? Thanks again, Maggie. I guess I'll see you around the hallways."

The CEO surprised Angela by coming around the desk to hug her. "I'll make sure I check in on you sometime next week to see how you're doing."

Angela smiled. "Thank you. I mean it."

"No, Angela. Thank *you*. You're an inspiration to the rest of us."

As Angela left the office, Maggie's assistant was staring at her with a look of apprehension and curiosity.

"Are you okay?" Angela asked the young woman, who quickly nodded her assent before returning her attention to the computer.

Angela took the elevator to the Cardiac Surgery department on the fifth floor and used her key card to access the clinical area. She entered her office to find Liz sitting at her desk.

"Well, well. Am I being replaced or is this always where you do your notes?"

Liz smiled. "It's quieter in here than in the nurses' suite and I knew you wouldn't mind."

"Of course not."

"Plus, I made the mistake of checking my email and Bernard wants all medical notes related to the Ava Sinclair case."

Angela's brain twisted in thought. *Ava Sinclair. The woman who died six weeks ago.* It felt like an eternity had passed since then.

"Why does Bernard want her notes?"

Liz paused. "How was your meeting with Maggie?"

"It was good. I'm returning on Monday."

"Great!"

"Uh huh. Liz, you didn't answer my question."

Liz grimaced. "I didn't want you to know about this yet, because I wasn't sure you could handle it."

"What, Liz? Just tell me."

"Mr. Sinclair is filing a wrongful death case against the hospital and you're named as the principal defendant."

Prior to the accident, this news would have felt like a sucker punch, but given the circumstances, Angela simply nodded. "Makes sense."

"Angela . . ."

"It makes sense, Liz. Mr. Sinclair is looking for someone to blame. And I'm where the buck stops. Of course he'd come after me."

Liz stood. "You don't need to worry, though, because your malpractice insurance is covered through the hospital. You'll be okay."

Angela smiled. "I never doubted it, Liz. That must be why Maggie had in-house Counsel and Risk Management at our meeting, and why her assistant was staring at me. I wonder why she didn't mention it, though?"

"She probably thought that you might not be able to handle it right now."

"Maybe. So why is Bernard asking for the information? Why not someone from Risk Management?"

"Honestly, I think he smells blood and is gunning to become chairman of Cardiac Surgery."

Angela burst out laughing. "He's barely out of his fellowship, Liz."

"Yes, but he holds an MBA from Stanford and he's smart and a really good surgeon, as you know. And honestly," she made a face, "I think Maggie thinks he's capable."

Angela thought a moment and nodded. "Yes, I can see it. Well, in order to keep Bernard in check, how about you and I gather the data the hospital needs to defend me in the lawsuit?"

Liz stood and gestured toward the chair. "Madame, your throne."

Angela sat and leaned back in her chair. "Feels good to be back, Liz. Thanks for all of your help. You and my parents have kept me alive these past weeks."

"Honestly, you look like shit, Angela. You must have lost fifteen pounds."

"I know. How about you and I go back to the range tonight?"

"Sounds good. I'll meet you there at seven."

They reviewed the list that had been given to them by the hospital's attorneys and assembled all necessary items in thirty minutes. As Angela stood to leave, Bernard Smythe walked through her door.

"Dr. Brennan . . . what a surprise to see you."

"Hello, Dr. Smythe. I hear you've been busy in my absence. You'll be happy to know that I'll be returning to work on Monday and plan to resume my full load of office patients and soon thereafter, my surgery schedule. So your leadership services will no longer be required." She smiled.

He paused, looking from one woman to the other. "Of course. Well, I was glad I could be of help in your extended absence. I'm sorry for your losses, by the way. I hope you received my flowers?"

"Yes. Thank you." She stared at him, her head high and her gaze unwavering.

"Okay. Well, I guess I'll be going."

"I guess you will."

She waved as he turned and walked away, and then shared a high five with Liz.

"And that," Liz said, "is how it's done, ladies and gentlemen."

CHAPTER 14

~

Angela had worked a half-day seeing patients as her clinical nurse, Karen, hovered and ensured that she had everything she needed. At lunchtime, she had been informed that she had no more scheduled patients and that she was to return home until the following day. Angela didn't want to admit it, but she was grateful, having underestimated how exhausted she'd be after only a few hours of patient care.

When she arrived at home, however, her energy had returned, motivated more by not wanting to be in her big house all alone than any other reason. Her parents had taken a break to spend some time at their second home in Ft. Myers, Florida, so it was the first time she'd been alone in the house since the accident. She had changed into some running clothes, dug out a backpack from the hall closet, loaded it with her cargo, and taken off.

Angela ran up Rumstick Road and took a left onto Nayatt Road. The backpack pounded in time with her footfalls, and she turned left again to shorten the distance to the beach. Cresting the hill on Water Way, she sprinted the remaining distance and slid to a stop on her knees in the warm sand, absorbing the beauty of the water in the afternoon sun. Boats dotted the bay as she recalled the many evenings that she and Tony had spent reading books on the beach during sunset. Sometimes the kids would ride their bikes to the beach and disrupt their solitude, begging to order pizza. Tony would inevitably give in and the four of them would enjoy an impromptu pizza dinner until the mosquitoes started biting. Although she had enjoyed those family moments at the time, she had no idea how precious the memories would become.

The sound of laughter pierced Angela's reverie.

Most of the people on the beach at two o'clock on a Monday afternoon were stay-at-home moms whose children were working very hard to ensure that sand found all the crevices in their small bodies. Squeals of delight echoed along the beach, but one woman's voice crescendoed above the others.

"Alexis! *Really*? Do you have to actually roll in the wet sand? Is it not enough to shovel it or build with it? Or even throw it at your brother's head, for goodness sake?"

The woman turned to Angela and rolled her eyes. "Honestly, having children is like being pecked to death by a duck. It doesn't hurt at first, or maybe ever, but it's incredibly irritating, you know?"

Without waiting for an answer, the woman chased her daughter, who had taken her mother's advice and thrown sand at her brother's head. The girl was running down the beach to escape her screaming sibling, who was vowing vengeance.

Angela regained her breath while watching the familiar scene unfold as if it were a movie from her previous life. Alexis and her brother were younger than Emily and Liam but had the same love/hate relationship that her children had enjoyed. Angela focused on the mother, wondering what she'd do when she caught up with her kids. Based on the woman's duck comment, Angela thought she'd overreact, but she didn't. She grabbed each child's arm and spoke sternly but fairly, doling out punishment with firm kindness. *She's a good mom*, Angela thought as she remembered her mission and stood.

Because the woman and her kids had gone right, Angela turned left and walked quickly down the beach, scanning for people she knew. Although all beaches in Rhode Island were public, she couldn't walk far before encountering private docks, the pilings driven deep into the bay's floor to withstand the wind and rough currents. She came upon a dilapidated dock and realized it belonged to an abandoned home on Rumstick Road. The end of the structure draped in the water, the wood rotting and gray, as if the dock knew that no one lived in the home anymore and had given up trying to survive. Angela understood how it felt.

She examined the incoming waves and verified that the tide was on its way out. As she backpedaled to avoid a particularly aggressive wave, she tripped and fell, her backpack flipping up and over her head. She righted herself while removing her pack and noted the cause of her fall. A rock sat half-emerged in sand, the water engulfing it and then releasing it as the waves ebbed.

Looking around, she decided that this was a good hiding place. The large dock pilings hid her from view, and no one had reason to come down to this section of the beach, especially because it was often completely covered in seawater. She had checked the tide schedule prior to her run and as she glanced at her watch, she determined that in another ten minutes the rock would be completely free of wave action. She removed the plastic package from the backpack and stretched as she waited. Within eight minutes, the rock was completely free of water, so with great effort she rolled it aside, clawed at the sand to dig a hole, and placed the tightly wrapped bundle in it. After ensuring that no one had seen her, she filled the hole with sand and returned the rock to its original location. She had just finished when she heard rustling.

"Hello."

Angela jumped. Searching for the source, she found herself alone.

The voice giggled. "Up here."

Angela looked up to see a little girl wearing a pink tutu standing on a boulder next to the decaying dock.

"Hi."

"What are you doing?"

Angela looked at the rock and the open backpack. "Oh, um—"

"Are you peeing?"

"What?"

"Because sometimes people pee here, and it makes my mommy mad, especially 'cause there's a bathroom right up the beach."

"No. I wasn't going to the bathroom here."

"It's okay. You can say 'peeing.' It's not a bad word."

Angela smiled. "Okay. I wasn't peeing."

"Then what are you doing?"

"I was resting before I ran back to my house."

"Oh. My name is Taylor. What's yours?"

"Angela."

Taylor tipped her head sideways and narrowed her eyes. "I think I've seen you on TV."

Angela looked down while zipping the backpack. "Yes, that's me."

The girl twisted her long, red hair around a finger and kicked at some pebbles. "I'm sorry that your family died. I have to go to dance soon, but if you want, I can stay and talk for a little bit."

Of all the opportunities Angela had been offered—free counseling sessions, attending dinners at friends' homes, girls' nights out—it was the sincerity of this child, this stranger, that touched Angela where up until this point, no one had been able to reach.

"That would be nice, Taylor. Thank you." Angela climbed the rocks and sat next to her on the edge of the boulder, their legs swinging in unison over the breaking waves.

"How old are you?"

"Seven-and-a-half. How old are you?"

"I'm forty-eight. And a half."

"When's your birthday?"

"November. Yours?"

"Mine is in November too. That makes us twins!" Taylor grinned. Her two front teeth were missing.

"I see you've lost some teeth."

"Yup."

"Did the tooth fairy come?"

Taylor nodded and tossed an oyster shell into the water. Seagulls dropped them from great heights in an effort to obtain a good meal when the shell cracked open. "Sure did. She left me five dollars!"

"Wow. That's a lot of money."

"I know!"

They sat quietly for a moment, listening to the water lapping gently against the dock pilings.

"Do you have siblings?" Angela asked.

"What's a sibling?"

Angela smiled. "Do you have brothers and sisters?"

"Nope. Just me. My mommy was supposed to have a baby last year, but she lost it. That's what she told me anyway. I hope she finds it because I'd like to have a sister. Not a brother, though."

"Why not a brother?"

Taylor scrunched up her face. "'Cause boys are dirty and gross."

A light breeze blew off the water, cooling Angela's perspiration. A fisherman appeared in a small skiff, cut his engine, and lay anchor in the bay. As he worked his rods, he waved at them and they waved back. "Were your children as old as me?" Taylor asked as she smoothed the hot pink tutu against her thighs.

"They were twelve and nine."

"What were their names?"

"Emily and Liam."

"I have a friend named Emily. But I don't know anyone named Liam." Taylor squinted and pointed. "Hey, there's an osprey!" They both watched the bird, screeching as it searched for an unsuspecting late lunch. All of a sudden it dove straight down and punctured the surface of the water, swooping up again with a wriggling fish in its talons.

"Wow," Taylor breathed. "That's amazing."

Angela observed the girl. "Do you like birds?"

"Uh-huh. I think they're kind of the most amazing things in the world. I want to be an ornith– . . . ornithol–"

"Ornithologist?"

"Yeah, I want to be that when I grow up."

"You may want to learn how to pronounce it first," Angela joked.

"Hey, that's what my mom says!"

"Why do you love birds?"

Taylor shrugged. "I dunno. They're beautiful, first of all. And it's amazing to watch them fly. I wish I could fly."

Angela thought about that for a moment, wondering if Emily and Liam had ever thought of flying like Taylor did. "That would be cool," she agreed.

"Yeah. And there's a nest in that tree over there." She pointed to a lilac tree about ten yards away. "Wanna see it?"

"Sure."

Angela shouldered her backpack and followed Taylor to a compact, well-built nest that housed three featherless birds. Their mouths gaped in anticipation of their mother's return with regurgitated food.

"Aren't they beautiful? They were born four days ago." Taylor spoke so quietly that Angela had to lean in to hear her.

A clipped chirp caught Angela's attention. She turned to find the mother bird perched on a nearby branch. Her head was bobbing up and down as she emitted short, loud bursts meant to scare away the intruders. Angela's heart went out to the desperate mother doing what she could to protect her offspring, when in reality she was completely dependent on the trespassers' intentions.

"Yes, they are beautiful, but we should leave them alone. Their mother is upset."

"It's okay," Taylor said, her eyes locked on the little birds.

"No, it's not. The mother thinks we're going to hurt her babies."

"But we're not."

"She doesn't know that, Taylor."

The girl pulled her eyes away and searched for the mother. Seeing the bird's distress, she sighed. "I didn't know. I feel bad." They returned to the boulder. "That must be how you felt, huh?"

Angela's muscles involuntarily twitched as if she'd been shocked.

"I mean, when you lost your babies. You must have felt like that mother bird."

Angela watched the mother return to her nest and feed her young, then groom them as she perched on the edge. Taylor reached out her hand and placed it in Angela's, entwining their fingers. Angela examined the girl's hand, so similar to her own daughter's, and gently squeezed it.

"That is exactly what I felt like." Her raspy voice sounded foreign and faraway.

"Taylor! Time to go. Come on!" Angela turned to see a well-dressed woman calling from the driveway next door.

"Okay, Mom! I need to go to dance now, Angela. It was nice meeting you. Maybe I'll see you again."

"Sure, Taylor. Thanks for talking."

The girl scampered away, leaving Angela alone. Glancing at the nest once more, Angela did something she'd been waiting for and dreading since the accident. She cried.

CHAPTER 15

“It’s been two months since the accident and I finally cried the other day.” Angela took a tentative sip of scalding coffee as she observed a twenty-something patient attempt to find an empty table in the hospital cafeteria. His portable IV pump trailed behind him.

“I’m glad to hear that. I know it was bothering you that you hadn’t,” Liz responded.

“Actually, the crying jag was two weeks ago, but it’s only now that I can talk about it without bursting into tears.” The young man secured a table and waved to a woman.

Liz offered a tight smile. “There’s no schedule for grief, you know.”

Angela raised her eyebrows. “That’s what the grief counselor told me.”

“I’m glad to hear you’re talking to someone now.”

Angela recalled the conversation in which Maggie had all but demanded that Angela seek therapy. Angela had been angry at the time but now had to admit that therapy had been a good recommendation. “Well, Maggie kind of insisted.”

“What do you mean?”

Angela shook her head. “She still thinks I’d be a good CEO

candidate, so she's pushing me to 'get better.'" She used her fingers to make air quotes.

Liz made a face. "Get better, huh? I'm not sure that's how this death thing works."

"I know."

The woman arrived at the young man's table carrying a tray full of food. They bickered as she tried to help him arrange his IV tubing. Angela pictured Emily's last minutes when she had been attached to machines like the patient before her. She allowed herself to feel the sadness that accompanied her memory, as instructed by the therapist, then mentally wiped away the vision.

"I had a dream last night about that man from the waiting room. He was sitting under an oak tree with Tony and the kids, and they were reading. Actually, he was reading, and Tony and the kids were listening. Tony looked at me and smiled. He seemed so . . . at peace. He looked from me to the kids and then back to me. It was as if he was telling me that they're safe. They're okay."

Liz looked at the ceiling in an effort not to cry. When she had regained her composure, she smiled. "Honey, they *are* okay. I don't know how you feel, but when my mother passed, I felt her presence more strongly than I ever had when she was alive. It's almost as if her spirit became part of me, so I was able to carry her with me all the time. Obviously, I miss being able to talk to her on the phone and give her a hug, but those are only physical things. It doesn't mean I don't miss them, but they're small potatoes."

"They don't feel like small potatoes, Liz."

"I know."

Angela's stomach dropped as she voiced a thought she'd harbored but not yet spoken. "Kids aren't supposed to die before their parents. It's not the natural way."

"And yet it happens every day, Angela. You're unique in that you've seen both sides now. As a doctor and as a parent."

Angela looked into her coffee cup and swallowed the lump in her throat. "That's true."

"The question is, what are you going to do with this new information?"

"What do you mean?"

"I know you, and you're questioning why this happened. Why you survived, but your family didn't. Maybe there's a reason."

"Like what?"

Liz shrugged. "That's your job to figure out, my friend. But I'm a true believer that things happen for a reason."

Angela shook her head and struggled to remain calm. Liz had done so much for her and she didn't want to lash out. "I cannot believe that my entire family died so that I could learn a lesson, Liz."

"There's a school of thought called Deliberate Creation that believes that our souls manifest events in an effort to achieve the goals for which they were incarnated."

Angela squinted at her longtime friend. "I didn't understand a word you just said."

"All I'm saying is that our souls attract the stuff that happens in our lives in order to learn something."

Angela shook her head again as her frustration grew. She leaned forward and whispered because she was afraid she might yell otherwise. "You're saying that my soul *wanted* my family to die?"

"Absolutely not. I'm saying that your soul was put on earth to learn something, and that the accident furthered that education."

Angela glared at Liz and then guffawed, her strong emotions finding relief in the outburst. "You're out of your fucking mind, Liz. I had no idea you were into all of this woo-woo shit."

"Okay, maybe you're right. Look at it this way, then. What good are you going to take from this horrific situation?"

Angela scowled at Liz, then at the food court patrons, many of whom were laughing. She felt her temper flare at all of the mindless automatons whose minuscule worries occupied their days. Their loved ones were still alive, and she resented them for it. She glanced at the millennial who had managed to arrange a semi-comfortable seat for himself, his IV tubing wrapped around him like a feather boa. His head had dropped to the table and the woman rubbed his back as a tear ran down her cheek. *No one deserves to be so sick that he can't hold up his head*, Angela thought.

Angela opened her mouth, ready to blast Liz with a litany of reasons why she didn't know what the hell she was talking about. Punishing sentences that were littered with curse words sat poised on the edge of her lips.

"Angela," Liz hissed as she looked past her friend. "Mr. Sinclair at six o'clock."

Before she could register Liz's meaning, Angela felt a hand on her shoulder. She turned to find Ava Sinclair's husband standing behind her. She rose to face him.

"Mr. Sinclair."

"Hi, Dr. Brennan. I saw you sitting here, and I thought I'd come over to tell you how sorry I am about your family."

Angela was caught off guard by his kindness. "Thank you."

"I kind of feel like it's my fault."

Angela pulled back. "What do you mean?"

The bereaved man looked around the cafeteria as he searched for words. "I wished this. Not that your entire family would be killed. But I wished that something awful would happen to you so that you would know how I felt when my Ava died."

Angela held the man's gaze and tears filled her eyes. "Now I know," she whispered.

Mr. Sinclair's face twisted as a spasm of grief swept over him. "Now you know. And I'm sorry. I'm sorry that you know what this feels like. And I'm sorry that I wished this on you."

Angela looked away, realizing that she was at a crossroads. She wanted to lash out at this man who had wished her family harm. She wanted to punish him, as if the accident were his fault. But it wasn't. It was a confluence of events that had begun before Ava Sinclair died. Angela searched his eyes and saw a reflection of her own grief, a shared bond that is known only by those who have lost greatly.

"Thank you, Mr. Sinclair. And let me say that I'm truly sorry for my role in your wife's death. I am so sorry." As Angela spoke, she realized with alarm that it was the first time she truly meant the words that she'd spoken so many times. Prior to this moment she had tossed "I'm sorry" around as if the mere statement automatically absolved her of guilt or wrongdoing. The sudden awareness left a pit in her stomach and the acrid taste of self-loathing in her mouth.

"I forgive you, Dr. Brennan. Ava's death should not have happened, but I forgive you."

Mr. Sinclair extended his hand and a shocked Angela took it in both of hers. They stood like that for a moment until a younger man approached and glared at Angela. His lip curled as he grabbed Mr. Sinclair's arm. "C'mon, Dad. Let's get out of here."

Angela met the younger man's angry eyes and then dropped her gaze to the ground.

"Ava comes to me at night, you know."

"Oh?"

Mr. Sinclair smiled. "Yes. She's often sitting in her favorite chair, knitting. She loved to knit, you see. She's so peaceful, sitting there with our daughter who we lost when she was three. Leukemia."

A renewed grief stabbed Angela's gut. She didn't know what to say.

"Dad, let's go."

Mr. Sinclair turned to his son. "Okay, just a sec."

He returned his intense gaze to Angela. "Listen, the pain doesn't go away, but it changes. Don't give up, Dr. Brennan." He offered her a genuine smile that crinkled the skin around his eyes. "It gets better."

The two men walked away, leaving Angela rooted to the spot, her legs heavy but her soul a little lighter. Her eyes found the young man and the woman, who held hands as they ate. Both were smiling now and Angela's heart lifted.

"You okay?" Liz asked.

Angela nodded, dazed. "Did you hear what he said, Liz? Ava comes to him at night and she's knitting in her favorite chair. Similar to what I dreamt with Tony and the kids sitting under a tree reading. Tony used to love to read to them when they were little. They'd sit under the oak tree on the side of our house."

"I know."

"What do you think it means?"

"I think it means that Ava, Tony, Liam, and Emily are in the Light. They're safe and at peace. Did you hear the other thing Mr. Sinclair said, Angela?"

Angela looked at Liz, confused. "What?"

"He said that he forgives you."

Angela reviewed the conversation. "He also said that Ava's death shouldn't have happened."

"That's true, but he forgives you. So maybe you should forgive yourself."

Angela sat heavily. "I wish it were that easy."

"It is."

Angela shook her head. "Do you think that means he's dropping the lawsuit?"

"Let's hope so."

Angela looked into her coffee cup and considered whether or not Mr. Sinclair should drop the lawsuit. Maybe she deserved what was coming to her.

"Hey, do you want to go to the range tonight?" Liz asked.

"No. I think I'm done with target practice. I packed my pistol away for a while. Until I'm ready for it again."

Liz cocked her head. "What does that mean?"

Angela looked at her friend and shrugged. "I just don't feel like shooting anymore, that's all."

"Okay. Is your gun locked away in a safe place?"

Angela thought about where she'd hidden the gun. "You know how Tony felt about guns, Liz. He never would have allowed one in the house. I'm honoring his wishes."

Liz squinted. "So, where's the gun?"

Angela gave her an enigmatic look. “It's not loaded, and it's packed away in a very safe spot.”

Angela watched Liz's face contort as her friend wrestled with her answer. Angela knew that Liz was considering how much to push, but after several moments, Liz nodded. “Okay then.”

CHAPTER 16

Angela removed her bloody surgical garb and scrubbed her hands and arms in the large, stainless sink before attending to the patient's waiting family. As she approached the apprehensive group, she was reminded of her own stint in the waiting room and the anguish she had felt while waiting for Emily to emerge from surgery. Her heart skipped a beat as she observed the patient's wife chewing on a thumbnail while her knee bobbed up and down. Another, younger woman, presumably the patient's daughter, paced the waiting area. Angela came to the self-realization that her perspective had surely changed, as she was certain that she had witnessed the same behaviors in waiting family members but had never taken note of them. Or if she had, she'd chosen to ignore them. Pushing her own emotions and thoughts aside, she donned a broad, confident smile to set the family at ease.

"The surgery went well. You can visit him in recovery room D in about a half hour. Just give the nurses a chance to get him settled."

"Oh, Dr. Brennan. God bless you. Thank you!" Angela smiled as the family collapsed in on itself, each member hugging another until they had coalesced into a mass of sniffling joy.

Her smile slowly faded as she returned to her office, collapsed in her chair, and rubbed her eyes. She stretched and leaned back, mentally reviewing the surgery.

Bernard Smythe had assisted and had remained extremely quiet as she and Liz had chatted. When she'd asked him about his silence, he'd said, "I have nothing to add. That's all."

Angela had noted that Dr. Smythe's attitude toward her had changed since she had returned to work. Liz's opinion was that Bernard was having a tantrum, plain and simple. She'd said, "He saw an opportunity for advancement and is pissed that you returned because it means that he lost his leadership position."

On multiple occasions Angela had tried to engage him, but he had resisted, and Angela was finished trying to appease him or his ego. Suddenly exhausted, she glanced at the time and decided she'd complete her surgical notes and call it a night. As she turned to her computer, her sleeve brushed against a piece of paper that gently floated to the ground. She leaned down to retrieve it and froze, mid-bend, as her eyes scanned the message.

I'm not sure that the cause of your daughter's death is what it seems. I thought you should know.

The ticking of the clock felt ominous as Angela slowly retrieved the note and stared at it for a full minute, wondering who wrote it and why. Suddenly aware that the note's author might be waiting for her to discover it, she jumped out of her chair and rushed to her open office door, glancing right and left down the wide hallway. But the area was completely empty, save Ronin, the evening housekeeper assigned to her department.

"Ronin, have you cleaned my office yet?"

The young man shook his head.

"Did you see anyone in my office?"

The man nodded. "Yes. Dr. Toner."

Frank Toner had sent a kind note to Angela three weeks after burying her family, as if he'd known that the initial onslaught of visitors would have subsided and that she'd be feeling particularly lonely and vulnerable. Of course he had known. He had buried a wife several years before and had been in practice long enough to understand the business of death, as well as the intricacies of its aftermath.

"Thanks." Angela picked up her cell phone and found Frank's name in her list of contacts. She pressed his name and he answered on the fourth ring.

"Hello?"

"Hey, Frank. It's Angela. I hope I'm not calling too late."

"No, no, it's fine, Angela."

"You sound like you were sleeping."

"No. Just resting my eyes." Angela smiled. Tony had used that same expression when Angela would catch him napping while he was supposed to be taking care of Emily and Liam.

"Do you want me to call back another time?"

"Absolutely not. How are you today?"

"I'm good."

"Really?" His tone cut through all of the bullshit that she normally fed people who didn't want to hear the truth.

She sighed heavily. "Good days and bad days, Frank. Today is good. Just had a good surgery and I'm working on my notes. I still have my health."

He chuckled, a warm but phlegmy sound that simultaneously concerned her and drew a smile to her face. "That's my girl."

"Hey, Frank, did you leave a note on my desk today?"

"No. Why?"

"Ronin said that you stopped by."

"I did, just to see how you were faring. But I didn't leave you a note."

"Oh." Anxiety prickled her skin.

"What does the note say?"

Angela read it aloud and asked, "What do think it means?"

"You have no idea who it's from?"

Angela thought through who might have left the note and came up empty. "No."

"Well, I would think that it was written by someone within

the hospital. Is there anything special about the paper on which it was written? A header from a particular department perhaps?"

Angela searched the paper for any identifying characteristics. "Honestly, it looks like a piece of printer paper. And the note is written in regular blue ink. Nothing special as far as I can tell."

"Have you asked people in the department about it?"

"It's seven p.m., Frank. Everyone's gone except for Ronin and me. I came to my office to complete my surgical notes and then I was heading home."

"Well, ask people about the note tomorrow when you arrive."

"I will. You didn't answer my question though."

"What question?"

"What do you think the note means?"

Frank sighed. "Who knows, Angela? I mean, obviously you need to find the person who wrote it. It could be some sick person's idea of a bad joke. Or it could be someone who believes that Emily's death might have been . . . was there a . . ." Frank paused, unsure whether to venture down this particular path.

"Was there a what, Frank? An autopsy? You can say it. Believe me, that's the first idea that popped into my head when I read the note."

"Was there?"

"No."

"Why not?"

Angela sorted through her mental closet to find the box that contained the events immediately following Emily's death. "If I remember correctly, my parents asked for one but were told that it wasn't necessary."

"By whom?"

Angela furrowed her brow as she tried to recall the conversation she'd had with her mother. "I don't know, now that you ask."

"I think you should figure that out too. Emily died from an overdose, right?"

"Yes. She went into seizure at the end and died."

"Was Narcan administered?"

"Yes."

"But not in time?"

Angela's brain reeled as it relived the horror of watching her daughter's body shut down. Froth around her mouth as she whispered, "You can't come." Angela started shaking and found that she couldn't stop.

"Angela? Are you okay? You're breathing funny."

Angela forced herself to breathe slowly. *Inhale. Exhale.* "Sorry, Frank. What was the question?"

He paused. "Why don't you get some sleep, Angela. Do your surgical notes tomorrow."

Angela found relief in returning to solid, clinical ground. She straightened in her chair and willed her body into stillness. "Dr. Toner, a very wise physician once told me to never, *ever* leave one's notes to the next day, as the brain has a tendency to marinate overnight and alter important findings."

"Hmmm. I did say that, didn't I? Well, maybe this one time it might be alright to ignore my sage advice."

Angela realized with embarrassment that she hadn't inquired about his health. "Frank, what's happening with your illness?"

"It's still there."

"Ever the father figure, Frank, not wanting to worry me. What's really going on?"

He paused. "Colon cancer."

"What stage?"

"Four."

Angela was silent as she digested the startling information. He'd said that he was sick, but she hadn't imagined it was that bad. Fatigue wrapped in darkness threatened to overwhelm her.

"Cat got your tongue?"

"God, Frank, I don't know what to say."

He tutted. "That's why I didn't tell you before, Angela. I don't want to do all of the sad stuff with you."

Honoring his wish meant that she couldn't allow him to hear her sadness. He had done so much for her; this was the very least that she could do. Swallowing hard, she forced a smile. "Okay. But have you exhausted all of the options?"

"You mean surgery, radiation, chemo? Yes, all of them. I'm done, Angela. I'm waiting for the pain to worsen and then I'll check myself into hospice or something."

"What does 'or something' mean?"

The ticking clock echoed throughout the room as silence buzzed over the line. She strained to hear his response, but none came.

"Frank, you're not talking about—"

"I'd like to go out on my own terms, Angela."

"Yes, but—"

"Haven't *you* thought about it?" he interrupted her.

The abruptness of his question shocked her into silence. Shame brought blood rushing to her cheeks and she opened and closed her mouth several times.

"You don't need to answer my question, Angela. I know you have. Liz told me that you bought a gun."

"That's not why I bought—"

"Stop it!" he ordered. "Don't lie to me, of all people. It's insulting."

She was seven years old again, caught with a spoon in the cookie dough while her mother's back was turned.

"Are you going to do it?" he asked matter-of-factly.

Angela's voice shook as she answered, never intending to have this conversation with anyone. "I don't know."

"Well, don't tell me not to do it if you're still thinking about it."

"I guess that's fair."

"Tell you what. Let's make a pact that neither of us will follow through on our plans without talking to the other person first. Deal?"

Relief slid down Angela's back and she realized how heavily her indecision had been weighing on her. It felt good to share the burden with a friend. "Deal."

"Now, go home, get some sleep, and in the morning figure out who sent that note."

Angela was transported back to her residency when Frank would speak sternly to the residents in one breath and then follow up with a kind word to restore their egos. "Thanks, Frank."

"My pleasure, Dr. Brennan."

"Frank?"

"Yeah?"

"You asked if the Narcan was administered too late. The answer is that I'm not sure. Emily was talking right until the shot was given, but her speech was garbled, and her mouth was . . ." Angela paused to suck in some air, ". . . frothy. And then she started seizing." Angela's knuckles kneaded her forehead as she described Emily's last, terrifying minutes.

"An opiate overdose can cause all of the symptoms you just mentioned, as you know," Frank reasoned.

"That's true."

"So it would stand to reason that given the prescription misdosage, she died of an opiate overdose. But two questions remain. Why didn't the Narcan work? And why did someone leave the note?"

Angela sat up straighter, her head tilted to the side. "Both good questions, Frank. I don't know."

"And no autopsy was completed."

Angela's arms started to tingle. "No."

"So, really, we don't know why or how Emily died."

Angela couldn't breathe as the ticking of the clock drilled into her head.

"Find the person who wrote that note, Angela."

CHAPTER 17

The morning sun shone through the window and Angela noted that the oak tree's deep-green leaves were large and veiny, an indication that the tree had received enough water and sunshine throughout the spring and summer. She lay in bed and thought about the day ahead of her, realizing that it was the first time since the accident she hadn't awoken with a sense of foreboding. Guilt descended quickly, however, followed by a healthy dose of anger. Guilt that she was alive when her family wasn't, and anger because the person who had left the note on her desk was either a crackpot whose aim was to hurt her or someone who knew more than they were willing to admit publicly. Either way, Angela was determined to unearth the note's author, and grill him for answers.

She dressed quickly in a navy-blue linen suit, brushed her teeth, and applied light makeup. She styled her hair in a loose bun before descending the stairs to find her parents sitting at the kitchen table drinking coffee and reading the newspaper. They looked tanned and well rested, and her heart surged at seeing them again. Angela smiled and kissed each on the cheek before pouring herself a cup of coffee.

"What are you doing here? I thought you weren't coming back from Florida for another couple of days."

Her mother rolled her eyes. "Somebody was worried about his little girl."

Her father folded the newspaper and placed it deliberately on the table. "Yes, and I'm not ashamed. How are you, angel?"

Angela sat at the table and squeezed her father's hand. "I'm good today, Dad. You both look well. A little sun has done you good. How was Florida?"

"Hot," her mother answered.

"It *is* Florida in the summer. Anyway, thanks for coming back, but you don't need to worry about me, really."

Her father gave her a look that indicated he knew better.

"I'm serious. I still have bouts of anger and I miss Tony and the kids more than anyone can imagine, but I know that I need to move forward. It's good to be back at work."

"Liz tells us that you're doing fairly well."

Angela regarded her parents, amused that they had been discussing her mental state with Liz. "You don't need to go through a back channel to keep tabs on me. I think I've been open with my feelings."

Her mother stifled a laugh. "Angela, my love, your feelings are never clear. You've developed a glorious wall behind which you hide."

"What do you mean?"

"What your mother means is that you're an expert at allowing people to see only what you want them to see."

"Doesn't everyone do that?"

Her mother shook her head. "Not like you. You're an Olympian at creating a façade."

Angela wasn't sure if she should be offended or pleased as she considered her parents' comments. "I don't think it's a façade, Mom. I think it's a protective barrier."

"To keep the pain in or the world out?" her father asked.

Caught off guard, Angela realized that she didn't know the answer to his question. What's more, she reasoned, she wasn't sure she wanted to know the answer.

"Either way, you lose," her father continued as he rose, pulled her out of her chair, and embraced her. "We just want you to be happy again, angel. Please know that you can come to us about anything at any time. Okay?"

Angela surrendered to her father's hug and sagged against him, reveling in the ever-present scent of his aftershave that whisked her back to childhood. "Okay."

"Now," her father said as he pulled her away from him, "go heal some sick people. That's an order."

He took her face in his large hands and kissed her forehead. She smiled, then grabbed a banana and a granola bar on her way out. "See you tonight."

"I'll have tacos waiting for you," her mother called after her.

Angela made it to the hospital in fifteen minutes and realized that she felt a little lighter knowing that someone was waiting for her at home. She walked straight to her office where she found Tony's business partner, Sean, sitting at her small table. After first registering shock at seeing him, she felt a rush of joy at being so close to someone whom Tony had cared for so much, but she also felt an irrational annoyance that he was sitting at her table when it should have been Tony. Sean's hair was mussed and his face registered worry—or was it guilt?—as he looked up from his phone. Angela hadn't seen him since the funeral and couldn't imagine why he was in her office.

"Sean, what are you doing here?"

He stood quickly and gave her an awkward one-arm hug. "Hi, Angela. Sorry to just bust in on you like this, but I was in the neighborhood so I thought I'd stop by."

Angela threw him a disbelieving look. "You were 'in the neighborhood'? You paid for parking in the garage and took the elevator to the fifth floor, whereupon you negotiated the maze of hallways to arrive in my office?"

Sean grinned. "Yeah. Is that so hard to believe?"

"Yes. What's up?" Angela sat in the chair opposite him and crossed her legs, deciding that she was genuinely happy to see him. His mere presence brought Tony back to life, if only for a moment.

"I was wondering how you are, that's all."

"I'm okay, thanks. How's Melanie?"

"Thrilled to be home with the kids in the summer, as usual. Although by the end of August she's always ready to go back to teaching."

"And the kids?"

"Connor is great, doing a summer soccer league, and Victoria is busy with lacrosse. That kid, she's always up to something. In fact, last week—" Sean cut himself off as he noted Angela's strained expression. "Anyway, everybody is good. Thanks for asking."

Angela smiled tightly. "Good to hear. How are you and the firm?"

"Crazy. The firm, not me. Business continues to pour in, and I'm busy training the new guy. Oh, I hired a new architect to replace Tony." Angela watched his eyes widen as words tumbled from his mouth. "Not that Tony's replaceable, because he's not. It's just that I couldn't handle all of the work, so I hired another person . . ."

Angela held up her hand to stop him. "I understand, Sean. Tony was discussing hiring someone before the accident. I'm glad business is good."

Sean nodded and looked at his hands.

"Why are you here, Sean? Don't get me wrong. It's nice to see you, but . . ."

"Sure, sure. Well, I wanted to talk to you about the business."

"What about it?"

He took a deep breath and exhaled quickly. "I was wondering if you'd be interested in selling Tony's portion of the firm to me."

Angela unconsciously drew back in shock, but then realized that his request made sense. When she considered the idea, however, she concluded that she didn't want to sell Tony's share. Her husband had built the firm from the ground up. It had been his dream and he had molded it carefully, coddled it during bad times, and pushed it forward in good times. The firm had come second only to his family, and Angela realized that she felt an obligation to continue his legacy.

"No. I can't, Sean. I hope you understand."

She could tell that Sean had been expecting a different answer. He sat openmouthed while composing a response.

"Angela, please understand that it's next to impossible to find experienced architects to replace—I mean, to help me out. I've interviewed six candidates and each of them has requested some ownership of the firm."

"Then split up your half, Sean. Give them ten percent and you keep forty. I'm sorry, but I can't do it. I can't sell Tony's dream."

Sean leaned across the table and took her hands in his. "Each candidate has asked for fifty percent, Angela. It's standard these days when you're searching for experienced, well-known talent. They have no reason to accept less than that. And you wouldn't be selling Tony's dream, Angela. You'd be furthering it. The firm can't grow if I can't hire a talented partner. This is what Tony wanted. You said it yourself."

Conflict muddled her thoughts. Sean was correct in that Tony had wanted to grow the firm, but he would have wanted to be a part of it. And since that was no longer possible, wasn't it her responsibility to carry it forward on his behalf?

"You can be involved in the hiring if you want. You can help me interview people to ensure that Tony would have liked them."

"I thought you already hired somebody."

"Technically I did, but he's waiting to see what you say about percentage ownership. Would you like to meet him? I know Tony would have liked him."

Angela stared at Sean, whom Tony had loved like a brother. His look was pleading, and she realized with melancholic clarity that Tony would want Sean to move on without him. She breathed deeply as she came to a decision. "Tony trusted you, Sean, so I'm going to trust you to hire someone whom Tony would have respected. And I will sell Tony's half of the business. Have your attorney draw up the paperwork and I'll sign."

Sean was visibly relieved as he squeezed her hands. "Thanks, Angela. You're doing the right thing, for Tony and the firm."

Angela offered a weak smile. "Don't make me regret it, Sean."

"I'll call you soon," he said and exited her office.

Angela was still deciding how she felt when Liz sauntered in. "Hey, was that Sean?"

"Yeah. I'm selling Tony's half of the architecture firm to him."

Liz's eyebrows rose. "Wow. That's a big step."

Liz's reaction cemented the mixed emotions roiling inside of Angela. "I know. And it's not easy. But I think it's what Tony would have wanted."

"Good for you then, Angela. Now, let's talk about your day. You've got—" she consulted her wrist watch, "exactly twelve minutes before your first patient."

Angela rose, happy to focus on something else. "Hey, did you leave a note on my desk yesterday?"

"Nope. Why?"

Angela produced the note and Liz read it, her eyebrows raised. "What the hell is this, Angela?"

"I don't know. I'm going to ask around to see if anyone wrote it or saw who left it on my desk yesterday. I'll be in clinic right after that."

"Sounds good."

Angela walked around the department asking everyone she encountered if they had either left her a note or seen anyone in her office. Within ten minutes she had interviewed the Cardiac Surgery office staff and received no new information.

Frustrated, she decided to go to clinic, complete her patient care schedule, and then resume her investigation in the afternoon. She donned her lab coat, looped a stethoscope around her neck, and entered the elevator. She had depressed the button for the second floor when she heard someone call out, "Hold the elevator!" The department's daytime housekeeper ran in.

"Hi, Ingrid."

"Hi, Dr. Brennan. Thanks for holding the door. Hey, did you get that note I left on your desk yesterday?"

Angela's head whirled toward her. "*You* left that note?"

"Yeah. You got it?"

Angela stepped quickly toward Ingrid until they were inches apart. "And what, exactly, did you mean by saying that the cause of my daughter's death wasn't what it seems?"

Ingrid looked terrified and took a step backward. "I didn't read the note. Is that what it said?" The rational side of Angela noted that Ingrid's voice shook, and she looked like she was going to cry.

The irrational side of Angela continued speaking. "That's what it said. You didn't write it?"

The terrified woman shook her head quickly, as if to absolve herself of her role.

"Then who did?"

The elevator arrived at the second floor and the doors opened. Ingrid backed out quickly and Angela followed, looming over her as the small crowd waiting to enter the elevator looked on.

"Answer me!" Angela ordered.

"I don't know. I don't know," Ingrid stammered.

"Where did the note come from?"

"The-the-the—"

"*Where*!" Angela roared, surprisingly herself with her tone.

"The front desk. D-d-downstairs in the lobby. Th-th-that's all I know. I swear." The woman stuttered, genuinely scared.

Angela bolted toward the stairs, threw open the door, and took them three at a time until she arrived at the hospital lobby. She ran to the front desk, where an elderly, smiling woman whose nametag read Esther sat with folded hands.

"Hello, Doctor. How can I help you?"

Angela breathed deeply and tried to gather herself. "Ingrid, the cleaning lady from Cardiac Surgery, said that a note was given to her yesterday by someone at the front desk. The note was for me. Did you give Ingrid the note?"

Esther smiled. "Yes. That was me. Did you receive it?"

"Yes, I did. Who gave you the note, Esther?"

Esther's head bobbed back and forth. "Well, I'm sure that I can't tell you that, my dear."

Angela closed her eyes, willing her mind to calm so that she didn't reach across the desk and grab the poor woman by her shirt. "And why is that?"

"Because I don't know her name."

Angela's head fell to the desk.

"Are you alright, dear?"

"No," she mumbled, suddenly exhausted. Short of dusting for fingerprints or a writing analysis, Angela had no idea how she was going to find the person who'd left the note.

"Oh, but I can tell you one thing."

Angela's head lifted, resignation in her eyes. "What's that?"

"The young lady that left the note was very sweet. Oh, and she had a prosthetic leg. I definitely remember that. Does that help?"

CHAPTER 18

After speaking with Esther, Angela wanted nothing more than to find Lauren Kirk, but logic required her to go to clinic and see her scheduled patients. After all, she reasoned, Emily was gone, and nothing would bring her back—not even discovering why Lauren had left the note with Esther. Nevertheless, Angela's lack of concentration in clinic wasn't lost on Liz, who had insisted on replacing Karen as Angela's clinic nurse since she'd returned to work after the accident. Liz needed to redirect Angela several times throughout the morning.

"What's going on, Angela? You're completely off-task today. Is it because of the note?"

Angela grabbed Liz's arm and dragged her into an empty exam room.

"The note in my office was left by Lauren Kirk."

"Who's Lauren Kirk?"

Angela's misdirected frustration boiled over and she huffed, "Emily's nurse right after her surgery when she, you know, died."

Angela watched Liz assemble the puzzle pieces, her face registering confusion, then understanding, then confusion once more. "But that doesn't mean Lauren wrote the note, you know."

"True, but at least I know who left it for me. I'm going over to the pediatric ICU right now. I want to talk to Lauren."

"Jesus, Angela, I'm surprised you lasted this long in clinic." Liz consulted the patient schedule and nodded. "You have only one more patient—in room eight."

"I thought I was done after my last patient."

Liz shrugged. "Me too, but scheduling must have added this guy into your extra slot."

Angela grumbled, "Dammit."

"Want me to reschedule him?"

Angela shook her head. "No. It wouldn't be fair to him. I'll see him."

The medical assistant had collected the patient's medical history and Angela reviewed it on her iPad as she walked toward the exam room. The man's name was Martin Stevens, and he had been referred by his primary care physician for shortness of breath and fatigue. He was sixty-five years old and was otherwise in good health.

Angela announced her entrance with a perfunctory knock on the door before entering.

"Mr. Stevens, it's a pleasure to meet you. I'm Dr. Brennan. I understand your primary care doc referred you for fatigue?" Throughout her introduction Angela had been consulting her iPad. As she raised her eyes to meet his, she gasped and dropped the device, which clattered to the floor. "It's you," she breathed as she backed up against the wall.

The man looked around and spread his hands. "Yup. It's me."

"What—" Angela's unbelieving eyes scanned his body. "What are you doing here?"

The man smiled. "Um, I don't know how to answer that. I'm here because—"

"You look so different. So . . . clean." Her eyes locked on his as she slid along the wall toward the door.

The man's eyebrows rose, and his mouth formed an 'oh.' "I feel like I should be offended but . . . are you okay, Dr. Brennan?"

Angela knelt and retrieved the iPad. She stood, grabbed the door handle, and mumbled, "Excuse me. I'll be right back" while sliding through the door opening.

Once in the hallway, she breathed way too quickly and doubled over. Liz came running down the hall. "Angela! What's going on? Are you alright?"

"Liz, that man . . ." Angela pointed to the exam room as she fought to regain her breath.

"Angela, you need to calm down. You're hyperventilating. What about him?"

"He was the guy who spoke to me in the waiting room. Remember I told you that a man said that everything was going to be okay? And then I went back to thank him after Emily's surgery, and he was gone. And the woman in the waiting room told me that it had been only her and me for the last hour. You had even suggested that maybe he was my guardian angel. Remember?"

"Yes, yes. I remember."

"Well, he's sitting in that exam room, but he looks completely different."

"Different how?"

"The man in the waiting room was really messy and had a missing tooth. His clothes were old and crumpled. This man is clean cut, handsome, and is wearing a really nice suit."

Liz regarded her friend. "Angela, perhaps the man in the exam room is the brother of the man you spoke to in the waiting room that day. Did that occur to you? Honey, it's okay."

Angela's wide eyes locked onto Liz's, seeking assurance that she wasn't losing her mind.

"Do you want me to reschedule him? I think Lauren's note is messing with your head. I'm not sure you're okay to see patients right now."

Angela leaned toward Liz. "If you're correct about the two men being related, then don't you find it odd that the brother of the man I saw in the waiting room the day Emily died is now in my exam room the day after I receive a note indicating that there's something weird about Emily's death?"

"You're not thinking that the two events are related in some way, are you?"

Angela threw up her hands. "You tell me, Liz. You're the one who got me thinking about all this psychic mumbo jumbo."

"I guess it *is* quite a coincidence."

The door opened, and Mr. Stevens' head emerged. "Excuse me, Dr. Brennan, but are you coming back in or should I reschedule? Or perhaps see someone else?"

Angela looked from him to Liz and back again. Feeling ridiculous, she took a deep breath and said, "Absolutely not, Mr. Stevens. I'm coming right back in."

He smiled, unsure. "I'll be in here waiting." He closed the door and Liz stared at Angela. "Are you going to be able to keep it together?"

Angela nodded, smoothing her lab coat. "He thinks I'm crazy, but that's okay. Thanks, Liz. You're right. It's probably just a coincidence." Liz patted her back, nodded reassuringly, and opened the door for her.

Angela reentered the room and focused only on the clinical aspects of the case seated before her. Leaving all personal feelings or opinions outside the exam room, she attended to Mr. Stevens' physical needs, completing an initial cardiac work-up that included scheduling a stress test and some blood work.

After telling Mr. Stevens he could get dressed, Angela removed her latex gloves and crossed to the sink to wash her hands.

"I don't mean to pry, Dr. Brennan, but what was happening when you first came in to see me?"

Angela dropped her eyes. "I'm very sorry, Mr. Stevens."

"Please call me Marty."

Angela smiled. "Thank you, Marty. I'm Angela." They shook hands. She paused, uncertain how to explain the bizarre situation without sounding like a nut case. "You see, I lost my husband and son several months ago in a car accident."

"Oh my goodness. I'm sorry."

"Thank you. My daughter survived the accident, only to die after surgery due to a drug issue."

"How awful!"

"Yes, it was awful. And still is."

"Had she been using for some time?"

"What? Oh, no. She wasn't a drug addict. A miscalculation of drug dosages administered after surgery caused her death."

Marty shook his head. "I can't even imagine what you've been through. I'm so sorry."

"Thank you."

"Did your daughter's death occur at this hospital?"

Angela nodded silently, then took a deep breath. "Anyway, that's part of the reason I was acting so strangely today. I'm sorry."

"Please don't apologize. You've been through so much. I can't imagine how I'd feel." He paused, and then said, "I know my next question will seem extraordinarily indelicate, but do you plan to hold the hospital responsible? Financially, I mean."

Angela furrowed her brow. "I don't understand."

Marty hesitated. "I know you work here, but have you thought about suing the hospital for the wrongful death of your daughter?"

Angela stared at him, unsure how to respond. The thought hadn't even crossed her mind, and yet she imagined that she had every right to do it. In fact, she reasoned that she'd probably win. Then her thoughts wandered to Mr. Sinclair, the man who had named her as primary defendant in his own wrongful death case against the hospital. The truth was that she felt responsible for Ava Sinclair's death, no matter what decision a jury might render. She wasn't sure she could hoist that same guilt on a colleague who had made a simple mistake. Sure, she was angry, but what good would it do to play the blame game and pass on her own guilt to someone else?

"No. I haven't thought about it."

Marty Stevens removed a business card from his suitcoat pocket. "Maybe that's why I ended up seeing you today, Angela. Maybe I'm supposed to take your case." He handed her his card.

"You're an attorney?"

He smiled broadly. "One of the best."

Angela nodded. "I'll think about it. Thanks." She slipped the card into the breast pocket of her lab coat, fully intending to throw it away after he left.

"Now I understand why you acted so strangely when you first came in the exam room. I thought it had something to do with me."

Angela blushed. "It did, actually. You might think I'm crazy, but when I first saw you I thought you were a gentleman I'd spoken to while my daughter was in surgery."

Marty was taken aback. "Really? Did he look like me? That's funny, isn't it?"

Angela laughed nervously and rolled her eyes. "It is funny. Especially because the man with whom I spoke that day was disheveled and—"

"Dirty? That would explain your comment about my being clean." He smiled.

Angela wrinkled her nose. "Yeah. Sorry about that. He was wearing cargo pants and a grungy hoodie. He had a tooth missing, too. But he was so comforting to me. So kind. You don't have a brother like that, do you?"

Marty was squinting at her, nodding slowly. "Yeah, I do. A twin actually."

Angela drew back. "Oh my goodness! It must have been him. Next time you see him, please tell him that I say thank you for his kindness."

Angela noted the sad smile on Marty's face. He tilted his head. "I will tell him, Angela. The next time I visit his grave."

CHAPTER 19

~

"Excuse me?" The oxygen in the room evaporated and Angela struggled to breathe.

Marty leaned forward quickly and grabbed Angela's arm, leading her to a chair. "Here. Sit down. Can I get you some water?"

"Yes, please."

Marty disappeared for a moment and then Angela heard Liz and Marty talking. Although they were right outside the open door, their whispered exchange sounded muffled to Angela's ears, as if she were listening from under water.

"I don't think Dr. Brennan is okay. Can you get her some water?"

"What happened?"

"It's kind of hard to explain."

"Try."

Marty sighed. "Dr. Brennan saw my brother in the waiting room while her daughter was in surgery."

"And?"

"My brother's dead. For seven years, actually."

Angela lifted her head and stared at Marty's profile as she registered what he'd said. *How did I see a man who's been dead for seven years?*

Liz replied to Marty. "Go to the desk and ask a nurse for some water. Don't tell them why. Say it's for you. Then come back here. I'll stay with Dr. Brennan until you return."

Angela allowed her head to fall into her hands as Liz entered and closed the door.

"Angela? You okay?"

Recently Angela felt like she had made some progress in the grief department, yet Marty's revelation about his brother sucked her back into the endless well of despair. Not only had she seen the man in the waiting room, but she had spoken with him as well. He had seemed as real to her as Liz. She was questioning every interaction she'd had since her family died. Her body trembled violently as her grief twisted into a morose humor that erupted in barks.

"Angela, you're scaring me."

Angela removed her hands and lifted her head to look at Liz. Tears ran down her face as her sporadic laughter continued. Liz watched cautiously, unsure what was happening.

Wiping her eyes, Angela asked, "Why aren't you laughing, Liz?"

"Should I be laughing?"

"Absofuckinlutely!"

Liz stood motionless. "Angela, let's talk about this. Tell me what happened."

"Okay, okay, Liz. Where shall we start? With the fact that I've lost my entire family? No, no. I know. Let's talk about the fact that I'm losing my fucking *mind*!" Angela stood quickly and started pacing the small room.

"You're not losing your mind—"

"How do you know, Liz? You're not a shrink. Maybe the stress has cracked my brain." Her hands clawed at the air.

Liz sat in the chair that Angela had vacated. "Angela, I can't imagine what you've been through in the last few months, but I've been with you almost every day since then and I can tell you with certainty that you are not losing your mind."

Angela stopped abruptly. "Then what's happening to me, Liz?

Because I really don't know. And I'm terrified. Absolutely terrified." She choked out a laugh. "It's ironic, isn't it?"

"What?"

"That I'm terrified when I've already gone through the most horrific loss imaginable. I mean, what's left to be scared of?"

Liz was quiet a moment. "Why do you think you're scared?"

Angela leaned against the wall and then sank to the floor. "God, I don't know." Her head dropped to her hands and she shook it slowly back and forth. "I've always been taught to be in control, you know? Even when I wasn't completely sure, I was taught to act confident, so the patient felt more comfortable. Nobody wants to hear a doctor say, 'Gee, we're gonna do a load of tests because I have absolutely no idea what's going on and some blood work might give me a sense of where to start looking.'"

Liz nodded. "True."

"I was born into a good family, I went to the best schools. I married a solid guy and had two beautiful kids. I followed the rules, Liz. All of them. And I was rewarded for it. A great job, strong family, good friends." She smiled weakly at Liz, who offered a sad smile in return. "And then everything disappeared in an instant. Poof." She snapped her fingers. "It was all gone." "And it was awful. Absolutely awful. The worst-case scenario in anyone's imagination."

"Oh, honey—"

Angela held up her hand. She wasn't done. "But I was getting through it. I was choosing to wake up every morning, although I've considered a different option." Angela glanced up quickly before continuing. "Yeah, I know you spoke to Frank Toner about me. And to my parents. Thank you for all of that."

Liz nodded once, then said, "You'd do the same for me."

"You're right. I would. Anyway, I was managing to move forward and create some semblance of a life without Tony and the kids. It was horrible, but I was doing it. Tony, Emily, and Liam were gone, but I was still here, so I had to keep going." She sighed heavily. "And now I find out that a dead guy came to visit me *before* Emily died. Like maybe he knew she was going to die and was comforting me *before the fact*. You asked me what I'm afraid of. I think I'm scared because I've lost complete control over my light."

"You mean your life."

Angela looked at Liz. "Yes. My life."

Liz raised her eyebrows. "You said 'light,' not life."

"No, I didn't."

"Yes, you did."

Angela shook her head. "That doesn't make sense, Liz. Why would I say that?"

"Because your light *is* your life, Angela. Do you remember what Emily was saying right before she passed? She told you that she'd seen Liam and that he had light emanating from him. That was his light shining brightly, inviting Emily to join him. Whether you like it or not, and whether you understand it or not, you're being invited into the fold."

"So you're saying that I'm going to die, too?"

"Do you want to?"

Angela looked away and considered Liz's question. Immediately following the death of her family, she had wanted to join them, simply because she couldn't imagine being left alone. Then the guilt had kicked in. Why was her life spared? There must be a reason, she had thought. But as time passed, the reason had not been made clear to her. Until now.

"I want to find out why Emily died."

Liz nodded. "Okay. Then focus on that. One day at a time."

A soft knock sounded, and Marty entered the exam room with a large glass of water. "Sorry, Dr. Brennan. I had to go to the cafeteria to get this." He handed her the cup and glanced at Liz, who nodded.

Angela stood, accepted the water, and drank it slowly. When she had drained the cup, she threw it away and turned to Marty. "Thank you. Now can you please tell me more about your brother?"

Marty Stevens' gaze fell to the floor. "Sure, but there's not much to tell. Reggie was a great guy. Always protected me on the playground. He was the bigger twin, you see. He was only three minutes older than me, but he never let me forget it. Anyway, while I went to college, he was drafted and shipped to Vietnam. After he returned, he wasn't the same. Prone to mood swings he called the black-and-blues. Blue because he felt sad, and black because that's what color his eyes were after bar fights. He started drinking too much and developed cirrhosis. He lost his wife, then his house and car. Soon he was living on the streets. While I went to law school and built my practice, he was in the gutter scrounging for food."

"How sad," Liz commented.

Marty swiped at a tear that trickled down his cheek. "Yeah." He cleared his throat and breathed deeply before continuing. "Our parents were long gone, so it was just him and me. I really tried to help him, but he was such a proud son-of-a-bitch. Wouldn't accept a dime from me. After a while I guess I just sort of gave up. And then one day I got a call from the precinct about two blocks from my office. They'd found Reggie curled in a ball. He had frozen to death overnight right in front of the precinct. Can you believe that? My twin brother froze to death outside a precinct less than two blocks from my office." Marty ran his hands over his face.

Angela touched his shoulder. "I'm so sorry for your loss," she said softly.

"Thank you." Marty breathed deeply and straightened his jacket. "And you saw him. You saw Reggie in the waiting room, and he comforted you?"

Angela nodded. "He really did."

"And he looked dirty?" The heartbreak in Marty's expression gave Angela pause. "It's okay, Dr. Brennan. I need to know."

"Yes, he was dirty, but you should also know that he was smiling. He was very happy. So happy, in fact, that I had trouble understanding how someone of his—" She broke off, not wanting to offend.

Marty continued her thought. "Social standing?"

Angela smiled. "Yes. I didn't understand how someone of his

social standing could be so happy. He seemed like he didn't have a care in the world. He was . . ."

"At peace?" Liz offered.

Angela tilted her head, thinking. "Exactly, Liz. He was at peace."

"Now it's my turn to thank *you*, Dr. Brennan. I've felt incredibly guilty since Reggie died. I should've tried harder, done more to help him." He stopped as his voice caught.

"We all do the best we can, don't we, Mr. Stevens? We can't control other people's lights." She glanced at Liz.

"You mean lives?" Marty asked.

"Those, too."

"Anyway, now I know that he's safe."

"He's more than that, Mr. Stevens. He's genuinely happy." Angela smiled. "Actually, I had a dream that your brother was reading to my family."

Tears filled Marty's eyes. "Really?"

Angela nodded. "The four of them were sitting under a tree. I know how happy your brother was when he appeared to me in the waiting room. I can only hope that my husband and children are that happy."

"I'm sure they are, Dr. Brennan." Marty smiled warmly, sniffled, and then checked his watch. "I hate to leave, but I have an appointment. Thank you for everything. And please consider what I said about mounting a case against the hospital."

Angela reached into her pocket and closed her hand around Lauren Kirk's note. "I'll think on it, Mr. Stevens. I'll think on it."

CHAPTER 20

As a cardiac surgeon, Angela spent a lot of time in the Adult Intensive Care Unit, but she avoided the Pediatric ICU as much as possible. Prior to the accident, seeing children in life-threatening situations had been discomforting, but now she wasn't quite sure how she was going to handle the stress. She had not returned to the Pediatric ICU since Emily died, and as she approached, her breath quickened and she tightened her grip on the paper in her pocket. The responsibility of determining the provenance of the note lay like a wet wool cloak on her shoulders, but she owed it to Emily and was determined not to back down. Angela tried to appear casual as she approached the desk with a smile fixed on her face.

"Hi. How are you?"

A young nurse lifted his head and took in Angela's efficient hairstyle, expensive suit, and white coat. His eyes darted to her blue, embroidered name, and he returned the smile. "I'm great. How are you, Doctor?"

"I'm well, thank you. Tell me, is Lauren Kirk working today?"

"Who?"

"Lauren Kirk. She attended to my daughter after her surgery several months ago."

"Hmmm. I don't know anyone by that name." A momentary panic ran through Angela as she briefly considered the terrifying idea that Lauren had been another figment of her overactive, exhausted imagination.

She shook her head to clear it as movement out of the corner of her eye caught her attention. The Pediatric ICU nurse manager, a pudgy brunette named Barbara Royes, was rounding the corner. When she saw Angela, she turned quickly and disappeared. Angela's eyes narrowed and she returned her attention to the desk nurse.

"Are you new here?" Angela asked.

"Yes. I started about four weeks ago."

"Thanks. Best of luck." Angela turned and followed the path Barbara had taken. She spotted her at the end of the hallway and called her name. Barbara paused and then continued walking, her hips swinging quickly. Surprised that Barbara had chosen to ignore her, Angela increased her pace and watched her enter a patient room. Angela approached quietly and waited outside the door.

Three minutes later, Barbara exited the room and turned right to return to the nurses' station. Angela emerged from her waiting spot and fell in step beside her.

"Hi, Barb. How are you today?"

Barbara jumped at Angela's voice and folded her arms over her chest while increasing her pace. A frustrated Angela grabbed her arm, forcing her to stop.

"Barbara, stop! What's going on?"

Barbara shoved an unruly curl behind her ear. "Hi, Dr. Brennan." She shifted her weight back and forth while her eyes danced around, unable to focus on Angela's face.

"Look at me please, Barb."

"What do you want?"

Although Angela hadn't known what to expect, she certainly had not anticipated this reception. After the ordeal of the last few months, she was flummoxed as to why she'd be treated in such a hostile manner.

"What do I *want*? First, I'd like you to look me in the eye."

Barbara stopped moving and lifted her round face to meet Angela's gaze. Her large brown eyes softened and she offered Angela a weak smile.

"That's better. Now, how are you?"

Barbara slumped and shook her head. "Fine."

Angela dipped her head and squinted at her. "Your body language says otherwise. What is it, Barb? You and I have known each other a long time. What's going on?"

Barbara glanced around quickly, and Angela's eyes followed. "Come here." Barbara motioned for Angela to follow her into an empty patient room. Once inside, she placed her iPad on a table and rubbed her eyes. "Jesus. What a mess."

Angela waited. She didn't know where her patience was coming from, but she embraced it. Eventually, Barbara spoke. "I owe you an apology."

"For what?"

"For the medication error that killed your daughter."

There it was. Spoken bluntly and aloud. The reason her daughter died. The very simple error that could have been avoided. But wasn't. And Emily was dead. Before Angela could process the words that escaped her lips, they were released into the ether.

"I forgive you."

Angela was taken aback at her own response. It was as if a stranger had uttered the words, as if they'd come from somewhere else, deep inside where she hadn't known she housed that level of compassion. The stranger continued to speak. "Barb, it was a mistake. A heart-wrenching, life-changing, devastating mistake. But a mistake nonetheless. It could have happened to anyone, including me."

Tears formed in the nurse's eyes and her face contorted as she stared at Angela. Angela opened her arms, and Barbara rushed forward, her quiet sobs echoing throughout the small room. Angela cried with her and found that her apprehension about the note had dissipated. She had nothing left to give and no one left to give it to. All that mattered was the moment, and Angela was surprised to feel a sense of tranquility and relief in forgiving someone who had been directly involved in Emily's death. Barbara Royes was a good person and a talented nurse. She didn't deserve to have her career derailed because of a mistake that Angela herself could have made.

Several minutes passed before Barbara withdrew. She removed a clean tissue from the package in her pocket, blew her nose, and wiped the mascara from her eyes. "I'm sorry I've been avoiding you, Angela. I haven't been able to sleep or eat since Emily . . . you know."

"I understand. Me neither."

"I'm just so sorry."

"Me too, Barb."

They stood quietly as Angela searched the room. Her eyes found the patient confidentiality sign. "What room are we in?"

"Um, twelve. Why?"

"This is where it happened, Barb. This was the room Emily was in when she died."

"Oh my goodness. I'm so sorry, Angela."

Angela nodded as her hand found the piece of paper in her pocket. "I want you to look at something." She removed the note and handed it to Barb, who read it quickly and then looked at Angela with a horrified expression.

"Who would write this?"

"I'm told that Lauren Kirk left it at the lobby desk."

"Why would she do that?"

"I don't know. That's why I came here, actually. I know that she's not working today, but when will she be in next?"

Barbara frowned. "Actually, she was fired."

Angela's eyebrows drew together as she processed the news. "Why?"

"For her part in Emily's death."

Angela shook her head as if ridding her hair of snow. "No. That doesn't make sense. She simply handed Emily the meds. She didn't order them. She's not responsible."

"We're all responsible, Angela. Me, her, Stan Jacobs. All of us."

Angela couldn't argue with Barb's logic. "But why was *Lauren* fired?"

"Someone had to take the brunt of the blame. Maggie and some attorneys met with the staff that was on duty the day Emily died. She asked us, one by one, to describe exactly what had happened. Stan told me that in his meeting with Maggie he threw Lauren under the bus and blamed her for the medication mix-up. Apparently, the attorneys told Maggie that if she didn't fire someone, you might sue the hospital for not taking Emily's death seriously. Given what Stan had said and the fact that Maggie felt compelled to let someone go, she fired Lauren. Well, technically, I fired Lauren, but you get the point."

Angela was incredulous. "That's ridiculous. I could still sue the hospital."

"I know, but apparently firing someone who was involved goes a long way in avoiding a lawsuit, or so I'm told."

Angela thought back to her meeting with Maggie, and how obsequiously the CEO had acted. She had gone beyond offering her condolences to Angela by reminding her that the CEO position was still available for her consideration, and she had repeatedly told Angela that she was part of the hospital family. Angela remembered the seemingly impromptu conversation with Maggie while Emily was in surgery. Even then Maggie had an attorney and a Risk Management employee in tow. What were their names? Darlene Rancon and Bud Blake? And those same two people had appeared at her last meeting as well. Did they simply follow Maggie around all day? Was it coincidence?

A bolt of anger surged through Angela as she considered that fact that the lowest level employee bore the entire weight of the enormous error that had caused Emily's death. There was plenty of blame to go around, so why did Lauren carry the load alone? "That's not right. I'm going to talk to Maggie. But first, how can I get in touch with Lauren?"

"I don't have her home number or address. You're going to have to call Human Resources. Or better yet, when you meet with Maggie, ask her."

"I will. Is Stan Jacobs around?"

"Yeah. He's in his office."

"He and I are going to have a chat."

"Angela?"

"What?"

"Be careful."

Angela made a face. "What's that supposed to mean?"

The nurse shrugged. "I don't know. This whole thing seems . . . dicey. You're a good person and . . . just be careful."

"I have absolutely nothing to lose, Barb. Besides, I'm just asking questions. Trying to understand what happened and why."

"Let me know if I can help."

"You already have."

"I'm sorry I stuck my head in the sand, Angela. You deserve better than that."

Angela stared through Barb as she envisioned Emily being loaded onto the stretcher after the accident, then her waking up from her surgery and asking for water. And finally, her awful, last moments. "Thank you, Barb. But this isn't about me. This is about Emily. And you're right about one thing—my daughter deserves better than that."

CHAPTER 21

The discussion with Barb had boosted Angela's confidence that she'd get to the bottom of Emily's death. The weight of responsibility felt slightly less onerous as she walked toward Stan Jacobs' office with Lauren's note held tightly in her closed fist. What had begun as a simple search to find the note's author had blossomed into something larger, and Angela felt drawn—*no*, she thought, *compelled*—to follow it through.

Angela's last encounter with the chief of Pediatric Orthopedics had occurred as Emily lay dying. She closed her eyes and was back in Emily's recovery room, imagining she could feel Stan's chest against her fist as she struck him repeatedly. "*You tell me what happened, Stan! My baby is dying! I don't know what to do!*" She shivered as the memory replayed in her mind, then breathed deeply and turned her focus to the upcoming meeting. She entered Stan's office suite to find his assistant on the phone. The young woman seemed surprised to see Angela but recovered quickly and pasted a pout on her face as she hung up the phone.

"Oh, Dr. Brennan. I'm so sorry for your loss." Her hollow words floated away as Angela stood before her.

"Is Stan available?"

"He's not here."

Angela glanced at Stan's closed door and smiled. "I know he's here because he leaves his door ajar when he's out of the office. I'll just go in." Before the assistant could stop her, Angela opened the door.

"Hi, Stan. Got a moment?"

The person sitting across from Stan had his back to Angela, but turned upon hearing her voice. Angela smiled. "Mr. Bud Blake, what a pleasant surprise. You certainly do get around the hospital, don't you?"

The Risk Management director stood and shook her hand. "Good to see you again, Dr. Brennan."

"Angela, Bud and I are in a meeting, but how about I call you when we're done?" Stan suggested.

Bud said, "Actually, Stan, I think we're about finished here. I'll attend to what we discussed and get back to you with my thoughts."

Stan nodded, and the man exited, closing the door behind him. "Angela, please have a seat. What can I do for you?"

Angela regarded the barrel-chested man, his black hair slicked back like some mafia wannabe. His chest hair peeked out from his Hermes dress shirt and he wore his red tie too long, as if to draw attention to his groin. His five o'clock shadow seemed forced, like he was trying too hard to fit in with a younger crowd. The image of an overgroomed bear popped into her mind.

"Your assistant seems to think you're not here. At least that's what she told me."

Stan smirked and threw his arms wide. "You caught me. When I don't want to be disturbed, that's what I instruct her to tell people. Sorry about that."

"What if she gets in trouble for saying you're not here, Stan? Have you thought about it from her perspective? You're asking her to lie for you, and she takes all of the shit when people get frustrated."

He fixed her with a condescending stare. "Angela, is this why you're here? To lecture me on how I handle my staff? I know you've been through a lot but—"

Angela suppressed a sharp retort and shook her head. "No, that's not why I'm here. I want to know why Lauren Kirk was fired for completing your directive in giving Emily the second dose of medicine. You know, the one that ultimately killed her."

Stan's chair squeaked as he leaned back and tented his fingers. Angela watched a myriad of emotions play across his face, which ultimately settled into a mask of stone. "Angela, please understand that the hospital is sad to see one of its employees, one of its family members, go through this hell. Lauren made a mistake and had to take ownership of it."

Angela nodded sagely. "I see. Tell me, Stan, are you taking ownership of your part?"

He leaned forward quickly, his cologne beating him by a margin. "I was just doing my job."

Angela inhaled quickly and quietly in an effort to stifle the urge to scream. "So was Lauren, Stan."

He sighed and stood facing the window, his fists shoved deep into his pockets. "Are you planning on suing me?"

Angela was shocked that the conversation had turned so drastically. "What? No, of course not. Don't get me wrong. I've been approached by an attorney who seemed eager to take the case. But in the end, Stan, it was a mistake. Having said that, I *would* like to hear you say that you understand your role in this disaster."

"I can't do that."

"You can't say that you're sorry?"

"Listen, Angela. Am I sad that your daughter passed away? Of course I am. I'm human, for goodness sake. But I did nothing wrong and I'm not going to apologize for something I didn't do."

Ants crawled up Angela's back as she sifted through Stan's speech. "Stan, I'm hearing lots of words, but nothing related to how sorry you are for your part in Emily's death." He stared at her mutely, his dark eyes unreadable. Angela nodded slowly. "I came here to understand why, Stan. Why someone in your position would dump all of the responsibility on a young nurse who was just following your orders. It's not right and you know it."

Stan placed his hands on the desk and leaned forward. "I don't know what you want me to tell you, Angela. I bear no guilt over her dismissal." She looked up at him and realized with astonishment that he was trying to intimidate her. He towered over her as he glared, and she suddenly wondered how she ever felt this man worthy of her collegiality.

Holding his stare, Angela stood, straightened her lab coat, and cleared her throat. "You, Dr. Jacobs, are a pompous ass."

Turning on her heel, she marched out of his office and slammed the door. She paused for a moment, aware of the assistant's eyes, and took stock of her emotional state. Her heart felt like it was going to explode, and she focused on deep breaths for several moments before turning to Stan's assistant. "Have a nice day."

She took the elevator to Maggie's office and asked the assistant if Maggie had time to talk.

"Please take a seat, Dr. Brennan, and I'll see if Ms. Donnelly is available."

Angela did as instructed and waited only three minutes before the large double doors opened to reveal a smiling Maggie dressed in a light-blue Givenchy linen suit.

"Angela, so great to see you. How's clinic going? Are you happy to be seeing patients again?"

After her discussion with Stan, Angela was relieved to be received so openly. Her adrenaline dissipated quickly, leaving her tired but focused as she smiled. "Absolutely. It's going well. Thanks."

"Sit, sit. Coffee, tea, soda, water?"

"No, thanks, Maggie. Listen, I'm here because I understand that Lauren Kirk has been fired from the Pediatric ICU."

"Lauren Kirk? Oh, right. The nurse. Yes, that's right."

"I'm wondering if you might reconsider her dismissal, seeing as she was following Stan Jacobs' orders when she gave Emily the medicine."

Maggie's eyebrows knitted. "Angela, let me understand this. You're asking me to reinstate the young woman that killed your daughter?"

Angela understood Maggie's reaction but pressed forward. "Lauren did not kill my daughter, Maggie. The drugs killed Emily. But to answer your question directly: yes, I'm asking you to reinstate Lauren."

Maggie shook her head. "It wasn't just that, Angela. Lauren was let go because of some other infractions."

This was new information and Angela's determination faltered. "What other infractions?"

"I can't tell you that, Angela. That's between me, Human Resources, and Lauren. But let me just say that she was given ample opportunity to improve and, unfortunately, she failed. We had no choice but to let her go."

"Huh. It's funny, because Barb Royes didn't mention any performance issues when I spoke with her about Lauren."

Maggie held Angela's stare and then offered a tight smile. "Why would she mention it to you? It's none of your business."

The sudden change in Maggie's demeanor and tone caught Angela off guard and she stared at Maggie. "It wasn't my business before now, Maggie. In fact, I came to you, just as I came to Stan Jacobs, to get some answers. But instead, I've been met with arrogance and condescension. You should know that an attorney approached me asking if I wanted to sue the hospital for wrongful death. I was surprised when he asked because I had never considered it. I know what it feels like to be on the receiving end of a lawsuit, and I wouldn't want to put anyone here through that. After all, we're a family, isn't that what you said? But having had two conversations today in which I am clearly a second-class citizen have made me rethink my position."

Maggie held up her hands. "Angela, let's not jump to conclusions. What do you want from me?"

"I want you to reinstate Lauren Kirk."

"I cannot do that."

Angela set her jaw. "Okay. Give me Lauren's home address or phone number, and I'll be on my way."

Maggie sighed. "I can't do that either, Angela. Legally, I mean. I can't just give out employee information."

Angela stood, her betrayal and anger barometer rising quickly. "I had a feeling you'd say that. I'm going to talk to her one way or another, Maggie." She crossed to the door. "You know, it didn't have to be this way. I've been very happy here. And you yourself said that I have what it takes to lead."

Maggie stood, removed her glasses, and placed them carefully on her desk. She raised her eyes to meet Angela's and folded her arms across her chest. "I did say that. But perhaps I was mistaken."

CHAPTER 22

Angela channeled her frustration into the accelerator and drove home way too fast. She felt reckless, a part of her secretly hoping that an officer would pull her over so that she could scream at him. The conversations with Stan and Maggie had left her emotionally drained but had also injected her with a new sense of purpose, and she felt a swirling energy building. But by the time she pulled into the garage, she had completed the emotional roller-coaster ride and exhaustion consumed her. She entered the house and called out to her parents. Receiving no answer, she went to the back yard and found her father sitting by the pool reading the local newspaper, the *Barrington Times*.

Angela stared at the water. "When did we open the pool?"

"It's been open for about a month, angel. I think you've been too preoccupied to notice. Care to take a swim?"

"No, thanks." She plopped in the chaise next to her father and noted how the gentle breeze rippled the chlorinated water. The sun's rays dove to the bottom and flitted among the tiles. "Hey, Dad, why did you name me Angela?"

Her father closed the paper. "Because right after you were born, I felt a tightening in my chest, followed by a fluttering in my stomach. When I told your mother, she said that it was just love and nerves combining to create a parent. I told her that I had a different theory." He smiled and waggled his eyebrows until she laughed.

"I give up. What was your theory?"

He leaned forward conspiratorially. "I told her it was because I had been touched by an angel."

Angela raised an eyebrow and smirked. "Really? An angel?"

"Yes. You. You're the angel. You touched my soul when I first saw you. So right then I decided to name you Angela."

"Mom didn't have a say in naming me?"

Her father chuckled, a warm, throaty sound that reminded her of happier days. "You know your mother. When she has something to say, she says it. The reality was that I wanted to name you Angel, but she thought it was, and I quote, 'tacky,' so we called you Angela instead."

She scrutinized her father and noticed the toll the past stressful months had taken on him.

"When did your hair turn white?" she asked playfully.

"About the same time that we opened the pool," he shot back.

She leaned back, closed her eyes, and reveled in the warmth of the sun on her face. The last time she could remember enjoying the sun was her family's last day together on Cape Cod. Her memory replayed their last hours together, and her heart soared as she remembered her children's laughter and the love in Tony's eyes.

"What are you smiling about?" Angela opened her eyes to find her father leaning over her. He was holding a glass of lemonade.

"I was thinking about our day at the beach before the accident."

"You were laughing in your sleep, so it must have been a good memory."

"Sleep? What do you mean? I just closed my eyes for a moment."

Her father smoothed her hair. "You were out for about an hour, angel."

Angela looked at her watch. "Wow. You're right. That's the deepest sleep I've had in a long, long time." She yawned, stretched, and accepted the lemonade.

"And your memories were happy, Angela. That's good. You told me that since the accident you dream only about the bad stuff. You're making progress."

"Yeah, I guess." She sipped her drink. "This is good."

"Mom made it. You know how she feels about lemonade. Homemade or bust."

Angela sighed, enjoying the simplicity of the moment, and how the experience of a shared history enabled effective communication using so few words. A year ago she wouldn't have made time to sit by the pool, with a glass of lemonade, no less, and chat with her father about nothing in particular.

"Hey, Dad?"

"Hmmm?" he answered as he perused the sports section of the *Times*.

"You said that I touched your soul when I was born."

"Uh-huh."

"Do you think that's actually true?"

Her father closed the paper and turned toward her. He looked intently in her eyes and nodded his head. "I've been waiting to have this conversation with you."

"You have?"

"Yes, but I was waiting until you were ready."

"Ready for what?"

"Listen. The first time I saw you, I knew without an iota of doubt that I would lay down my life to protect you. The feeling I'm talking about goes way beyond rational thought."

"I felt the same way when I saw my babies."

He nodded. "Exactly. Now, as a person whose life has been based in science, one might argue that a parent's drive to protect and defend its offspring is primal, in order to ensure survival of the species. That the entire parenting paradigm is science-based. But you and I both know that it goes way deeper than that. I would do anything to ensure your happiness. If I could go back in time and undo the accident, I would. Those feelings are not science-based. They're soul-based."

"I'm not sure what you're trying to tell me, Dad."

"This is my very long answer to your question: Do I really believe that you touched my soul when I first saw you? Absolutely. The tightness in my chest and the flutter in my stomach were physical representations of you reaching across space to become part of me. It's ironic, if you think about it. You physically exist because of your mother and me, but I spiritually exist because of the connections our souls made upon your birth. Does that make sense?"

Angela nodded, mesmerized. She had no idea that her father thought about things like this. "I didn't know you were a religious man."

Her father swallowed some lemonade and waved his hand. "I'm not religious, but I do consider myself spiritual. And before you ask, I think the connections we make while we're on this earth last well beyond the physical time we spend here."

"So you're saying that in some way we live on after we die?"

Her father shrugged. "Something like that. I'm no expert in this stuff, but I've seen too many unexplainable events in the operating room to dismiss the idea."

Angela leaned forward in her chair. "Like what?"

"Like a strange light floating above someone I was operating on immediately before his heart stopped. The light hovered as we performed CPR, and then rose quickly when we pronounced him dead. Another time a patient started talking, clear as day, even though she was under deep anesthesia. During the conversation, the OR lights flickered several times, even though no other area in the hospital was experiencing a power issue. The patient later told me that her conversation was with someone who had been dead for fifteen years. I have other examples, but the point is that interesting things have happened for which I don't have satisfactory scientific explanations."

Angela wasn't sure whether to scoff or be jealous. "I don't have any juicy stories like those."

"Keep operating and you will."

Angela glanced sideways at him, unsure whether her

emotional health could handle treading further. "Have you ever seen a ghost, Dad?"

"No. I'm not sure how I'd handle it if I did."

Angela sighed heavily. "Yeah."

He appraised her. "Have *you* seen a ghost?"

She felt like she was on a precipice, uncertain whether to take the leap, unsure what awaited her if she did. Finally, she spoke quietly. "I thought I was losing my mind." She recounted the events at the hospital—seeing Reggie before Emily's death, finding Lauren's note, meeting Marty, and her conversations with Barb, Stan, and Maggie.

When she was done, her father blew out a mouthful of air. "Oh, angel. No wonder you fell asleep when you got home. What are you going to do now?"

"I need to find Lauren Kirk."

"I've got friends who can get her address."

Angela turned quickly. "Really?"

"Really. I'll take care of it. What about that lawyer? Are you going to take him up on his offer to represent you in a suit against Stan Jacobs and the hospital?"

Annoyance poked at her conscience. "I don't want to. It goes against everything I stand for. Plus, I'm being sued right now as it is. I know how it feels, and it's not good. Stan may be a jackass, but he's a good surgeon who made a mistake."

"That's very kind of you, taking the high road like that, Angela. I'm not sure I'd make the same decision if I were in your shoes."

Angela turned, a perplexed look on her face. "To be honest, I'm not sure where my patience is coming from. I think this hell I'm walking through has awakened me somehow. I know that I can't get my family back, and I'm not sure how being vindictive would help me. Maybe it would. I'm just not sure. I keep remembering what Reggie said."

"Who's Reggie again?"

"Reggie Stevens was the brother of the attorney who came to see me." She rolled her eyes and added, "The dead ghost guy from the waiting room."

"Oh, right. What did he say?"

"He said, 'God looks out for us, so we're going to be alright no matter what happens.'"

"Do you believe that?"

"Frankly, I'm not sure what to believe."

"Would it help you to believe it?"

Angela thought a moment. Could she actually believe that there was an old guy somewhere in the sky that oversaw everything that happened? No. But would it provide comfort to think that some larger-than-life presence was looking out for her best interests, despite all of her recent loss? "Yes, Dad. I think it might."

"Then believe it. Sometimes it's only when the Devil visits us that we can find the grace and humility to forgive. Not because of him, but in spite of him."

Angela turned to her father, astonished at his wisdom. "How did you get so smart?"

"Hanging around with your mother," he deadpanned.

"Dinner!" Sally called.

Her father pulled her out of the chair and held her close, rocking her like he did when she was little. His scent and warmth drew her in, and for a moment, she allowed herself to be comforted. Her sadness faded to the background as she absorbed his love.

"Tomorrow is a new day when you can tackle gargantuan problems. But tonight, my angel, you're mine."

An overwhelming sense of love and loss filled her as she laid her head against his chest and whispered, "Thanks, Dad. I love you."

CHAPTER 23

~

Angela awoke to the sound of her grumbling stomach. The scent of pancakes and bacon wafted from the kitchen, and she realized that she hadn't remembered smelling any food for the last few months. Although her mother had crafted spectacular delicacies in an effort to entice her underweight daughter to eat—including Tony's favorite entrée, chicken Parmesan, which had ended with Angela crying and refusing food—Angela had eaten sparingly, ingesting only enough to keep her alive. Now it felt as if her body were reawakening, discovering little joys she had ignored or been unable to experience since the accident. She lay on her side of the bed and caressed Tony's pillow. Leaning into it, she could barely discern his scent. She had allowed her mother to launder the sheets, but Tony's pillowcase and the dirty clothes he'd left in the hamper were off-limits. It was all she had left of him, and they made her feel less alone.

"I miss you," she whispered. "My heart breaks each day I wake up without you and the kids." She turned to the window where the oak tree's branch was gently tapping on the glass. "Do you hear the branch scraping the glass? Is that you talking to me?" She smiled, remembering her husband's touch, the tilt of his head when he laughed, the way he gathered Liam and Emily into a hug before falling to the floor in giggles. Then a veil of melancholy floated down and settled into the lines around her mouth, erasing the fleeting happiness that had rented space there.

"Angela? Are you awake? Breakfast!"

"Coming," she called. She turned to the pillow. "I'll see you tonight." She kissed two fingers and placed them on Tony's pillow, then dressed quickly and descended the stairs to find her aproned mother standing in front of a sizzling frying pan. A plate heaped with bacon and buttered pancakes was placed at her spot at the table. She sat and evaluated her immaculately dressed father, his creased salmon-colored shorts perfectly paired with a crisp, Vineyard Vines oxford shirt.

A neatly folded piece of paper lay next to her plate. "What's this?"

Her father answered without looking at her. "Open it."

Inside was an address and a phone number. Smiling, Angela asked, "How did you get this, Dad?"

He glanced at her and winked. "I know people."

"What's that?" her mother asked as she loaded Jim's plate with food.

"It's the phone number and address of the nurse who attended Emily when she died. I want to talk—" Angela stopped when her father shook his head quickly, indicating that he hadn't told Sally about Lauren's note. He probably didn't want her to worry. "I just want to talk to her."

"Okay. Well, eat up so you can be on your way. When will you be home, dear?"

Angela drenched a pancake in syrup and stuffed it in her mouth. "I dunno, Mom," she mumbled.

"Honestly, Angela! How old are you? Stop stuffing your mouth, for goodness sake."

Angela stood and smiled as best she could with a full mouth. "Gotta go, Mom. Thanks." She kissed her mother on the cheek, leaving sticky lip marks behind, then grabbed some bacon and dashed from the kitchen.

"Angela!" her mother yelled after her. She heard her father laugh. Just for a moment, she felt fifteen years old again, her biggest concern who she'd go to prom with. She got in the car and grinned as she pulled out of the driveway.

After a full morning in clinic, Angela sat in her office dictating patient notes. Liz knocked on her open door and plopped down in the chair opposite her friend.

"What's happening? You seem different today. A little lighter."

Angela paused. "Do I?"

Liz nodded. "It's nice."

"It's strange, Liz. Sometimes I feel like I can't remember what they look like and it scares me. But then I get this feeling. It's difficult to describe, but it almost feels like they're inside me. And then I feel better. Lighter, like you said. Does that make sense?"

"Completely. It's like what I told you about my mom. After she passed, I felt like she was with me all the time. I think that's what you're saying. It doesn't mean you don't want to touch them. But you know you can't, so you're filled with their presence in a different way."

Angela stared into the distance. "I miss them so much."

"I know you do." They sat quietly for a moment and listened to the noise of a busy hospital. The sound of laughter floated down the hallway. "What happened with the note yesterday?"

"I'm still working on it."

"Want to go to lunch?"

Angela shook her head. "Thanks, but I'm going to make a call and then head home."

Liz stood. "Sounds good. Say hi to your parents."

"I will. See you tomorrow. Close the door behind you please, Liz."

After Liz left, Angela removed the piece of paper her father had given her. She dialed Lauren Kirk's number and the call went straight to voicemail. "Hi, Lauren. This is Angela Brennan. I wanted to chat with you about what happened the day my daughter Emily died. If you could give me a call back, I'd appreciate it. I assume this is your cell phone, so you'll have my number on your screen. Thanks so much."

She disconnected and returned her attention to the computer screen. Sixty seconds later, her cell phone buzzed.

"Hello?"

"Hi, Dr. Brennan. It's Lauren. Sorry I didn't pick up your call, but I didn't recognize the number and I was worried it was another weird phone call."

"What do you mean?"

A long sigh came across the line. "Ever since I was fired, I've been getting calls where the person will disconnect when I answer. It's happened at least thirty times. But when I heard your voice, I was relieved. I'm glad you reached out to me, actually. I was trying to work up the nerve to contact you."

"Why?"

"Because of what happened the day that Emily died."

Angela's heart skipped a beat. "Did you leave the note at the lobby desk for me?"

"Yes."

"Why didn't you just call my office or bring the note to me directly? Or better yet, have a face-to-face conversation?"

"Well, after what happened I wasn't sure you'd want to see me. Plus, after I was let go, I was told not to step foot into the hospital again or they'd get a restraining order against me. And no one wants to hire someone who has a restraining order against them."

"I was told that you were fired because of the medication error, that someone had to shoulder the blame."

"I accept full responsibility for that, Dr. Brennan. I cannot express to you how sorry I am. Emily was an amazing child and I've been sick about her death. Literally, sick."

The sincerity of her words wrapped around Angela and warmed her. "Thank you, Lauren. I accept your apology. Now, I want you to do me a favor."

"Absolutely anything."

"I want you to let go of the burden you've been carrying. Grab the cawing black crow that sits on your shoulder and toss it high in the air. Let it fly away along with your guilt. Emily's death was tragic, and I'm sick about it too. But it was an accident, and I don't hold you responsible. I forgive you."

Lauren was silent so long that Angela asked, "Are you still there?"

Lauren sniffled. "Yes."

"Now that we've discussed the elephant in the room, I have some questions."

"Okay."

"Maggie Donnelly told me that you'd had some performance problems in your job. The medication error was simply the last straw."

"That's not true. My performance record was impeccable the entire time I'd been employed there."

"Then why would she say that?"

"To shut me up. To impugn my character."

"To what end?"

"I don't know. Maybe so no one will listen to me or trust what I have to say. What did Barbara Royes say? Have you talked to her?"

"I did. She told me that you were relieved of duty because of the medication error."

"But she didn't say anything about my having performance problems, did she?"

"No."

"Because I didn't."

Angela closed her eyes, reviewing the events surrounding Emily's death. "Lauren, can you walk through what you remember about the day my daughter died?"

The young nurse inhaled deeply. "Sure. Emily got through surgery like a champ. Her vital signs were strong during and immediately following surgery, and in recovery she was hooked up to an IV that contained saline and Fentanyl. You came into the room and we chatted for several minutes, and Dr. Jacobs changed the medication orders."

"Why did he alter them so soon after surgery?"

"I'm not sure, but it's not uncommon for that to happen in orthopedic cases. We've found that patients do almost as well with a strong anti-inflammatory as they do on a narcotic like Fentanyl."

"Okay. Go on."

"I came into the room and changed the IV that contained the Fentanyl and replaced it with a regular saline solution, and then you saw the rest. You watched me give her the pill that contained 30 milligrams of Oxycontin."

"Twice the dosage she should have had."

Lauren broke down crying. "I know. I relive it every day. If only I hadn't given her that damn pill!"

"Lauren, you have to trust me when I say that I understand the guilt. I've gone through the entire day a thousand times. If only we'd left the beach earlier. If only I hadn't given Tony my sunglasses. If only I'd asked what the dosage of her meds was. If only we'd gotten the Narcan to her in time. We could play the 'what if' game all day and end up with nothing but migraines and suicidal tendencies. Please stop."

The sniffling slowed. "That's the part I don't understand."

"What?"

"I feel like we *did* get the Narcan to her in time. It should have worked."

Angela reflected on her conversation with Frank Toner, who had said the same thing. The injection to reverse the accidental overdose should have worked.

"Why do you think it didn't?"

"I don't know, but it was bothering me, so I started asking questions."

"Of whom?"

"Dr. Jacobs. When I first asked him why the Narcan didn't work, his response was, 'That's a good question. Let me think about it and get back to you.' When I followed up several days later, he told me to drop it. And then, when I pushed him further, he told me to shut up and let it go."

"Did you?"

"No. I went to Barb Royes and told her what had happened with Dr. Jacobs. She tried talking to him and when that didn't get her anywhere, she went above his head to Maggie. Next thing I know I was in Barb's office being severed."

"Severed?"

"Yeah. Let go. Fired. But they gave me a severance package of six months' salary, so I have time to find another job. You tell me, Dr. Brennan, why would I have been given a severance package if I'd been fired for bad behavior?"

"I don't know. So why did they tell me that you had performance issues?"

"Maybe so you wouldn't talk to me."

"But here we are talking. Why did you leave the note for me, Lauren?"

"Because my gut says that something isn't right about Emily's death. The Narcan should have worked. Dr. Jacobs was originally as curious as I was to find some answers, but then, all of a sudden, he clammed up and ordered me to do the same. Does that seem right to you?"

The lightness Angela had been feeling evaporated, replaced by a hollowness in her core. "No, it doesn't seem right to me at all. I'll be back in touch. Thanks for your time, Lauren."

CHAPTER 24

Angela disconnected the call, gathered her belongings, and dialed Frank Toner's number while walking to her car.

"Frank, hi. It's Angela. Can I come see you?"

"Of course. You okay?"

"I don't think so. I know this sounds crazy, but I think the hospital might be hiding information about Emily's death."

"Doesn't sound crazy to me. Come on over."

As she drove, her thoughts drifted among various scenes. Liam proudly holding his most recent Tai Kwon Do trophy, Emily braiding her hair for the fourteenth time in one day, Tony offering to cut back his work schedule so she could pursue an MBA. She had always been so busy thinking about the "next thing" that she hadn't paid attention to whait was happening right in front of her. *And now it's too late*, she thought. Her mind wandered to the man in the waiting room, Reggie Stevens. *Did I really see him or was he in my mind? All those things that he said to me—was I speaking to myself? And if so, perhaps I really am losing my mind.*

Angela pulled into Frank's winding driveway and marveled at the magnolia trees that lined each side. Powering down her window, she inhaled the blooms' intoxicating scent. Frank was waiting for her on the front porch, a blanket draped over his bony shoulders. He looked frail and tired, and Angela's heart sank at the sight of his sickly state.

"Don't look at me like that," he ordered as she approached. "I'm still your superior, you know."

"In so many ways." They embraced, and he ushered her inside where two glasses of ice water and a tray of cookies sat on a table in the sunroom. "Quite a reception," she commented.

"Only the best for my favorite resident. Please sit, Angela, and tell me what's going on."

Angela updated him on her conversation with Lauren Kirk. He listened with a furrowed brow and attentive eyes. When she was finished, she took a sip of water and said, "So, that's it. I don't know what to think. I'm way too close to the situation to know what's real and what I'm imagining."

"It sounds like they bribed her not to talk, without her even knowing it."

"What do you mean?"

"Why would they give her a severance package if she were fired for incompetence?"

Angela shrugged.

"They wouldn't, Angela. The money was to shut her up. And they told her that they'd get a restraining order against her if she returned to the hospital? That doesn't sound right. They want her to go away and not ask any more questions. Did you talk with Stan Jacobs?"

Angela rolled her eyes. "Yes, and he told me in no uncertain terms to mind my own business. He accepts no responsibility in Emily's death, even though he was the physician that ordered the meds that killed her."

Frank coughed. "Maybe you should come at the problem from a different angle."

"What do you mean?"

"You've hit the problem head on, asking the people who were directly involved in Emily's care. But what about the people behind the scenes? I'm talking about Housekeeping, Nutrition, Pharmacy."

"Emily wasn't in the hospital long enough for there to be any interactions with housekeeping or nutrition."

"Stan Jacobs ordered the drugs, but who filled the order?"

"Pharmacy."

"Exactly. Talk to them. They should have, at the very least, caught Stan's error. Or—" Frank was interrupted as a coughing fit racked his body. Angela jumped up and handed him some water, which he drank as she watched nervously. "Thank you." After catching his breath, he finished his thought. "Or perhaps there was something wrong with the Narcan that was injected. Maybe that's why it didn't work. And maybe Stan and Maggie know it."

Angela leaned forward. "Are you serious, Frank? I find it hard to believe that the Narcan was compromised in some way. And honestly, even if there was something wrong with it, I can't imagine that Stan or Maggie, even as arrogant as they are, would allow any death to go unaddressed by hiding the truth. But I'll do as you suggest and follow up with Pharmacy."

Frank was quiet a moment as he stared past Angela. "Did you know that I had a daughter?"

Angela was taken aback. "No."

"She died forty-five years ago, from being given a vaccine that had not been adequately refrigerated. The virus had spoiled, if you can believe that, and it killed her. An immunization to protect her ended up killing her."

"Oh, Frank. I'm so sorry. I had no idea."

"It was a long time ago. I still think of her often, but like your family, she's in a far better place now. It wasn't just my daughter who died. Seven babies were given vaccines from the same unrefrigerated bottle, and they all died. We filed a class action lawsuit against the manufacturer that lasted twenty years in the courts. Twenty years!" He shook his head and shifted in his chair.

"What happened?"

"In the end, the judge found in favor of the pharmaceutical company. All of our time and money wasted."

Angela took her mentor's hand. "I'm sorry, Frank."

"Do you know that afterwards, the president of the pharmaceutical company called me and apologized for the company's mistake? He actually admitted to me over the phone that they knew about the vaccines and let them be administered anyway, hoping for the best. That's what he said—that they had been 'hoping for the best.'"

"Oh my God."

"My point is, Angela, that people in power will do unthinkable things to remain there. Even when they know what they're doing is wrong." He blew air though his nose. "Yes, people get crazy when it comes to power and money."

Angela held his gaze for a moment and then sighed. "I guess I need to talk to the director of Pharmacy at the hospital."

"I guess you do."

She smiled, stood, and hugged him hard, his wasting body tensing with the pressure. "Sorry. Did I hug you too hard?"

"It's okay."

"Frank, honestly, how long do you have?"

He lifted his head and smiled crookedly. "Angela, does it matter? How much time do any of us have? The fact is that we don't know, which is why we have to enjoy every day. Not just live but *thrive*. Do you hear me?"

Angela's eyes welled with tears. "Oh, Frank. I'm not sure I can handle losing you too."

"You'll be okay. You'll hurt for a little while, but you'll rally. Because that's what we do, isn't it, Dr. Brennan?" Suddenly he rose to his full height and became the attending physician she had worked so hard to impress.

"Yes, sir."

"That's my girl. Now, get out of here and let a man rest. But do me a favor."

"What?"

"Go home and sleep on our discussion. Plan out your strategy and be dogmatic in your questioning when you speak to the Pharmacy director."

"Got it. Thanks again, Frank."

"My pleasure."

Angela walked to her car and turned around to wave. The porch was empty. Frank had already returned to the comfortable cocoon of his house.

CHAPTER 25

After eating ten bites of her mother's specialty, chicken cordon bleu, Angela begged off dessert and retreated for a warm bath and a glass of wine. She lay in the tub and asked Alexa to play some classical music. Relaxing with her wine, she opened her iPad and googled Joseph Kaiser. He had received his doctor-ate-of-pharmacy at the University of Michigan and had worked in various health systems throughout the years until landing his current job as Pharmacy director. For the last seven years, Angela had worked peripherally with him, engaging directly only once when they'd both served on a communication improvement task force. Overall, she had found him to be effective, intelligent, and highly likeable. She felt confident that when she approached him seeking information about Pharmacy's role in Emily's death, he would be accommodating.

After her bath, she laid her head on Tony's pillow, thinking about Frank's advice to be deliberate and organized in her discussion with the Pharmacy director. As she drifted off to sleep, she pictured Emily's last moments and vowed to herself that she would discover the truth behind her death.

Emily and Angela walked together in a cornfield. Emily told a story and they both laughed. Suddenly, the ground trembled and cracked, leaving Angela on one side of the divide and Emily on the other. As the gap widened, a bridge appeared, and Angela rushed toward it, only to find that the cornfield had morphed into a swamp. With Liam and Tony standing behind her, urging her on, Angela trudged forward in a desperate attempt to reach Emily. She arrived at the edge of the swamp and put one foot on the bridge, only to feel it give way beneath her. As she fell into the chasm, she saw Emily's face appear over the edge. She was screaming for Angela to come back and save her.

The alarm sounded, and Angela awoke, agitated and out of breath. The details of the dream gnawed at her, and she realized how chaotic her life still felt. *One step forward, two steps back*, she thought. She moved slowly through her morning routine and arrived at work to find Bernard Smythe sitting at her desk, rifling through files. She stood in the doorway, torn between curiosity, confusion, and anger. After several moments, she decided on curiosity.

"What are you doing?"

"Hello, Dr. Brennan. Maggie asked me to obtain Ava Sinclair's last test results before she underwent surgery with you."

Bernard didn't seem surprised to have been caught and didn't get up from her chair. Her curiosity quickly turned to anger. "You mean surgery with *us*, don't you? You were there too. Don't forget that."

"But I wasn't in charge. You were. Don't forget *that*."

Angela felt as if she'd been slapped. "Oh, I haven't forgotten. All of her test results should be online. Why are you going through my desk drawers?"

"Because her records seem to be missing."

Angela couldn't hide her surprise. "*All* of them?"

"Every one. Maggie was wondering if you'd kept hard copies."

"No. Why would I?"

Dr. Smythe shrugged. "I don't know, but she wanted me to check. She also wants to talk to you about where Mrs. Sinclair's test results might have gone."

"How would I know, Bernard? Have you talked to the Information Technology people?"

"No. She told me to ask you."

Angela closed her eyes and massaged her forehead. "Tell Maggie that I have no idea where Ava Sinclair's records are, and that I have not touched them since the lawsuit was filed."

"Okay." He stood and walked slowly toward her, a half smile on his face. As he was passing, he bumped against her. "My apologies," he mumbled.

Angela watched him walk away as Liz sidled up beside her.

"What did Captain Marvelous want this time?"

"Honestly, I'm not sure. Listen, can you cover for me while I go speak with Joe Kaiser in Pharmacy? I was going to chat with him after seeing patients, but I'm not sure I can wait that long."

"Actually, I was coming here to tell you that your first two patients cancelled. They're a husband and wife and their daughter had a baby—"

"So I have some free time?"

"Bottom line? Yes."

Angela patted Liz's back and said, "I'll be back as soon as I can. Thanks."

She trotted to the elevator, smiled at its occupants, pressed the B button, and faced the closing doors. A little girl in a wheelchair looked Angela up and down, unabashedly examining her clothing.

"Are you a doctor?" she asked. Angela smiled and nodded.

"Are you a good doctor?"

Angela glanced at the other passengers. "I try to be."

"Has anyone that you've taken care of died?"

"Eleanor, that's rude!" the girl's caretaker admonished. All eyes turned first to Eleanor, and then to Angela, who said, "It's okay. It's a good question." She knelt by the little girl and said, "Sadly, yes. I do the best I can, but sometimes I can't save someone."

Eleanor squinted at her. "I'm going to die."

Angela glanced at the girl's caretaker, seeking assistance, but found a blank stare. "You don't know that, Eleanor."

"Yes, I do. I have cancer all over my body. But it's okay." Angela couldn't tear her gaze from the little girl's face. Her large green eyes were sincere, and her forehead was high with a sassy cowlick at her widow's peak. A light dusting of freckles covered her blunt nose and the area around her lips was very chapped. She was no more than six years old yet possessed the solemnity of an aged woman.

"Why is it okay?" Angela whispered.

The frail child smiled and said, "Because He's with me." She pointed to the roof of the elevator. Angela stopped breathing for a moment, acutely aware that everyone was awaiting her response. She looked into Eleanor's clear green eyes and saw not resignation and despair, but acceptance and contentment. She saw peace.

Angela fought back tears and tried to smile. "Then you *are* going to be okay."

The little girl nodded, took Angela's hand, and said, "And so are you. It's going to get better. You'll see. Everything's going to be alright."

Speechless, Angela stared at Eleanor as the elevator stopped and the doors opened. Eleanor kept smiling as she was wheeled away followed by the other passengers, leaving Angela alone. *What the hell just happened?* Angela thought as the doors closed and the elevator descended. *Did I imagine her?*

Arriving on the basement level, the doors parted, revealing a brightly lit corridor. The last time she had been in this hallway was when she had identified Tony's and Liam's bodies. Pushing the thought aside, she walked quickly to Pharmacy and asked to speak with Joe Kaiser. A minute later a bald, overweight man sporting a warm smile and an extended hand rounded the corner and took Angela's hands in his own.

"Angela, I'm genuinely sorry for your loss of your family. My parents passed recently. I'm not saying that it's the same as losing your husband and children, but I empathize with you."

His quiet kindness touched her. "Thank you, Joe. I'm sorry about your parents as well."

He nodded and escorted her into his office. "What can I do for you?"

"As you probably know, my daughter Emily died from an accidental overdose here at the hospital."

He nodded and then shook his head. "Awful."

"She was given a Narcan injection, but it didn't work, and I'm trying to understand why."

Joe cocked his head. "I was told by Stan Jacobs that your daughter's overdose was too far advanced for the medicine to have worked."

"That's what I originally thought, but that fact is that Emily was able to speak right up until the very end. Her lungs were filling with fluid, but she could still speak."

"I didn't know that."

"So I'm wondering if maybe there was something wrong with the medicine itself that rendered it ineffective."

Joe twisted his mouth in thought and then turned to his computer. After working through several screens, he turned the monitor toward Angela. "As you can see, Angela, your daughter's Narcan dose was taken from vial thirty-five of shipment number sixteen."

Angela quickly reviewed the information on the screen. Her daughter's name, birthdate, medical record number, current medication list, primary and secondary diagnoses, primary care physician, and specialist names were listed, along with progress notes from Stan Jacobs. The current medication list included Narcan, the surgical anesthesia, the Fentanyl IV drip, and the acetaminophen with hydrocodone. Next to each medication was the dosage and the batch from which it was drawn. As Joe had said, the Narcan was listed as being from vial thirty-five of shipment number sixteen.

"Yes, I see that."

"Now," he typed rapidly, and another screen appeared with a list of patient names and medical record numbers. "Every single one of the patients whose names you see on the screen was treated with Narcan from the same shipment, and they all survived. In fact, the three names at the bottom of the screen were given injections from the exact same vial as your daughter, and they're fine." He turned the monitor back around. "My point is that the Narcan wasn't compromised."

"But if the Narcan was effective and the overdose didn't kill her, then . . ."

"Maybe it *was* the medication error, Angela. Maybe her body was just too weak to handle that much medication in her system."

Angela dropped her head in thought. "No. Emily was stronger than that. It couldn't have been a negative reaction to surgical anesthesia, because she was fine immediately after surgery. It has to have been something else that we haven't yet considered."

"Angela?"

She lifted her head, not realizing that she'd been mumbling to herself.

"I'm sorry that my people didn't catch the dosage error. I accept full responsibility on behalf of Pharmacy. I want you to know that based on what happened to your daughter, we've put new measures in place to ensure patient safety. I know it won't bring your daughter back, but I thought you'd like to know."

"What measures?"

"Well, now when a clinician orders medication, it's entered into the online system, reviewed by the Pharmacy staff, and then sent back to the ordering clinician for final approval, so it's now triple-checked. So far, the medical staff hasn't complained about it too much. I think they understood that the system needed to change. Unfortunately, Emily's death was the impetus to make the change happen."

Angela slowly shook her head. "I appreciate that the system has been improved, Joe, but why is it that we need something awful to happen in order to alter a damaged system?"

"Good question. I think it's because people, for the most part, despise change."

"True." Angela glanced around his small office and pointed to a picture. "Is that your family?"

Joe swiveled his chair around. "Yes. That's me with my wife, Amelia, and our three kids."

"You have a beautiful family, Joe. Cherish every minute." Angela patted her thighs and stood. "Anyhow, I've taken enough of your time. I appreciate your directness and honesty. That seems to be in short supply around here recently."

"My pleasure, Angela. Let me know if there's anything else I can do for you."

They shook hands and Angela walked out of his office. As she passed the Morgue entrance, she clenched her jaw as she pictured her beautiful girl lying on the cold, steel table. Her visit to Pharmacy had succeeded in crossing off another potential cause of Emily's death, but had gotten her no closer to the truth. Angela was convinced that Emily had not died from a drug overdose, and as she continued the long trek to the elevator, she made a silent promise to Emily that she would rest only when she had more answers.

CHAPTER 26

~

"Dr. Smythe, can you please finish here?" Angela caught his eye across the operating table.

"Absolutely, Dr. Brennan."

Since the altercation in her office four weeks ago, Dr. Smythe had been polite, but cool toward her. Liz believed that he was still hoping to take Angela's position as chairman of Cardiac Surgery, but Angela had a different theory. Much like a three-year-old, she believed that Dr. Smythe was testing to see how far he could push her. Her response had been to treat him like she would her children if they were having a tantrum—with patience, firmness, and kindness.

Angela nodded once and removed her gloves, scrubbed up, and changed back into her street clothes before meeting the family. They were relieved and grateful, as was she, as the complicated surgery had gone better than expected. The focus that surgery required brought a refreshing distraction from the yawning emptiness of recent events and offered her the sense of control she so desperately sought, if only for a few fleeting hours in the operating room. When she deliberated on the pact that she and Frank had made about end-of-life considerations, she would remember what the grief counselor had said: "Although your life will never be the same, you will carve out a new normal which, in time, will become a happy place." Surgery had always been a happy place for Angela and aided in her search for a "new normal."

Angela returned to her office to find Sean examining the family photos she kept on her credenza. "Sean, good to see you."

He turned quickly. "Sorry, Angela. I was just—"

"It's okay. I like to look at them too." She walked over, picked up a picture, and ran her fingers over it. "This was taken the day Tony and Liam died. And Emily would be gone the next day. It's all so . . . unbelievable. It's still so unbelievable."

Sean gently removed the frame from her hand and replaced it, then gathered her in his arms and held her. She tensed at first, not understanding his motivation, but then relaxed as she realized his intention was simply shared grief and comfort. She returned the embrace, and they stood like that until Liz cleared her throat.

"Should I come back?"

They parted, and Angela smiled. "No. Come in, Liz. You remember Sean?"

"Of course. Hi, Sean." He waved his hand in greeting and sat down.

"Angela, I need to talk with you when you have a moment."

"Okay. I'll be right there."

Liz left, and Angela leaned against the edge of her desk. "What's up?"

Sean removed a folder from his briefcase. "I brought the paperwork for you to sign over Tony's half of the firm, along with a check made out in your name."

Although Angela had known this moment was coming, she panicked and felt an absurd urge to run from the room. Even more than burying her family, the act of selling Tony's pride and joy felt so final, an exclamation point on the fact that Tony was never coming back. She felt as if she were betraying him, yet knew it was the smart decision for her financial well-being, as well as her psychological health. She gathered herself and nodded. "Of course."

Sean placed the paperwork on the table and opened to the last page. He adjusted his glasses and proffered a pen. "Are you sure, Angela? Because you don't look sure."

She swallowed. "Give me the pen before I change my mind." A swoop of ink and the act was complete. "There. It's done."

Sean placed his hand over hers. "I promise you that I will carry on the business as Tony would have wanted. He was your husband, but he was my best friend and partner too." Angela smiled tightly and nodded, the lump in her throat the only thing blocking a devastating emotional release. Sean gathered the papers, kissed her cheek, and disappeared.

Liz wandered in as Sean left. "Oh, I know that wasn't easy. You okay?"

Angela nodded as she grabbed a tissue and swallowed her sadness. "It was the right thing to do. You needed to talk to me?"

"It can wait."

"Go ahead. I'm okay, Liz. Really," Angela said as she dabbed her eyes and drew staggered breaths in an effort to steady herself.

Liz regarded her friend with an apprehensive look. "You're not going to be happy, Angela."

Angela spread her arms. "Do I look happy now? What's a little more unhappy? Bring it on." She attempted a smile.

Liz shook her head and slapped down a copy of the *Barrington Times*. On the front page was a picture of Angela in her favorite lab coat standing next to a beaming Emily, their arms wrapped around each other's waists. A renewed round of sadness took hold as Angela remembered Barrington Middle School's Bring-Your-Parent-to-School-Day. Emily had been so proud to introduce Angela, who had spoken to Emily's class about what it's like to hold someone's heart in her hands. Angela envied the casual assuredness with which she and Emily posed, as if nothing could impose on their perfect world. She switched her attention to the headline, which read, "Local Doctor Sued for Malpractice."

"What the—?" She quickly scanned the column and then stared at Liz. "What the hell is this?"

Liz's eyes were huge. "I have no idea. It was laying on a table in the cafeteria, so I picked it up and came straight to you."

Angela shook her head as she read. "It keeps referencing a source close to Dr. Brennan. Listen to this."

> Dr. Angela Brennan, chairperson of Cardiac Surgery, is the primary defendant named in a lawsuit for the wrongful death of Ava Sinclair of East Providence. Dr. Brennan has been in practice for over twenty years, and sources close to her say that this is not the first time she's been named in a malpractice lawsuit. Health systems are not legally obligated to release information regarding their physicians and pending litigation, making it all the more curious as to why hospital sources would approach this reporter.
>
> Dr. Brennan lost her husband and son several months ago in a car accident, and her daughter died of a drug overdose shortly thereafter. Sources say that Dr. Brennan's actions have been erratic following the loss of her family. Indeed, she only recently resumed her surgery schedule, but some are questioning her competence.
>
> Given recent developments, one wonders if the pending lawsuit might be a wake-up call for Dr. Brennan. Perhaps it's time for her to hang up her scalpel.

~

Angela finished reading and slowly lifted her head. She met Liz's gaze. Her stomach flipped and blood rushed to her cheeks. The newspaper shook in her hands. "They make it sound like Emily was a drug addict."

"Who would do this, Angela?"

"I don't know, but there's one way to find out." She picked up her cell phone and googled the *Barrington Times* phone number.

"Angela, you may want to calm down before you call. Remember, this is a small town."

"That's right, Liz. It *is* a small town, which means that all of Emily's friends will be reading this asinine piece. I have to make this right." She held up her pointer finger toward Liz as someone answered.

"Get me Jesse Callaghan. Tell him it's Dr. Angela Brennan. He'll definitely want to speak to me."

Ten seconds later a male voice came on the line. "Jesse here. Is this Dr. Brennan?"

"Yes, it is."

"I'm glad you called."

"How dare you write about my daughter! You can say anything you want about me, but how dare you disparage a dead twelve-year-old girl! What's *wrong* with you?"

"Dr. Brennan, I—"

"She did not die doing drugs, you sick bastard! She suffered an overdose of medications that were administered by clinicians at the hospital. You made her out to be some kind of addict in your ridiculous column!"

"I didn't mean to make her sound that way."

"And what do you know about my situation? If you lost everything you might act a little erratically too. How dare you suggest I stop practicing medicine, you, you . . . snide sycophant!" She stabbed at the 'end' button and slammed the phone onto her desk. Breathing hard, Angela looked up to find Liz staring at her with wide eyes.

"You look scared. Or surprised. Or both," Angela commented.

"Both. In all the years I've known you, I've never heard you speak like that. Do you feel better?"

"I do, actually."

"Do you feel like you accomplished anything?"

"Absolutely not. In fact, he may write another piece about my continuing erratic behavior." Suddenly, Angela started laughing and found that she couldn't stop. After a moment, Liz joined in. When their laughter had been spent, Liz caught her breath and said, "You called him a snide sycophant, Angela. Awesome!"

Angela rolled her eyes and picked up the paper. "The real question is, who was the hospital source he references in the article?"

Angela squinted in thought and then looked at Liz, who was smirking and nodding her head. They answered in unison: "Bernard."

CHAPTER 27

Angela wanted to find Bernard Smythe immediately, but Liz advised against it. "Did you learn nothing from the phone call with that reporter, Angela? Don't speak to Bernard when you're so angry. If he's the source, then you'll only be giving him more ammunition for future defamation and more reason to speak ill of you." Angela had glared furiously at her friend, but acknowledged the logic behind her advice. Instead, Angela had finished her patient notes and spent a somewhat enjoyable evening with her parents, drinking wine and watching a Netflix movie as she ruminated on the conversation she'd eventually have with Bernard.

By the next morning, the searing ball of fiery anger had dissipated enough so that she could form coherent thoughts. She drove to work and found Bernard in the cafeteria hunched over some early morning coffee and in deep conversation with another male physician she didn't recognize.

"Hello, Dr. Smythe. May I have a moment?"

"Of course."

Angela glanced at his companion, but neither he nor Bernard made any move to get up. "Okay. I guess we'll do this right here. Did you happen to read the column in the *Times* yesterday?"

"I did."

She had expected him to be smug, but his expression was ambiguous. "What did you think?"

"Frankly, I thought it was an unfair characterization of you."

The comment caught her by surprise, but she rallied. "Thank you. I agree. Do you happen to be the source with whom Jesse Callaghan spoke?"

He appeared shocked, and then wounded. He stood and said, "Dr. Brennan, you and I have had our differences, but I would never denigrate your surgical expertise. You are the best surgeon with whom I've had the pleasure of operating."

Angela had anticipated resentment and was unsure how to respond, so she remained silent.

"Furthermore, I have an idea who might have spoken to that reporter."

Angela's eyebrows rose in silent inquiry as she repositioned her anger.

"Maggie."

Angela glanced at the seated doctor, who was openly observing their conversation. Annoyed, she cleared her throat. "Why would Maggie do that?"

"I don't know."

"Why do you suspect it was Maggie then?"

Bernard's bony shoulders lifted quickly and dropped. "Just a hunch."

Angela stared at Bernard's angular face and noted the dark half-moons under his eyes. She thought about her most recent discussion with Maggie, and how she had flatly denied Angela's request to reinstate Lauren Kirk. Although they had different viewpoints on the issue, she couldn't see any reason why Maggie would proactively reach out to a reporter to trash her reputation.

"I guess I'll ask her. Thanks for your time." Angela turned and started to walk away.

"Dr. Brennan?"

Angela turned. "Yes?"

"Watch your back."

Angela raised an eyebrow, ready for a fight. "Is that a threat?"

Bernard shook his head. “No. It’s a warning.”

Angela tilted her head and evaluated him for a moment before nodding. His expression was open and seemingly sincere. “Okay.” She started to walk away and then turned around again. “Bernard?”

“Yeah?”

“Get some sleep. You look tired.”

She walked quickly to Maggie’s office, Bernard’s words ringing in her ears. She wasn’t sure if she should trust him, but she had every intention of heeding his advice.

After checking in with Maggie’s assistant, Angela heard Maggie call through her closed door. “Angela, come in!”

She entered Maggie’s office to find Darlene Rancon and Bud Blake seated at the CEO’s conference table. Shaking her head in amazement, she quipped, “Do you two travel with Maggie all the time?”

Maggie smiled. “No. Only when they’re needed.”

Angela pulled a face. “That’s odd, because I’ve seen them with you each time we’ve met.”

“Sit down, Angela.”

Maggie’s tone was directive and put Angela on guard. She glanced at Darlene and Bud, neither of whom acknowledged her. She sat, and as she opened her mouth to speak, Maggie held up a finger to stop her. “What opportune timing on your part. We have some items of importance to discuss. First off, Ava Sinclair’s medical records are missing.”

“I’m glad you brought that up, Maggie, because I entered my office to find Bernard Smythe rummaging through my desk looking for them, which I didn’t appreciate, by the way. Let me save you some time. I don’t have a hard copy and I have no idea where the electronic files might have gone.”

Maggie nodded. “Obviously the missing records are of great concern. What if they’re released to the public? Can you even imagine?”

“I can imagine, and it would be awful, for us and for Mrs. Sinclair’s family.”

"And your name is all over them as the attending surgeon. You were responsible, so that would be a huge problem for you, wouldn't it?"

Angela glared at Maggie. Fury seized her, tightening her jaw. Maggie smiled sweetly. "Well, I'm sure it won't come to that."

Angela felt her nostrils flare and pictured a skewered bull facing its tormentor in a Spanish arena. Ensuring that her breath was even, she asked, "Can I ask you a question?"

"Of course."

"Were you the source in Jesse Callaghan's story about me in the *Times*?"

Maggie pursed her lips. "Story?"

Angela smirked and shook her head as another barbed arrow entered her hide. "Why, Maggie? What do you have to gain by denigrating my reputation?"

"I don't know what you mean."

"Is it because I asked you to reinstate Lauren Kirk?"

Maggie sighed. "Angela, I just want you to do your job. No more, no less. You've been through so much, and I know you've been incredibly stressed. That's probably why you misplaced Mrs. Sinclair's medical records."

"I didn't—"

Maggie held up her hand. "All I'm saying is let's go back to the way things were. You remain chair of Cardiac Surgery. I should have never rocked your boat by asking you to consider the CEO position. You're a very effective surgeon. Let's leave it at that. I'm sure Mrs. Sinclair's records will turn up once everything has calmed down."

Her tone exuded warmth and caring. It was almost motherly. Angela decided to play along and smiled. "I think I understand."

Maggie sucked in a big mouthful of air and clapped her hands. She faced the Bobbsey Twins, who had followed the verbal jousts with bored expressions. "See, Darlene and Bud? I told you she was rational. Now on to the next item of business. Darlene, I'll let you take this one."

Darlene's impossibly light-blue eyes were framed in large, square, black-framed glasses. She sported no makeup and her pie-shaped face wore no expression whatsoever. Her short, blond hair was styled in a no-nonsense cut and her navy-blue blazer over a white blouse and tan pants bespoke efficiency and practicality. "I have something for you to read, Dr. Brennan," Darlene stated. When she spoke, her monotone, even voice completed the picture that her outward appearance created. *She's beige*, Angela thought as Darlene opened a file, withdrew a sheet of paper, and pushed it across the table to Angela.

"What's this?" Angela scanned the document and a whooshing sound filled her ears. "Does this say what I think it says? I no longer have malpractice insurance?"

"Actually, it turns out that your policy was never valid," Darlene said. "Apparently you misrepresented your cardiac surgical fellowship dates on your insurance application, so the entire policy is invalidated."

Angela's head swiveled between Maggie and Darlene, thinking that this was some sort of bad joke. "What are you talking about?"

Darlene's face was impassive as she responded. "Back when you were first hired, you indicated on your malpractice insurance application that you completed your cardiac surgery fellowship on September 21, 1997, when you actually completed it on October 1. That misrepresentation invalidated your application."

"No. That can't be right."

Darlene shrugged and looked to Maggie, who nodded slowly. Panicked, Angela closed her eyes and tried to recall the details. She had had one month remaining in her cardiac surgery fellowship at a Boston hospital when she had accepted the job offer from Maggie. She remembered completing the new-hire paperwork while sitting at a conference table with a representative from Human Resources. Suddenly she nodded. "When I completed the insurance application the dates were correct. My fellowship was supposed to wrap up on September 21, but on September 19, they asked me to stay an additional week and a half to cover for another physician who had given birth early. So, you're correct that the dates were wrong, but not intentionally."

"It doesn't matter whether the mistake was intentional or not," Darlene said.

Angela shook her head and closed her eyes. "This is ridiculous. Can't you just alter the dates?"

"Then we would be committing fraud," Maggie said as she brushed some lint from her jacket sleeve.

Angela shifted her attention to Maggie and saw the play for what it was: a desperate attempt to control her. "This is ludicrous, Maggie. I've been here for years and it's never been an issue before."

Maggie spread her hands and then clasped them, as if the entire situation were out of her control. "I don't know what to tell you, Angela. You've not been the primary defendant in a malpractice case before, so the issue never came up. It was Mr. Sinclair's attorney who noticed the error. He's making a big stink about this, not us. We have no choice but to go along."

"That's not true, Maggie. You could step up and defend me. This is a choice you're making."

"Angela, the hospital is larger than any one of its employees. I must consider the hospital's well-being first."

Angela's head dropped. Maggie was planning on hanging her out to dry. "So you're telling me that the hospital's lawyers won't be representing me in the Sinclair case?"

Maggie leaned forward, her eyes full of concern. "Darlene is working hard to get your malpractice insurance in place, but it will take a while. Given the current lawsuit against you, your premium is going to be very high. But to answer your question directly, past infractions on your part cannot covered by the hospital."

Angela looked at each of them in turn. She leaned back in her chair, an incredulous look on her face. "You realize that if Mr. Sinclair wins his lawsuit against me, I could lose everything."

Maggie shook her head. "Don't be so negative. It's not going to come to that. But Bud pointed out to me that you can no longer practice until you have coverage. I'm sure you understand."

Angela looked at Bud, whose eyes wore an expression of apprehension mixed with melancholy. He clearly did not relish his role in the debacle unfolding before him. Bringing a hand to his mouth, Angela noted his chewed nails as he nodded in agreement with Maggie's statement and mumbled, "It's true. Sorry."

Angela looked around Maggie's large, graciously appointed office and shook her head. She had thought that she'd lost everything when her family was destroyed, but she now realized that she still had a strong career ahead of her if she wanted it. And now Maggie was threatening to take that away too. Not just her career, but her good name and reputation. *Why?*

Angela leaned forward and looked into Maggie's eyes. "I do understand, Maggie. For some reason I cannot fathom, you're holding my career hostage."

"I'm doing nothing of the kind, Angela. You're the one who made the mistake on your application. I think you're being a little paranoid."

Angela laughed. "Am I supposed to believe that you're *helping* me?"

"Angela, since your husband and children passed, all of your family at the hospital have done everything in our power to support you."

Angela stood and meticulously replaced her chair at the table. Leaning on the back of the chair, she said, "This isn't a family, Maggie. A family is a cohesive unit that works together for the betterment of each member. Since I've started asking questions about Emily's death, I've run into roadblock after roadblock, which makes me think that there's more to her overdose than you're willing to share."

"I'm sorry you feel that way."

"The good news is that because I can no longer see patients, I'll have lots of time on my hands to investigate."

Maggie smiled and placed her palms on the glass tabletop. "I wouldn't do that, Angela."

"Why not? Are you going to fire me? Do it. Oh, that's right. You can't because I haven't done anything wrong. But that probably won't stop you, will it? It didn't stop you from firing Lauren."

Maggie removed her hands and placed them in her lap. Angela noticed that there were condensation marks on the glass where her palms had been. *She's nervous.* A sense of warped satisfaction emerged as a small smile on Angela's lips.

"Angela, you need to see someone. You're starting to lose it."

Angela backed toward the door. "No need, Maggie. I've already lost it, according to the column in the *Times*. Thank you for your time."

Angela felt almost giddy as she walked quickly to the Cardiac Surgery department. But by the time she reached her office, she was exhausted, so she closed the door and placed her head on her desk. After a moment she heard a soft knock, followed by the door opening and closing quietly. Liz cleared her throat.

Her head still on the desk, Angela muttered, "What do you want, Liz?"

"I want to know what happened."

Angela lifted her head and rubbed her eyes. "I'm not exactly sure why, but Maggie's nervous and wants to shut me up. She denies being Jesse's source, and apparently I don't have malpractice insurance, so I can't see patients."

"What do you mean you don't have malpractice insurance?"

Angela waved her hand. "It was an error in my application and Maggie is choosing to be a coward."

"What about the current lawsuit against you? Is the hospital going to cover the attorneys' costs?"

"Not if I don't have insurance."

"What are you going to do?"

Angela's eyes fell to her desk. The check from Sean was lying on the top of her to-do pile, waiting to be deposited. She couldn't imagine that Tony would want her to use the money this way, but what choice did she have? Picking up the check, she said, "Divine providence, I guess. I have five hundred thousand dollars at my disposal. It's a start."

CHAPTER 28

Angela watched a white heron, jealous of its patience as it awaited an opportunity to strike. Occasionally it flicked its head to gain a new vantage point on the pond water, luring the hapless fish into a false sense of safety, but for the most part it remained completely still. *Dead fish swimming*, Angela thought. After an eternity, the bird's head sliced into the water and snatched a wriggling fish. The heron turned to Angela, seemingly surprised to find her so close, and then began its awkward ascent toward the sky.

Angela watched the bird fly until it was out of sight, then turned to the three headstones. "It's beautiful, isn't it? I wonder if you see birds like that where you are."

Tony's headstone had arrived first, solid and pristine granite engraved with his name and pertinent dates. The children's markers had arrived just recently, as Angela had insisted that their pictures be inlaid into the stone. She traced her finger along the lines of Liam's hair. "Are you chasing your sister up there?" she asked, smiling. "I bet she's kicking your butt." Joy sprouted at the thought, only to be quickly replaced by the weeds of melancholic apathy that had taken root in her soul.

It had been two weeks since Angela's insurance had lapsed,

and she was finding it challenging to stay busy. She had cleaned the house, then organized it, and had started running each evening in an effort to find relief from the thoughts that swirled upon awakening each day. Liz had told her that Bernard had been appointed interim Cardiac Surgery chief, and that although he had accepted the role with gusto, recently his energy seemed to be flagging. Liz attributed his dispassion to taking on more than he could handle and said that she thought Bernard now realized what a tremendous job Angela had done as chair, although he'd yet to say it aloud.

Angela had hit an impasse regarding the cause of Emily's death. Frustration had led to despair as her one remaining reason for living dwindled to nothing. She was becoming despondent and had considered contacting Frank to have another end-of-life discussion. Liz and her parents, ever vigilant, had urged Angela to focus her energy on trying to see patients again. To that end, she had checked in every day with Darlene Rancon and had been told that her insurance had not yet been approved. No surprise there. Angela wondered how long she'd be kept in purgatory, unable to see patients, yet still on the hospital payroll. Finally, there was Mr. Sinclair's lawsuit, currently scheduled for November, looming heavily like a bloody morning sunrise that portended a powerful afternoon storm.

Angela returned her attention to Tony's headstone and brushed some dirt from its base. "I hope you're okay with my selling your half of the firm, Tony. Sean feels good about its future now that he's hired a new partner. I hope you don't mind, but I know you wanted the business to grow. I think you would've wanted me to do that." She glanced upwards. "But really, who knows what you would have wanted? I'm just doing the best I can down here." A tear trickled down her cheek and she placed her forehead against the cool stone. "I'm so alone here, Tony. I'm an island surrounded by a sea of good-meaning people who can't possibly understand."

Sudden movement out of the corner of her eye drew her attention. A coyote as large as a Labrador retriever stood no more than fifteen feet away. Its dark-brown fur was splotchy and its ears were fully erect as it evaluated her. The animal remained perfectly motionless as its bright, yellow eyes locked on hers. She felt the hairs on her arms rise in response. She had read in the paper that the coyote population was on the rise in Barrington but had not yet seen one herself. Her mother's warnings of rabies flew to her mind, and she briefly wondered whether it was normal for a coyote to be traveling alone in broad daylight. She didn't think that it would attack, but she stood slowly and picked up a nearby stick just in case. The coyote broke eye contact and lay down, resting its head on its crossed paws. It was clearly not threatened by her proximity.

"Is this your territory?" she asked. The animal raised its head, blinked once, and then resumed its relaxed position. "Are you here to hunt?"

Without taking her eyes from the coyote, Angela slowly sat down with her back against Tony's headstone. "Aren't you supposed to be with your pack? What happened? Where'd they go?"

The coyote tilted its head. Its large ears twitched.

"I know how you feel. All alone. Me too."

As she observed the wild animal, Angela felt a bizarre calm settle over her. They sat in silent camaraderie, listening to the birds chatter.

Suddenly the coyote's nose bolted up and sniffed the air. Its eyes widened and its hackles stood on end. "What is it?" Angela asked as she stood and searched the area. The animal jumped to its feet and darted away, much faster than Angela could have imagined. She shuddered as a sudden breeze crossed over her.

"Angela."

She whipped her head around and was shocked to see Frank Toner standing behind her. "Oh my goodness, Frank. You scared me! What are you doing here?"

"I thought I'd find you here. I stopped by your house, but you weren't there. And I know you're not at the hospital these days, so it was either here or the beach."

"You're looking better than the last time I saw you, Frank."

"You think so?" He approached her. "I'm going to be leaving soon, Angela."

She stared, unwilling or unable to comprehend his words.

He smiled patiently. "It's okay, Angela. It's time."

Refusing to accept his unspoken meaning, she babbled. "I'm sorry I haven't come to visit you, but I don't know what to do these days. The promise I made to Emily to discover why she died has gone nowhere. I keep hitting dead ends and don't know how to proceed. I'm just . . . lost."

"That's why I'm here."

"I thought you came to say goodbye."

"That too." He smiled. "I contacted Lauren Kirk last night."

"What? How do you know Lauren?"

"I got in touch with her because I think you two need to put your heads together. You should call her."

"And say what, Frank? I can't advocate for her with Maggie anymore. Shit, I can't even advocate for myself."

He nodded. "I understand. But take some advice from an old man. Call her."

"Okay. When I return to the house, I will."

"You know that I love you like a daughter."

Of course she had known that he cared for her, but he had never spoken of it. "I do know that."

"You're an incredible surgeon, Angela. Your compassion and empathy have grown since you lost your family. You now truly understand the value of human life."

Tears fell as Angela absorbed his words. "Thank you, Frank. But it was a big price to pay."

"You have more to learn, my dear. And that's why you need to call Lauren."

Angela wiped her cheeks. "I don't understand."

"I need to leave now. I won't see you again."

She stared at him. The finality of his statement was unacceptable. "You and I made a pact, remember? You're not going to—"

He waved his hand in the air, disrupting the dust particles that floated in the sunlight. "No. Nothing like that. It's just my time."

She wanted to disagree with him, to cry out and beg him to fight a little longer, not to give up. But something in his eyes commanded obedience as he regarded her with a serene gaze, his composure a more powerful statement than any words.

She nodded once. “I understand.”

She approached to hug him, then remembered the last time she'd accidentally hurt him. She felt him brush a kiss across the top of her head. “Everything is going to be alright. You're going to be okay.”

She smiled sadly. “You say that like you know it to be true.”

“That's because I do.”

He withdrew and slowly made his way back over the hill to the parking lot. Angela watched him walk away and promised herself that she would call him tomorrow. She didn't want him to spend his last days feeling alone. When he'd crested the hill, she returned her attention to the grave markers.

“I'm leaving now, you guys. But I'll be back soon. Maybe tomorrow.” She kissed her hand and placed it atop each stone. “You're always in my heart and mind. I love you so much. Take care of each other.”

She turned to walk away and noted the coyote standing at the edge of the woods. A beautiful white rabbit was draped in its jaws. The lifeless rabbit was dripping blood, and Angela was grateful that it wasn't still alive. Hopefully it hadn't suffered much.

“Late lunch?”

The coyote darted away, its prize swinging jauntily from its maw.

Angela was thoughtful as she drove home, reminiscing about her tutelage under Frank and how quickly her perfect life had turned upside down. She considered the daughter Frank had tragically lost and how he'd just told her how much he loved her. Then her mind turned toward the interesting behavior of the coyote and she wondered if, indeed, the animal was sick and she'd been fortunate in not having been attacked. She pulled into the garage and entered the kitchen to find both of her parents seated at the table, their expressions sullen. Her apprehension grew as she looked from one to the other.

"What is it? What's wrong?"

Her father stood and embraced her. "Oh, angel." She pulled away from her father and stared at him. "Dad, it can't possibly be any worse than what I've already gone through, so just say it."

He took a deep breath and his eyes creased at the corners. "It's Frank Toner, Angela. We just got a call from the hospice people. He died earlier today."

CHAPTER 29

~

Angela shook her head in disbelief. “It’s impossible that Frank Toner is dead.”

Sally glanced at Jim with a concerned expression. “You see, Jim? I knew we shouldn’t have told her this way.”

“How else should we have told her, Sally?”

“I don’t know, but now she’s upset.”

Her father rolled his eyes. “She was going to be upset however we told her.”

Angela listened to their verbal volley but couldn’t make sense of their words as she replayed the conversation with Frank in her mind.

Shaking her head, she said, “You’re wrong. There’s no way he died earlier today. I just saw him in the cemetery.”

Her parents ceased their bickering. “What do you mean?”

“Right now. I just came from the cemetery and he was there talking to me.” Another worried glance flitted between her parents. “I’m serious. I saw him. I spoke to him. He gave me a kiss, for God’s sake!”

“What did he say?” her father asked as her mother turned away, her hand over her mouth.

Angela looked down, thinking. “He wanted me to call Lauren

Kirk. I'm not sure why, but he was adamant about it. He told me that I had grown as a surgeon since Tony and the kids died. And he told me—" She stopped talking and held her breath as she looked at her dad. "He told me that he wouldn't see me again because he was going to die."

Her father rubbed his face with his hands. "Jesus."

Angela's face crumpled. "What's happening to me, Dad?"

He stood and drew her close. "Nothing, angel. You're just processing your losses. It takes a long time."

"I saw him. I *felt* him, Dad. He was *there*!"

"I believe you."

Angela addressed her mother. "Mom, do you believe me?"

Sally turned, her face impassive. "You're asking me if I believe that you saw Frank in the cemetery even though he died earlier today? No. I don't think you saw him."

"So you think I'm lying?"

Her mother shook her head. "No, honey. I think your brain is trying to reconcile incredible tragedies and is finding ways to deal with them."

"You think I'm crazy."

"I didn't say that."

Angela glared at her mother. "You didn't have to."

Sally had given voice to a fear Angela had been silently harboring. *Maybe the* Times *column was correct. Maybe I* am *going insane. Is this what it feels like?* Terrified, Angela bolted upstairs, collapsed on the bed, and sobbed herself into exhaustion.

Through the haze of half-sleep, she heard a cell phone ring followed by her father's baritone voice. "Um, I'm not sure. I'll check." She listened as he climbed the stairs and opened her door.

"Angela? Honey? There's someone on the phone for you."

She shook her head without opening her eyes. "I don't want to talk to anyone right now."

Her father paused. "She kind of insisted on speaking to you. And I think you'll want to speak to her."

Lifting her mascara-stained, blotchy face, she glowered at her father. "What's so damn important that it can't wait? My entire life has been on hold for the last few weeks, and now something is critical? Who is it?" she growled.

"I think it's the nurse who was fired from the hospital. What was her name? Lauren?"

Frank's words flew through her mind. Angela extended her arm toward her father and wiggled her fingers. "Quick, Dad, give me the phone."

He handed it to her and left.

"Lauren?"

"Yeah. Hi, Dr. Brennan."

"How are you?"

"I'm okay. Closing in on another job. It's in Warwick, so it's kind of a schlep from my house, but that's okay."

Angela realized that she'd been carrying some guilt related to Lauren's dismissal and was relieved to hear she'd found employment. "I was going to call you."

"Were you?"

"Yes. A friend thought that you and I should talk, although I'm honestly not sure why."

"That's odd. Well, I'm calling because I had a really strange dream last night, and when I woke up, I felt compelled to contact you."

"What kind of dream?"

"I was sailing on Narragansett Bay and it started snowing."

Angela waited impatiently for additional information. When none came, she prompted, "And then what?"

"Nothing. That's it."

"And when you awakened you felt the need to tell me that?"

"Uh-huh."

Annoyance swelled quickly and she fought the urge to slam the phone down. Anger would do no good. "What am I supposed to do with that information?"

"I have no idea."

Angela pinched the bridge of her nose and sighed. "Okay."

"The snow was weird, though."

"Weird how?"

"It was heavier than regular snow. Almost like sleet. Little crystals. And it wasn't cold."

Angela closed her eyes and pictured the scene. "Were you sailing alone?"

"Yes, and when the snow hit the water it sank, but I could still see it."

Intrigued, Angela opened her eyes. "You mean like when you pour powdered drink mix into water and then stir it up?"

"Yeah. In fact, now that I think of it, I draped my hand in the water and stirred it, like you just said."

"And what happened?"

"It disappeared as it blended with the bay water, but it took a lot of effort."

Angela glanced at the oak tree and pictured little white crystals that didn't mix easily into a liquid. "Was the snow more like sugar . . . or salt? They both take a while to mix."

Lauren was silent.

"Lauren, you still there?"

"Oh . . . oh," she stammered.

"What is it?"

"Sailing. Salt."

"Yes. What about them?"

"Sailing sounds like saline, which is made with sodium chloride."

"Salt, yes. So what?"

"Emily's death."

Angela massaged her scalp to calm a throbbing pain that had taken root. "Lauren, I really can't do this—"

"The saline solution, Dr. Brennan. Maybe the Narcan injection did work but there was something wrong with Emily's saline IV. Maybe Emily didn't die from a drug overdose. Maybe she died because of the saline."

Angela winced with irritation and fatigue. Lauren was grasping at straws. "Lauren, as you well know, saline solution is simply sodium chloride mixed with water—it's used to keep people hydrated."

"I know, but what if there was something wrong with the saline we used? As I've been going over and over Emily's death in my head, it's literally the only thing I hadn't considered."

A branch scraped the window, drawing Angela's attention to the oak tree. The commitment she'd made to Emily ran like a ticker tape through her mind. She had an obligation to check out every lead, every possibility, no matter how unlikely it seemed to her rational mind. "Okay. You're not allowed back in the hospital, so I'll go and check it out. I'll call you if I learn anything."

Lauren sucked in a breath. "I feel better."

"I'm glad. I don't."

"I'm sorry to dredge this up again for you, Dr. Brennan."

Angela sighed. "It's not your fault. Actually, your phone call is kicking me back into gear. The cause of Emily's death has been like an anchor weighing me down. If we can get to the bottom of it, I think I'll feel better. And even if I don't, at least I'll know the truth."

"That's true."

"Hey, I heard that you spoke with Frank Toner last night."

"Who's that?"

"My friend who told me to call you. He said that he talked to you."

"I haven't spoken to anyone by that name."

Angela felt a rush of adrenaline climb her back and nestle into the base of her skull as Frank's exact words flooded her brain. He hadn't told her that he'd spoken with Lauren last night. He'd said that he'd *contacted* her. Like a fog being burned away by a rising sun, she felt light-headed as the potential reality became clear. She shook her head to clear it of the possibility that a dead man had somehow communicated with Lauren. *But what other explanation was there?* She laughed as she accepted the unlikely truth.

"Dr. Brennan. Are you okay?" Lauren's voice sounded far away as Angela continued to put the pieces together.

Lauren's dream. Sailing in snow. The clue was a final gift

bestowed on his favorite resident, a surrogate for the daughter he never had the opportunity to see grow into adulthood.

Thank you, Frank, Angela thought.

"Yes. I'm fine. As for my friend, I must have misheard him. My mistake. I'll talk to you soon."

CHAPTER 30

~

The next morning Angela awoke with an unsettling sense of peace. Her emotional existence had been unpredictable for so long that she had forgotten what it felt like to be anything but sad and angry. She wondered whether this was her new normal or whether it was yet another track on an endless roller-coaster. She found herself thinking about happy moments with her family as she showered and dressed, and by the time she descended the stairs and entered the kitchen, she was feeling hopeful.

"Are you sure you're okay to drive?" Sally asked.

Angela hugged her mother. "Mom, please stop worrying. I'm fine. I slept really well last night, and for the first time in several weeks I have some focus. I'm going to the hospital to talk to some folks. That's all, okay?"

Her mother pursed her lips and lowered her eyebrows. "Okay. But for the record, I don't like it. After yesterday . . . " Her mother's words faltered.

Angela smiled and kissed Sally's cheek. "I love you, Mom."

"Hey, what about me?" her father asked as he entered the kitchen. "Where's my kiss?"

Angela rolled her eyes. "Enough. You both need to go back to Florida. Those tennis balls aren't going to hit themselves, Dad.

And Mom, who's running the neighborhood association while you've been gone?"

"Good points," her mother said as she glanced at her husband. "We're not leaving until we feel you're truly back on your feet, angel. No discussion."

Angela looked from one parent to another and sighed. "Well then, I guess I need to get back on my feet."

"That's my girl."

"I'll be back later."

Angela drove slowly and inadvertently ended up in front of the Barrington Middle School. She pulled into the parking lot and cut the engine, thinking how excited Emily would have been to be an eighth grader. Oldest kids in school. And Liam would have been entering the middle school in the fall. For the first time in years, her two kids would have been in the same building, and back-to-school-night would have been a breeze. She and Tony would have divided and conquered, he going to Liam's classes and she going to Emily's to understand what their kids would be learning for the year. She used to dread those evenings after a long day in surgery. She now realized that she'd give anything to get five minutes in one of those classrooms, listening to a well-meaning teacher describe her children's curricula. Black anguish prodded at the edges of her mind, seeking an entrance, but the hope she'd gathered in the morning pushed it away and she restarted the car.

Arriving at the hospital, Angela maneuvered to her reserved parking spot, only to find that it was already inhabited. Not wanting to steal someone else's parking place, she drove to the general garage and spent ten minutes searching for an empty space. She felt annoyed, even more so when she realized that her cardiac patients had to negotiate the parking structure each time they came for an appointment. After parking, she gathered her purse and walked to the hospital's front entrance.

She entered the hospital through the lobby doors, where she spotted Esther sitting primly at the front desk.

"Hello, doctor. So good to see you. Did you talk to the nice young woman who left the note?"

"I did. Thanks."

"Did it help?"

"The jury's still out on that one, Esther." Angela pressed the elevator button.

"Have you heard the good news?"

"Good news?"

"About the new CEO?"

Angela turned fully so she was facing Esther. "New CEO? No, I haven't heard. What's the good news?"

"It's just wonderful! Dr. Jacobs has been named Maggie Donnelly's successor. The Board voted unanimously last night."

Angela was convinced she had misheard Esther. "I'm sorry. What did you say?"

"I know. It's simply great! He's a really good doctor and such a nice man. Don't you agree?" The older woman clapped her hands together.

The elevator arrived, and Angela entered before her vicious thoughts could find voice. At the end of their last meeting, Maggie had intimated that Angela might not be named her successor. And given the current state of Angela's life—her family tragedy, the lawsuit, her malpractice insurance fiasco—she didn't really expect that she was still in contention. But *Stan Jacobs*? He was less qualified than Angela, and he was a jerk to boot.

As the elevator arrived on the fifth floor and the doors opened, Liz rushed forward to hug her best friend.

"Soooo glad to see you!" she gushed. Angela couldn't help but laugh as she disentangled herself from Liz's embrace. "Why on earth are you so good to me, Liz?"

"Hey, you've been there for me many a time, my friend. I'm like an elephant. I don't forget."

Angela smiled and squeezed Liz's hand, then glanced at the elevator door. "How in the world did you know I was going to be on the elevator? Or do you just wait here and hug everyone who exits?"

"Esther texted me."

Angela raised her eyebrows and shook her head. "She has your cell number? Why? Never mind. That old lady gets around. Talk about efficient. Wow."

Liz linked her arm through Angela's. "Anyhow, why are you here?"

Angela updated Liz on her visit with Frank in the cemetery and Lauren's dream. Liz's eyes grew as the story unfolded. When Angela finished, Liz said, "Frank is looking out for you just like he did when he was alive. You always said he was like a father figure."

Angela nodded. "Yeah. In fact, he told me that he had a daughter who passed away years ago. So, I think in his mind, I've replaced her."

Liz stared into space and slowly nodded. "Holy shit. I told you that you were being invited into the fold, but this is on a whole different level. That's the second time that you've seen a ghost, Angela."

"You don't need to remind me, Liz. And why are you looking at me that way? You're the one who believes in all of this crap."

Liz shook her head. "It's amazing, that's all. I wish I could see ghosts."

Angela turned on her. "No. You don't. It's terrifying. Really messes with your head."

"Only after the fact, though."

"What?"

"Think about it. When you were talking to Reggie in the waiting room and Frank in the cemetery, everything seemed perfectly normal and rational, right? Two people having a conversation."

Angela grimaced and bobbed her head from side to side. "I guess."

"It's only afterwards, when you realize that you were speaking to a ghost, that things get wonky."

Angela stopped walking. "Wonky?"

"It's only weird because you're trying to put your experience into an earthly box. Maybe if you open your mind to allow conversations with ghosts to be normal, then it won't mess with your head." She smiled, clearly proud of herself for having made such a fine point.

"It's all so simple to you, isn't it, Liz? Because it's not happening to you." Angela started walking again and Liz fell in step beside her. "But I think I understand what you're saying. Maybe you're right. Maybe it's my new normal. Weird, but normal."

"Exactly." Liz bumped against Angela, prompting her to smile.

"It doesn't mean that it's not scary though."

"I know."

"I suppose you've heard that Stan is to be Maggie's replacement?"

"Of course. Maggie disseminated a hospital-wide email this morning."

Angela looked around and noted people congregating, chatting in an excited air. "People seem to be happy about it."

Liz shrugged. "It gives them something to talk about."

"And you?"

Liz stopped and regarded her friend. "You would've been a rock star, Angela. But I think your opportunity has passed. At this hospital, at least."

Angela thought a moment, deciding how she felt about it. As she considered, she realized that although she wasn't happy about the current situation, she wasn't disappointed that she wasn't going to be CEO. "Yeah, you're probably right. Hey, someone's car was in my parking spot."

Liz sneered and stuck out her tongue. "Bernard."

"Are you kidding me?"

"I am not."

Angela looked at the floor and marshaled her patience. "Okay. Listen, I have to go. I'll talk to you later."

"Maybe we can have drinks this week?"

"Sounds good."

Angela made her way to the Pediatric ICU and found Barbara Royes at the nurse's station.

"Angela, so good to see you."

"Hi, Barb. Can you show me where the supply closet is?"

Barb looked confused. "Sure. Why?"

"I just want to look at your saline."

"Why?"

Angela smiled patiently. "Barb, can you please show me to the closet?"

Barb paused, but then walked quickly to the supply closet with Angela in tow. She entered the access code on the security panel and opened the heavy door. An automatic light illuminated the small space as they entered.

"What are you looking for, Angela?"

Angela's eyes took in the well-organized room. "Who's responsible for stocking?"

"Me."

"The day my daughter died, would the saline have been stocked where it is now—on the upper right side, top two shelves?"

"Yes. I haven't altered the layout in years. People want to be able to get supplies quickly. If I change where items are, they might grab the wrong one."

"I don't suppose that this is the same saline that was stocked when Emily died?"

"My goodness, no. We go through at least thirty-five bags of saline per day. In general, I keep only three hundred bags here."

"So you restock once per week?"

"Approximately. What's going on? Why so many questions?"

"Can I trust you, Barb?"

The nurse manager crossed her arms over her chest. "You know you can."

"We think that Emily might have died because of the saline that was administered through her IV."

"Who's 'we'?"

"Lauren Kirk and me."

"Lauren? You've been talking to Lauren?"

Angela nodded. "Both she and I think that Stan is hiding something. We think that maybe the Narcan injection did work and that Emily died of something other than the overdose. The only item we haven't considered is the saline."

"Or another underlying condition."

Angela stopped short. She had used the same logic regarding her own role in Ava Sinclair's death, and had most likely been correct. So maybe Barb was right. Perhaps Emily did have an underlying condition of which she was unaware. Maybe the saline angle was a wild goose chase that she and Lauren had concocted out of frustration or desperation, or both.

"You might be right, Barb. But I have to consider all possibilities."

"I understand. As a parent, I think I'd do the same thing." She glanced at the bags on the shelves. "If you want to know about the saline we had in stock the day Emily died, you need to talk to the IT people. They'll be able to retrieve records going back that far. I'd look for you, but I can only access information within the last six weeks."

"Thanks, Barb. Oh, and you and I never had this conversation. Okay?"

Angela noted Barb's disbelieving look. "Really, Angela? It's that cloak and dagger?"

"Really, Barb."

Angela watched Barb's face go from doubtful to confused to determined. "Then you have my word that I won't speak of this to anyone, ever."

CHAPTER 31

Angela's only interactions with the Information Technology department had been in interdepartmental meetings and short phone calls that started with phrases like, "This is Dr. Brennan in Cardiac Surgery and I need help." She entered the IT suite where a waif with spiked purple hair leaned against the front desk while munching on a granola bar. Her translucent skin boasted several tattoos, and Angela was reminded of an inked Tinkerbell. Angela smiled as she read her T-shirt: I'M ONLY HERE BECAUSE YOU BROKE SOMETHING. The young woman caught her staring and said, "It's true, you know. We only get called when all hell's broken loose and people panic."

"You're not wrong," Angela conceded. "Guilty as charged. I'm one of those people."

Purple hair squinted and examined Angela with a sideways glance. "Funny, though, you don't look like one of them."

"Really? What do 'they' look like?"

"Well, let's see. They normally have white coats and often have a stick up their—"

"Sonny! I see you're chatting with Dr. Brennan. How about I take over?" interrupted a middle-aged, balding man sporting a brown, rumpled suit.

"Sure thing, boss man," Sonny mumbled as she sauntered away.

"Sorry about that, Dr. Brennan. Some IT people can be . . . challenging."

"No need to apologize, Nick. A lot of doctors can be that way too. How long have you been IT Director?"

"Five years. It's been a blessing and a curse, if you know what I mean."

She smiled. "I know exactly what you mean."

"Listen, Dr. Brennan, I just want to say how sorry I am for your loss. I can't imagine what you've been through."

Angela appreciated his kindness. "Thank you. Please call me Angela."

"What can I do for you? Are you having some issues in Cardiac Surgery?"

You could say that, she thought. *Major issues.*

"Not IT issues, but I do have some questions for you, if you don't mind."

"Sure, sure. Let's go to my office." She followed him down a long, tiled corridor, past a large room whose walls were lined with black, wire shelving. Electronic, blinking boxes of various sizes were arranged from floor to ceiling. "What's in that room?"

"That's where we keep the servers. Every piece of electronic information related to the hospital is kept on those machines."

They walked past large, open spaces where young people sat hunched over computers, typing madly. Angela's smile caught his eye. "What's so funny?"

"What are they doing?"

"Coding. Maggie wants us to create our own proprietary medical record software. In my opinion it's silly because there are so many good out-of-the-box alternatives available. But she insists."

"This might sound strange to you, but watching those young people type reminds me of Schroeder at his piano in the *Peanuts* cartoon strip."

Nick followed her gaze and chuckled. "I can see that." He brushed his hands over his wrinkled suitcoat. "I guess that would make me Pig-Pen. Here we are. My glorious office." He cleared some thick coding manuals from a chair and plopped them on the floor. "Please sit down. How can I help?"

Angela sat and crossed her legs as he sank into his desk chair. Once seated, his large brown eyes found hers and in them she saw genuine concern. She liked the way they crinkled slightly at the corners. It made him look perpetually happy. "Nick, long story short, I'm hoping you can help me take a digital look at the stock of saline solution in the Pediatric ICU supply closet the day my daughter died."

"Did you talk to Barb Royes?"

"Yes, but she said that she can access information only as far back as six weeks, and Emily died the morning after Memorial Day."

"Ah. Good point. Okay." He turned to his keyboard and typed so quickly that Angela lost sight of his fingers. After scrolling through several screens, he asked, "What was the date that your daughter died?"

"May twenty-ninth."

"Ah. Here it is." He squinted at the screen. "May twenty-ninth was a Tuesday, and restocking occurs each Monday in the Pediatric ICU. So the saline used on your daughter would have been the batch that was logged into the system and delivered the day before she died."

"Okay. Can you see on your screen what type of saline it was?"

"I can tell you that it was from the same manufacturer that we always use, Laird Pharmaceuticals. The rest of the information is numerical, though, so I'm not sure if it's the same saline that the Pediatric ICU normally orders. I'd have to compare this batch against others they've ordered in the past. Do you want me to do that?"

Angela's pulse quickened. "Yes, please."

"Sure thing." His fingers took on a life of their own once more. "Alright. Here's a list of all saline solution ordered and delivered to the Pediatric ICU in the last six months. You can look at the list yourself and see if anything stands out."

The overhead lights flickered, and Nick's screen went black. "What the hell?" He pressed the enter key and nothing happened.

"What's going on?"

"Probably a momentary power outage, but don't worry. The back-up generator will kick in. Oh, here it comes."

His screen lit up. "Let me just pull up that information again." He reentered the parameters to create the same report. "Huh, that's weird."

"What?"

"I'm not sure, but it seems like the information I requested before is gone."

Paranoia prickled Angela's scalp as she considered the ramifications of what he'd said. She wondered, just for a moment, if the power outage had been deliberate. She shook her head, realizing how crazy her thoughts had become. "That can't be the case."

Nick stared at the screen. "It's telling me that the data I requested before is no longer in the system. Let me try requesting a different report."

His fingers tapped the keys quickly and loudly. After another minute, he leaned back and ran his hands over his face. "It's like the saline orders just disappeared."

Refusing to accept his explanation, Angela asked, "Has this happened to you before?"

He shook his head. "Never. All of the other information related to the Pediatric ICU is here, but the saline is gone. I don't understand." He glared at his screen as if it were a cheating lover.

"Can you ask someone for help?"

He dropped his head to the side and smiled. "I *am* the help people call, Angela."

Fear nibbled at the edges of her brain as she looked from the computer to Nick. "So what do we do?"

He threw up his hands. "I'll keep trying, but it seems like the information has been deleted."

"How can that happen?"

Nick stared into space as he thought. After a moment, he waggled his finger in her direction. "There was only one time since I've worked here that I've been asked to destroy information, and it had to do with a billing issue that had been resolved."

"If the issue was resolved, then why was the data deleted?"

"I don't know. I was new and eager to please, so I didn't ask too many questions. If the same situation arose today, I'd treat it very differently."

Angela worked her mouth as she thought. "There has to be a way to get the saline information. I thought I read somewhere that data is never truly deleted."

"That applies to your home computer. For example, if you drag a file into your digital trash bin on your desktop, you believe that it's gone, but in reality it's still retrievable."

"And the same rules don't apply here?"

"Absolutely not. Like I said, Maggie has insisted that our IT systems are home grown, proprietary. I'm where the proverbial buck stops."

"Could someone in your department have deleted the information?"

"I hate to say it, but yes."

Angela eyed Nick, wondering if Maggie had somehow gotten to him. "How is it that you're not aware that one of your employees has deleted pertinent information?"

He raised his eyebrows at her. "Angela, if you're thinking that I had something to do with the information deletion I can assure you that I did not. Besides, are you aware of every single movement in Cardiac Surgery?"

His countenance remained open and kind, so either he was a really good liar or he was telling the truth. Angela thought back to Bernard and how she'd had no idea that he'd been working Maggie behind-the-scenes in an effort to take her job. A lump of humility sat like a stone in her stomach.

"Touché."

"Bottom line is that I'm not sure I can get the information you've requested."

Angela nodded and looked at her hands as she considered her options. "I want to ensure that I understand, Nick. Is it possible that the saline-related information was deleted by accident because of the momentary power loss?"

"If other information had been lost, then I might say yes. But it seems as if only the information related to your request was deleted, at least as far as I can see right now. So, no. I don't believe that the power loss caused the disappearance of your data."

Angela set her mouth and steeled herself for the anticipated answer to her next question. "So someone, somewhere, deleted the saline data at the same time that I happened to be requesting it?"

"It certainly seems that way."

Angela's tone was even as her stomach rolled. "Do you know anyone on your staff that would be capable of doing that?"

Nick's gaze went past Angela, into the hallway. "Angela, you need to understand that many of the IT people who work here are hackers in their spare time. They live, eat, and breathe code. If someone were presented with a challenge to remove sensitive information without being caught, they might take it."

"Even though it's illegal?"

"Especially if it's illegal." Nick chuckled. "So the real question isn't who might have done this in my department, but rather who *wouldn't* have done this, especially if they felt they wouldn't be caught."

Angela closed her eyes. Another dead-end. *But you're on the right track*, a voice in her head said. *Otherwise they wouldn't have deleted the data.*

Opening her eyes, she stood and shook his hand. "Nick, you've been incredibly helpful."

"I'm really sorry, Angela."

"It's okay. One last question. When you were new here, who directed you to delete that resolved billing issue information?"

"Maggie."

Angela nodded as a vice tightened around her skull. "That's what I thought. Thanks again, Nick."

CHAPTER 32

With a sense of grim determination, Angela left the IT department and walked straight to Maggie's office. She wasn't exactly sure what she was going to say, but she wanted to see Maggie's face when she asked her about the data disappearance. As she approached Maggie's assistant, the woman stiffened and picked up her phone.

"If you're planning on telling Maggie that I'm here to see her, don't bother. I'll take care of that myself." Angela opened Maggie's door to find the CEO staring out the window, her hands clasped behind her back. She didn't turn around as Angela cleared her throat.

"Hello, Angela. Please sit down."

A river of defiance ran through Angela's veins. "I'll stand, thank you. I understand that Stan Jacobs has been named as your successor."

"That's correct. I genuinely wish it had been you."

Angela closed the door behind her and stepped to the front of Maggie's desk. "Really? Because I don't. Now that I understand what kind of ship you're running here, I'm not sure I want to be a part of it."

Maggie turned. "Are you offering me your resignation?"

Her question threw Angela. "What? No."

Maggie walked around her desk and stood directly in front of Angela. Staring into Angela's eyes, she offered a half smile and asked, "What, exactly, kind of *ship* do you think I'm running?"

Her sudden closeness rattled Angela's confidence, but she rallied and lifted her chin. "One that breaks hospital rules, all ethical standards, and potentially some laws."

Maggie's eyes flared and her tone became clipped as she abruptly turned away and crossed behind her desk chair. "I don't know what you're talking about, Angela. Sit down and be rational. You're speaking in riddles."

Angela balled her hands into fists in an effort to cease their trembling. "I thought I was losing my mind, Maggie, but I'm not. My daughter didn't die from an overdose ordered by Stan. She would have if Liz hadn't injected her with the Narcan, but Liz got to her in time. Emily died of something else, and I think you know the cause. Furthermore, I believe that you're covering it up."

Maggie's eyes narrowed as she leaned on the back of her leather chair, her face a mask of worry. "Angela, I think the column in the *Times* was accurate. I think it's time for you to call it quits. Have you seen someone? Because honestly, you sound crazy. You know that, right?"

Angela leaned forward too, incredulous. "I cannot believe that you are standing there claiming that I'm the one who's crazy, when you're covering up a major hospital mistake that claimed the life of my daughter!" Angela suddenly straightened as a horrible thought struck. She cocked her head like a bird. "Unless it wasn't a mistake. Did you kill my daughter on purpose?"

Maggie rolled her eyes theatrically. "Angela, my God! What are you talking about? Seriously, sit down and let's talk. We can start at the beginning, and you can tell me what you're so upset about." Maggie pulled out her chair and sat, then motioned for Angela to sit across from her.

Angela backed away as her wild eyes scanned the room. "Where are the Bobbsey Twins, Maggie? I thought they traveled with you everywhere."

"Angela, please—"

Angela shook her head. "No, Maggie. I know there's more to this. Did you erase the saline data?"

"I don't know what you're talking about. What saline data?"

"There was a power interruption today when I was talking with Nick Papadopolous in IT, and when the power returned, the information he'd gathered for me was gone. Disappeared."

"That's odd."

"I thought so too. And Nick said that he'd been asked to delete data in the past. That you, specifically, had asked him to make information disappear."

Maggie shook her head. "He's mistaken. I've never requested anything like that. My goodness, that would be illegal."

"I know. But he was new and eager to please you."

"Does he have proof of this supposed request?"

"I don't think so."

Maggie nodded and smiled, as if finally understanding the solution to a pesky problem. "Then it never happened."

Angela gaped openly at Maggie. She knew that there were people in the world whose decisions were mandated by what could be proven. Indeed, Tony had said that you could tell a lot about a person by the way they played golf. Did they move the ball when they thought someone wasn't looking? Did they take extra shots and not mark them on their scorecard? But Angela had never imagined that Maggie would be one of those people. "Is that the way it works, Maggie? If there's no proof, then it didn't happen?"

Maggie shrugged, seemingly unconcerned.

"It's like you don't have a conscience, Maggie. How do you sleep at night?"

"Like a baby. You?"

Angela felt something crack inside that revealed a terrifying hollowness. "I don't. Not anymore. Not for several months now."

"Lack of sleep might explain your current behavior, Angela."

"That was mean, Maggie." Angela's understatement lay like a wounded child between them. The two women stared hard at each other with unblinking eyes. The emptiness that had revealed itself continued to expand inside Angela until she thought it might reach outside of her and drag its unwilling host into the depths of nothingness.

Finally, Maggie clapped her hands. "Well, it's been lovely seeing you, Angela, but some of us have work to do. By the way, Darlene told me that your malpractice insurance is not going to be active for some time, so you may want to think about doing something else for a while."

Maggie's announcement forced Angela from her darkness. "Like what?"

"Take a trip, learn a new hobby—something, anything, to get your mind right again."

"My mind is just fine, Maggie."

"Are you sure, Angela? Because it certainly doesn't seem that way. Oh, also, before I forget, Dr. Smythe has been appointed as acting Cardiac Surgery chair. He's been doing a bang-up job, so if your insurance isn't in effect by the time the state does its annual inspection, I'll have no choice but to officially place him in that position."

Angela's anger flared once more. She was surprised that she had anything left. "You're going to fire me?"

"No, no. Of course not. You'd be placed on administrative leave pending your insurance issue. That's all."

Maggie made it sound like it wasn't a big deal. Without insurance, Angela couldn't practice at the hospital. And given her damaged reputation, Angela doubted whether she could find employment elsewhere either. And Maggie knew it.

Angela's anger quickly contorted into frustration, and she fought back tears. "I thought you had integrity, Maggie. I used to look up to you as someone I could emulate. And now I realize that you're bloodsucking and power hungry. I want you to understand that whatever you're gaining by hiding the truth isn't worth the death of a young girl." Angela's tears spilled as she continued. "My daughter died, Maggie. She *died*! She's not coming back. And I think that you know why, but you won't tell me."

Suddenly, a thought exploded in Angela's mind like a firecracker on July fourth. "Does Stan know too? Is that why he's going to become CEO? A reward for keeping your dirty little secret?" Maggie came around the desk as Angela continued. "Oh my God, Maggie, nothing can be worth the life of a child! Do you understand? No amount of money or power can be worth the guilt you should feel. Do you *hear* me?"

Tears streamed down Angela's face as Maggie approached, speaking soothingly. "I wasn't blessed with children, Angela, so I don't know how you feel. But you and I have been friends and colleagues for a long time, and I don't like to see you hurting." Before Angela could react, Maggie pulled her in and embraced her. Confused, she resisted at first, but then gave into exhaustion and let herself be comforted. After a moment, Angela felt the tension in both of their bodies release, and she wondered in confusion if she had misjudged Maggie. When they separated, Maggie had tears in her eyes. She took Angela's hands.

"Angela, I am truly sorry for the loss of your daughter. I would never do anything to purposely hurt you or anyone else. My obligation is to this hospital, its board, and its employees. I have to do what's right for the organization. You are correct when you said that Emily is gone and not coming back. So I need to move forward appropriately. I hope you understand."

Angela examined Maggie's eyes and recognized genuine sorrow. For a moment she opened her heart and allowed Maggie to witness the boundless grief that had taken up residence within her. But then Maggie blinked and there, silently lurking behind the sincerity, was a hardness, a determination, and Angela immediately intuited that her initial inclinations about Maggie were correct. She would get nowhere with this conversation.

Pulling her hands from Maggie's grasp, Angela said, "I completely understand, Maggie. Thank you for your time." She crossed to the door, and added, "By the way, I'm still chair of Cardiac Surgery, right?"

"Technically, yes."

Angela opened the office door, then turned around. "Great. Can you do me a favor then?"

"Sure."

"Would you please tell Bernard to get the fuck out of my parking spot? Thanks."

CHAPTER 33

Angela returned to her car and sped out of the parking garage, infuriated that she had to pay for parking. She called Lauren and updated her on the meeting with Nick Papadopolous and the follow-up conversation with Maggie. She finished by saying, "Honestly, I'm not sure if there's a cover-up, and if there is, if Maggie's involved or not. She basically told me that I'm losing my mind and that I should talk to someone. Maybe she's right."

"Dr. Brennan—"

"Angela."

"Angela, from what you've told me, I find it impossibly unlikely that the information you were about to obtain from Nick disappeared during the brief power outage."

"But how would Maggie have known I was even talking to Nick? After I spoke with him I went straight to her office and walked in unannounced."

"Did you talk to anyone prior to seeing Nick?"

"Yes. I talked to Barbara Royes . . . oh no."

"Maybe she's involved, too."

"I can't imagine she would do anything to hurt me this much. Unless I've completely misread her personality." Angela rubbed her face. "I don't know, Lauren. I just don't know anymore."

"We still need to get that report that outlines the stocked saline."

"I know. And I'm at a complete loss as to how to do that."

"I'm not."

Angela felt a surge of hope, even as she rationalized that she was probably chasing rainbows. "What do you mean?"

"I have a friend who might be able to help us."

"Who?"

"My college roommate at Brown. She's a computer genius. I texted her while we were talking, and she can meet us at 5:30 at the pizza place in Barrington. Piezoni's. You know it?"

"Of course."

"Can you be there?"

Angela glanced at the clock and shrugged. "It's not like I have a lot going on."

"That's a yes?"

"That's a yes."

"Great. See you then." Angela disconnected the call, threw her phone on the passenger seat, and continued her trek down Route 114 toward Barrington. She passed the high school and felt a surge of sadness that she'd never attend a graduation there. Further on, she passed the town hall where they'd attended Christmas-tree lightings on cold December evenings, and the library where she'd often taken the kids for reading groups when they were small.

She stopped at a red light near the hardware store, and her phone buzzed. The light turned green, and as she accelerated, she leaned over to read the text. She picked up the phone, and when she returned her eyes to the road, there was a stopped car no more than ten feet in front of her. She slammed her foot on the brake and yanked the wheel hard to the left in order to avoid rear-ending the SUV in front of her. Her car completed a half circle, coming to rest facing oncoming traffic. Angela looked up, straight into the eyes of a shocked motorist. Shaking badly, she held up her hand in apology, backed up quickly, and then hung a hard left to resume her short trip home. *I've got to keep it together for at least a little while longer,* she thought.

She pulled into the garage and took a moment to allow some of the adrenaline to be reabsorbed by her body. Glancing at the text that had drawn her attention from the road, she read, "Gone for groceries. Dad and I back soon."

This is the text that almost killed me? she thought as she entered the empty house. She dropped her keys into the bowl by the door and imagined how the near-accident might have played out differently. She envisioned that as she'd rear-ended the car in front of her, her airbag had not deployed. She pictured her neck whipping forward and slamming against the steering wheel and then back against the headrest as her car came to an abrupt, violent stop. Her mind wandered to Tony's last moments, and she imagined joining him, entwining her fingers with his as he ushered her away. She smiled as she saw Emily and Liam running toward her, toppling her with their energy as they competed to hug her. Angela wandered into the living room and picked up the latest school picture of Emily, her hair a raven mane that framed her expressive face. Her body involuntarily shivered as Emily's words wafted on the air: "You can't come, Mom." Angela whipped her head around, convinced that she would find Emily somewhere near her. The room became suddenly quiet, the only audible sound the endless ticking of the grandfather clock in the foyer.

"Are you here?" she called out. "Em?"

Troubled, she continued to wander the first floor of the house, caressing pictures and objects that held significance in their life as a family. Her body felt heavy and her chest hurt as she continued to fantasize about rejoining her family.

A sudden sound from the garage stole her attention and she sprinted toward it, only to find her parents returning from their grocery run. Feeling stupid and vulnerable, she decided to get out of the house. She bolted upstairs, changed into running clothes, threw a backpack on, and slipped out the front door as her parents entered from the garage, arguing about the price of milk.

She channelled energy into her legs, but started the run too quickly, and by the fourth mile she was spent. Ignoring the pain, she pushed forward, punishing herself.

She crested the hill on Chachapacasset Road and remembered her kids trying to sound out the street name when they were learning to read. To her left, the water of Narragansett Bay glistened, and she allowed herself a moment to catch her breath.

Approaching Barrington Beach, Angela was amazed to find it relatively empty. She approached the dock where she'd buried the gun and glanced around to ensure that no one was watching—especially Taylor, the little girl who'd surprised her last time she'd visited. She knelt and vigorously dug with clawed hands, unearthing the carefully wrapped bundle. She removed the plastic cocoon and was pleased to find that the unrelenting tide had caused no damage to the pistol.

As she stared at the gun, she considered the harm she'd caused. Four people were dead: Tony, Liam, Emily, and Ava Sinclair. She glanced across the water, wondering if she should add a fifth.

If she ascertained that Maggie had lied to her, if she discovered that Emily had needlessly died due to avarice and arrogance, she knew she'd have to set things right. And although Angela wasn't sure exactly what that meant, she wanted to be prepared.

Angela wrapped both hands around the pistol, enjoying the weight of the cold steel against the warmth of her palms. She turned around and aimed at the lilac tree where Taylor had shown her the mother robin with her babies. As she drew a bead on a branch, a small, newly feathered bird emerged from the greenery. She lowered the gun as the chick stumbled awkwardly to the end of a branch, and then took to clumsy flight. She watched it circle the tree once and return to the safety of its mother, who stood on the edge of the nest chirping, no doubt encouraging her offspring's efforts.

"Good for you, baby. Fly," she whispered. She looked at the

gun, returned it to its plastic shroud, and placed it carefully inside the backpack before running home.

She found her parents in the kitchen where her father held the end of a pencil in his teeth as he struggled with the daily New York Times crossword puzzle. Sally stood behind him, offering answers and rubbing his back. Angela smiled at the familiar scene and Sally looked up.

"Went for a run?" her mother asked.

Angela nodded, out of breath.

"What's in the pack?" her father asked.

"Oh, just a change of clothes in case I didn't have time to come back before meeting a friend at Piezoni's for dinner."

Her mother looked crestfallen and her entire body sagged. "Angela, I was planning your favorite meal."

Angela hugged her mom. "No can do, but thanks."

"Oh, you're sweaty. Go away," her mother squealed as she poked at Angela's midsection.

Angela winked at her dad. "I'm gonna shower and go."

"You're suspiciously happy today. What's going on?"

"I don't know what you mean, Dad."

"Yes, you do."

Images flashed through Angela's mind: the eyes of the driver after her near-accident, the emptiness of the house upon returning home, Emily's voice echoing through the living room, the imaginary reunification with her family, the weight of the gun against her back. "I feel like I'm starting to get some control over my life again. I'm not all the way there yet, but I'm on the road."

Her father squinted at her. "You've said that before and then things went south again, angel."

Angela made a face. "As Liz has said, there's no schedule for grief, Dad. I just feel good today, that's all."

Jim scrutinized her. "You're sure that's it? Because I feel like there's something you're not telling us."

In response, Angela donned her best innocent mask.

"Oh, now I *know* something's going on," her father said. "The last time I saw that face, you and Tony had eloped!"

Angela stuck out her tongue at him and then kissed his cheek. "One way or another, Dad, this whole hospital fiasco is going to be done."

Her mother whirled around. "Has your malpractice insurance been cleared up?"

"Nope, but I'm taking care of things. No need to worry." She trotted upstairs, tucked the backpack on the top shelf of her closet, showered quickly, and drove to Piezoni's, arriving at exactly 5:32.

She entered the Barrington landmark, and Lauren waved from a booth in the back. Angela approached the table and slid in next to Lauren. Across from her sat a young woman wearing a T-shirt that read: I HAVE NEITHER THE TIME NOR THE CRAYONS TO EXPLAIN THIS TO YOU.

Angela regarded the shirt's tattooed, purple-haired occupant. "Nice shirt."

Lauren laughed. "She has tons of these shirts. She's a freakin' riot, this kid. Dr. Angela Brennan, I'd like you to meet—"

"Sonny," Angela finished.

Lauren drew back in surprise. "Yeah. Sonny McIsaac. How did you know?"

"Because the good doctor here stopped by the IT shop today to chat with Mr. Wonderful," Sonny said.

"Nick Papadopolous is Mr. Wonderful?" Angela asked.

Sonny rolled her eyes and spread her skinny arms, palms up. "Thinks he's God's gift to us."

"And he's not?"

Sonny cringed. "Hardly."

"They used to have a thing," Lauren said under her breath.

"We did not!"

Lauren faced Angela and mouthed, *Yes, they did.*

Sonny's pierced eyebrows shot up and she said, "Lauren, you know what?" She waved her hand. "Whatever."

Lauren twisted her mouth as she considered her friend. "It's okay to be vulnerable, Sonny."

"Oh my God, enough!" Sonny said, and slapped the table.

Angela looked from one woman to the other. "You two have been through a lot together, huh?"

"Yes, we have," Lauren said as she kicked Sonny under the table. "A lot."

"Anyway, can we talk about why we're here?" Sonny snapped, kicking back.

Lauren straightened. "Angela would like you to hack into the hospital's IT system to find some data she was told has been deleted."

"That's it?" Sonny asked, disgusted.

"Can you do it?"

Sonny threw Angela a brief, but very dry look. "Of course I can do it. But why *should* I do it?"

Angela had been unprepared for this question, but the answer materialized instantly. "Because you would be sticking it to the man."

The two younger women shared a strained look and then laughed. "I have no idea what that means," said Sonny.

Angela leaned forward. "How do you feel about authority?"

"Nick's a good dude, but only because he lets me do my thing. Overall, in general, I'd say that authority is overrated," Sonny said.

"How would you like to get the best of the powers-that-be at the hospital?"

Sonny crossed her arms and narrowed her eyes. "Aren't *you* one of the powers-that-be?"

"I used to be, but I'm not anymore, and now I see things differently. Will you help?"

"What can you offer me?"

"You'd be helping me."

"Obviously. What else?"

Angela sighed and attempted to put herself in Sonny's shoes. A female information technologist who had perhaps been ignored, or worse, bullied and demoralized. Angela's answer was simple and direct. "If you help me you would earn my unending respect, admiration, and gratitude."

They locked eyes and Angela could see that she'd hit a nerve. "Deal," Sonny said as she slid a piece of paper across the table.

"What's this?" Angela asked.

"The report you want."

Angela looked from Sonny to Lauren, confused and amazed at the same time. "I don't understand."

The IT guru shrugged. "I overheard you and Mr. Wonderful talking, so I took it upon myself to mine the info during your conversation. See? I *am* better than him. I was able to generate and print this report faster than him, before the power cut out! And he's *my* boss? I don't think so." She leaned back in the booth, crossed her arms, and smiled smugly.

Angela looked at Sonny, trying to figure out her out. "So why did you have me go through the entire story and ask for your help if you already had the report I needed?"

Sonny shrugged again. "For fun."

Angela glared at her and couldn't decide what she felt: monumental anger or begrudging respect. As she was staring, Sonny winked at her. A smile spread across Angela's face and she slowly shook her head.

"Remind me to never get on your bad side."

"Noted," Sonny said.

Angela leaned back and said, "You really don't like authority, do you?"

Sonny offered a mischievous smile. "Lady, you have no idea. Let's order. I'm starving. Oh, and by the way, dinner's on you."

CHAPTER 34

Angela managed to engage in actual conversation even though 90 percent of her attention was on the report she'd stuffed in her purse. The young rebel sitting across from her had an annoying habit of stuffing her mouth and then launching into a diatribe. Her topics ranged widely, from the environment ("Global warming is so real and why can't the alt right accept it?") to the government ("We need someone in office who understands how shit works and don't even get me started on the Congress"), to income inequality ("I did an informal survey and discovered that I'm making only eighty-seven percent of what my male co-workers make, so don't tell me there's no glass ceiling"). Angela nodded and tutted in all the correct places but found it increasingly challenging to focus on her words. When she could stand it no longer, she glanced at her phone and said, "I should get home."

Sonny stopped, mid-chew, a scornful look on her face. "Yeah, it's, like, 6:10. You'd better get home. Bedtime is right around the corner."

Angela glanced at Lauren, who said, "Ignore her. Go. I hope the report helps. Let me know if you need anything else."

Angela smiled and placed two twenties on the table. "This should cover the meal and a nice tip. I can't thank you enough, Lauren. Keep me posted about that new job, and if you need a reference, I'd be more than happy to provide one."

"Thanks."

"And you," Angela looked at Sonny. "Thank you for your kindness in getting me this report."

Sonny rolled her eyes. "I didn't do it for you, *Doctor*."

"I know. You did it for Lauren, and I think that's awesome."

"I didn't do it for her either."

"Then why did you do it?" Angela asked.

Sonny put down her slice and wiped her hands on a napkin. She leaned forward and stared hard at Angela. All pretense was set aside as she spoke. "I did it for your daughter, who should have had a chance to grow up, but doesn't because of some asshole that wants to maintain a ridiculous status role in a brick and mortar institution. If people are covering up a mistake that led to Emily's death, it needs to be exposed. They need to be held accountable. That's why I did it." She picked up her pizza slice and resumed eating, seemingly unaware of the impact her words had made on Angela, who struggled to maintain her composure. Angela swallowed hard, then stood, nodded once to Lauren, and drove home in complete silence as she replayed Sonny's words.

Sonny was correct. Emily should have been given the chance to grow up. And the report might go a long way in informing Angela of the reason why her daughter was robbed of that privilege.

Angela entered the house to find her parents playing gin rummy. "Angela, darling, come play a hand with us," her mother said.

"No, Mom. I'm beat. I'm going up for the night."

"Angela, please come here," her father said.

Angela dropped her head in defeat. She walked into the kitchen and sank into a chair at the table. "What, Dad?"

"How was dinner?"

"Fine."

"You don't seem as happy as when you left."

Angela gripped her purse tightly. "I just want to go upstairs and do some research, that's all."

"On what?" her mother asked.

"Oh my goodness. Stop, please! I just need some time to myself."

Her father held up his hands. "Okay, okay. Are you jumpy because of tomorrow?"

"What's tomorrow?"

Her father's face fell. "I thought you might have forgotten. Tomorrow is the sentencing hearing for the man that hit you."

Angela felt as if she'd been struck. "No, no. That's not tomorrow. That's in late August."

"Sweetheart, it's August thirtieth," her mother said quietly.

Angela looked around the room as if searching for the lost time. "Oh. Yeah."

"You don't have to go, angel."

"Yes. I do have to go. I have to tell the judge—"

Her father placed his hand over hers. "You already attended his initial hearing, angel. You don't have to go this time."

Angela took a deep breath. She didn't have a choice. Not really. She had to go in order to speak for those who could no longer speak for themselves. She stood and said, "I'm definitely going. That guy is going to hear from me and hopefully go away for a long, long time."

"Then we'll go with you," her mother said. "Gin, Jim."

Her father's head swiveled toward the array of cards Sally had splayed on the table. "Darn it! You win every time. How do you do that?"

Sally smiled and gathered the cards as Angela made her way upstairs.

Alone in her room, she removed the piece of paper from her purse and smoothed it out on the bed. She grabbed her laptop and powered it up as she reviewed the report. There were seven columns: Person Ordering, Supply Name, Supply Number, Order Date, Quantity, Delivery Date, and Date Stocked.

All orders had been placed by Barbara Royes, and all dates corresponded to the week of Emily's death. The only columns that varied were the supply name, number, and quantity ordered. She ran her finger down the column of supply names: paper towels, toilet paper, syringes, gauze, and saline.

Tracking the saline row with her finger, she noted the supply number associated with the product. Then, using her hospital identification number, she accessed the supply company's website, Laird Pharmaceuticals, and typed the product number into the search bar. The screen changed to show a picture of a rubber bag of saline with black writing that defined the level of salinity at 0.9%. Angela referred to the report and noticed that Barb had ordered and stocked 300 bags of 0.9% saline. Angela noted that there was nothing abnormal about the order, as saline was often used in post-operative care. She traced the supply name column down further: emesis basin, rubber tubing, catheters, saline—

Her finger stopped. *Why would saline be listed twice?* She compared the supply number of both saline orders and discovered that they were different. Turning to her laptop, she typed in the second saline supply number and the same picture of a plastic IV drip saline bag popped up on her screen. She leaned back and sighed. *Why would there be two different serial numbers for the same product? There wouldn't. They have to be different.* She dragged the two pictures so that they were side by side on her screen. The bags were identical, except for a small red box on the top left of the second bag's picture. She highlighted the picture, double-clicked to enlarge, and then zoomed in on the red box. She leaned in toward the screen and froze. Her brain was unwilling to accept what her eyes were seeing. It took several moments for her to fully process, and when she did, she leaned back and stared at nothing as the blood drained from her face to support her hyperactive heart.

"Oh my God. It was hypertonic. They gave my baby hypertonic saline."

As if in a trance Angela repeated the mantra three times, then watched her hand reach for her phone, only to drop it twice because she had no feeling in her fingers. She willed her trembling hands to still long enough to grab the phone and enter the security code. Once unlocked, she dialed Lauren, who picked up on the second ring.

"Hey, Angela. I'm still at Piezoni's with Sonny. We decided to—"

"You gave her hypertonic saline, Lauren."

"What?"

"Do you remember when Stan changed Emily's medication orders, you removed the IV bag that contained saline and Fentanyl and replaced it with another bag of saline?"

"Yes."

"The saline you used was hypertonic. Instead of a 0.9% saline solution, you gave Emily a 3% saline solution."

"No, no, no. I went to the supply closet and got the saline solution that had been ordered for Emily by Dr. Jacobs."

"Hold on."

Barely breathing, Angela put the phone down and accessed the hospital's online medication ordering system. She had been so focused on the medication overdosage that it had never occurred to her to check the saline order. She found Stan's online orders for Emily on May twenty-ninth. There, in black and white on her screen, was the request for 3% saline.

A little box that had an "X" in it.

A click of the computer mouse had killed her daughter.

Angela's hand flew to her mouth. Emily had not died from the overdose. She had died because the high saline levels in her blood had sucked the water out of her cells, causing them to shrivel, which in turn led to seizures and, ultimately, her body shutting down.

A choked bark erupted from Angela and the room started spinning. She gulped for air and desperately tried to control the sounds coming from her mouth. Eventually she allowed them release and sobbed. "I'm so s-s-sorry, baby girl."

"Angela, are you there?" Lauren's frantic voice yelled through the phone.

Angela stared at her phone, afraid to pick it up. If she said the words out loud, then it would all be real. She'd have to face the truth—that she was a party to her own daughter's death. She shouldn't have trusted Stan. She should have checked the orders herself. She should have overseen Emily's care more closely. How could *she*, of all people, have allowed this to happen?

Angela observed her hand pick up the phone and raise it to her ear. Lauren was babbling about the medication ordering system and how easy it was to make a mistake. How small and closely aligned the boxes were and how normal saline and hypertonic saline were right next to each other. Angela absentmindedly glanced at the ordering screen and noted with detachment that Lauren was correct. *We should fix that*, she thought. *Have other people died because of ridiculous, preventable errors too?*

"Angela, are you still there?"

Lauren's voice reached her from far, far away. "Yes. I'm here," she heard herself respond.

"I'm so sorry, Angela. I don't know what to say. There are no words, really. It's my fault. And I completely understand if you hate me and never want to see or talk to me again. I accept full responsibility and will never, ever get over my role in Emily's death. I will carry it with me for the rest of my life." She was crying openly, and Angela could hear Sonny in the background trying to console her friend.

As the seconds ticked by, feathers of calmness tickled the tension out of Angela's face and shoulders, and she imagined that she could feel the blood running through her veins. Her heart slowed from a violent thud to a gentle pulse and she experienced the sensation of a shadowy veil being lifted from her face. "No."

Lauren's tears subsided in her confusion. "No?"

"You will not carry Emily's death with you for the rest of your life. I forbid it. You're too young to place a burden like that on yourself. It would literally ruin your life. You will learn from this mistake and become a better nurse because of it. That's what Emily would want and it's what I want."

"I don't know what to say, Angela."

"There's nothing to say. It was a mistake. That saline should never have been ordered by Stan, but it was." Angela glanced at the computer screen and stared at the two saline bags, side by side. "And the fact is that the 0.9% and the 3% saline bags look almost identical. Should you have noticed the error? Yes. Should I have noticed it? Yes. All of us should have, but we didn't, and there's no sense destroying your life because of it."

"What are you going to do now?"

Angela looked around her bedroom until her gaze settled on the last formal family portrait they had taken two years ago. "I'm going to take a long rest. I'm tired, Lauren."

"Are you going to be okay, Angela?"

"Honestly? I don't know. Take care."

CHAPTER 35

Angela awoke the next morning to her phone vibrating against her cheek. When she opened her eyes, she was staring at a black laptop screen, and the conversation with Lauren from the previous night came back in waves. The dread of facing another day without her family, coupled with her own guilt in Emily's death, smacked her like a gut punch. She glanced at her phone screen, ready to let the call go to voicemail, but saw it was Liz and fumbled to answer it.

"Hey."

"Oh, did I wake you? Sorry!" Liz said.

"No, no. It's fine."

"I wanted to know what happened with Maggie yesterday."

Angela's foggy brain slowly sifted through recent events to extract her conversation with Maggie. Given last night's revelation, that interaction seemed like a week ago. "Let's just say I'm going to get my parking spot back from Bernard."

"Nice!"

"Yeah." Angela rubbed her eyes and sat up, reticent to say the words aloud. "Listen, it turns out that Emily died from hypernatremia."

"What? High sodium levels?"

"Yeah. Stan ordered hypertonic saline by accident, and Lauren administered it."

Liz blew out a mouthful of air. "Oh, Angela. I'm so sorry."

"Yeah."

"So we did get to her in time with the Narcan."

"Well, the drug overdose didn't do her already-weakened body any favors, but yes, Liz, you got to her in time. Thanks for that, by the way."

"A fat load of good it did, Angela. Don't thank me."

"No, I do need to thank you. You're a great nurse and an even better friend. And I'm sure you were a kick-ass soldier."

"I was, actually."

Angela attempted a smile but couldn't summon one. "I don't doubt it."

A sudden exhaustion overcame Angela and she struggled to find words. She hadn't realized until now how much energy conversations required. "I have the hearing today."

"For the guy that hit you?"

"Uh huh."

"Do you want me to come? I'm sure I can get someone to cover my shift."

"No, but thanks. My parents are coming with me."

"Alright. Good luck. Hang in there."

Angela looked at the computer screen and then at her closet. It occurred to her that she had a job to do. "Listen, Liz, I need to get dressed, but let's meet later for a drink or something."

"Okay. Good luck today."

"Thanks."

Angela dragged herself from her bed and showered, mentally replaying the moment Lauren entered Emily's room to change the saline bag. Had she not been so focused on telling her daughter about Tony and Liam, Angela might have noticed the different bag. In her imagination, she caught the difference and Emily was alive, and in her bedroom, fast asleep. Angela opened her eyes and realized that she had sunk to the tile floor of the shower. Her knees were hugged to her chest and her tears blended with the shower water as it circled the drain. She forced herself to focus on the upcoming hearing and pictured herself speaking to the judge, asking for the death penalty. She dried her hair, donned minimal makeup, and dressed in her best Donna Karan power suit, the red one, before sweeping her blond hair into an elegant French twist. She wanted to look the part when she doomed the monster who had robbed her of happiness. She descended the stairs and her father smiled as he handed her a banana and a granola bar. "Breakfast of champs."

"Thanks, Dad."

They drove in silence to the Barnstable, Massachusetts, courthouse where the hearing was scheduled for 10 A.M. Angela sat in the front row and waited through two cases before the assistant district attorney appeared and sank onto the bench next to her.

"I'm not late, am I?" she asked.

"No. I think we're next, though."

As if on cue, the bailiff stood and announced, "The Honorable Christian Vasquez will hear case number 24601, a hearing to pronounce sentencing on defendant Jonathan Dale, who has pled guilty to vehicular manslaughter thereby causing the deaths of Anthony Brennan and Liam Brennan. All rise."

Hearing Tony and Liam's names stripped Angela of the illusion of control that she'd harbored. She squeezed her thighs together in an effort to quell her quaking knees, and her breath came in shallow, rapid bursts. Per the bailiff's directive, her attorney helped Angela stand as Judge Vasquez entered. On shaky legs, Angela and her attorney crossed to the table reserved for the prosecution. The judge adjusted his glasses and cleared his throat as the gallery chattered. Not receiving the reaction he'd desired he brought his gavel down, his bass voice booming throughout the courtroom. "Order!" His mouth was set in a perpetual frown as his glare alternated between Angela and the defendant. "Are all of the requisite parties to this case present?" he growled.

"Yes, Judge," the bailiff answered.

Judge Vasquez lifted his caterpillar brows to gaze over half-glasses at the defendant. "Please rise, Mr. Dale."

Jonathan Dale stood and placed his hands on the table for support. Angela hadn't seen him since the plea hearing and noted that he had lost a significant amount of weight. He was sweating, causing his limp, long, dirty-blond hair to stick to his protruding cheekbones, and as his red-rimmed eyes darted around the courtroom, he reminded her of a terrified new addition to the zoo, desperately searching for an exit that didn't exist. The attorney touched Jonathan's shoulder and spoke to him, which prompted the defendant to stand up straighter. The effort seemed to have exhausted him, though, and his head hung as the judge spoke.

"Mr. Dale, you have pled guilty to reckless endangerment and vehicular manslaughter. According to the laws of the Commonwealth of Massachusetts, I have the obligation to pass sentencing upon you. Before I do so, do you have anything to say?"

Angela saw Jonathan sway as he tried to find a comfortable stance. For a split second, she realized that she and Jonathan were most likely sharing similar feelings. *How did my life veer so badly off course? My life will never be the same and I will never again feel true happiness.* The difference was, she noted, that he had *caused* her to feel these things, whereas she was simply the recipient. When he spoke, his voice sounded small and hollow. "I just want to say that I'm sorry. The only reason I looked at my phone that day was because my wife was in labor. It's not an excuse. I shouldn't have looked. I'd always heard that it only takes a second to end a life, and now I know that to be true. I'm just so sorry. So sorry." He shook his head as grief overcame him. His shoulders slumped, and he sank into the chair, sobbing.

Angela's entire body tensed at his words and her attorney reached over to still her trembling hands. She swallowed repeatedly to calm the disquiet brewing in her stomach as she focused on Judge Vasquez.

"Stand up, Mr. Dale," the judge bellowed. Jonathan's attorney helped him to his feet.

"I do believe that your sorrow is genuine, and I commend you for accepting responsibility for your actions, something that seems to be lacking in this day and age." The judge cleared his throat and glared at the gallery, as if admonishing those seated there.

Angela leaned forward in her seat and stared at Jonathan. He was haggard and pale, but there was something else that caught her attention. Angela squinted at his wrinkled, untucked plaid shirt, thinking that she'd seen it before. *Did Tony have one like it?* Realization dawned, and she closed her eyes in disbelief. Reggie Stevens, the ghost who had chatted with her during Emily's surgery, had been wearing the same shirt when he appeared to her in the waiting room.

"Nonetheless, your negligent behavior that led to the death of two people needs to be accounted for. Therefore, under the laws of the Commonwealth, I sentence you—"

"Wait!" Before she realized what she was doing, Angela was on her feet.

The judge's eyebrows rose and he slammed the gavel down. "Order! Bailiff, who is this?"

Angela ignored the large court officer stalking toward her. "My name is Angela Brennan and I'm the widow of the man that was killed in the accident caused by Mr. Dale."

Jonathan Dale stared at Angela, open-mouthed. His face wore a tired look of defeat as he discerned Angela's intentions in attending the hearing. Judge Vasquez, taken aback, said, "I'm sorry, Mrs. Brennan. I saw you sitting there and assumed you were an attorney. I apologize that I was not made aware that you were attending today. Would you like to speak prior to sentencing?"

Angela swallowed and nodded, unsure if she could actually carry out what she'd started.

"Please step up to the podium so that you may address the court."

Angela walked forward and placed herself behind the lectern. She inhaled slowly, willing her heaving heart to settle. This was her one chance to speak for her family and she felt the weight of the responsibility like a yoke on her back. She tucked a wayward hair behind her ear and clasped her trembling hands, surprised to discover that she had been subconsciously reciting a prayer. Gathering her thoughts, she glanced at her father, who nodded once in encouragement.

"Um, I wasn't sure if I was going to speak today. In fact, I really came just to ensure that Mr. Dale got locked away." She looked at the defendant, who was openly crying and averting his eyes. Angela took a deep breath before continuing. "But since coming here and seeing Mr. Dale, I feel compelled to say something." She looked at her mother, whose facial expression encapsulated her unwavering love for her daughter.

Angela then focused on Judge Vasquez, not trusting herself to look anywhere else. "I was angry. Furious, actually, when my family was demolished. No, that's not true. I was despondent at first. And then the sadness morphed into an incredible anger that burned inside my entire body. A massive fury that threatened to consume me. I bought a gun with the intention of killing myself." An audible gasp from her mother drew Angela's attention as the rest of the gallery twittered. Her father reached across and took her mother's hand, squeezing it tightly. "But then some strange things happened that made me rethink my decision. Additionally, recently I almost caused an accident because I glanced at a text on my phone." Angela turned to face Jonathan. "Your wife was in labor. I can understand how strong the urge was to just glance at the screen to see how she was doing in your haste to get home. You're a landscaper, right?"

Jonathan nodded, confused as to where Angela was headed with her speech.

"I would imagine that you make, what? About thirty thousand dollars a year?"

Jonathan Dale looked at his attorney for direction and then nodded to Angela.

"Who's going to take care of your family while you're in prison?"

The man looked to his attorney once more and then to the judge, who said, "You may respond, Mr. Dale."

He spoke quietly. "We have no family in the area, ma'am. I'm not sure, to be honest."

"Did your wife have a boy or a girl?"

"A girl."

"What's her name?"

"Angelica Rose. She's right there with my wife and other two children." Jonathan pointed to the back of the courtroom, where Angela saw the woman that she'd met during the bail hearing. Jonathan's wife was crying as she met Angela's eyes. She mouthed, "I'm sorry," then dropped her gaze.

Angela nodded and returned her eyes to Jonathan. *Of course your daughter's name is Angelica, just as Mrs. Crowe's grandbaby was named Liam as my Liam was passing. Of course you're wearing the same shirt as Reggie Stevens.* "It's all supposed to be this way," Angela whispered.

"Can you please speak up, Mrs. Brennan? The court cannot hear you," Judge Vasquez said.

Angela cleared her throat. "Like I said, I wasn't planning on speaking today, and to be honest, I'm not sure what prompted me to stand in the first place. But now that I'm here, I want to say one thing and ask another." She turned to face the man who had taken everything from her. "Mr. Dale—"

Her breath caught, and she was unable to bring herself to speak the words that perched on her lips. Fat tears sprouted and rolled freely down her cheeks.

Suddenly she felt as if someone were standing next to her. She turned and heard Liam whisper, *It's okay, Mom. I'm here.*

She gasped and frantically searched the gallery. Liam's voice was so clear that she was sure she'd see him standing somewhere nearby. A warmth rushed up her back and hovered around her shoulders, and she felt an elation she never would have thought possible. Then, as quickly as it had come, the euphoria vanished, leaving her cold and alone.

But it had been there. She had felt it, and she knew without an ounce of doubt that she had just experienced something profound.

"Mrs. Brennan, do you need a minute?" The judge's booming voice fractured her reverie, and for a moment, Angela wondered if she'd broken with reality.

When she finally spoke, her voice was clear and unwavering. "No. I'm fine. Thank you, Judge. I apologize." Turning to the defendant, she smiled. His confusion was evident as he struggled with a facial response. Through her tears she said, "I forgive you, Mr. Dale. I know that the state cannot, but I do." She finished speaking and felt weightless, as if she were being carried by a river rushing towards some unknown end.

She turned to a surprised Judge Vasquez and said, "I leave his punishment to you, but I agree that Mr. Dale understands what he's done and has accepted responsibility for it. I'm not sure if that matters, but I'm requesting that you take his contrition into account during sentencing. Please excuse me." Angela dashed out of the courtroom, trembling uncontrollably. She found a nearby bench and put her head between her knees in an effort to slow her breathing. Her parents rushed over.

"Angela, what happened in there?" her father asked.

Without looking up, she said, "Liam came to me. It was incredible. Literally. I think I'm going to vomit."

Her mother sat next to her and rubbed her back. "I think you need to go home and relax."

Angela slowly sat up, swallowed, and shook her head. "No. I need to go see an attorney about suing the hospital for wrongful death."

"I thought you said that you weren't going to do that because you know what it's like to be on the receiving end of a lawsuit."

Angela stood, gauging her stability. "I did say that, and I don't want to sue. But if my plan doesn't work, then I'll have no choice."

"What plan?"

Angela hugged both of her parents. "The one I came up with while I was in the courtroom."

Angela noted the anxious glance that flitted between her parents. "Honey, you're not really making sense right now."

"Mom, I know what I have to do now."

"That's what we're worried about," her father said.

CHAPTER 36

The waiting room of Simon, Simon, and Blair reminded Angela of Maggie's office, and for a moment, she questioned her motives. As her parents had listened, she had telephoned Martin Stevens from the car, asking if he might have time to see her today. She'd been told by Marty's assistant that he'd see her when he could, but that he was a "very busy man who doesn't usually manage his schedule in a willy-nilly fashion, but rather by appointment." Angela had accepted the not-so-subtle reprimand and had said that she'd be happy to wait until Mr. Stevens had time to see her.

She glanced at the wall clock. Marty's assistant had not been joking about his busy schedule, as two hours had passed since she'd taken a seat. She'd ordered her parents to leave an hour ago because they were making her nervous by repeatedly asking unanswerable questions like, "Are you sure you know what you're doing?" and "Barrington's a small town. Do you really think this is a good idea?" She had exhausted all of the waiting room magazines and was questionably proud of the fact that she now understood that Heddon Spooks and Booyah Blade Spinnerbaits were the best lures to attract the fickle smallmouth bass.

The door to Marty's office opened and laughter emerged, followed by a man she didn't recognize, and then Marty, who stopped abruptly when he saw her. Before she could speak, the assistant intercepted and spoke quietly to Marty, who patted his shoulder and said, "It's okay, Robert. I'll see Dr. Brennan now. If you could reschedule my lunch with Tyler, I'd appreciate it. Thanks."

Robert threw Angela a supercilious glance that simultaneously gave her permission to see his boss and dismissed her. Angela felt annoyed but appreciated his commitment to protecting Marty's time.

"I didn't think I'd see you outside of the hospital. You're looking well." They shook hands. "I hope you haven't been waiting long."

"Not long at all," Robert answered for her as he trailed Angela into the office. "Dr. Brennan, something to drink?"

Angela turned around to face the assistant. "Nothing. Thanks."

Robert vanished and Angela perused Marty's office. The actual space wasn't large but boasted a beautiful view of the Providence River. Angela smiled as she remembered walking along the bank with Tony during WaterFire, a summer event in which bonfires are lit in large basins that sit atop the water. The fires are stoked by black-clad performers as visitors are entertained with great music and even better food. She and Tony had so enjoyed the brief and wonderful evening getaways when they could find the time. She closed her eyes and imagined the crackle of the pine logs and the wood smoke tickling her nostrils.

"Have you been to WaterFire?" Marty asked as he followed her gaze.

"That's what I was just thinking about," Angela answered.

"It's amazing, isn't it?"

Angela nodded and noticed two millennials sitting on a cement bench. They were holding hands and laughing.

"Please sit. To what do I owe the pleasure?"

Angela turned away from the window and sat in an overstuffed black leather armchair opposite Marty. "I've been thinking about your offer of representation against the hospital."

"Really?"

"You sound surprised."

"I am. Why the change of heart?"

"You know that my daughter was given an incorrect dosage of medication."

Marty nodded.

"Well, she was also given a hypertonic saline solution through her intravenous line."

Marty gave her a perplexed look. "Can you spell out the issue for the nonmedical personnel in the room?"

"Of course. Sorry. Our cells are filled with water. When you feel thirsty it's because your cells have less water in them than they should to maintain a healthy balance. When you drink to quench your thirst, water reenters your cells through a process called osmosis."

"I've heard of osmosis. My ninth grade biology is coming back slowly," Marty interjected.

Angela stood and began pacing in front of Marty's large, oak desk. "Okay, so you know that when osmosis occurs, water moves from a place of higher concentration to an area of lower concentration. So if there is more water outside your cells then inside, the water will move into the cell through its membrane. When the concentrations of water inside and outside the cell are equal, we call that isotonic." She abruptly stopped pacing. "You with me so far?"

"Yes."

Angela placed her palms on Marty's desk and leaned forward. "When extra sodium chloride, or salt, is in the blood outside the body's cells, it draws the usable water from inside the cell to the outside, leaving the cell smaller and too dry. Normally, when that happens, at the beach for example if you ingest seawater, you feel thirsty and drink something to help your cells regain an isotonic state where the amount of water is equal inside and outside of the cell. But if you don't drink enough water to restore the necessary water inside the cells, they start to shrivel up and die."

"Like dehydration?"

Angela pointed at Marty, pleased that he was following her narrative. "Yes. That's what it is. Now, if you inject a salty solution directly into someone's veins, the process is much quicker because the high levels of salinity in the blood draw water out of the cells at a rate in which water cannot be replaced fast enough. The cells start to die at a rapid rate, causing the kidneys to fail, and eventually, the heart as well." Angela stared at Marty as she finished and then sank, exhausted, into the chair across from his desk.

Marty tented his fingers and pulled them to his lips, as if he were praying. "And that's what happened to your daughter?" he asked quietly.

Angela nodded. "0.9% saline solution is often used after surgery to replenish the body. Emily was given 3% saline."

Marty's eyes widened. "So, two major mistakes were made in Emily's care?"

"Exactly. And just to be clear, I'm not here because two mistakes were made. I'm here because I believe that Maggie Donnelly, the current hospital CEO, knows about the hypertonic saline and is covering it up."

Marty leaned forward, causing the chair's worn leather to squeak. "That's a serious allegation, Angela. What makes you say that?"

"Several things. Maggie was wonderful to me right after my daughter died, and then as I started asking questions about Emily's death, suddenly my malpractice insurance was invalid, leaving me unable to practice and financially exposed in the wrongful death suit pending against me. In addition to that, a column was published in the *Barrington Times* that painted me as a washed-up has-been, leaked to the reporter by Maggie, I'm sure. Finally, the medical records of my patient who died after surgery have vanished, and I'm being blamed. Another set-up to make me look bad."

Marty was staring at Angela in disbelief, a pained look in his squinted eyes.

"I know it sounds crazy, Marty. Believe me. I used to scoff at all those doctor TV shows that made hospitals sound like breeding grounds for insanity, but it's all true. I swear."

"Anything else?"

"Yes. Before the accident, I was Maggie's pick to be her successor. And now Stan Jacobs, the surgeon who operated on Emily, has been named as incoming CEO, even though he has less experience than me. I think it's payment for keeping his mouth shut regarding the hypertonic saline. Oh, also, Lauren Kirk, the nurse who attended Emily after surgery, has been fired. I was told it was because of performance issues, but Lauren had an unblemished record. Lauren believes that she was let go because Maggie was concerned that she might discover the truth. She was given a nice severance package to bribe her to keep quiet."

"How did you discover all of this?"

"I've had a lot of time on my hands since I'm not seeing patients. I went to see the Information Technology director, who accessed information for me, only to have the data disappear as he was printing the report. Luckily the nurse who was fired, Lauren, knows someone who hacked the IT system. That's how I figured out that Emily actually died from the hypertonic saline." She drew a deep breath and blew it out. "That's everything."

Marty spread his hands. "So what do you want to do?"

"I want to threaten Maggie with exposure."

"To what end?"

Angela paused. She didn't approve of America's litigious culture and had never imagined that she'd be sitting in an attorney's office outlining a plan to use the legal system for personal gain. Then again, she'd never imagined that she'd lose her entire family within twenty-four hours and be attacked by the very people with whom she'd shared common goals.

Sensing her hesitation, Marty continued. "I only ask because people who come in here often have visions of *Law and Order* in their heads. You know, where the defendant's on the stand and feels the pressure and blurts out a confession."

Angela's face reddened. That's exactly what she'd been hoping for.

Marty smiled kindly and leaned forward. "Just like you think the doctor shows on TV are ridiculous, I think the law programs are preposterous. In the real world, people lie, cheat, and steal to protect what's theirs, including committing perjury on a daily basis. It's infuriating, but it's true. If you're looking to have Maggie admit to covering up Emily's death, I am 110 percent sure that will *not* happen, as the admission would ruin her as well as the hospital. Who knows? The hospital board might even be involved."

Angela closed her eyes. She hadn't thought of that.

"I'll do whatever you want, but it's important that you understand what you're getting yourself into, that's all. I know what you've already been through is unthinkable, but wait 'til you see what people do when they're backed into a corner. They lash out like an angry, caged animal. And from what you've told me so far, this Maggie person seems like she's ready for a fight. Are you?"

Angela stared at Marty for a long time as she reflected on his question. She remembered Liam coming to her in the courtroom and wondered if someone would offer her guidance as she faced another major decision. After a few moments of silence, Angela asked, "Where are they when you need them?"

"I'm sorry?"

"The ghosts, or whatever they are. Where are they when you need them?"

Marty smiled and looked around the room. "You mean to tell me that they're not here, offering sage advice on how to best legally tackle your foe?"

"Sadly, no."

They were both quiet a moment. "I guess they'll come when I really need them. It seems to work that way. So maybe I don't really need them right now. Perhaps I can figure this out myself. In fact, another idea has just occurred to me. Maggie used the press against me. Maybe it's time that I returned the favor." She stood quickly. "Keep our conversation on hold, Marty. I may be back in a week or so and still need you."

"Where are you going?"

Ignoring his question, she walked toward the door. "Thanks for your help. Even just talking it through made me feel better."

She turned to leave, and Marty said, "Did it ever occur to you that they might have sent you the idea that seemingly just popped in your head?"

"The ghosts?"

He nodded. "Maybe they're with you after all."

Angela smiled. "You might be right. They are pretty sneaky."

CHAPTER 37

~

Angela ran a finger around the rim of her martini glass while she waited for Liz. The Wharf Tavern was busy tonight, so she was fortunate to have snared two bar seats that overlooked the river. Angela watched sailboats float by, manned by children on the Barrington Yacht Club sailing team. She recognized one of Emily's friends, and the girl waved wildly from her seat at the tiller, prompting Angela to smile and wave in return. Her happiness was short-lived, though, as she realized that sailing was yet one more thing that Emily and Liam would never do again. A seventy-something, well-dressed lady wearing too much perfume was eyeing the stool next to Angela, so she grabbed her phone and stabbed out a text to Liz. "Hurry up or I'll be sitting with an old coot instead of you."

Thirty seconds later Liz appeared. "An old coot? Really?"

Angela smiled and patted the stool. "Sit. I have some news."

Angela recounted her conversation with Marty Stevens and how it helped her formulate next steps.

"So your plan is to make Maggie come to you?"

"Yes."

"How?'

"By working with him." Liz followed Angela's pointed finger and saw a tall redhead walking toward them. He was blue-eyed and broad shouldered, and sported a light beard made fashionable by the millennial crowd.

"Hi, Angela. I'm glad you called."

Angela rose and shook his hand. She turned to Liz and said, "Liz, I'd like you to meet Jesse Callaghan. Jesse, this is Liz."

At her full height, Liz stood a foot shorter than Jesse. Angela saw Liz's eyes light up as she recognized the reporter's name. "So you're the snide sycophant that wrote the scathing column about Angela."

Jesse held up his hands in surrender. "That's me. But I believe we've gotten past that."

He glanced at Angela, who nodded. "It turns out that Jesse had contacted the hospital's Public Relations department in an effort to speak to me about the column and had been told to take a hike. I'm sure Maggie didn't want me to know about the story before its release."

"Ah. Makes sense," Liz said.

"Like I said, I'm glad you called because it gave me a chance to explain my side of things. And then when you told me everything that's happened to you since I wrote the column, I felt that I had an obligation, journalistically and morally, to follow up with another story."

"So you're not actually a snide sycophant?" Liz joked.

Jesse turned an appraising eye toward Liz and smiled. "Liz, I'm never snide, sycophantically speaking." He rolled his eyes at his own bad joke and Liz laughed out loud.

Angela looked from Liz to Jesse and back again. An idea blossomed, followed by a large grin. "Listen, I need to run, but why don't you two stay and have dinner?"

"Angela, you haven't even finished your drink," Liz said.

Angela waved her hand toward the martini. "You have it. I need to go, but I insist that both of you stay." Liz looked at Jesse, who shrugged and said, "That might be nice." Liz blushed and turned back to her friend, gave her a hug, and spoke quietly. "You're unbelievable. I'll call you tomorrow."

Angela squeezed Liz's hand as they parted. Turning to Jesse, she said, "Take care of her. She's priceless. And get me the new column when you can. I'll need it when I confront Maggie."

"It's already in your email. I wrote it when we got off the phone. Let me know what you think. If I don't hear from you, it'll run in tomorrow's edition."

Angela returned to her car and accessed email on her phone, then opened the attachment Jesse had sent.

Hospital Targets Local Surgeon
By Jesse Callaghan

Several weeks ago, I published a column outlining the downfall of prominent local cardiac surgeon Angela Brennan. At the time I had reached out to Dr. Brennan through the Public Relations department at the hospital and had been told that she had no interest in speaking to me about the story.

I have come to learn that what I was told by the PR people is not true. Dr. Brennan was very interested in speaking with me and, after talking with her at length, I have learned that she has an amazing and terrifying story to tell.

Just to recap, Dr. Brennan lost her husband and son in a car accident in May of this year. Her daughter, who had been badly hurt in the crash, was taken to the hospital where Dr. Brennan is employed and died after undergoing surgery for her injuries.

In my previous column I had written that Emily Brennan died from a drug overdose. What I should have said is that she died from an erroneous dosage of medication administered by hospital clinicians. But I now know that even *that* statement would be incorrect. The truth is that Emily would have survived the medication error if the hospital had not made a *second error* in giving little Emily an intravenous solution that was too high in saline.

You read that correctly. Our award-winning hospital made not one, but *two* major medical mistakes that cost Emily Brennan her life.

Her mother is angry. She should be. How would you feel if this had happened to you?

Maggie Donnelly is the current hospital CEO and was looking to step down and hand the reins to Dr. Brennan. Following the hospital's missteps, Ms. Donnelly has rescinded her offer to Dr. Brennan and has offered it to Dr. Stan Jacobs, who happened to be Emily's surgeon and the person who ordered the medication overdose.

I also spoke with a former Pediatric Intensive Care Unit nurse named Lauren Kirk, who was released from employment shortly after Emily's death, despite an unblemished employment record.

Dr. Brennan does have a lawsuit pending against her in an unrelated wrongful death case, and although the hospital has not fired her, they are no longer covering her malpractice insurance, leaving her no way to make a living and open to potential bankruptcy due to legal costs associated with the case.

You do the math here. Something doesn't add up, right? The hospital made two catastrophic medical errors that led directly to the death of a twelve-year-old girl, yet Dr. Brennan and nurse Kirk are the ones who are out of jobs.

Dr. Brennan has met with Martin Stevens, a local attorney who has agreed to represent her in her wrongful death case against the hospital. Mr. Stevens believes that given the strong facts, the jury will find in Dr. Brennan's favor and will award her a sum that is, as he describes it, "substantial."

Ms. Donnelly and Dr. Jacobs were unavailable for comment. They must be wondering if they should be worried about more than a simple lawsuit against the hospital. The missteps that led to Emily Brennan's death were tragic and awful, but they were human errors. If, however, Dr. Brennan and her attorney can prove that Maggie Donnelly and Stan Jacobs actively concealed those blunders, then they can be held liable both civilly and criminally.

~

Angela smiled. Jesse had done a thorough job in creating a factual column that tugged at her heartstrings. More importantly, he'd managed to implicate Maggie and Stan without going so far as to accuse them. She texted Jesse, "It's perfect. Thank you."

She started the drive home and powered down the window to enjoy the humid bay air. She smiled and inhaled the scent of a brewing summer storm, the kind that Liam had loved. He used to bundle himself in a blanket, sit on the front porch, and sing quietly as the thunder rattled the dormers. Angela would watch him from the window, marveling at his innate ability to become part of the landscape as he sat for an hour or more, just watching.

"Hey, buddy. Hope you're okay up there. How are Dad and Em? I miss you guys so much."

Her eyes became dewy as "Bridge Over Troubled Water" came on the radio. She had sung it to the kids when they were little, and over time they had begun to sing it back to her, joking that when she was old and gray they'd be her "bridge." She allowed herself a good cry, but when the third verse began, she listened to the words as if hearing them for the first time. Paul Simon and Art Garfunkel crooned about a silver girl whose time had come to move on, but lest she ever feel alone, they reminded her that they were behind her if she needed them. Although she'd listened to the song over a hundred times, she'd never paid particular attention to that verse. But now it held special meaning for her.

She was the silver girl. It was time for her to move forward, knowing that her family had her back. Not just Tony and the kids, but Marty, Liz, her parents, and Reggie and Frank, too. Angela realized with alarming and sudden clarity that Liz had been correct when she'd said that the dead were no longer physically with us, but they live inside of us, in our souls. They live through our actions and memories. They are alive when we remember them or do something positive. We are their legacy.

She pulled in the driveway, wiped her eyes, and entered the house.

"Angela, is that you?" her mother called out.

"Yeah. Hi, Mom." Her mother came around the corner with laundry in her arms. "Let me take that, Mom. Why don't you sit down?"

"Have you been crying? Are you okay?" Sally asked.

Angela put the laundry on the table and pulled her mother in for a hug. "I'm fine, Mom. No, I'm more than fine. I'm good, working toward really good."

Her mother withdrew, giving her a suspicious look. "What's going on?"

"I've been focusing on what I've lost, which is a lot. But recently I've realized that I haven't lost everything, like I thought I had. I still have so much to be grateful for. I don't like to throw the word 'blessed' around, but that's what I am."

"Where is this coming from, Angela?"

"I don't know. I just feel like I'm moving forward, informed by my past. Empowered by my past. The good, the bad, and the ugly parts of it. Does that make sense?"

"It does to me," her father said from the doorway. "It makes perfect sense to me." He turned to Sally. "Dear, I think we should be packing up soon to return to Florida."

Sally looked at her only child. "Oh, I don't know if that's a good idea, Jim. Not until this whole thing is settled."

Angela hugged her mother. "I agree with you, Mom. I think you should stay a little longer. Besides, when you go back to Florida, who knows how long it'll be before I see you again?"

CHAPTER 38

~

The next morning Angela glanced at the clock and was shocked to see that it was 9:20 A.M. She couldn't remember the last time she'd slept so long or so well. Her phone vibrated on the nightstand. She picked it up to discover that she'd received four texts and two voicemails in the last hour. Smiling, she reviewed all of her messages and went downstairs.

Sunshine streamed through the kitchen window and highlighted a stained-glass ornament that Emily had thought too beautiful to pack away last Christmas. The prism of light splashed a rainbow of color across the wall.

"Good morning, angel."

"Good morning, Dad."

He pushed the *Barrington Times* across the table. "Have you seen this?"

"Yup."

"Might this column have something to do with your good mood last evening?"

"It does."

"Are you ready for the fight that is surely coming your way?"

"The fight's been in progress for a while now, Dad. And it certainly wasn't started by me."

"But you're going to finish it?" her mother asked.

"Abso-fucking-lutely."

"Angela, my goodness. Language, please."

"Sorry, Mom."

"Has Liz seen this?" her father asked as he pointed to the paper.

Angela held up her phone. "Liz, Lauren, Sean, Sonny. They've all seen it and have contacted me about it."

"What about Maggie?"

"Nothing from her yet."

"She may skip the small talk, Angela, and go right for your jugular. You know that, right?"

"Let her come, Dad. I met with an attorney who says that I have a great case against the hospital. If she wants a long, protracted legal battle, I'm up for it."

"Honey, how can you afford that, especially with no insurance and the other suit still pending?" her mother asked.

Angela shrugged. "I have the money from Tony's half of the architecture firm. And I have some funds in savings and retirement."

"Angela, you can't take money out of your retirement accounts. Dad and I can help you."

"No, but thanks. I'm serious. I'm ready for this. I think a part of me wants a good fight. It'll give me somewhere to put my residual anger."

Angela's phone buzzed, and she held up her finger toward her parents as she answered. "Hi, Liz. Sorry I haven't responded to your text. Believe it or not, I just woke up."

"That's okay. The column was great, wasn't it?"

"Sure was. How was dinner with Jesse?"

"Amazing, actually, but we can talk about that later. Listen, I have someone here who came looking for you after she read Jesse's story."

"Who is it?"

"A woman named Melinda. Hold on." Angela listened as the phone was passed to someone.

"Hello? Dr. Brennan?"

"Yes. Who is this?"

"This is Melinda Nuñez."

Angela closed her eyes, trying to remember where she'd heard the name. She couldn't place her.

"I was the assistant in the hospital morgue."

A flash of white sheets on cold steel and a tearful woman standing between the tables. "Of course. I'm sorry that I didn't recognize your name. How are you, Ms. Nuñez?"

"I'm fine. Actually, I'm not fine." Her voice dropped to a whisper. "Dr. Brennan, I need to speak with you."

"You are speaking with me."

"No, no. I need to speak with you in person, but right now I need to return downstairs before I'm missed. Can you come see me at noon? I can meet you in the parking garage."

"In the parking garage? Why don't we meet in the cafeteria?"

"No. It must be somewhere more private."

Angela paused, wary. "Why?"

The woman sighed heavily. "Just please come to the parking garage at noon." Angela heard rustling as the phone changed hands again.

"Angela?"

"Yeah, hey, Liz. That was weird. Did she give you any indication as to why she wants to meet me?"

"No. She came here looking for you. She seemed nervous and insisted that she speak only to you, so I called."

"Huh. Well, I guess we'll see. So, switching subjects, tell me about the date."

"He's a really cool guy, Angela. A little young for me, but so delicious. Did you set me up, by the way?"

"No. I thought he might join both of us for drinks and we could discuss the column, but when I saw you guys looking at each other I made different plans. Talk about chemistry."

"It seems that we do have that. Like you and Tony had."

Angela smiled, remembering the first time she'd met Tony and how smitten she'd been. He'd arrived for their blind date in seersucker pants and white oxford bucks. She had decided right then and there that he was either supremely confident or crazy. Turns out he had been a little of both.

Liz interrupted her reverie. "Oh, I'm being paged. I need to go. But let's meet for lunch in the cafeteria, okay?"

"Okay. I'll see you there at 11:45 for a quick bite before I meet Melinda. Thanks, Liz."

Angela disconnected. "What's going on now, Angela?" her mother asked.

"I need to go to the hospital and talk to some people."

"Well, eat something first."

Angela stood. "I'll get something there, Mom, but thanks."

"Honestly, you're shrinking down to nothing!"

Angela watched her father take her mother's hand and gently pat it. She smiled, marveling at how two souls could become so aligned that a single touch was enough to calm a troubled heart. She and Tony had shared such a bond, and a surge of panic gripped her as she fully understood that she would never again have the privilege of his warm caress. She breathed deeply and tore her eyes from her parents' hands. "I'm going to get dressed."

Angela showered and took her time dressing in a stylish, blue, linen suit. She wasn't certain as to why she was taking so much care in her appearance, but the return to a part of her former daily routine felt comforting. She brushed her hair and noticed that a white streak had appeared on either side of her natural part. She was genuinely perplexed as to when that had happened but decided that she liked it. It spoke of experience, wisdom, and hard-won emotional battles, and she decided to wear it with pride. The bags under her eyes, however, were another matter altogether, and she applied a full face of makeup in an effort to look put together. Finally, she returned to her walk-in closet and perused her large collection of designer handbags. After trying several options, she chose a Chanel purse that was spacious enough to carry indispensable items she might need. Having completed her preparations, she stepped back and evaluated herself in the full-length mirror Tony had hung two years prior.

"Well, Tony, what do you think?" she asked aloud. She heard him whistle behind her, as he had done so many times when he was alive. She smiled. "Thanks."

By the time she arrived on the hospital grounds, it was 11:20 A.M. On a whim, she drove to her parking spot, only to find Bernard's car parked there. She sat in her idling car, deciding how best to deal with the situation. After considering several options, including keying his car, she decided to ignore the blatant slight and park in the main garage. Clearly Maggie was not taking her seriously or she would have forced her plebe to vacate Angela's parking spot. *But maybe she's read the column by now*, Angela thought as she parked her car and walked to the front entrance.

Angela entered the sliding doors to find Esther gesturing in her direction. "Hello, Dr. Brennan. I read the story in today's paper. Is it true?" she asked breathlessly. "Did Ms. Donnelly know about the reason your daughter died?"

Angela smiled but remained silent. Marty had warned her to speak as little as possible with people who might later be called as witnesses if her case went to trial.

"It's good to see you, Esther. What a good-looking sweater."

The distraction worked, and the old woman preened. "It's new. Thank you. My son gave it to me. I know it's silly to wear a sweater in the dead of summer, but it gets so cold in here."

"Well, you look lovely," Angela gushed as she walked toward the IT suite.

She entered the waiting area and spoke to the receptionist. "Hi. I'm looking for Sonny McIsaac. Is she available?"

"Hold on. Let me check." The young lady typed on her keyboard and within seconds Sonny appeared donned in a T-shirt that read "WILL CODE FOR PIZZA."

Angela nodded toward her shirt. "Your shirt speaks the truth."

"Well, well, if it isn't the good doctor all dressed up," Sonny said. "Let's take a walk, shall we?"

"Actually, I don't have a lot of time, so—"

"Just walk with me."

Angela glanced at her watch, keenly aware of the tight schedule she'd created for herself. Sonny exited the building without looking to see if Angela was following. Consternation crossed Angela's face, but not seeing an alternative, she hurried to catch up. They walked until they encountered a grassy quad that doubled as an ultimate Frisbee field in the summer. A game was in progress, so they skirted the unmarked field until they were out of earshot of any potential eavesdroppers. The sun was high and warm, and Angela noted how quickly time seemed to have passed since the accident. *Was it really only three months ago that Tony and the kids were playing Frisbee on the beach?*

"Hello . . . did you hear what I said?"

Angela shook her head. "Sorry. I was just remembering . . . never mind. What did you say?"

"I said that I didn't want to talk where people could overhear us. Hence, the walk."

"Ah."

"The *Times* column was good," Sonny said.

"Thanks to your hard work."

Sonny blew out air and watched a guy crash to the ground, Frisbee in hand. "Yeah, well, the little favor I did for you could get me fired. And don't you think there's enough of that going around?" She gave Angela a pointed look.

Angela looked away. "True. Sorry. Anyhow, I came by to thank you, Sonny."

"You're welcome. And?"

Angela turned back to her. "And what?"

"I can tell you want something else."

"No, I don't."

"Are you sure?"

Angela tightened her mouth, irritated but impressed. "How could you possibly have known that I wanted something else?"

"Because people like you don't seek out people like me simply to say thank you."

"What's that supposed to mean?"

Sonny rolled her eyes. "This isn't my first rodeo, Angela. I know that you and I don't travel in the same social circles, so why would you come to me unless you needed something?"

Angela was offended. "What if I just wanted to say thanks?"

"But you didn't."

"But what if I did?"

Sonny stood on her tiptoes and leaned forward so her nose was touching Angela's. "Tell me I'm wrong."

Without moving, Angela replied, "You're not wrong, but I want you to know that the incredibly large chip on your shoulder is going to become very heavy over time, perhaps even disabling."

Sonny smiled and pulled away. "Nicely worded, Angela. Now, what can I do for you?"

Angela glanced at her watch and then spoke quickly. "I'm being blamed for the disappearance of some medical records of a former patient of mine named Ava Sinclair. I'm wondering if you can find them and get me a copy. And this is all under the radar, of course."

Sonny's eyes shifted left, then right, as her brain processed Angela's request. Finally, she nodded. "Give me an hour. I'll text you when I find something."

CHAPTER 39

It was 11:45 A.M. Angela ordered a chocolate croissant and a large coffee with one sugar and extra cream. She deposited herself at a corner table so she could observe the microcosm of society that had found its way, for one reason or another, into the hospital. She blew on her coffee while marveling at the socioeconomic differences that were so apparent among the people in the cafeteria. As a physician she had noted these differences, but it had been with an air of detachment, secure in the knowledge that she would never be "one of them."

Now she wondered what she'd meant by that phrase. *One of them*. Did it refer to money? Power and influence? Was it in reference to control or freedom? Intelligence? Education? Her brain went on and on outlining the options. Then Sonny's words floated into her mind. "We don't travel in the same social circles." She suddenly realized that by creating the divide of "us and them," she had not only locked people out, but she had shut herself in. *That must be what Dad meant when he asked me if I build emotional walls to keep people out or the pain in. Either way, I lose*, she thought.

She shook her head, astonished by her own lack of self-awareness and flat-out stupidity. *I* am *one of them. The wounded, the suffering, the doing-your-best-just-to-get-through-the-day kind of person. That's me. Silver girl.* She nodded, liking the new her just a little bit.

"Why are you nodding?" Liz asked as she placed her tray on the table and plopped down in a chair.

"It's amazing, Liz."

Liz smiled. "Angela, it's so great to see you look happy. What's amazing?"

"This." Angela spread her arms across the eating area.

Liz looked at her askew. "The cafeteria is amazing? I'm not sure I'd agree with you on that one."

"No, not the cafeteria. The people. They're wonderful, conflicted, confused, passive-aggressive, kind, and impatient."

"Are you okay? Now I'm a little worried."

Angela laughed. "I'm fine. I'm just . . . noticing things. Seeing things differently now. It's so much clearer, Liz. It's like putting on eyeglasses for the first time. You didn't know what you were missing until you can actually see."

Liz followed Angela's gaze, her mouth in a frown. "I'm not sure I see what you see, my friend."

"Well, I hope someday you can, Liz, because it's beautiful. But I hope you don't have to go through what I've endured in order to see it."

"From your lips to God's ears."

Angela glanced at the wall clock. "I'm meeting Melinda Nuñez at noon. I'll see you later."

Liz spoke through a mouthful of cheeseburger. "Okay. Let me know how it goes."

Angela made her way to the hospital's parking garage. The structure had four stories, and Angela realized that she and Melinda should have been more detailed about their exact meeting point. Angela entered through a side door and evaluated the two sets of stairs in front of her. "Up or down?" she asked aloud.

"Dr. Brennan?"

Angela jumped. She turned to find a fidgety Melinda Nuñez standing behind her. The assistant wore well-pressed scrubs, and her matching Crocs squeaked as she shifted her weight. She repeatedly brushed a wayward piece of hair away from her face.

"Hi, Ms. Nuñez. You scared me. How are you?"

Melinda's small eyes darted around the stairwell, unable to settle.

"Ms. Nuñez, what's going on? Why did you want to see me?"

The question focused her, and she looked directly at Angela. "It's not right. What they are doing to you. So I wanted to give you this." She handed Angela a piece of paper with handwritten scrawl on it.

"What is this?"

"You know how we always take a blood sample before releasing a body to the family?"

"Yes."

She pointed to the paper. "You're holding Ava Sinclair's blood results."

Angela glanced at the paper and then at Ms. Nuñez. "I thought Mrs. Sinclair's records were missing."

"They are, but I always retain a hard copy of my work in case the computers go down. These blood results are from the day she died. I hand wrote them because I was afraid to give away my only hard copy. If I were found to be speaking to you . . . well, I really need to keep my job, Dr. Brennan."

It was the second time in one day that Angela had been associated with people losing their jobs. She felt terrible, but she pressed on. "Why are you giving me this?"

Melinda's wary eyes started dancing again. "Check out her sodium level."

Angela ran down the blood results list until she found sodium. "It's high."

"Remarkably high, don't you think?"

Like puzzle pieces floating in space, her brain started logically assembling the parts, trying this one and that, turning them until the full picture began to emerge. Angela looked at the number again and then at Ms. Nuñez, who nodded in encouragement, willing Angela to find the solution. As her mind came to the inescapable, terrible conclusion, the skin on Angela's scalp tingled and she felt the back of her neck tighten. "She was given the wrong saline bag, just like my Emily." Angela stared at the paper and tears pricked her eyes. Through her awful epiphany, she was able to appreciate the risk Melinda had taken. "Ms. Nuñez, I understand the potential peril you're in because you've shared this information with me, and I can't tell you how much it means to me. Thank you." She hugged the assistant, who stood awkwardly in Angela's embrace.

"You're welcome. You are very kind, Dr. Brennan. You don't deserve all that has happened to you. I just want to help. I need to go now."

"Okay. Thanks again."

As Melinda scooted away, Angela crumpled the piece of paper in her fist and returned to the cafeteria to find Liz emptying her soda can. Angela sat down heavily in a chair and slid the ball of paper across the table, her face a mask of grim determination.

"What's this?" Liz asked as she smoothed the paper.

"It's what Ms. Nuñez wanted to show me. Those are Ava Sinclair's saline levels. The blood was drawn and analyzed prior to her body being released to the family."

Liz ran a hand through her platinum hair. Her eyebrows came together in concentration as she read the results. After a moment, she looked straight at Angela. "Was she given—"

"The wrong saline? Yes, I believe so."

"You know what this means, don't you?" Liz grabbed Angela's hand.

"What?"

"That you didn't cause Mrs. Sinclair's death."

Angela leaned back in her chair and stared at the floor as she was carried back to the moments after Mrs. Sinclair died. If Mr. Sinclair had allowed an autopsy, she might have understood the true cause of death and Emily's life might have been spared. "That's true. It won't bring her back, but at least I didn't kill her."

"She must have been given the wrong saline bag in post-op."

Angela's eyes went wide with panic. "But what if I ordered that saline by mistake? After all, when we place an online order for saline, the boxes we check are right next to each other."

"With her medical records missing, I don't know how we're going to figure that out."

Angela's phone buzzed, indicating a new text. Absent-mindedly, she read it aloud. "'*Found what you asked for.*'"

"Who's that from?"

"Sonny McIsaac. I asked her to dig up Mrs. Sinclair's records, so we should have an answer about which saline I ordered."

They looked at each other, neither willing to voice their fears. Instead, Angela said, "Melinda risked everything to help me."

Liz nodded. "She did. Sometimes you just have to do the right thing."

"Speaking of which—" Angela stood. "I have a date with an IT guru who doesn't seem to like me very much. Talk soon."

Angela entered the elevator and depressed the button. Arriving on the first floor, the doors opened to reveal Sonny walking toward her. Angela opened her mouth to speak, but Sonny handed her an envelope and entered the elevator without a word. Angela turned, and as the doors closed, a stone-faced Sonny winked.

Angela returned to the lobby and found a seat in a corner facing the window. With shaky hands she opened the envelope and found a typed note.

A—

It turns out that it took me only 35 minutes to mine the data you needed. Just so you know, it wasn't deleted, but it was buried under a mountain of recently completed code. I know the digital signature of the person who wrote the code. It's an ex of mine. A real asshole, by the way, but I guess that's beside the point. Anyhow, based on the type of code he used and the complexity with which he wrote it, he was clearly trying to ensure that this information never saw the light of day. The one thing he didn't count on was me. Ha ha! Take that, Bruce!

—S

P.S. I know you think I don't like you. I actually haven't decided yet. I'll let you know when I do. Right now I'm leaning toward liking you.

Despite the situation, Angela smiled as she removed the rest of the folded paper from the envelope. She quickly scanned the medical records to ensure that they hadn't been altered and noted nothing out of the ordinary. She reviewed Mrs. Sinclair's blood work prior to surgery and noticed that her sodium level was normal. Taking a deep breath, she then turned to the notes from the day of the surgery. At the end of the surgical notes was a list of medications Angela had ordered for post-operative care. She felt light-headed when she saw that she'd ordered normal saline at 0.9%. *My order didn't kill her. But her sodium levels were lethally high. Someone must have grabbed the wrong saline bag because they looked so similar. How many others have died—*

Angela's thought was interrupted when her phone vibrated in her pocket. Still riding a small high, she removed the phone, expecting to see a text from Liz asking about the medical records. It was a text, but it wasn't from Liz.

"Bernard saw you in the cafeteria. I think you and I should have a chat in my office. Now."

Angela took a deep breath and stared out the window, garnering her anger and focusing it into an orb of hard courage that burned brightly in her core. She rose, straightened her jacket, and swung her purse over her shoulder.

"It would be my absolute pleasure, Maggie."

CHAPTER 40

~

Angela nodded as she walked past Esther, who smiled brightly in return. Colors intensified and sounds magnified as adrenaline pumped through her body, readying her for the anticipated battle. She closed her eyes and breathed deeply in an effort to calm her rapid heartbeat. She must maintain her composure, as losing her temper would only feed into Maggie's goal of disposing of her. After so much chaos and competing emotions, an unexpected calm spread through her as she waited for the elevator.

The doors opened, and a surprised Angela shook her head and addressed the single occupant. "How is it that in a hospital of this size, you and I keep running into each other, Bernard? Are you following me?"

She watched Bernard recover quickly from the shock of recognition by rearranging his face into a stoic veneer. "I think you're being paranoid, Dr. Brennan. I'm far too busy to be following you."

"You're the one who told me to watch my back, Bernard. But I can understand why you're busy. Between acting as Maggie's snitch and your actual work as a physician, you must be absolutely exhausted." Angela pressed the button for the administrative floor. They rode in silence and Angela enjoyed watching Bernard fidget in discomfort.

"Going to see Maggie?" Bernard asked.

"Yes. I've been summoned."

Bernard cleared his throat as the doors opened. "Good luck with that."

Angela exited the elevator and turned around to face Bernard. She stuck out her hand to stop the closing doors. "Do you remember what I told you, Bernard? That we're all replaceable? What's happening to me could happen to you as well. It's a shame, because you're a good surgeon, but you've done the one thing I warned you against."

He lifted his chin in defiance and crossed his arms. "What's that?"

Angela felt genuine sadness for the promising surgeon. "You've let your success go to your head. Can I give you some last advice?"

Dr. Smythe pursed his lips and raised his eyebrows. "Sure."

"Distance yourself from Maggie. She's going down hard, and if you're not careful, you'll go down with her. Good luck, Bernard. You're going to need it."

Angela removed her hand and the doors closed, leaving her alone in the mahogany-paneled hallway leading to Maggie's office. Hugging her purse tightly against her side, she walked slowly, taking in the lemon scent of the freshly treated wood and the plushness of the royal-blue rug. She thought back to when she and Tony were first married. How their dreams had shone like a beacon! She smiled at their youthful audacity, how it had never occurred to them that their life together might not evolve as they had planned. They had worn their arrogance ignorantly, as if their place in the world had been carved entirely by them, never questioning how or why things worked so well.

Now she knew better.

It was all a façade.

Dumb luck encapsulated in a good education, a true partner, and hard work.

Angela entered the Administrative suite and Maggie's assistant smiled. "Good to see you, Dr. Brennan." Her grin was genuine. Angela took it as a sign of support. "She's waiting for you. Go ahead in." She held Angela's eyes longer than necessary, and Angela intimated that this woman understood the import of the meeting and was on her side. Angela offered her a quick, grateful nod in return. "Thanks."

Angela entered to find Maggie leaning over architectural plans, reading glasses perched precariously on the end of her aquiline nose. She glanced up.

"Look at this, Angela. Plans for the new cancer wing to be completed by next year. It's going to be beautiful."

Angela didn't move, and Maggie continued as if she hadn't noticed. "Now that Frank is gone, I think we'll have enough votes on the Board to move this thing forward."

Angela was shocked that she didn't feel a rush of anger at Maggie's thoughtless phrasing, but she realized that she felt devoid of emotion. "Now that Frank is gone?"

Maggie removed her glasses and crossed to her spacious, leather desk chair. "Yes. Like you, he tended to be . . . How shall I say this so I don't speak ill of the dead . . . difficult. The rest of the Board was ready to move forward with the cancer center, but Frank was lobbying hard to wait."

"He was a good man, Maggie."

"I know he was. But he didn't understand the financial end of the healthcare business. Another thing that you and he have in common." The barb was launched carelessly, a shot across the bow.

"And you do?" Angela's voice was low and even.

Maggie narrowed her eyes. "Of course I do, Angela. I understand what it takes not only to survive in the ever-altering healthcare landscape, but to thrive. Much like the banking industry, healthcare is consolidating. If we want to compete, we have to grow. And in order to grow, we need money."

Maggie stood and walked to the front of her desk, then leaned against it with her arms crossed tightly over her chest. "This hospital has 719 beds, and our occupancy rate was 79 percent last year. That's up from 68 percent the prior year. Given the rise, we saw a fifteen-million-dollar profit, but it's still not enough, Angela." She inclined her head toward the blueprints. "The new cancer center will produce millions in additional revenue, allowing us to purchase outpatient sites that will bring in even more money." She approached Angela and locked eyes. "And I can't have you, or anyone else, getting in the way of that."

Angela noted how Maggie's pupils dilated as she spoke. Her body was betraying her fear and frustration. "At what cost, Maggie?"

Maggie shrugged and returned to her desk. "Whatever it takes."

"Are you serious?"

"Dead serious. Do you hear me, Angela? Dead. Serious."

Maggie's eyes drilled into her, and Angela felt the verbal threat like a physical blow. The sphere that contained her emotions started to crack and anger leaked out like radioactive uranium, poisoning her desire to maintain her composure. Without warning, Emily's voice surrounded her, *You can't come, Mom.* A rogue wave of anguish crashed over Angela and the room whirled around her. She struggled to retain her balance and hugged her purse tightly.

Angela swallowed twice in an effort to quell the bile that rose. When she spoke, her voice sounded strained, as if she were being strangled. "My daughter died from the wrong saline being administered. It was an easy mistake to make because the two types of saline are right next to each other in the online ordering system. And no one noticed the wrong saline percentage because the IV bags are almost identical."

Maggie waved her hand in Angela's direction and sat heavily in her chair. The small gesture, meant to dismiss and belittle, injected Angela with renewed adrenaline, and she took a step forward, determined to see her mission through.

"No, Maggie, you will hear me out. Emily's death was an accident, as was Ava Sinclair's."

Maggie's head swiveled quickly. Angela continued, her voice finding strength. "Yes, I did some digging and found Mrs.

Sinclair's medical records, even though they were buried under new computer code. I didn't lose them, as you had said. You ordered them to disappear."

"That's ridiculous, Angela."

"I can prove it, Maggie. And you can bet that my attorney will be very interested, as will every paper in Rhode Island, Boston, and maybe nationwide."

Maggie laughed. "You've lost your mind, Angela. We've all seen it coming."

Angela felt giddy and envisioned a wounded ship turning on its side, sinking slowly into the ocean. She shook her head. "No, Maggie. I thought I was losing my mind, but I'm clear as a bell now. I looked up to you as a mentor. I had no idea the depths to which you'd sink. And for what? That's the part I don't understand. When Lauren Kirk started asking questions about Emily's death and approached Stan Jacobs, he came to you and—" Angela snapped her fingers, "—Lauren was fired. Tell me, was it you or Stan who determined that Emily shouldn't be autopsied?"

"Neither of us—"

"It was at that point that the cover-up began. But why? Were you afraid I'd sue?"

"Angela, we didn't bring you into the loop simply because we didn't think you needed the extra stress."

Angela laughed, a manic croak that made Maggie physically withdraw. "That's bullshit, because you then blamed me for Mrs. Sinclair's missing records. You were trying to get rid of me, to make it look like I was incompetent. Why?"

"I don't know what you're talking about."

Angela's anger gathered momentum and propelled her forward toward Maggie's desk. "And then Mr. Sinclair filed a wrongful death suit against me and suddenly you noticed that my malpractice insurance wasn't valid. That's quite a coincidence, isn't it?"

"That was your mistake, Angela. I don't know what to tell you."

"Did you urge Mr. Sinclair to file the suit against me? I know you talked to Jesse Callaghan at the *Barrington Times*. You were the source for the scathing piece about me."

"Angela, please, let's—"

"And then Stan was named as your successor. I assume that the Board approved that decision?"

"Of course they did. You were no longer a viable candidate, so Stan was the next obvious choice."

"The obvious choice? Maggie, he's not even qualified. He was awarded the position as payment for his loyalty and complicity."

Maggie threw up her hands and raised her eyebrows. "Angela, there is no cover-up!"

Angela took a step back and narrowed her eyes. Her lips involuntarily curled into a sneer. "I know that Ava Sinclair's saline levels were also incredibly high, Maggie. I bet if I do some more research, I'll find evidence that someone grabbed a 3% saline bag by mistake. The two bags are almost identical. I would bet my life that Ava Sinclair died of an improper saline dose—"

Angela stopped abruptly. Her face dropped as a thought took shape. It started as a vague outline, but then crisp edges emerged to form a grotesque picture. Ants crawled up Angela's back as the full impact of Maggie's treachery crystallized in her mind. She stared at Maggie as if she were analyzing a patient whose cardiac issues were particularly challenging. Her voice dropped to a whisper because she could barely stand to ask the question. "How much are they paying you, Maggie?"

Maggie shook her head. "I don't know what you're talking about."

"Is Stan taking a cut too? Does he even know about it?"

"Angela, I've had enough. Get out."

Angela could see that her interpretation was accurate and it sickened her, but she had to know. "How much, Maggie? A million dollars? More?"

"Angela, I'm going to call security."

Angela clutched her purse and walked in circles, her left hand gesticulating as her voice rose. "No! I want to know what my daughter's life was worth. And Mrs. Sinclair's. My God, Maggie, are there others?"

Maggie stalked toward her and stood within inches. Her hands closed into fists and her face morphed from a blank mask to seething rage. "As I said, *Dr*. Brennan, you have absolutely no idea what it takes to run a profitable hospital in today's competitive financial climate."

Angela wasn't intimidated. She pushed her face into Maggie's. "Don't make this about the organization, Maggie. This is about you. It's always been about you. Saving your ass from going to hell when the truth comes out. How much did Laird Pharmaceuticals pay you to keep quiet about the high saline bags? How many others died, Maggie?"

"Stop it." Maggie walked away. Angela followed.

"The 0.9% and 3% saline bags look almost identical. When Stan discovered the mistake that had been made in Emily's case, you saw an opportunity. You went to Laird and threatened them, didn't you?"

"No."

"You explained what had happened and threatened to bring a lawsuit against them. To protect the hospital in case I sued. I sue you for Emily's death and you sue Laird for disseminating saline bags that are so close in appearance that it's almost impossible to tell them apart."

"That's ridiculous, Angela. Stan ordered the wrong saline. The onus is on him. Why would I sue Laird?"

Angela's eyes bored into Maggie. "Because Stan's legitimate mistake made you realize how similar the saline bags are in appearance. And you figured out that Ava Sinclair died from the mix-up." Angela shook her head as her brain continued to process. "Actually, you're right though. You would never have sued Laird because a lawsuit would have required you to admit the hospital's role in this disaster. No, you didn't threaten Laird with a lawsuit. You blackmailed them, didn't you?"

Maggie lifted an eyebrow and tilted her chin in defiance, then crossed behind her desk and picked up the phone.

"I'm calling security if you don't stop with these ridiculous accusations."

"And Laird acquiesced because they knew that paying you would be cheaper than going to court, or worse than that, having to face the court of public opinion if the truth got out."

Maggie's finger paused over the phone's buttons, receiver in her other hand.

Angela nodded as the entire plot unfurled before her eyes. "That explains the quick retirement plans, Maggie. Get out with your payday and move somewhere far away. Maybe somewhere that doesn't cooperate with U.S. extradition? It's brilliant. I would bet that Stan doesn't know the position you're putting him in. Leaving him to take the fall when the truth spills out."

Maggie gently replaced the receiver in its cradle and held Angela's gaze. Her eyes softened and her voice was defeated. "Stop talking, Angela. You just don't understand."

Angela narrowed her eyes. "I understand perfectly, Maggie. Tell me, did you really think I'd make a good CEO, or was I just another pawn?"

Maggie crossed her arms.

Exhaustion overcame Angela and she swayed on her feet. She closed her eyes and her body started trembling as she pictured Emily's last moments. "How much was my daughter's life worth, Maggie? I need to know."

"It wasn't like that, Angela."

Angela opened her eyes and took a step toward Maggie. Barely audible, she whispered, "How much?"

"You don't understand."

Her emotions flip-flopped again and fury tightened the vise around her skull. Her head felt as if it might explode. Her lips drew away from her teeth in a snarl as her blazing eyes torched Maggie. "How much!" she hissed.

Maggie's head bobbed violently back and forth, and her breath came quickly as sour words poured from her mouth. "The amount isn't important, Angela. All you need to know is that Laird is giving us the money to build the cancer center. Not only that, but an endowment that will ensure the growth of the hospital for decades to come."

Angela glowered, her rage barely contained as she spoke through gritted teeth. "And how much did you personally receive to keep quiet about Emily's death?"

Seconds passed as tears formed in Maggie's frantic eyes.

Angela shook her head and backed away, her inner self disintegrating into rubble that lay scattered around her feet, threatening to take her down at any moment. Jabbing her finger toward Maggie, she clutched her purse and cried, "No! You don't get to cry, Maggie! How many others have died?"

Maggie looked down. "I don't know."

The shocking news should have caused a reaction, yet simply fell among the rest of the appalling debris. "Why?"

"Why what?"

"Why didn't you just tell the truth?"

Maggie choked out a cough. "Angela, you really don't understand. The hospital would have been destroyed, along with Laird Pharmaceuticals. Sure, I gained financially in the process, but that fact is that I saved this place."

Angela stared disbelievingly at Maggie. "People *died*. Do you hear me? They're dead! There is no price you can put on the value of human life."

Angela's heart galloped in her chest while awaiting Maggie's response.

"But Angela, the hospital will survive."

A rushing sound filled Angela's ears. She placed her hands on either side of her face and slowly shook her head. "No, it won't, Maggie. By the time I'm done dragging Laird and the hospital through the legal system, there will be nothing left of either one of them."

Maggie regained her composure and straightened her back. "I wouldn't do that, Angela. The Board will fight you tooth and nail."

Angela paused as she assimilated the new information, her

taxed brain unwilling to accept the repercussions. "So the Board was aware of the cover-up?"

Maggie shrugged. "Some of the same people who sit on our Board also sit on Laird's."

The blood drained from Angela's face. The depths of duplicity bordered on obscene. Angela faltered and Maggie took advantage of the momentary weakness to press her case. "Just go away, Angela. Move somewhere and start over. I'm sure I could arrange some financial help if necessary."

Angela's scalp prickled and a wave of cold passed through her. "You're actually standing here offering me a bribe?"

"No. Not a bribe. Just one friend helping another."

Fuzzy-edged memories clicked through Angela's brain as if on an old movie reel. Her wedding, Tony standing proud and confident beside her. Her first surgery as a cardiac specialist. Emily's birth. Liam's first T-ball game. Her family's last weekend together. She returned her attention to Maggie, and time seemed to slow as furniture edges came into stark focus and colors leapt from their palettes. Her eyes scanned the room to find the excruciating sound of a ticking clock that hung on a wall. Her shoulders slumped as she crossed to the conference table and placed her purse on it. The metal studs on the bottom of the bag tapped against the glass. With her back to Maggie, she reached into the purse and slowly withdrew her gun. Pointing it at the ground, she realized that her heartbeat had returned to normal. *Let the ballet begin*, she thought as she turned slowly. Maggie gasped.

"Angela, Jesus! What are you thinking? You're a doctor, for God's sake!"

Maggie's words sounded muffled as Angela shook her head slowly. "No, Maggie. I was a doctor, but you robbed me of that privilege. I was also a mother, but you stole that as well. And now? Well, now I don't know what I am." Angela looked around the room as if searching for her identity. Her gaze returned to Maggie and she lifted the gun. Maggie's terrified eyes darted to her phone.

In a voice completely devoid of emotion, Angela said, "You should know that I'm a very good shot. Ask Liz."

Maggie threw her hands up in a defensive position, and Angela noted with grim satisfaction that they were shaking. "Please, Angela."

"I didn't want to do this, Maggie."

"You don't have to."

Angela unlocked the safety and saw a puddle of urine pooling at Maggie's feet. She felt nothing but detached disgust as she stared at the yellow liquid. "Quite frankly I don't know what else to do to get your attention."

Maggie began babbling incoherently.

"I can't understand you, Maggie."

"I'm t-t-trying to s-say that you h-have my att-tt-ention."

A single tear traced Angela's cheek as she looked directly at Maggie. "Yes. I see that. And look what it took for you to take me seriously."

Angela recognized genuine terror in Maggie's eyes. She also perceived reluctant resignation to her current circumstances. She saw that Maggie understood that there was no way out of this predicament, save Angela finding the grace to back off. Satisfied that she had achieved her desired outcome, Angela lowered the gun and opened the chamber, holding it toward Maggie so that she could see that it was empty.

Flabbergasted, Maggie gawked at the gun and then at Angela as her legs gave way beneath her. Breathing heavily, she said in a shaky voice, "You have seriously lost your mind, Angela."

Angela moved robotically as she closed the chamber and put the gun in her purse, then shouldered the bag. Turning to Maggie, she was momentarily shocked that she had brought another human being to the state in which she found Maggie as she sat in a puddle of her own making. "No, Maggie. My mind is clear, as is my conscience, at least as it pertains to you." Angela crossed to the door and nodded toward the stained rug. "You may want to clean that up before it begins to smell."

She opened the door and started to leave, then wagged her finger in the air as if she'd forgotten something. She turned around and said, "If I were you, I'd keep this conversation between you and me, Maggie. And expect to hear from my attorney in the coming days. You may want to rally your legal forces. As battles go, this one is going to be epic, as my son would have said."

CHAPTER 41

~

February 2019

Ignoring the stares of fellow patrons, Angela and Marty walked toward the back of the bar in search of a quiet place to celebrate. She had become somewhat of a regional celebrity as the media outlets had reported on the unfolding saline scandal.

"How do you feel?" Marty asked Angela.

She thought for a moment, reliving recent depositions and negotiations. "Tired."

Marty ordered a bottle of the bar's finest champagne and three glasses. The waitress brought the bubbly and smiled at Angela. "Nice job, Doc. Sticking up for the little guy. I'm sorry about your family."

Angela smiled politely in return. "Thanks."

Liz slid into the booth next to Angela. "What did I miss?"

"Angela was just telling me that she's tired."

"Well, of course she is! She just struck a blow to a pharmaceutical company in a—how shall I say this—*generous* settlement agreement."

"And the hospital as well. Don't forget that," added Marty.

Angela looked from one to the other. "I'm not proud that

I've damaged two companies and that people are probably going to jail."

Liz dropped her head. "Angela, give yourself a break, will you? You didn't hurt Laird. They did that to themselves when they chose to hide the fact that their saline bags were so close in appearance. I mean, even when Maggie brought it to their attention they still didn't pull the bags from the shelves nationwide. They chose to pay Maggie to keep quiet and prayed that no one else noticed. It took your potential lawsuit for them to come clean. And the hospital? Don't worry. It will survive. It'll be a rocky for a while, but under new leadership, it will come back. The community needs it."

"I guess."

"Hey, Angela, you've helped a lot of people by exposing the truth," said Marty. "And the fact is that Laird never would have agreed to a deal if they thought they could win the case at trial. Between Sonny McIsaac's deposition regarding the IT cover-up and Stan Jacobs flipping on Maggie, we had all we needed to get the hospital to play ball."

"Barb Royes' testimony was a nice touch too," Angela added. "She really came through."

"Not to mention the hospital Board rolling over like the cowards they are," Liz added. "The way they piled on Maggie was nothing short of remarkable."

"I wonder where Bernard will end up," Angela mused.

Liz waved her hand. "He's a cat with nine lives, Angela. And, like a cat, he'll land on his feet. Last I heard he was on his way to California. Probably wanted to get as far away as he could from this mess."

A pang of loss speared Angela and she winced. "He has a bright future if he can find some humility on his way to the West Coast."

Liz rolled her eyes. "Maybe."

"I owe Ingrid an apology," Angela said quietly.

Marty looked at Liz and then Angela. "Who's Ingrid?"

"You mean the cleaning lady in Cardiac Surgery?" Liz asked.

"Yeah. She's the person who left Lauren's note on my desk and I inadvertently terrorized her when I was trying to determine who had written the note."

Marty looked disbelievingly at Angela. "After the hell that you've been through, that's who you're thinking about right now? The cleaning lady?"

"Who should I be thinking about, Marty?" Angela asked, legitimately curious. Liz patted her hand and nodded. "That's really kind, Angela. I bet Ingrid would appreciate an apology, even though I'm sure she understands why you acted the way you did."

As Angela leaned over to pick up her napkin that had fallen, she caught the tight smile that passed between Marty and Liz. She knew that they were worried about her, even if she wasn't.

"Angela, I know that Tony, the kids, and Frank would be proud," Liz said.

Angela nodded silently and stared into her glass of champagne. The never-ending bubbles were mesmerizing and she traced one from the bottom of the glass to the top, only to be replaced with another. "Yes. I think you're right. They would be proud."

"I think they would especially like the foundation you've created. The Brennan Foundation has a nice ring to it."

Angela shrugged. "What else am I going to do with so much money from a crooked hospital and pharmaceutical company?" Angela wished that she could share in her friends' elation, not because she was happy, but because she knew they wanted her to. But her body felt like a dried gourd, cracked on the outside and hollowed out on the inside. The anger that had fueled her quest fizzled in the judge's antechamber where the settlement had been negotiated. Although she had smiled and hugged her legal team, the final decision, announced by the judge earlier that afternoon, had left her feeling empty and without purpose.

"Are your parents still here?" Marty asked.

"They're packing as we speak. Their plane to Florida leaves at eight o'clock tonight."

Marty raised his glass. "To the bravest, smartest, and most driven person I know—Angela Brennan."

Angela looked from her best friend to the man who had aided her in finding justice for Emily. A man who had come to her as a patient, perhaps led to her by his deceased brother. She was so grateful to these two people who had put their own lives on hold in order to support her. She raised her glass. "And to both of you, friends who have helped me through an unimaginable time in my life. And to your brother, Reggie, who was with me right after the accident, preparing me for what was to come." They paused, digesting Angela's words, then touched glasses and drank.

"Have you seen him again?" Liz asked.

"Reggie? No. And I haven't seen Frank either, not since the incident in the cemetery. It seems like they come when I need them most and then retreat to the background when I don't."

Liz nodded. "Sounds like my mom. Even though I don't see her, I know she's got my back. She's my guardian angel."

Angela smiled, thinking how far she'd come in her belief in the beyond. "I suppose all of us have guardian angels now."

"Lucky us," Marty said. He raised his glass again. "To our guardian angels." They clinked again and Liz drained her glass. Angela sipped politely and then placed her champagne on the table.

"How's Jesse?" Angela asked.

Liz knocked on the tabletop. "Five months and counting. We're good."

Angela regarded her friend as her mind wandered to Tony. "That's something positive that came out of this mess. You guys seem really happy together."

"And your husband's firm? What's happening with that, Angela?" Marty asked.

"I just spoke to Sean two days ago and they're doing well. In fact, he hired another architect, so now there are three of them. Tony definitely would have liked that." Angela glanced at a man walking past their table. After he passed, he turned and winked at her. Just for a moment, she was staring at her dead husband. She blinked, and Tony turned into a man of about the same height and build, with wavy dark hair and stormy eyes. She tore her gaze away, downed the rest of her glass in one gulp, and stood. "I need to get home to say goodbye to my parents. Thanks for everything, you guys."

Liz stood and embraced her friend. "Are you sure you can't stay a bit longer?"

Angela glanced toward the spot where the stranger had been standing, but he had melted into the crowd. "Um, no. I have to go."

"I'll call tomorrow, okay?"

"Sounds good."

Marty smiled at her from the booth. "I'll be in touch, Angela. We need to iron out the details of the Brennan Foundation."

"You handle it, Marty. I trust you. I'm tired." Angela smiled weakly.

Arriving at home, she found her mother in the kitchen mumbling to herself while labeling Tupperware dishes and carefully placing them in the freezer. Her mother didn't notice her, and Angela watched Sally work. Although she and her mother had not always seen eye to eye, Angela knew that Sally's love was unwavering, a bulwark against any unforeseen evil. Sally communicated her love through fussing over physical things, like clean laundry and frozen meals. As Angela watched her mother organize a whole lot of love in the freezer, Sally noticed her and jumped. "Oh my goodness! What are you doing skulking around like that?"

Angela smiled. "I wasn't skulking, Mom. I love you." She gathered her mother in her arms and held her for much longer than Sally felt comfortable. Finally, her mother withdrew and shooed her away. "Go see your father. I have more meals to put away. You should have enough food for about three weeks."

"Thanks, Mom." Angela left the kitchen and found her father by the pool.

"Mom's overcooked, I see," she said. She sat next to him.

"She thinks you're not eating enough."

"She always thinks I'm not eating enough."

Her father's kind eyes gazed at her, and he dropped his head in her direction. "Well, then. Maybe you're not."

She slapped his arm playfully and noted new lines around his eyes where extreme loss had carved its mark. "You guys should get on the road, Dad. It's 5:10." He sat up and turned toward her. "I know. But we hate to leave you, angel."

"No, you don't."

He smiled. "No, we don't. But we do. You know?"

"I do know. But I'll be okay."

She could feel his stare, as if he were judging whether or not she was telling the truth. She fidgeted, remembering what it was like as a child to be scrutinized by Jim Barckett. "You know if you need anything, *anything*, you can call us, and we'll be on the next plane."

"I know. Thank you. And thank you for being here through all of this," Angela said as she watched the dipping sun cast shadows throughout the pool.

Jim stood and held out his hand to his only child, who took it and stood. They embraced, and for a moment Angela felt like a six-year-old girl who had fallen off her bike. Scooped up and comforted by her hero—a tall, strong father who would protect her from all that was bad in the world. She yielded to the feeling, allowing herself a moment of complete surrender, before gathering her adult self again.

Jim held her at arm's length and searched her face. "You do understand that none of this is your fault, right? None of it. Not the accident. Not the saline screw-up. Not Ava Sinclair's death. None of it."

Angela's eyes wandered down his face and she realized, to her surprise, that he was correct. On some level, she had been blaming herself for surviving when everyone around her was dying.

But none of it was her fault.

She had managed to find forgiveness for the driver that had killed Liam and Tony, and for Stan Jacobs, who had ordered the wrong saline that had killed Emily. But she'd not found the time to consider that perhaps she should forgive herself. She nodded silently.

"Good. I'm glad you understand." He hugged her hard and then kissed her cheek. "Okay. We'll gather our things and go. But we'll call you tonight when we land."

She smiled. "Okay."

After receiving a tutorial from her mother on the freezer food layout, her parents packed their suitcases into the trunk of the Uber and waved goodbye.

Angela reentered the house and took a long, hot bath. She dried her hair, taking time to brush it carefully, and slipped into her favorite polka-dotted, cotton pajamas the kids had given her for Christmas the previous year. She descended the stairs, removed the lasagna her mother had left for the evening's dinner, and heated it in the microwave. Pouring herself a glass of merlot, she put on Verdi's *Requiem* and sat at the kitchen table, savoring each bite of the delicious pasta dish. After dinner, she looked through all of the family photo albums, alternatively smiling and crying as she reminisced. The silence in the house was deafening and she closed her eyes, recalling the heavy footfalls of Liam as he tumbled down the stairs, and Emily's voice yelling at her brother to vacate her room. She felt Tony's hands on her shoulders and she leaned back, relishing the warmth of his touch. The grandfather clock struck eight, drawing her from her reverie. She glanced at the clock, yawned, and touched the last photo of her family at Truro Beach. "Time to go to sleep, guys."

She placed her dishes in the dishwasher and tidied the kitchen before ascending the stairs. After brushing her teeth and pulling her hair into a neat ponytail, she crossed to the closet and removed her backpack. She unzipped the bag, removed the gun and laid it gently on the comforter before replacing the backpack in the closet. She sat cross-legged on the bed and smiled at the oak tree that brushed gently against the window.

"I know that's you, Tony," she whispered. A lone tear traced her cheek. "I also know that you and the kids are okay. I'm okay now too." The sound of giggling floated from the corner of the room. Angela turned her head toward the sound and laughed through her tears. "I was beginning to forget what your laughter sounded like, you guys."

The branches scraped the glass again and the laughter faded. Angela's heart seized. Her children had departed.

The sound of wood on glass persisted and she sensed Tony's arms wrapping around her from behind. She shivered at his touch, closed her eyes and leaned into him, surrendering to the warmth and complete peace. His lips brushed her ear and his words came quickly, reverberating inside her head long after his touch had evaporated.

"Stay the course."

CHAPTER 42

~

May 2019

Small, gray snow mounds huddled against the spring warmth, defiantly refusing to melt. The piles stood in stark contrast to the bright-pink ribbons that fluttered in the breeze off the bay. Barrington residents chatted and laughed as their children played tag among the white, wooden chairs arranged in tight rows. The town manager expected a large turnout and had requested extra chairs from a neighboring town to ensure that each person had a seat for the remembrance service.

The town clock struck 12 P. M. and the manager approached the mic, asking everyone to find a seat. Once settled, he cleared his throat and began. "Good afternoon. It was one year ago that we lost three members of our special, little town when Tony, Emily, and Liam Brennan lost their lives in a terrible accident. But through Angela Brennan's efforts, not only do their memories live on, but through the Brennan Foundation, their legacy will continue to help children for many years to come. We have a special guest speaker with us today, specifically requested by Angela herself. Ladies and gentleman, Jonathan Dale."

The audience clapped politely as a man rose and slowly

approached the podium. Obviously terrified, he cleared his throat and stared at the large crowd. He withdrew a crumpled piece of paper from his pocket and smoothed it on the podium before taking a deep breath. "Good afternoon. My name is Jonathan Dale and I am the person who hit the Brennan's car, killing Liam and Tony."

There was an audible gasp from the crowd, followed by nervous twitters and swiveling heads. Jonathan shifted from one foot to the other as he waited. When the hubbub had subsided, he dropped his gaze to his prepared statement. "Per Angela Brennan's request, I was granted a one-day pass from prison today specifically to speak to you. Afterwards I'll be returning to complete my sentence." He cleared his throat again. "A day does not go by where I don't think about the damage I have done, and it took me a long time to be able to even think about what the rest of my life might look like. Against my attorney's advice, I pled guilty to the charges of reckless driving. I felt it was important to take responsibility for my actions, despite what it might mean for my own family. I assumed that I would go to jail for a long time because I deserved it. On the day of my sentencing hearing, though, something amazing happened. Dr. Brennan showed up and forgave me."

Murmurs shot across the rows of well-dressed Barringtonians. This information had not been previously reported.

"Not only that, but she asked the judge to give me a lighter sentence because I had taken responsibility. To this day I don't know why she did that. If I ever see her again, I'll ask her." He looked up at the clear, blue sky and started to cry. "And then I found out that she had set aside money from the Brennan Foundation for my children's education." He looked around as if searching for an answer. "I mean, who does that? I killed her family, and she's made sure that mine is taken care of." He wiped his eyes on his sleeve and nodded. "Dr. Brennan found kindness where I would have found only despair and hate. There is no way I can ever repay her. But I can pay it forward, so to speak, and I now strive every day for that purpose. Thank you."

The stunned crowd sat silently as he finished, not knowing if it was appropriate to applaud. The town manager approached the mic and cleared his throat again. "Ladies and Gentleman, Mr. George Sinclair."

A visibly nervous Mr. Sinclair leaned into the microphone and said, "Is this thing on?" much too loudly, sending feedback through the speakers. He cleared his throat and chuckled uneasily. "I asked if I could speak today. My wife always said I should do more public speaking, but I'm not sure this is what she had in mind. You see, she died after undergoing surgery with Dr. Brennan." Again, the crowd drew a collective breath. "I know, you probably wonder why I'm here. But the fact is that my wife, Ava—her death wasn't Dr. Brennan's fault. Even when I knew that for sure, I still blamed Dr. Brennan. I guess it's because I didn't have anyone else to blame. I was just so damned angry. Oh, sorry for the curse word, kids. Anyway, I dropped my lawsuit against her when I found out that the pharmaceutical company had screwed up. I'll be seeing a bunch of money from them, I'm sure, but following Dr. Brennan's lead, most of that will go toward charity. It's the least I can do. Thank you." Before anyone could react, the large man lumbered off the stage and the town manager hustled back on. Caught off-guard, he consulted his notes and mumbled, "Um, please welcome Liz Rumsey."

Liz glanced worriedly at Jesse, who nodded encouragement as she took the stage. "Hi. My name is Liz Rumsey, and I'm proud to call Angela my friend. Angela couldn't be here with us today, but she wanted me to tell all of you that she appreciated your graciousness in the months following the accident. Before all of this happened, Angela wasn't sure what she believed regarding Heaven and God. But I'm confident that she now knows what she believes. Thank you." Liz almost ran off the stage into the waiting arms of a smiling Jesse Callaghan, whose eyes flitted in Angela's direction.

Angela smiled at Liz's choice of words as she observed the proceedings from afar. A small breeze ruffled her hair and she looked to her left to find a coyote seated about ten feet away. "I remember you. What are you doing here?"

The coyote lay down. A few moments later its mate approached and lay beside it.

Angela smiled. "I'm glad you're not alone anymore. Me neither."

ACKNOWLEDGMENTS

I would like to thank my husband, Kevin, who supports my writing habit as he has supported my other artsy endeavors throughout our many happy years together. He told me two real-life stories and suggested I write about them, but it wasn't until I wove them together that *Devil's Grace* came into existence.

I was busy writing another novel when my woo-woo friend Michele McIsaac (no relation to Sonny McIsaac, but just as wonderfully sassy) instructed me that I was supposed to be writing about the Light: forgiveness, kindness, compassion. I literally dropped what I was doing and wrote the *Devil's Grace* prologue that day. In fact, towards the end of the book, Tony tells Angela to "stay the course." That is a direct quote from my writing angels when I had asked for some guidance in this massive endeavor. I am grateful to Michele, as well as Jack and Bob for their inspiration.

I would also like to thank When Words Count Retreat/Competition and its CEO Steve Eisner, as well as the judges Ben Tanzer, Dede Cummings (Green Writers Press), and Marilyn Atlas. I have done my best to ensure that their faith has not been misplaced. Additionally, I'd like to give a shout-out to some other fine writers who supported and encouraged me: Matt

Fitzpatrick, Kathy Haueisen, Renate LeDuc, Karen Kaiser, and Stephanie Schorow.

The breathtaking cover was designed by a talented artist named Asha Hossein, who did a remarkable job capturing the stormy beauty that all of our lives possess.

My wonderful editors, Rose Alexandre-Leach and Sarah Ellis, made this novel so much better with their gentle suggestions and guidance. I am very grateful.

Many thanks to my sons, Jake, Jesse, and Max, who (have no choice but to) listen endlessly as I dream up scenarios and test them out on unsuspecting and helpless ears.

And to my beta readers, who suffered through many rounds of reading, sometimes only four chapters at a time, I cannot thank you enough. Katie and Bill McMillan, Thelma Grace Mayer, Lisa Roots, and Jackie and Ed Splaine.

My heartfelt thanks to Dr. Charlie Payne for his invaluable advice regarding medical (and legal) details.

And to the person reading *Devil's Grace*, there is no more wonderful feeling in the world than a hug from someone you love. But second to that is the feeling I get when I hear from readers, either via email or a review on Goodreads or Amazon and the like. You can contact me via my website www.elizbethsplaineauthor.com. I always do my best to return the note. Thank you for reading *Devil's Grace* and please post a review if you're able.